Dear Carol,

Health is a human necessity —

human right!

CONVERSATIONS FOR PACO

a novel by

Enjoy!

JAMES LENHART

SLEEPING GIANT

Sleeping Giant Publishing, LLC
www.sleepinggiantpublishing.com

First Edition hardcover and paperback printing 2011
Second Edition hardcover and paperback printing 2012
Third edition hardcover and paperback printing 2013
Fourth edition hardcover and paperback printing 2014
v.3

Cover design by Jonathan Sturak
Manufactured and printed in the United States of America

To learn about the author visit him at
jameslenhart.net

1. Medical – Fiction. 2. Suspense – Fiction. 3. Satire – Fiction.

ISBN: 978-0-615-47109-9
Library of Congress Cataloging-in-Publication Data

To Nancy

For all
Who embrace
Healthcare
as a
Human right
... and
For
all
those
Who don't

CONVERSATIONS FOR PACO

PROLOGUE

The Hippocratic Oath

I swear by Apollo the Physician and Asclepius and Hygeia and Panacea and all the gods and goddesses, making them my witnesses, that I will fulfill according to my ability and judgment this oath and this covenant:

To hold him who has taught me this art as equal to my parents and to live my life in partnership with him, and if he is in need of money to give him a share of mine, and to regard his offspring as equal to my brothers in male lineage and to teach them this art - if they desire to learn it - without fee and covenant; to give a share of precepts and oral instruction and all the other learning to my sons and to the sons of him who has instructed me and to pupils who have signed the covenant and have taken an oath according to the medical law, but no one else.

I will apply dietetic measures for the benefit of the sick according to my ability and judgment; I will keep them from harm and injustice.

I will neither give a deadly drug to anybody who asked for it, nor will I make a suggestion to this effect. In purity and holiness I will guard my life and my art.

I will not use the knife, not even on sufferers from stone, but will withdraw in favor of such men as are engaged in this work.

Whatever houses I may visit, I will come for the benefit of the sick, remaining free of all intentional injustice, of all mischief and in particular of sexual relations with both female and male persons, be they free or slaves.

What I may see or hear in the course of the treatment or even outside of the treatment in regard to the life of men, which on no account one must spread abroad, I will keep to myself, holding such things shameful to be spoken about.

If I fulfill this oath and do not violate it, may it be granted to me to enjoy life and art, being honored with fame among all men for all time to come; if I transgress it and swear falsely, may the reverse be my lot.

Hippocrates of Cos ~ 400 BC

CONVERSATIONS FOR PACO

PART I

"Health is a moral imperative ... it is also a social and economic imperative. It is a central determinant in the quality of our lives, from a child's capacity to learn in the classroom to a parent's ability to provide for her or his family. It is the foundation on which so much else depends."

~ Georges C. Benjamin, MD, FACP

JAMES LENHART

SUMMER 2002

Conversation 1

Los Angeles, California, USA

Friday, July 26, 2002; 10:26 p.m.

Humanitarian Hospital intern Jerome Spivey approached the nursing station, set Paco Sánchez's chart on the counter and extracted a Palm Pilot from his white waist coat pocket. He tapped *e*Procrates Essentials, scrolled to the subject 'pharyngitis' and refreshed his memory. *"Pharyngitis: most cases are viral. A bright red posterior oral pharynx, pustular tonsils, fever and swollen glands support a diagnosis of Streptococcal infection but may also indicate Epstein-Barr (mononucleosis), Cytomegalovirus or gonorrhea."* Spivey frowned and whispered to himself, "Gonorrhea? Really? Hmmm."

The young doctor scratched his head and read on.

"Untreated complications of Streptococcal infection include rheumatic heart disease and kidney failure. Penicillin class antibiotics are the preferential treatment. If gonorrhea is suspected treat with intramuscular Rocephin 250 milligrams stat." He slid the Palm back into its case, began writing and motioned to nurse Adderley. "Linda, I want to get a complete blood count, throat culture for Neisseria gonorrhea, a Rapid Strep and a sed rate on the guy in bed nine."

"Mr. Sánchez?" the nurse asked.

"Yeah. Whatever his name is. The guy in bed nine."

"Can't Spivey, unless it is life-threatening. He's category 3."

"What do you mean category 3?"

The nurse shrugged her shoulders, "New Humanitarian policy since February. Patients with bills past due over 120 days get treated and streeted. No tests unless it's an absolute, life threatening emergency."

"What? You're kidding? What kind of policy ... that's bullcrap."

"It may be Dr. Spivey but that's administration's policy. Category 3."

"You're kidding. What about making the diagnosis?"

"No joke, no kidding, he has to go to County Hospital for follow-up too. Make sure you tell them."

"But how do I know what to treat, if I don't know what he has?"

"That's what you had all the high-flalutin' medical school for Dr. Spivey. Take your best shot. Make an educated guess."

"Guess?" Spivey retorted. "What about the patient?"

"That's what I asked Mr. Smarty-pants. He just ..."

"Mr. Smarty-pants?"

"The CEO of Humanitarian Hospital. Geoff Boyer. I call him Mr. Smarty-pants. Thinks he's so mighty mucky-muck. He puts on employee forums every once in a while. So at the last one I asked him the same question. He danced around the answer. In the end told us we needed to understand the hospital's responsibility to its stockholders. Gave us some jibber-jabber about balancing quality patient care with the financial well being of the company. Talked in terms of contribution to margin, which in the end is no different than Exxon or IBM yapping about their profits as far as I'm concerned.

"So guess," the nurse looked at him again and winked. "Just make sure you guess right. Pretend this is a Monopoly game. Take a Chance card. By the way, did you get a past medical history? Medical records will bounce the chart back if you didn't. It's another new rule. Administration wants *complete* past medical histories on everyone – improves reimbursement – and believe me, around here it's most often all about the money."

Spivey glared at the nurse, then looked back at Paco's chart. The words on the Emergency Department patient encounter form blurred. He couldn't think, he couldn't write. He even felt a little short of breath. Shoulders drooping, he made his way back to the cubicle to gather Paco's past medical history mumbling, "This is nuts. Guess? *Chance card?* Monopoly? Who for God's sake wields the power to make taking care of patients some sort of charade or entrepreneurial hoax? *Who?* What about the patient?"

NINETEEN YEARS EARLIER – SUMMER 1983
Conversation 2
Guadalajara, Jalisco, Mexico
Wednesday, July 27, 1983; 11:56 p.m.

Little Paco Sánchez slept against the intersecting walls of a dark corner. A straw mattress covered in coarse burlap insulated him from the dank earthen floor. His brothers Emilio and Jesus and sister Margarita lined up in a row, slept alongside him. In the opposite corner, Mamacita turned in her sleep to dodge the full moon showering her corner with bright, silver light. Outside crickets chip-chirped; a bullfrog croaked; mongrel dogs howled; an iguana peered over the window ledge; rats scampered pitter-patter on the rooftop and a summer breeze rattled the slender leaves of nearby mesquite trees. Despite the eerie cacophony, Mamacita's family slept well; these nightly sounds – so natural in their lives – tranquilized them.

Their ramshackle, two-room shanty sat on the outskirts of Guadalajara, Mexico's second largest city. In its remote location, it had neither sewer nor running water. A shared well three hovels down and public outhouses situated on the village fringe served those purposes. Mamacita considered what she had good fortune; she thanked God daily. But caring for a home with dirt floors and unfinished adobe brick was another matter, and she obsessed with sweeping it twice, and as often as three times a day, to keep order in and critters out.

Water, condensed from the air of the hot, humid day, dripped from the ceiling and ran over the walls. On the uneven surfaces of the brick, the water formed in tiny lagoons and rivulet pools as it made its way down. A drop fell from the ceiling, splashed against Paco's forehead and, trickling down his face, transformed his slumber into nightmarish sleep.

"¡Papá! ¡Papá!" Paco exclaimed in his dream, dodging through the brush along the river's bank. "¡Toma mi mano; alcanzame!" (Take my hand; reach for me!). "¡Papá, toma mi mano!" He ran faster and harder, "¡Apurate, Papá! ¡Toma mi mano! ¡Ya no puedo correr más!" (Quick Papa! Take my hand! I can run no more!) Then he tripped on a branch, landed face down and the river carried his father away. "¡Papá! ¡Papá! ¡Ay papito!" he cried.

Another drop fell from the ceiling, disrupting his dream. But he rolled to his side, wiped the water away, coughed twice, and went back to sleep.

As if Paco's whoop were the creature's bidding, a sinewy leg extended from a crevice high on the wall. Using the parapet as a springboard, it popped out from its nest, landing motionless on the precipice. The thing rested there like it was dead. Then it moved, paused again and flashed its beady eyes about the room. Finding the moonlight in Mamacita's corner blinding, it looked away and below toward the sleeping children.

Avoiding the condensation on the surface of the calloused walls, *Loxosceles reclusa* moved right, then left, then down … the brown recluse was out. The spider started slowly at first; then in rapid spurts, abruptly stopping to gauge the landscape and define its path. What the spider wanted lay beyond Paco, so it had three choices – around his feet; over his body; or over his face.

Loxosceles reclusae are tiny creatures and by nature introverts – recluses if you will, hence their name. They come out at night and avoid light. Brown recluse spiders shun human interaction; yet if threatened, inject venom notorious for pain and grotesque scaring of skin. As legend has it, *reclusae* bites can even be fatal. So it goes … *legend has it.*

And the spider continued its deliberate descent.

Although Paco faced the wall, he could not see or hear *reclusa* coming. He could not see the violin facsimile on *reclusa's* back, nor its probing pincers, its spindly legs or vicious fangs. No, he could not see the spider's progression toward him. He was deep in nightmarish sleep. Besides, it was pitch black in Paco's corner and *reclusa* found that to its liking.

The spider scooted toward the ground. Then paused and peered around.

Certain of its path, the arachnid scampered down.

But three feet from Paco, slid in a vaporous pool, lost its grip and fell.

Landing on Paco's sheet.

Reclusa shook off the shock and resumed its trek – along the sheet, over the pillow and toward Paco's neck. Down toward the fissured floor.

Paco Sánchez could not see *reclusa* coming.

But he could *feel* it coming.

Paco could not hear *reclusa*, but *he could feel it coming!*

He could feel the rap-tapping claws dancing over his neck ... and he swatted.

But *Reclusae* are quick.

Paco missed.

Incited, the spider darted and dashed first under, then over, Paco's right ear and stopped at the top of it. It dug in its claws. It searched for asylum. It spied Paco's ear canal and started to go for it.

Paco swatted again.

He missed again.

The jolt knocked the spider off its perch.

And it landed.

On Paco's cheek.

Now fleeing for safety, yet running in circles, *Reclusa* flew over Paco's eye lids, ran through his lashes and scampered onto his brow. Then it hesitated.

Until it zigged and it zagged.

Shot between his eyes, and raced over his nose.

Where at last it found refuge.

In Paco's right nostril.

Conversation 3
St. Louis, Missouri, USA
Thursday, July 28, 1983; 12:03 a.m.

As Paco fought off the spider, fifteen hundred miles north two young physicians made their way into Hot Shots Sports Bar and Grill. Drs. Jack MacDougall and Edmund M. Pinkerton pushed their way past the crowded entrance and finally found two empty seats at a bistro table at the back of the bar. Pinkerton removed his windbreaker, hung it on the back of the chair and sat down. MacDougall stretched, took his seat and yawned, "I thought that game would never end. Whew, I'm beat."

Pinkerton grabbed a menu and began reading, "Me too, but I'm hungry. I could eat a horse. What do they have that's good in this joint?"

The Cardinals won the game in the bottom of the 15th inning when Tug McGraw, pitching in relief, threw Willie McGee a big sweeping change-up that he patiently waited on and drove into deep left center field for a walk-off home run. Game over. Cardinals 3, Phillies 2. "You having another beer?" MacDougall asked.

Pinkerton looked over top of his menu and snorted, "Hell yes. Why not?"

A young woman dressed in a referee's jersey and dungarees approached them. Hair in her face, mascara smeared and lipstick worn off, she looked like a wilted daisy. "What will it be, gents?" she asked, taking a deep breath and blowing the bangs out of her eyes.

Her prognathic jaw and pug nose rebuffed MacDougall, yet he winked at the waitress, flashed her a libidinous grin and drawled, "What 'ya got darlin'? Me and my friend Ed have never been in this here saloon. We're mighty hungry and its awful dusty outside."

The waitress warmed up to MacDougall's joust immediately, winked back and declared, "Folks say we have the best cheeseburgers in all of St. Louie – you can build your own. Our pizzas have a great reputation too. In fact, some say it's the best pizza west of the Mississippi. Been on a cattle drive mister?"

"Nope. I'm just a drifter passing through," MacDougall quipped, thinking that, coupled with her saucy wit and broad smile, maybe she wasn't so bad looking after all.

Pinkerton interrupted their banter, "What's on draft?"

"Just about anything you could ask for," the waitress sighed. "We've got Heineken, Pilsner Urquell, Michelob, St. Pauli Girl ... this being St. Louis, Budweiser is our special."

MacDougall turned up his nose and snickered, "Bud. Ugh."

"So bring us two Heinekens to get us started while we're making up our minds on what to eat," Pinkerton chirped.

The waitress looked at Pinkerton and then back to MacDougall. "Heineken okay with you?"

"Actually, I'd prefer St. Pauli's girl," MacDougall wisecracked. "But my friend Ed has the reins on me tonight. Heineken will have to do."

The waitress shook her head and looked away from MacDougall attempting to deflect his comment. "Sixteen or twenty-two ounce?" she blushed.

"Twenty-two," they responded in unison.

MacDougall stretched again and brought his forearms back to the table, fingers flipping the edge of the menu. "So what did you think of Petersdorf's introduction to the fellowship this morning?"

"You mean his arrogant rant?" Pinkerton frowned. "He's everything everyone said – his contemptuous reputation is well deserved. Then again, he has earned it – chair of neurology at Washington University, international stature in neurological science, a plethora of publications in every major periodical including the New England Journal of Medicine, therapeutic breakthroughs, diagnostic patents – the works. If that gives you the right to be a first class prick, so be it," Pinkerton shrugged. "I'm lucky to be here and so are you."

The waitress floated two coasters on the table and set the beers one each in front of MacDougall and Pinkerton. "So! Have you decided what I can get for you?"

"First tell us your name," MacDougall interrupted.

"Oops, I'm sorry. We're way too busy," she apologized. "It's Jennifer. What will it be?"

"Well it's nice to meet you Jennifer. I'll have the Frisco Melt, medium well with a side of fries and a little mayo."

Pinkerton cleared his throat, "And I'll have two of the Jalapeño Pepper Jack burgers medium rare with tomatoes, lettuce, red onion, Dijon mustard and mayo."

"Did you say two?" she gawked. "They're one-half pounders and kind of big."

"Yeah, well, I am *kind* of hungry," Pinkerton laughed. "And bring us some of the spicy hot chicken wings for starters. Would you Jennifer?"

MacDougall ran his fingers through his hair and rubbed his eyes. Pinkerton's appetite flabbergasted him. How could anyone consume so much food he wondered? "Eating like that will bust your gut Ed."

Pinkerton drank from his beer, wiped away a frothy moustache and retorted, "So be it. As far as I am concerned there's but three

7

pleasures in life – good food, great sex and buckets of money – not necessarily in that order."

Dr. Jack MacDougall hesitated, astonished by the abrupt twist in the conversation. Then he took a drink from his beer and jumped on it, "Okay ... so in which order?"

"Order? I've never thought about it like that – it's all good. Depends on the what, the why, the how and the where."

"Oh no. Huh-uh. I won't let you off with a shrug and an empty answer, Dr. Edmund M. Pinkerton. In our situation, and in this time in our lives, *this* is a sentinel conversation. *What are your priorities, Ed?* Look at me. I'm not Petersdorf, the Dean of the School of Medicine, the chair of the ethics committee or your wife Judi. I've been your best friend through some pretty intense times the past eight years – medical school, residency, best man at your wedding and now fellowship. Shoot it to me straight ... like a pledge between blood brothers. What's important and in which order?"

Pinkerton looked about the room and up at the television replaying Willie McGee's walk-off home run. He took another drink of beer. Sitting silent, calculating.

"For Christ's sake, Ed, this isn't quantum physics. Give it to me down and dirty. You're in the circle of trust," he declared making a closed loop with his thumbs and index fingers. "Give it to me from your gut. There's really not anything to think about."

The waitress slid the order of chicken wings between them and under Pinkerton's nose, rescuing him from MacDougall's interrogation. "Yum-yum," he smiled. "Looks *and* smells delicious."

She watched in awe as Pinkerton grabbed a wing, put the whole of it in his mouth and stripped the bone clean in a single pass. Pinkerton's gluttony made her wince, but she'd seen worse, so she dismissed it and asked, "Two more Heinekens while you're waiting on the burgers?"

Getting the nod, she slipped away to place their order.

Pinkerton devoured two more wings before he returned to his friend's question. "So it depends ... on my mood, what day it is. What appetite I last satisfied, so to speak," he chuckled.

"The way you're sucking down those wings, it looks like food is number one," MacDougall chided him.

"Maybe so. But money and great sex are nothing to sneeze at," he asserted wiping his mouth and licking his fingers. "Like I said, it's all good ... so what about you?"

MacDougall didn't hesitate a nanosecond, "Money, sex, food and golf – one, two, three, four – in that order."

Pinkerton swallowed the last bite of his fourth wing, "No shit? Just like that?"

"No shit. Just like that."

The waitress approached the table balancing Pinkerton's two burgers on one arm and carrying MacDougall's order with the other. "Here you go, gentlemen," she declared. "The Frisco Melt for you and the Jalapeño Pepper Jacks for your friend." Then she pulled a fresh bottle of Dijon mustard from her apron pocket and asked, "Anything else I can get you two?"

"Did you forget something? Like the brewskis maybe?" Pinkerton chastised her.

"Oh! Yeah. Sorry. Coming right up."

Pinkerton lifted the bun from one of the burgers, set the lettuce, tomato and onion to the side and spread generous dollops of Dijon, ketchup and mayonnaise over the beef patty. Then he reassembled his concoction, anchored both elbows on the table and took an enormous bite. Chewing, he wiped the condiments from both corners of his mouth and starred straight into his friend's eyes. "Money, sex, food and golf? You failed to include family, or medicine, for that matter."

Wiping the condensation from the mug with his index finger and thumb MacDougall pondered momentarily, and then went on, "When we started medical school I thought I was the outlier – what did we have, seventy-two students in the class? And I thought I was the only student who didn't come with a profound desire to care for the sick and downtrodden, eradicate disease and rid the world of social injustice. Uncomfortable as an outsider, I observed the other students and listened for subtle clues. As I got to know our classmates, I discovered they were more, not *less* like me. Medicine wasn't a calling for them either – most were there to attract prestige, a standard of living or a trophy bride. Worse yet, like yours truly, many were acquiescing to family pressures."

Pinkerton polished off his first burger, smacked his chops and said, "Uh-huh? Your Frisco Melt or whatever they call it is getting cold."

"So by the time we had finished the second year," MacDougall went on, "I knew I was the rule, not the exception. Hell, look at McAlister and Kipfer. The proof is in the pudding. Both so liberal makes you want to puke. McAlister goes into anesthesiology and Kipfer radiology – highly paid specialists I might add, that rarely interact with patients."

"Okay. So what's your point Jack?"

MacDougall lifted his sandwich, took a bite and deliberated with his mouth full of food. "If you want the honest truth, Ed, I'll give it to you. But if I ever learn that what I'm about to say gets back to Carolyn, I'll cut off your balls. Understood?"

Pinkerton read MacDougall like a book and knew he was serious. Jack's wife would crucify them both, "Understood ... just between us, circle of trust."

Measuring his friend, MacDougall drank from his beer, set the mug back on the table and deadpanned, "Family? Family is a *social necessity.* Medicine? Medicine, Dr. Pinkerton, merely provides the means to the ends."

Conversation 4
Guadalajara
Thursday, July 28, 1983; 12:04 a.m.

Eight spindly legs propelled *reclusa* up Paco's nose. He grabbed at the prickle. *What else could he do?*

Then the thing spread its fangs and bit little Paco.

The venom spread like fire, penetrating his tissues.

Paco lost his grip; he stood up in a bolt.

And *reclusa* darted deeper.

It scampered through the crevices and under the concha; along the meatus and past his soft palate. It dug into his pharynx, sped over the larynx and flew toward his lungs.

Its claws pierced the bronchus; Paco started to choke.

Then he grabbed at his throat.

And coughed.

It did not come out!

Still there!

He choked and coughed.

Still there!

He coughed again.

S*till there!*

Paco lurched back and hacked. A stupendous hack.

And the spider hurtled out. Over his tongue.

Out of his mouth!

Onto the moonlit floor.

Despite his terror, or perhaps because of it, Paco bent over the creature to see what had gotten him. He beat back his tears. He stared at the thing.

It didn't move. *Was it dead?*

But what he saw sent a chill up his spine.

The violin.

On the body.

Of the brown recluse spider.

"¡Mira mamá! Mira! Es la araña café! Me pico! Me pico!" (Look mama! Look! It is the brown spider! It bit me! It bit me!)

Then it moved, and Paco jumped back.

"¡Mira mamá! Mira!" he pointed. "La araña café! Me pico!"

Emilio ran to his side and stomped at the creature.

But like Paco, he missed.

And *reclusa* spun out.

Raced away from the moonlight and disappeared down a crack.

Paco dropped to his knees, gripped the whole of his face and wailed out again, "¡Es la araña café! Me pico! Me pico!"

Paco could not sleep the rest of that night, nor for many nights thereafter. The chip-chirp of crickets, the howling of dogs, the croaking of bullfrogs and pitter-patter of rats – soporific before – terrified him now. The shadows of night, and everything he saw or thought he saw, left him wide eyed.

Electrified.

Paco's insomnia drove the others mad too – Emilio chided him *afeminado*; Margarita wept as he paced the floor. Finally, Mamacita made a bed on their table, lit a lantern for light and held Paco's hand until he found sleep. Even then he dreamed of gargoyles and gruesome things. Nights *and spiders* would never be the same.

Three weeks following, Paco stood before a hazy mirror staring at his nose, tears streaming down his face. The spider's venom had etched his nostril nearly to the bone. The eschar extended down from the vestibule to the border of his upper lip, and then returning upward, cleaved a gap where the edge of the nostril met the skin of his cheek. The gash exposed the destructed tissues. It looked like the guts of a butchered chicken and he whimpered, "Paco el monstruo horrible ... Paco el monstruo horrible!" (Paco the grotesque monster ... Paco the grotesque monster!)

The fistulous tract that opened two centimeters in and dove three centimeters down, piercing his gums, the roots of his teeth and roof of his mouth, was no less repulsive. Putrefaction oozed from it. Paco could smell his own rotten breath. He incessantly poked his tongue in the crevice hoping to rid of it. But of course he could not.

The doctors in Guadalajara examined Paco, shrugged their shoulders and said there was nothing they could do – maybe in the United States – otherwise, Paco's nose would have to heal on its own.

"*¿Se cura sola?*" *(Heal on its own?)*

"Si amigo, sanara sola." (Yes my friend, heal on its own.)

Months later Paco glared back at the mirror. He set his jaw, threw back his shoulders and stood up straight. Paco knew what he had to do. Paco Sánchez, aged ten years, *knew* what he had to do.

TEN YEARS AFTER – WINTER 1993
Conversation 5
University Hospital, Los Angeles
Wednesday, January 19, 1993; 8:37 a.m.

Dr. George Alexandre, Chief of Plastic and Reconstructive Surgery at University Hospital inserted the retractor into Paco Sánchez's mouth, secured it firmly in place and located the fistulous opening through the lenses of the operating scope. He then asked his assistant for the ronguer, slid it into the cleft and deftly threaded it upward until it pierced the fissure in Paco's right nostril.

Smiling to himself as he prepared the ronguer for the most meticulous portion of the procedure, Alexandre recalled the initial encounter with his young patient. Presenting with his uncle Raphael, Paco first consulted the surgeon in late 1992. Several elements of Paco's story stuck out in Alexandre's mind. Paco had emigrated from Mexico with his uncle in 1988. He had a credible command of English as a second language, *and* the grotesque deformity created by the brown recluse spider bite obsessed him. Finally, despite having health insurance from his workplace, the insurance company rejected his claim for nasal reconstruction as both "preexisting" and "unnecessary" – labeling it cosmetic.

Alexandre liked Paco from the very beginning – strong hands forged hard by rough work – steel blue eyes that made contact. Smooth skin with rich, brown tones. The plastic surgeon's uncommon sense for symmetry and beauty saw beyond the obscene scar. Paco's was a handsome face with solid character.

Quirks of nature, fistulous tracts form when microorganisms and noxious toxins bore seamy tunnels through soft tissue spaces. Defiling elements render them resistant to healing. Most surgeons shudder at the sight of them. After thorough examination and considerable evaluation, Alexandre concluded that *reclusa's* venom had entered a small vein in Paco's nostril and – in combination with Paco's resident bacteria – burrowed the tract from his nasal passage through to the roof of his mouth. Entrenched for over 10 years, the challenge to obliterate it was indeed considerable. Dr. Alexandre tackled it like a high wire dare.

The surgeon checked the position of the ronguer for a final time, opened the ninja blades at its tip and under fluoroscopic guidance began the procedure to eradicate the fibrous walls of the fistula. Meticulous attention to detail during the pre-operative phase – three dimensional mapping of the tract with magnetic resonance imaging, development of a flexible ronguer calibrated to 1 millimeter greater than the widest dimension of the fistula, and research in his animal lab, gave Alexandre confidence his approach would lead to success this time.

Despite the delicate aspects of the procedure, Alexandre reflected on the details of his initial conversation with Paco as he proceeded. "So what brings you here, Mr. Sánchez?" Alexandre recollected asking.

Paco looked about the office, taking notice of the degrees and citations hanging on Alexandre's walls – medical school at Stanford, residency at University of Chicago, fellowship at Plastique International, Brussels, Belgium, presidential service awards for humanity in medicine and dual certification in plastic as well as head and neck surgery. Then he cleared his throat, looked the surgeon straight on, and pointing at his nose, said, "I have been – how do you say? – searching for someone who can help me with this. I want to look more better, not like a monster."

From the distance of his desk, Alexandre surveyed the devastation above Paco's upper lip and the cleft encircling his right nostril. He inwardly agreed – it *was* grotesque *and* deforming; then he asked, "How did this happen, Mr. Sánchez?"

"When I am 10 years old, I am sleeping. In the night, a brown spider, it crawled inside my nose, and it bit me. I now have this," he pointed again to his nose.

Alexandre rose from his chair, took a pen light from his coat pocket, and examined the wretched scar more closely, gently pushing back and forth and up and down on the nasal coumella. He shined the light inside Paco's nose, observing the disfigured tissue underlying the nostril and extending back along the floor of the passageway.

"Hmmm," he paused. "Open your mouth … I see. Interesting," the surgeon mumbled under his breath. "Let me have another look inside your nose. Bend your head back."

Alexandre shined the pen light inside Paco's nose again, examining the surface and said, "Once more inside your mouth."

As the light reflected off the fistulous opening in Paco's soft palate, a drop of pus oozed from it. The sight, and feculent odor, caught Alexandre off guard. He stood up straight to suppress nausea, returned the pen light to his pocket, and walked back to his chair. "That's quite an injury, Mr. Sánchez; very complex as a matter of fact."

"Yes, sir," Paco responded. "That is why I have come to you. For over ten years I have been looking in the mirror at my face. For over ten years I have been smelling and tasting what you call it – the pus – in my mouth. I have been working very hard with my Uncle Raphael to get the money to fix this, but all the doctors they tell me it is very expensive, maybe $15,000 or $20,000. I cannot save so much money fast enough for me. I have been saving and saving, but I must also send some money to Mamacita. When I finish high school, I get a green card and I take a job laying the bricks. When I get medical insurance with the company, the insurance says this is – what do you call it – cosmetic and they will not pay for it, so I am stuck day and night with this. All the people see that I am a monster. Even mi amigos tease me and they call me Caracortada."

"Caracortada?" Alexandre asked. "What does …?"

"Scarface," Paco interjected.

Alexandre instructed the assistant to engage the ninja blades on the ronguer. Through the fiber optic nasopharyngoscope he observed the glistening steel unfold and begin to whir in Paco's nasal passage. Satisfied with the position, he gently tugged on the ronguer and watched the blades disappear into Paco's flesh. Deftly rotating the ronguer under fluoroscopic guidance and the MRI map, he slowly and oh so carefully threaded the instrument down the fistulous tunnel toward Paco's soft palate.

Paco's reaction to the surgeon's proposal when they first met exhilarated Alexandre and nestled fresh in his memory. "Here's the way I put this together, Mr. Sánchez," Alexandre remembered saying. "You've got three, really four conditions in need of correction. The fistula that leads from your nostril into your mouth, the bed of scar tissue inside your nostril that inhibits nasal function, the cleavage extending to the outside at the nasal margin and, of course, the tissue destruction and scar above your upper lip …"

"Can they be fixed? I have to have them fixed," Paco interrupted. "How much money do I have to have? They say …"

"The entire process will require four surgeries, possibly more," Alexandre interjected. "With time to heal between each procedure, more than a year maybe 18 months, even longer – no little time – or commitment on your part. This is precise, meticulous, delicate surgery

15

Paco; it demands tedious aftercare and follow-up, especially the fistula."

"How can it be done?" Paco asked again.

Alexandre leaned back in his chair and pondered the question. Repair of the fistula could be streamed through the University's research on human subjects committee, the Institutional Review Board and his National Institutes of Health Wound Research grant – perhaps the same for repair of the nasal mucosa. The nasal cleft amounted to straightforward plastic surgery, which could be financed through the umbrella of research or his Plastic Surgery Foundation for Humanity. He wasn't certain what or how to cover the cost of the upper lip reconstruction, but he would figure something out. Of course, he had to pay his staff, the anesthesiologist, and facility charges. The costs were indeed considerable.

Finally, he broke the silence, "I will do this for you, Paco."

"What is it that you mean?"

"It means that I will repair all of this for you without cost."

Paco could not believe his ears and said, "I do not understand."

Alexandre smiled, "I will do all of this surgery for you without cost."

"How? The other doctors want so much. How can *you* do this?" Paco asked again.

"Research. I can roll your case into my research grant."

"You are going to do experiments on me?"

"Not exactly ... by applying established principles and thoroughly tested technology in your reconstruction, I'll refine the methods and procedures used in plastic surgery to repair your injury. When I publish the results others will benefit. Call it applied research, Paco, not experimentation."

Paco's face relaxed. At first he sat speechless and then he blurted, "Jesus Christ! Do you hear, Uncle Raphael?! Dr. Alexandre say he is going to fix my nose! I can no longer be *el monstruo horrible!*" Then Paco stood and with his left arm akimbo and right arm held high, he pirouetted like a gypsy dancing to flamenco. "Jesus Christ, Uncle Raphael! Jesus Christ!"

Alexandre's assistant tapped the surgeon's shoulder, interrupting his reminiscent thoughts, "Your secretary called to say your lunch with the Dean of the medical school has been cancelled ... something about the chancellor of the University and rescheduling next week."

"Again, Zuckerman is such a jerk," he grumbled glancing up at the clock – 9:47 a.m. – and then asked the anesthesiologist, "How's our patient?"

"Vital signs stable. Oxygen saturation 98%; heart rate, respirations and blood pressure rock solid."

"Excellent."

"Give me the high sign when you are five minutes from closure. I need to precisely titrate the propofol."

"Gotcha'," Alexandre responded without looking up.

To his dismay the first two procedures to correct Paco's fistula failed. Undaunted, and with Paco's acquiescence, Alexandre returned to his research laboratory. By creating fistulous tracts in Pit Bull Terriers utilizing a mixture of arachidonic acid and bacteria cultured from Paco's nose, he discovered that irrigation of the eradicated tract with antibiotics sensitive to his patient's bacteria and subsequent closure of each opening with cartilaginous plugs, improved the outcomes – 17 of 21 resulted in full closure of the fistulas created in the Pit Bulls. So when the tip of the ronguer appeared at Paco's soft palate, Alexandre set the instrument to the side, quickly but thoroughly flushed the tunnel with a mixture of the antibiotics cefotaxime and clindamycin and inserted 3mm plugs of cartilage harvested from Paco's ear into the fistulous openings. The surgeon then observed for blood oozing around the plugs – a good sign – as he discovered during his research that fresh red blood cells in the ronguered tracts formed cellular matrices, creating bridges for tissue growth.

Alexandre's investigations also confirmed that painstaking attention to postsurgical care, intravenous antibiotics and 14 one-hour sessions in a hyperbaric oxygen chamber at 6.9 psi ensured success. With the procedure complete Alexandre removed his surgical gown and ordered the anesthesiologist to reverse the propofol.

Pushing the gurney through the swinging doors, the hospital order-ly rushed Paco Sánchez from the surgical suite to the elevator on the 2nd floor that took them to the basement of University Hospital. The eleva-tor stopped with an abrupt clunk and the doors rattled open jostling Paco from the remaining haze of the anesthesia. The attendant pulled the gurney from the elevator, wheeled it about and headed down the corridor to another set of double doors above which a sign read The University Institute of Hyperbaric Medicine. The doors automatically swung open into a cavernous room where the orderly was greeted by Dr. Alexandre and a wholesome woman in her late forties wearing a badge labeled Chief Technician Hyperbaric Medicine.

"Good. You're here," Alexandre said. "Move the gurney alongside the steel chamber and help us transfer him."

Paco surveyed the room through the veil of residual anesthesia. It looked like the control tower for a space shuttle launch – grids flashing digital messages, computers, cathode tube monitors and whirring un-familiar sounds. Situated squarely in the room, Paco's eyes zeroed in on one of three hyperbaric chambers. Except for the electronics sur-rounding and attached to it, the thing looked like a miniature submarine – steel rivets the size of jaw breakers spaced evenly and continuously about the tubular hull, six inch portals on both sides and a door leading to the interior of the chamber fitted on the outside with a reduced rendi-tion of a nautical wheel. His muscles tightened.

"How are you feeling Paco? Anesthesia wearing off?" Alexandre asked.

"I am okay," Paco lied.

"You're trembling."

"Maybe I am a little nervous."

"Nothing to worry about Paco," Alexandre reassured him. "You're in capable hands. We'll be with you the entire time and we'll monitor your vital signs the whole way. And you'll have a headset to communi-cate with us whenever you need to. Any pain from the surgery?"

"Not so much," Paco hesitated and then asked. "Is that the thing that you are going to put me into? The what you call it – the hyperbaric oxygen?"

"A bit imposing isn't it? This one's a relic the University acquired from the U.S. Navy. Perfect for research," Alexandre said resting his hand on the chamber. "It's not so bad once you get over the sight of it. Patients often fall asleep during the treatment. Any other questions before we proceed? We need to get going."

Paco had a hundred questions but sensed the doctor's urgency – Dr. Alexandre had explained that his research on fistulas proved that post-operative submersion in high pressure oxygen promoted healing. After ten years of living with the smell and taste of pus in his mouth, and two failed procedures already, nothing took priority over surgical success. Paco put aside his questions and said, "No sir. I am ready."

The chief tech and the orderly slid Paco from the gurney onto the chamber's rolling table, pushed him into the hyperbaric unit, swung the heavy metal door into place and spun the wheel to lock it down. Paco's muscles stiffened. He clenched his fists. The eerie silence rattled him. Beads of sweat welled up on his forehead. A wave of nausea spread up and into his throat. "Am I going to die?" he wondered. Then the confident voice of Dr. Alexandre blotted his claustrophobic sense of doom.

"You all right in there, Paco?"

Paco looked at the surgeon through portal and spoke, "I feel very how do you say – closed in – and it is hard for me to breathe. But you say that this will make me more better, so I am okay."

"Slow your breathing down – long, slow, deep breaths," Alexandre instructed. "Your vital signs are stable. The temperature in the chamber is just 69 degrees, oxygen is flowing in and you are doing fine. I'm going to begin the pressurization now, Paco."

Alexandre signaled the chief tech, who in turn flipped two toggle switches and adjusted one dial, "You said 4.4 psi to initiate the dive sir?"

"Yes, let's see how he tolerates that and go from there. I don't want to overwhelm him and it's hard to know at this point if the pressure will increase or decrease immediate post-op discomfort."

Paco thought he felt the hyperbaric pressure envelop his body – wrapping him like a mummy; squeezing his insides. He quivered twice and suppressed another momentary wave of nausea. The beads of sweat on his forehead coalesced into rivulets and trickled down his temples

19

like summer rain on a windowpane. Finally, he took a deep breath, exhaled and closed his eyes.

"Four point four psi, Dr. Alexandre. Vital signs stable, sir."

"Good. Hold it there, then slowly increase it when I tell you."

Alexandre peered through the portal observing his patient. "How are you doing now, Paco?"

"I am doing okay. The pressure in my ears is the worse, but I am okay."

"Open and close your mouth like chewing bubble gum. That should help relieve it. And you can move around – wipe your forehead if you like – remember slow, deep breaths."

Paco feigned chewing gum, pulled the gown up to wipe his brow and took three deep breaths. His muscles suddenly relaxed and he felt the warm glow one feels just before passing off to sleep.

Alexandre watched Paco's eyes blinking shut and then glanced up at the chief tech, "Take the pressure incrementally to atmospheric 6.9 pounds per square inch and hold it there for sixty minutes. I'm going to run up to the cafeteria and get a Starbucks. You want something?"

"Caffé Mocha if you're buying, sir."

As Alexandre headed toward the elevator, he pondered the next steps for Paco Sánchez, thinking out loud. "So if this corrects the fistula – and it should – I can harvest buccal mucosa for a full thickness graft on the nasal passage and repair the nasal cleft ... perhaps in a single procedure. That leaves the hideous scar above his lip, and I haven't a clue what to do with that. One thing at a time I guess," he grumbled.

Then an idea came to him in the flash of an "ah-ha!" moment and he scurried toward the cafeteria, whistling.

Conversation 6
Rancho Palos Verdes, California, USA
Wednesday, January 19, 1993; 4:31 p.m.

A blustery winter wind from the northwest chilled the late afternoon as Carolyn and Jack MacDougall climbed toward the edge of the ravine to survey the vacant property. Walking behind her husband, Carolyn adjusted her shawl to fend off the cold. She wished he had warned her to wear different shoes – walking in high heels through weeds and rocks weren't Carolyn MacDougall's idea of a good time. "Can you wait up, Jack? I'm having trouble in these shoes."

MacDougall turned, glared at his wife, and reluctantly extended his hand, "Why did you wear high heels? I made it perfectly clear the property was undeveloped. You of all people should know better."

"Well I guess I didn't think," she declared taking his hand. "Who else is building here?"

"I haven't a clue. There are nineteen home sites of about one acre each – all with magnificent views, situated for absolute privacy. The developer says they will sell out fast in this market despite the steep price. Actually they are not even listed yet"

"How much?"

"For this one? Five-hundred grand."

Carolyn could not believe her ears, "Say again."

"You heard me," MacDougall retorted as they reached the edge of the ravine.

Carolyn caught her breath and then exclaimed, "Wow! What a view!"

"I thought you'd like it – would you look at the ocean from up here? And if we get this one, absolute privacy. I love it."

"But, Jack, the price. It's too much."

MacDougall put his arm around her shoulder and drew her in. He *had* to have this property, so he sold her. "Think of it. Custom design, custom built. Six, maybe seven thousand square feet. Huge master suite with a veranda looking out over this. A spa for a master bath. Home theater, exercise room, the works ..."

"Spacious bedrooms with separate bathrooms for the kids? A gourmet kitchen?" she broke in.

"Bedrooms for the kids, a gourmet kitchen *and* a wine cellar."

"How about a swimming pool?"

"But of course. Nothing's too good for you and the kids Carolyn."

SIX MONTHS LATER – SUMMER 1993
Conversation 7
University Hospital, Los Angeles
Thursday, July 21, 1993; 8:06 a.m.

The anatomy of the nasolabial triangle is defined by its borders – the nostrils, which serve as conduits for oxygen flowing to the lungs; the nasolabial folds that extend from the nostril ridges to the corners of the mouth, and the upper lip delineated by the vermillion border or "Cupid's bow" where the fleshy lip meets the skin above it. Within the borders there lies the columella – the partition between the nostrils; the philtrum – the depression above the center of the lip that begins at the demise of the columella and ends at the grip of Cupid's bow; and the philtral columns – the distinct linear folds that define the central depression of the philtrum. Many plastic surgeons embellish their financial largess by leveling nasolabial folds accentuated by aging, and injecting Cupid's bow to create petulant, "kissy" lips. However, for Dr. George Alexandre and Paco Sánchez, reconstruction of Paco's nasolabial triangle defined the essential purpose, art and science of plastic surgery.

Alexandre's strategy to eliminate the hideous scar cascading from Paco's right nostril came to him like drumfire. Rather than dermabrasion or skin grafting, and the specter of countless revisions, he opted to hide the deformity in the masquerade of a moustache. Although no easy task, and the thorny reality that he had never transplanted a moustache, Alexandre possessed the swagger to pull it off.

The multifaceted dimensions of Paco's case fueled Alexandre's resolve. He knew the cutting edge technique of "follicular unit transplantation" vastly improved hair restoration techniques and he surmised that by replanting follicular bundles, each containing 2 to 4 hair follicles replete with sebaceous glands, muscle, and connective tissue, he could overcome the consequences of the *reclusa* spider bite. Alexandre also predicted by harvesting from the donor area and immediately reimplanting into the moustache site, he could substantially improve graft survival. *It had to work.*

After months of experimentation and refining his technique in the canine lab, the prospect of actually performing the procedure on Paco left the surgeon giddy. Still, the entire procedure needed to be staged: electrolysis to remove all existing moustache hair above Paco's left upper lip; modifying the surgical chair, custom fit to support Paco's torso and mitigate fatigue during the lengthy surgery; repetitive, gentle dermabrasion of the scar to level the spider bite cicatrix; and finally, calculating the number of follicular units, as well as the precise angle of the grafts, to create a realistic moustache. Despite Paco's impatience and Alexandre's flurry, it simply couldn't be rushed.

"Unlike the other surgeries," he explained to his patient, "I am using an anesthetic technique called conscious sedation for the moustache transplantation. You will be sitting for two, maybe three – even four hours. I want you responsive yet comfortably in twilight sleep. You will be harnessed in the chair for support – like in a rollercoaster – and your head, neck, and chin will be stabilized by the collar we've developed.

"I'll be extracting the grafts from the back of your head with one of these," he said, handing Paco a direct hair implanter. "And immediately transplanting each one into the skin above your upper lip – one at a time, over and over – meticulous work, really. Make sense?"

A scowl enveloped Paco's face. "Yes, I understand what you say. But if you say I am only twilight sleeping, I want to know if this what you call transplantation is to hurt me. I have been so long to do this over and over. I sometimes want to give it up. Slowly I look more better, so it keeps me going. Slowly, Paco, the monster goes away … but I do not want to have to feel the pain."

Alexandre took a deep breath, "With Versed as the anesthetic agent and small amounts of local anesthesia, the discomfort should be minimal. I understand your desire to be done with this Paco. Your commitment has been unwavering and your resolve considerable. Our efforts have resulted in original contributions and knowledge to medical science. My hat is off to you. This should finish what we started together over two years ago – the fistula is obliterated, your nasal passage repaired; I am confident you will be happy with the result of the moustache as well – Paco 'the monster' no more," Alexandre smiled.

The surgical staff positioned Paco in the procedure chair securing his chest and abdomen with a contraption improvised from a baseball catcher's chest protector and aircraft seatbelts customized for an exact fit. Using Velcro, they strapped down his arms and legs. Finally, they immobilized his head and neck with a padded cervical collar that aligned and supported the base of his skull, mandible and chin.

"How does that feel, Mr. Sánchez?" one of the technicians asked. "Are you comfortable?"

"I think maybe you are going to launch me like a rocket," Paco frowned. "But yes, I am very comfortable."

"Good. I'm going to raise the chair. Then we'll start your IV and get set to go. Okay? Set to launch. Count down: 10, 9, 8, 7 ... 3, 2, 1, 0," the tech smiled pressing the hydraulic switch labeled "Up".

With the unit elevated to Alexandre's specifications, one tech started Paco's IV and attached the electrodes on his chest to the heart monitor; another shaved and prepared the donor area; while another prepped the moustache site with Hibiclens. The anesthesiologist infused the Versed. Alexandre performed a fastidious surgical scrub – *no infection on this one for God's sake* – donned his gown, sterile talc-free, latex-free surgical gloves, and the procedure began.

Alexandre calculated the area to be transplanted at just over 10 square centimeters. At 0.6mm per graft, 50 follicular units per square centimeter, 500 grafts in all. He slipped his magnifying loupes into place and with the direct hair implanter held perpendicular to the sagittal plane of Paco's scalp; he harvested the first follicular unit, walked around to face his patient, and transplanted the initial graft into the left upper corner of the philtrum, just below the columella. Although his heart raced, behind the surgical mask he glowed with satisfaction and said to himself, "This is the crown jewel of hundreds of hours and two years of research. Paco's monster – Scarface – obliterated! *And my work* cemented in the archives of Plastic Surgery." Then he repeated the process over and over, implanting perpendicular from left to right and down, philtral column to philtral column, until the entire philtrum was transplanted. Paco occasionally winced or groaned, but otherwise, held comfortably still. The clock read 10:42 a.m.

Alexandre next turned his attention to the right upper lip, implanting laterally from just outside the philtral column to the nasal labial fold in slight but ever increasing angles. At 12:17 p.m., he removed his gloves, consumed two oatmeal raisin cookies, drank 12 ounces of 2% milk, scrubbed once more and returned to his task.

The left side proceeded without delay. At 2:06 p.m., Alexandre dropped his gloves in the biohazard waste bucket, made his way to the surgeon's lounge, poured a generous cup of coffee and sank into an overstuffed chair, exhausted.

"Nice job, Dr. Alexandre, your transplant looks great," a voice came from behind.

Alexandre looked up and around to discover the operating room director. "Thanks. But save the congratulations for later. I'm confident that they won't ... nevertheless the grafts could fail," he frowned.

Conversation 8
Rancho Palos Verdes
Thursday, July 21, 1993; 3:26p.m.

Drs. Jack MacDougall and Edmund M. Pinkerton walked past the carpenters, stepped over the construction debris and climbed the temporary staircase leading to the future master suite. An electrician pulling Romex cautioned them to watch their steps, to which MacDougall grunted "thanks," largely ignoring the warning.

"So here's what I want to show you," MacDougall smiled as the two physicians made their way through the chaos of construction and out to the master bedroom balcony.

Pinkerton stepped over the threshold and looked out, "Holy cow!" he exclaimed. "It's everything you made it out to be, if not more. This view is out-fucking-rageous, Jack!"

"Carolyn's ecstatic. At first she was skeptical – too far to the kid's schools, not close enough to the malls, blah, blah, blah – I had to sell her. When she saw this, she knew I was right."

Pinkerton shook his head. "They never listen," he grumbled. "You putting in a pool?"

"You bet. We're thinking infinity edge. From up here it will really set things off – magnify the effect of the ravine and the ocean. What do you think?"

"No doubt in my mind," Pinkerton responded checking his watch. "Show me the rest of it, then how about we celebrate your good fortune at my place? I picked up a case of 1989 Château Beau-Séjour Bécot at Marché Bacchus – it's a St. Emillion premier grand cru classe' that is sure to knock your socks off."

"Good enough for me. And speaking of grape, let me show you the wine cellar," MacDougall chortled heading back to the staircase.

Conversation 9
University Hospital Clinics, Los Angeles
Tuesday, September 13, 1993; 3:23p.m.

Paco Sánchez leaned into the mirror inspecting his moustache and the results of months and months of painstaking surgery when the exam room door swung open and Dr. George Alexandre entered.

"So what do you think? You like it?"

Paco turned away from the mirror and faced the surgeon. "I have to say it look very good and I am very happy, Dr. Alexandre."

"Hop up on the exam table. Let's take a look."

Alexandre removed the magnifying loops from his lab coat pocket and slipped them on. Rubbing his thumb over the surface of the moustache, he peered between the hairs and down to the follicles. "Impressive. Very impressive," he hummed. "I can't see where you lost any follicles, Paco. It looks fantastic!

"Let's take one more gander at that nostril. Turn to the left. Now head back. Hmmm … back a little more. Okay. Sit up straight. Well," Alexandre paused, "your moustache is perfect. I'm still not entirely satisfied with the symmetry of your nostrils. What say we correct that?"

After so many months and countless procedures the thought of more surgery petrified Paco. Straight on and from the side the defect was barely perceptible. From below, looking skyward, the right nostril took a slightly crooked curl compared to the left, but all in all Paco thought it looked just fine. "I can think about that?" Paco asked.

26

"Certainly. No rush. Anytime," Alexandre responded. "Sit right here. I'm going to get my camera – as I told you I am publishing your case in the Journal of Plastic and Reconstructive Surgery – I have the 'before' photos; I need to get the 'after' shots. I'll be back in a flash."

Alexandre hurried back carrying a 35mm SLR digital Canon and the portfolio of photographs that memorialized Paco's reconstruction. After taking several shots from every angle, he laid the 'before' photographs out for Paco to examine – photos from the very first consultation revealing the hideous scars; photos immediately post-op, and 3 months after the repair of the nostril cleft; close-ups of the grafts of the nasal mucosa and more shots taken the afternoon of the moustache transplantation. They were all there, in vivid color.

Paco glanced at them, became suddenly pale, turned gray-green and suppressed the urge to vomit. Choking back his emotions, Paco broke out in a sweat and whispered, "I must have to sit down ..." The room went yellow, then grey, then black. And Alexandre looked up just in time to catch his patient crumpling to the exam room floor.

The nurse broke a pledget of smelling salts, ran it under Paco's nose and wiped his face with a damp cloth while Dr. Alexandre guided Paco into a chair. After several minutes he declared, "We lost you there for second, Paco."

"I was looking at the fotographia. I remember getting all the sweat ... then nothing. I think I am better now. Could I have some water?"

Alexandre's nurse brought Paco a cup of water and a fresh cloth to wipe his face and the surgeon sat with him while he recovered. When Paco seemed up to it, Alexandre spoke. "Well this is it, Paco. We're done. It's over. No more procedures. I know you are happy for that."

Paco managed a weak smile; tears welled up in his eyes. "Thank you. I am very pleased. I no longer look like a monster. People they do not call me a monster or Scarface."

"You never were, and you are not a monster, Paco."

"In my heart I know that," Paco said wiping his eyes while producing a thick envelope from his jacket and handing it to the surgeon. "But when I look everyday into the mirror for more than ten years, I cannot help but to believe that I am ... so this is for you, and what you have done, to make me more better."

Alexandre took the envelope, opened it and stared dumbfounded at the contents – a handwritten thank you note and several one hundred dollar bills. He looked up at Paco, and back to the envelope, speechless. Finally, he risked offending his patient, "I can't accept this Paco. I agreed to do your reconstruction at no cost to you. Your commitment and contribution to medical science is all the payment I asked."

"So you can give it to – what do you call it – the Foundation? Maybe it helps you to help others like me?"

Alexandre considered the offer and after a moment said, "Please do not be put off Paco. Your gift is generous and I am honored – the Foundation would be grateful, but I want you to use this to reunite your family – to move Mamacita and the others to the United States. Please Paco. Do this for you *and for me*," Alexandre pleaded handing the envelope back.

Paco's eyes glazed over again with tears, "To have family together is muy importante."

"Exactly!" Alexandre agreed. "Now get out of here. No more nonsense! I'm behind. My other patients are waiting."

Post-traumatic stress disorder or PTSD arises following perceived or real threat of death or disruption in physical, sexual or psychological integrity. Alexandre considered himself an avid student of the psychology literature – he co-authored with Sarwer one of the six epidemiological studies on the increased prevalence of suicide in women with cosmetic breast augmentation. Deblinger's research on PTSD in sexually abused children intrigued him. He embraced the essential theoretical constructs of the syndrome – re-experiencing the trauma through flashbacks and nightmares as the basis for the chronic symptoms – insomnia, anxiety, anger, hypervigilance and impairment of social functioning. Nevertheless, Paco's collapse at first flummoxed Alexandre. As he watched Paco leave his office he chastised himself and wondered how in his enthusiasm to make Paco whole, he had marginalized this essential point – no scalpel, no ronguer, no amount of surgical expertise or painstaking research could correct the psychological impact of the *reclusa* spider bite, ten years of living with a detestable scar and the many months of intense surgical reconstruction. Paco's resolve, steel blue eyes, strength of character and work hardened hands had buffaloed

Alexandre and he flogged himself for it. He knew better, although what could he do now? And what would he have done differently in any event?

"Holy moly," he whispered shaking his head. "What will become of Paco Sánchez?"

CONVERSATIONS FOR PACO

PART II

"Of all the forms of inequality, injustice in health care is the most shocking and inhumane."

~ Martin Luther King, 1965

JAMES LENHART

NINE YEARS LATER – WINTER 2002

Conversation 10
Bellflower, California
Friday, January 11, 2002; 8:17 p.m.

While Paco helped Mamacita put José and Miguel to bed, Sarita finished the dinner dishes. After the boys were tucked in, Paco took his jacket from the hall closet and asked, "You want to walk Muchi with me, Sarita?"

Sarita dried her hands and smiled, "I have to get my coat and be right with you."

Paco leashed Muchi up, held the door leading to the driveway for Sarita, and they were off.

Their home sat simply on a tidy lot. White stucco, three bedrooms, one bath; a living room and a kitchen decorated in bright, vivid colors. Paco hung his tools and lawn implements along the walls of the single-car garage. Nails, screws and fasteners; power tools, motor oil, Black Flag bug spray, Ortho 1-napthy N-methycarbamate insecticide, two Hudson tank sprayers, a blower-vac and chain saw were stored in the cabinet drawers and shelves along the back wall. Sarita's Caravan squeezed in next to their lawn mower, the hedge trimmer and a DeVilbiss power washer; Paco parked his pick-up outside on the drive.

Nestled in on Calderon Street, their house fit in with the rest of them. No white picket fences, but well-kept properties separated by painted concrete block walls laid out in a working class neighborhood. Bushes and shrubs, as well as flowers that bloom in the spring and in the summer, spruce up the surrounding homes.

In their backyard, a sandbox for Miguel and José occupied a corner next to a concrete slab just large enough for two lawn chairs and Paco's barbeque. There was room for little else, except a collapsible clothesline and the trellis roses – one Dream Weaver, two Mornings Magics, and a Blaze of Glory – that Sarita tended when Paco mowed the grass that grew both in the front and back.

Twinkling stars lit the black night sky; a crisp winter breeze caught Sarita off guard. "Burr-r-r. It is cold," she shivered. "Hold me."

31

Paco nuzzled the crest of Sarita's left shoulder in the hollow of his right underarm and wrapped the rest of his arm around her back, cradling her right elbow with his hand and drawing her in. She snuggled up, smiled and said, "That is better … it gets so cold these last days." Ambling together, arm in arm, Paco and Sarita Sánchez appeared as one – the matching pieces of a jigsaw puzzle.

On the leash, Muchi pranced like a Tennessee Walker; her rusty red head held high, ears pointed to the sky. Sarita and Paco shuffled behind her, making their way down Calderon to 59th Street, and turning two blocks north to the crosswalk leading to the entrance of Mancusso Public Park.

Beyond the arched portal, Muchi stopped to sniff, release her urine and kick up grass, certain to extinguish the scent of other canines claiming squatter's rights to *her* land. Then, holding her nose close to the surface of the ground, she pulled them along, sniffing for whatever it is that dogs smell between the blades of dormant grass.

Well past the entrance, Paco checked for other dogs and seeing none, unleashed Muchi. Free at last, she bolted like a Thoroughbred – legs flying parallel to the earth, leaping through the air. She ran straight, then darted, dodged and darted again, circling in and out between the trees and bushes. Finally out of breath and panting, Muchi tired and slowed her pace behind curious nostrils surveying the earth. Rambling about, she stopped at last to pass more urine and dump her load. Paco bagged the excrement, tied it with a knot and tossed it in the trash. When Paco gave Muchi her Milk-Bone, she knew the walk was over. Paco leashed her up and they headed back. Sarita nuzzled under Paco's shoulder again, walking quietly her face comfortable against his chest, eyes closed.

Near 59th and Calderon, Paco broke the silence. "Today on the way home from work I check out a bigger house for us, Sarita. It has four bedrooms, two-car garages and a big backyard for the children to play. It needs some work to fix it up, but that I can do. The price it is good and the neighborhood it is very nice"

"We have to sell this house first?"

"Yes, but the other houses here sell. With the baby coming we need more room."

Sarita looked up into Paco's eyes and smiled, "That is very nice. But I love our house. It is where our children first live. Our families never have a home so nice in Guadalajara. I am happy with what I have and that we have each other. I need nothing more, Paco. We can make it work."

"It is just my thinking," Paco shrugged. "Whatever we do now, someday I make a big house for us. I have for you a flower garden and for each of the children a bedroom. In this house, we have a garage for our cars and a kitchen made for a chef with terra cotta floors. Maybe I can build a casita for Mamacita."

At their side entrance, Paco took Muchi off her leash, opened the door for Sarita and let them in. Taking a deep breath, he followed Sarita and shut the door. Then he put away his Dodger baseball cap and windbreaker, hung up Sarita's coat and got ready for bed.

Conversation 11
Los Angeles
Friday, January 18, 2002; 4:25 p.m.

Winter sun ducked behind late afternoon clouds, casting magenta shadows across the western sky. Paco Sánchez set the trowel down and checked his watch – 4:25 p.m. He took a deep breath, pushed back his hair, wiped the sweat from his face with his forearm and signaled Emilio for more mortar.

With trowel back in hand, he scooped mortar from the palate, flipped it once or twice, laid fresh beads along the row of blocks and hoisted a new one in place. He tapped the corners, checked the mason's line for true, leveled it from side to side and rhythmically repeated the process until six more blocks were laid and the row completed. With his finishing trowel he scraped away the protruding mortar and smoothed out the joints. "Tomorrow we finish," he said to himself. "Four men, 27 days, 34,000 blocks, one magnífico warehouse."

Paco whistled a shrill note between his teeth and yelled at the men, "González, Jorge, Emilio. No más, amigos. Call it a day. Clean up and we go home."

Paco climbed down from the 30-foot rise of scaffolding, scraped and brushed his tools and loaded them into his pickup truck. As Paco arranged his trowels, hammer and plumb lines into a heavy canvas satchel, Sarita came from around the front of the building carrying a 12 pack of Modelo Especial and said, "Buenas tardes, Paco."

Paco did not see her coming, but turned to Sarita's voice. "¡Sarita, hola mi amor! (Sarita, hello my love!)

"Aha! Look what you have! Hey Emilio," he shouted. "Get Jorge, get González. Sarita brought cerveza!"

The men gathered around Paco's pick-up and Sarita, taking their beers, as she popped them open.

"¡Modelo Especial, que padre! ¡Como me las receto el doctor!" (Modelo Especial, super cool! Just like my doctor ordered!) Emilio declared. "Muchas gracias, Sarita. ¿Cómo esta el bebe?" (Many thanks, Sarita. How is the baby?)

"You are welcome," she blushed. "Due in three weeks. It is moving all the time. It never stops the kicking."

"Phew, I am tired," Paco said taking a long swig. "Mmmm, this taste good."

Sarita drank from a mandarin Jarritos looking over the workers and up at the new building, "The warehouse it looks like you have to be done."

Paco finished off the Modelo and threw his empty toward the construction debris. The bottle spun in an even spiral, one-hopped and landed on top of the pile. "Tomorrow we finish it I think," he smiled.

"Paco, I invite your uncle Raphael and aunt Graciela to dinner for green chili enchiladas, there is enough for everyone. You are done for today?"

"Done for sure, Sarita," Jorge laughed. "Let's go, I get more cerveza on the way."

Emilio climbed into Paco's truck. He shut the door and rolled down the window. "Jorge, no Tecate – just Modelo Especial."

"No problema, Emilio. See you at Paco's."

Paco leaned forward, looking around Emilio, "And Jorge. No tequila, cerveza only. Tomorrow we work and have to finish."

Emilio poured the tequila, one for Jorge, one for González, and one for himself. "Paco? Raphael?"

"No más, Emilio. I said no tequila. Now look at us. Shit faced pendejo Mexicans. All of us. Tomorrow our heads will be exploding, the walls will be crooked, and we will think they are straight! No más."

"Come on, Paco, one more. We wash it down with Modelo, sing the national anthem and then I go a la casa."

"Go ahead. Not me – and not the national anthem," Paco answered.

"Uncle Raphael?" Emilio asked.

Raphael stuck his hand up, palm forward, "No más. I have to drive."

"Have it your way," Emilio shrugged, lifting his glass. "Jorge, González. ¡Salud!"

"¡VIVA MÉJICO, SALUD!" they shouted in a chorus, throwing down the tequila and slamming their glasses to the table.

Emilio took a deep breath and broke out in song. Jorge and González followed suit. *"Mejicanos, al grito de ..."*

"González. Jorge. No more, Emilio! You wake the children and I said no anthem," Paco interrupted. "No más, I said before ..."

González and Jorge stopped but Emilio went on, *"Al sonoro rugir del cañón ..."*

"No more, Emilio!" Paco warned his brother.

Emilio laughed, whirled about and continued, *"De la Paz el arcángel divino ..."*

Paco grabbed Emilio, spun him about and threw him against the wall. Blood spurted from Emilio's nose splattering on the floor. "I said no más, Emilio. See what you make me do? What do not you understand? You are in the United States now. I bring you, my twin brother, from Jalisco. Give you my job. And all you do is shovel mortero, drink tequila, and sing the anthem of Mexico. In my house and on my job we speak English like the Americans. You learn English, take up the trade and stop getting drunk all the time, or I send you back to Guadalajara where you can work in the agave fields for 240 pesos per day and die the rotten death of poverty. Grab your stuff and get the fuck out of here, Emilio. All of you. Jorge, González, go home."

Paco sat alone at the kitchen table slumped in a chair, spinning the empty bottle of tequila. He reached for the shot glass filled with the last of it, put it to his lips and threw it down. The tequila burned his tongue and throat so he washed the sensation away with another slug of the beer. Staring at the Modelo Especial, he spun the bottle emptied of tequila, then glanced at the kitchen clock and realized it was way past time to go to bed, although he really didn't feel like it.

Except for the sound of Paco spinning the empty tequila bottle on the kitchen table, the house was stone cold quiet. The children were tucked in, and Paco had long since sent Sarita and Mamacita off to bed, after which he finished the dishes, cleaned up Emilio's bloody mess and took out the trash. The gloomy mood hanging over him came not from regret for his outrage aimed at Emilio or his own drunken stupor. More than once he had put his twin brother in his place – and for that matter, more times than one he'd had too much to drink. Tonight's funk emanated from a much thornier problem. So he asked once more the question that plagued him, "How can I tell what have happened at work to Sarita? And what will she say?"

Conversation 12
Rancho Palos Verde
Friday, January 18, 2002; 8:39 p.m.

Jack MacDougall donned a thick terrycloth robe, tucked his feet into lamb's wool slippers, and stepped out onto the balcony. Perched on the south end of a deep ravine, his view from the master bedroom veranda looked northwest into the night and the sprawling city below. He set a snifter of freshly poured Remy Martin X.O. on the end table and pulled a Bolívar Belicosos Finos from his pocket. Peeling away the wrapper, he ran the cigar under his nose, then licked the shaft of it sucking in the flavor off the tip of his tongue. Smacking his lips, he clipped and lit the cigar evenly in three rhythmic puffs. Clearing his throat, he sat back in an upholstered lounge chair, put his feet up on the ottoman and stared out at the city lights. Settling in, he sniffed the aromas of jasmine, candied orange, and hazelnut from the X.O. "What a beautiful evening," he pondered, "and, all things considered, a pretty decent week, then again, thank God it's Friday."

He took a long draw from the cigar, half inhaling and half exhaling – just enough to feel its buzz. Lifting the cognac to his lips, he inhaled its aroma again, and then took a sip letting it spill over his tongue and down his throat. "This *is* the life," he smiled to himself.

MacDougall laid his head back, closed his eyes and shut out the sparkling lights. It had not always been this way. To be sure, it helped to come from money, attend Johns Hopkins Medical School, take residency at Harvard, complete a neurology fellowship at Washington University he admitted, but the real money – the rocket that launched a life full of Cuban cigars and cognac – was shrewd investing during the 1991 Iraqi War, Desert Storm.

MacDougall remembered vividly the early spring telephone call. "Hey, Jack. Steve Wasserman, your eagle eye stockbroker from Smith-Barney. Listen, I have a deal. I've been talking to our Wall Street analyst. He says all indications point to the market going into the crapper on this Desert Storm thing. He recommends pulling the blue chips and tech stocks to the sidelines high and come back in low when the market bottoms out. What do you think? Donohue is a great analyst. Seems like a bull's-eye to me." MacDougall sat silent on the other end of the line pondering, and then set the broker straight, "My blue chips are parked, Steve. No matter how you try to convince me to the contrary, I'll leave those alone. They are well positioned, dollar-cost averaged and net a good return. But Intel and Microsoft, different deal. How many shares have I got of each?"

"Let me see. Open your account. Just a minute. Our computers are slow today …

"So. Damn. Slow. Come on. *Come* on … here we go, okay. Okay, Jack, Microsoft 5,000 shares at $53.00 a pop. Intel 2,000 shares at $107 and change … so what are your thoughts?"

MacDougall sipped from the Remy Martin and blinked at the city lights. He recollected not responding at first to Wasserman's question, penciling the math, and after some reflection saying, "Honestly, Steve, I don't give a blistering fuck what your analyst Donahue thinks. Here's what I am going to do. Sell the 2,000 Intel at $107."

"Yeah. Great. Good goin', Jack – what else?"

"Plow the $214,000.00 from the sale of the Intel back into Microsoft, add in another $55,000.00 on margin and make it a clean 10,000 share Microsoft holding."

"You know, Jack, that *is* good thinking, compromises you between your intuition, my expertise and Donohue's analysis. Yeah. Great. I like it."

"Don't give yourself too much credit and quit blowing smoke up my ass, Wasserman."

"I'm not blowing smoke. Look at your portfolio. It's stellar and you've called most of the shots."

"Yeah, yeah. So what commission are you charging me for *this* transaction?"

"You know Smith-Barney, they got this nailed. I can't change what's in the computer. You're at 3% going in and 2% coming out. Tell 'ya what though. I'll take you and the wife to dinner at Spago."

"Screw Spago, Steve, I hate that frou-frou shit. Just do the transaction."

MacDougall smiled and dragged from the Belicosos Finos tasting hints of earth and black honey. "Wasserman's such a stupid little prick," he chuckled to himself. Then he inhaled deeply, holding the smoke in his lungs. His lips tingled, a buzz meandered through the interstices of his brain. After he exhaled, he took a long sniff and another sip of the cognac and was high. A wry smile spread across his lips. "Ahhh, the good life," he whispered.

Conversation 13
Bellflower
Saturday, January 19, 2002; 5:37 p.m.

Paco Sánchez signaled and turned right onto Calderon. The incessant knock-knocking from Emilio's rot-gut tequila still pounded in his brain. For the 27th time that day, he winced and pushed the hangover from his head; for the 28th time that day he asked himself, "Why did I have to drink the rest of it?" He pulled into his driveway, turned off the Carlos Santana "Supernatural" CD and shut down his pickup. "Motherfucking alcohol," he whispered.

Paco opened the door, carefully stepped down from the truck and said to his pup, "Come on mi Muchi poochie, we are home."

Gray clouds hung low, dropping fresh rain across his face. Running his fingers through his hair, Paco took a deep breath, exhaled slowly and let the relief to be home settle in. He lifted the satchel of trowels, plumb bobs, levels, and mason lines from the back of the truck, dropped them under the canopy next to the side door and walked into the house. Muchi slid in behind.

Sarita sat in the rocker watching NBC's nightly news. Miguel and José ran around the room, ducking behind the rocker, playing Pancho Villa. José leveled his finger gun, took precision aim and yelled, "POW! POW! GOTCHA'! YOU ARE DEAD, PANCHO VILLA!"

Miguel swirled around, grabbed his chest and fell to the floor groaning, "Yes, I die. But I die for my country – just tell them I have said something."

José stood over Miguel, "Die! Pancho Villa! Die and I *cut off* your head."

Paco chuckled at their antics and said, "Buenas tardes, Sarita. Buenas tardes, mi niños."

"Buenas tardes, Paco. How was your day?"

Paco leaned over and kissed Sarita on her head. He ruffled Miguel's dark head of hair as he flew by, and sank into the chair.

"Paco … what is the matter?"

"I finished the job today, Sarita. It is done."

"Well, what is next?" she asked. "I hope you do not have to drive forever."

"I do not have to drive at all. They laid us off."

"Laid you off? What?"

"Francisco has no more work right now."

"But I thought … Francisco said …"

"I could not tell you. With the baby coming I did not want you to worry. But now I must. They hire a different company."

"How can they do that?"

"The contractors can do anything they want, Sarita. Francisco lost the job. Construction is so slow. The other company they came in low and they outbid Francisco."

"When will it be back? What will we do?"

"You do not have to worry."

"The children and Mamacita …"

"Francisco says he have bid another job and should find out in a month," Paco interjected.

"A month? You have never been out of work. A month? The house? The baby? What are ...?" she asked massaging her pregnant abdomen.

"See? I told you how you would worry, but you must not. I can work the Union Hall; I can do the handyman," Paco reassured. "It will be all right, Sarita. Please do not worry. I get the money. We keep the house, I promise."

Conversation 14
Los Angeles County Health District
Monday, January 21, 2002; 9:31 a.m.

Dr. Edmund M. Pinkerton founded Pinkerton Pathology Laboratories in a two-story structure near County and University hospitals in 1994 when he tired of working for healthcare conglomerate Medical Diagnostics. The initiative spoke neither of Pinkerton's genius nor his industry. Actually, the decision had been easy. The County Commission, perturbed by what they saw as unacceptable gouging by Medical Diagnostics, agreed to feed all basic clinical labs to Pinkerton for a fixed monthly price adjusted for volume, while negotiating rates favorable to Pinkerton for specialized testing.

Moreover, the contract permitted Pinkerton to maintain an independent arrangement with County Hospital for anatomic pathology. Pinkerton enjoyed autopsies or, as he put it, "discovering what disease hath rot" and the deal was struck. The flow of the negotiations surprised even Pinkerton. Of course, it didn't hurt that he and his wife Judi hobnobbed with the majority of the commissioners at the golf and country club, *and* contributed generously to their political campaigns.

In the end, the deal was ironclad; a base salary for anatomic pathology and a steady stream of revenue from County Hospital for tech fees and fixed laboratory costs. And of course, Pinkerton kept all income from professional fees generated by patient billings. The good doctor got giddy when he saw the numbers. The dollar signs exceeded his wildest expectations. When he showed them to Judi Pinkerton, she thought so too.

The commissioners applauded their decision as well. Edmund M. Pinkerton was a good friend they could trust.

Pinkerton Labs soared like an eagle. The pathologist, now entrepreneur, hired a seasoned, well-regarded technician as laboratory director, a certified public accountant as chief financial officer, and a taskmaster bitch as lab manager. All these he stole from Medical Diagnostics Labs, who in turn, raided MDL for lab technicians and support personnel. Pinkerton paid them well, expecting loyalty, hard work, and integrity in return.

His chief financial officer's nose for opportunity beyond the County contracts fueled the extraordinary growth of Pinkerton Laboratories as well. Crammed for space in 1999, Pinkerton purchased and expanded to the two-story building next door. The original owner constructed the newer of the two buildings just after World War II, right before stringent building codes. Just three feet separated the freestanding structures.

Salvatore Scarantino knocked on Ed Pinkerton's office door and entered, "Hey, Dr. Pinkerton, sorry to interrupt. I've drawn up and figured what you'll need to upgrade to high speed digital. Needless to say I've encountered a myriad of building regulations. To accommodate the changes, we'll need a 75 foot trench 3 feet deep to run underground cable between your two buildings."

"So what's the problem?"

Pinkerton's information technology contractor rubbed his chin and answered, "There's no trenching equipment narrow enough to fit between the buildings – it'll have to be dug by hand."

"Got somebody who can do it?" Pinkerton asked.

"Not really, Ed. Not my business. But you can run an ad. I guarantee some poor Mexican wetback will do it."

"I don't speak Spanish."

"Don't have to. Sign language. Take out a tape; point between the buildings, say 'dig' and then show them with the tape and your hands, 1 foot wide and 3 feet deep. You'll be surprised how they'll get it."

Conversation 15
Bellflower
Monday, January 21, 2002; 8:16 p.m.

José came up from behind Paco's chair dressed in pajamas holding Maximo, his well-worn teddy bear.

"Papá?"

"Yes, José?"

"Can you tell us a story?"

"What? You want me to tell you a story? It is already late and past your bedtime."

"Please, Papá, please," he pleaded.

"Go get Miguel," Paco frowned, "One quick story, but just one."

José shoved Maximo onto his father's lap, whirled about, and ran across the room screaming, "Miguel! Miguel! Where are you? Papá says he will tell us a story!"

Dressed in his pajamas, Miguel appeared from the bathroom sporting a wide grin that exposed his missing two front teeth. José grabbed his hand, turned and ran back to Paco, dragging his older brother behind him. Paco reached down, pulled José onto his lap, nestled him under the wing of his right arm and gave back the teddy bear. Miguel climbed up and sat on Paco's left side.

"So, what story do my little niños want tonight?" Paco asked.

"Fernando Valenzuela – El Toro," Miguel blurted.

"No! Pancho Villa" exclaimed José.

"Not again, you always get Pancho Villa," Miguel protested.

"Pancho ..."

"Fernando, Papá. Please?"

"Wait, wait, wait," Paco interrupted. "Last time you got your choice Miguel. So, tonight José get Pancho. Tomorrow you get Fernando, okay?"

"I'm tired of ..."

"Miguel, tonight José get Pancho, tomorrow you get El Toro, I promise."

"Promise?"

"I promise."

Wide eyed, the two boys snuggled down in Paco's lap and he began.

"So Pancho Villa he is a very brave man. A hero to all of Méjico – a revolutionary general. His real name was Doroteo Arango Arámbula, but he took the name Pancho Villa because he thought it sound very tough."

"You mean like Maximo?" José growled, pushing his teddy bear out at arms length.

"Just like Maximo," Paco smiled, and then continued. "Pancho Villa fought the Revolution in northern Méjico in the state of Chihuahua. He had many horses and he called his cavalry *Los Dorados*, 'the Golden Ones'.

"Pancho he hate Porfirio Días, the president and dictator of Méjico, because Méjico it has many poor people. Días, he rule very bad, and he kept all the money from the mines and gave nothing to the people. So they have no food. Some have no houses. The campesinos work for peanuts on the big haciendas and Pancho Villa say this is very bad."

José squirmed in Paco's lap, "Tell the story about the guns and the shooting, Papá."

"I am getting to that, but first you must know why Pancho Villa make the army and kill the people. You have to know why he was so mad that he kill people to free his country, José.

"So, there was another man – Victoriano Huerta – he want to be dictator too ..."

"What do you mean 'dictator'?" Miguel interrupted.

"A dictator tells all the people what to do and force them to do whatever he says. A dictator takes all the freedom. Do you see?"

"I think so Papá, but tell us about the shooting," Miguel answered.

"I am getting to that. You have to wait.

"Pancho Villa is very mad at Porfirio Díaz and this guy Huerta. Pancho he is very smart but he have no money. He needs horses and guns for his army. So he get them by stealing from the rich. He robs the trains and takes the silver to buy the things he needs to build his army."

"He stole and robbed, did he kill people?" José asked.

"He want very much to free his country. So, yes, he rob and steal and kill because he loves his country so much. Pancho Villa he was very brave.

"Finally, he had enough money and he commanded the *Los Dorados* in the battles of Ciudad Juárez, Tierra Blanca, Saltillo, and Zacatecas. The people are very happy. They think Pancho Villa free them because now Díaz and Huerta are gone and Pancho is the governor of Chihuahua.

"But another very bad man, Venustiano Carranza – Pancho thought he was his friend – betrayed him. Carranza want all the power and all the money just like Huerta and Díaz and he get the president of the United States on his side and together they hunt Pancho Villa down and all the poor people become very sad again."

Wide eyed, José asked, "What happened?"

"They kill Pancho. Many men run up to his car in Chihuahua and they shoot him many times. He had no gun, no nothing. They assassinated Pancho Villa."

"Assassinated? What did he do, Papá?" Miguel asked.

"He can do nothing. He only says, 'Yes I die. But I die for my country – *just tell them I have said something*'. Then he is gone."

"What else? What else?"

"That is all, José, he die and all hope for freedom for Méjico die with him."

"But you said they cut off his head." José declared.

"Some people say that without his head he can never rise again and Méjico will never be free."

"Is Mexico free now?" Miguel asked.

"Better, but many people are still very poor and live in poverty."

"What do you mean 'poverty'?"

"It means that you have no money – no money to have a house. No money even to buy food, so you have to go hungry."

"Is that why you and Mamá came here?" José asked.

Paco swallowed the large lump in his throat and pushed back his tears. "That is why, José," he frowned. "The United States makes us a better life for you and Mamá and Mamacita. But you always have to remember even here life it is not easy. When I came to the United States with uncle Raphael he says I cannot only work, I have to go to school and learn to read and write English and study the math. Still I have to work very hard, every day."

Miguel looked up at his father, "Did Mamá go to school Papá?"

"In Méjico, but not here. That is why I have the family speak English in our home. I help your mamá to read whenever I can and encourage her to become a citizen. We live in America. It is a land of hope, but still you must always work very hard for it. That is why you must have the education too …"

"I'm going to be doctor," Miguel trumpeted.

"A doctor? Really Miguel! That would make me very proud …"

"I'm going to be Pancho Villa," José blurted.

Paco chuckled, ruffled Miguel's hair and looked at his wristwatch. "Off to bed my little niños, it is past your bedtime."

Conversation 16
Los Angeles County Health District
Wednesday, January 23, 2002; 7:07 a.m.

The next morning Paco Sánchez answered Pinkerton's advertisement and agreed to meet Pinkerton, his lab director, and information technology contractor at Pinkerton Pathology Laboratories on Wednesday at 7:00 a.m.

At 7:03 Pinkerton grew impatient. "Where is he?"

"Ed, you heard me say it. Mexican's work on mañana time," the lab director chuckled.

"Well, I'm not standing around here forever," Pinkerton declared, looking at his watch again. "You had better get someone else to do it."

"Mr. Pinkerton?"

Pinkerton turned to the voice, "Yes?"

"I am Paco Sánchez. I answered the ad to dig."

"Hey, Paco," Pinkerton said, extending his big beefy hand. "Ed Pinkerton, here. This is my lab director, Richard Steinberg, and my IT guy, Salvatore Scarantino. We thought you weren't coming."

"I am sorry. The traffic it is very bad," Paco apologized. "You need to have something dug?"

Pinkerton took out his tape and pulled it open to one foot, pointed between the structures, cleared his throat and said. "Yes, my IT man here says I need a ditch dug between these buildings, one foot wide like this and three feet deep like this," Pinkerton continued, extending the tape to 36 inches.

Paco looked down the space, took out his own tape, and measured between the two buildings, "34 inches."

"Ahh-ha," Pinkerton said to himself.

Paco walked the space, kicking up dirt with his heel every few feet. At the end of the building, he turned around and walked in 6 foot strides, calculating the length. "Seventy-eight feet," he estimated; then turned and re-walked the distance to be certain.

"What is he doing?" Pinkerton whispered over the corner of his mouth.

"Figuring things out. Don't worry. You'll see," Scarantino said.

Paco turned and walked back to the men. "The space it is very narrow. I cannot get equipment in there to dig. It have to be dug by hand."

"I know that," Pinkerton said. "That's why we ran the ad."

"You want me to dig by hand?" Paco asked.

Pinkerton grimaced. He just wanted an answer. "Yes, that's right – by hand – can you do it?"

Paco looked at Pinkerton. "You want to have it one feet wide and three feet deep?"

"Yes, one foot wide by three feet deep, the length of the buildings."

Paco walked over to his pickup and brought back a mattock pick and a shovel. Ten feet into the space between the buildings he set the shovel against the wall and swung the pick end of the mattock into the dirt. The point landed with a thud. He repeated the motion, set the mattock aside and shoveled the loosened soil. "Very hard," he whispered.

Paco came back to the men, staring at all three waiting for them to speak.

"Well?" Pinkerton finally asked.

"I can dig for you." Paco said. "But the dirt it is very hard. It takes me a little while to do this."

"How long and how much?" Pinkerton asked.

"My wife she is very pregnant. She is due any day ..."

"What does that have to do with my ditch?" Pinkerton broke in.

"She is due any day so I have to get this done right away and get the money for the hospital."

"So how long, and how much?" Pinkerton asked again.

Paco looked at Scarantino, back at Pinkerton, and back to Scarantino. "Mr. Scarantino, you have the underground cable?"

"Of course. It's insulated underground CAT 5."

Paco removed his Dodger cap, scratched his scalp and asked, "Why do you not want to run a 3 inch or maybe a 4 inch pipe to put the cable through when you need to use it sometime later. That would be better."

Scarantino cleared his throat. "That's possible. Ed? He thinks we should lay a 3 to 4 inch chase to pull the CAT 5 and have access for future use."

Pinkerton grew irritated with the conversation, certain that Paco was stalling to up the price. He had heard about how Mexicans could never give a straight answer, always bargaining and forever upping the ante. He glared at Paco "Whatever. How long and how much to dig the trench?"

Paco looked at Scarantino, "You buy the pipe and you have one person to lay, at the same time that I dig?"

"I can arrange that," Scarantino answered.

"Okay, Mr. Pinkerton, you have someone to lay the pipe the same time that I dig, I think I can do this for you very fast."

"So how long and how much?" Pinkerton asked again. "I need a straight answer."

"Two, no more than three days – $300."

Pinkerton did the math, two days for $300. No way am I paying this smarmy Mexican prick $150 per day to dig a ditch, he thought. Besides he needs the money. "Make it $200 for the job. If you finish in two days, I'll bump it another $50."

Paco looked between the two buildings, then back at Pinkerton. Finally he said, "Okay. I can start tomorrow."

Conversation 17
City Centre, Los Angeles
Wednesday, January 23, 2002; 5:18 p.m.

Chairman and Chief Executive Officer of Humanitarian Hospital Corporation Geoff Boyer stood up from the desk of his 44th floor office, stretched, and ran his fingers through his hair. Expansive floor to ceiling glass provided an extraordinary view of the city both day and night. In the distance, freeway traffic built to a crawl. Brake lights flashing on and off signaled the stop and go pace. Boyer walked over to a walnut-paneled wall and pressed on one of the segments. It popped open to a neatly concealed, well-stocked bar. He took down the Chivas Regal, poured straight up an amount sufficient to break the day's stress, and secured his office. He swirled the Chivas, sniffed the aroma and took a drink.

As a graduate of the U.S. Naval Academy and former jet fighter pilot, Boyer aspired to CEO of Northrop Grumman Aircraft Corporation. With an Executive MBA from the Thunderbird School of Global Management and an extraordinary track record in senior leadership, he had the pedigree. And when he took the helm at Humanitarian Hospital Corporation, he did so knowing that making his mark on a $2 billion dollar corporation could land him the job of his dreams. So from the get-go, slashing expenses, doubling contribution to margin and "adjusting" the price-earnings ratio of Humanitarian's stock were strategies one, two and three.

A letter sized envelope marked "Confidential for Geoff Boyer Only" lay on the corner of his desk. He took a sterling silver letter opener inscribed with the initials GMB from his top drawer, sliced the envelope open, and removed the contents. A letter signed "Ralph Appleton, CFO, Humanitarian Hospital Corporation" covered the documents. He set the letter aside and turned to the top sheet, printed in color.

The header read, "Humanitarian Hospital Corporation, Consolidated Profit and Loss for the First Six Months Ending December 31, 2001." He took another drink, rolled the Chivas over his tongue and let it linger. Then he swallowed and leaned back to examine the financials. At first glance, he liked what he saw – no red ink. His attention turned to the revenue side. After adjustments, compared to budget they were up slightly, just north of $940 million, a 2.67% increase. He smiled. Expenses looked favorable as well. In aggregate, the cost of doing business came in 3.12% less than projected.

"Good work – well done," Boyer grinned.

His eyes roamed down the columns to the far right hand corner bottom line. "And contribution to margin?" he asked out loud. "3.73 %

or $35,062,000 smackers. Fucking A, Geoff Boyer; fucking A," the CEO snickered.

Boyer removed a calculator from the top drawer and crunched more numbers. With his calculations complete, he pushed the speed dial button on the speaker phone labeled RA. It rang twice.

"Ralph Appleton."

"Hey, Ralph. Geoff Boyer. I'm looking over the Six Month Consolidated."

Appleton chuckled, "Like those babies?"

"Impressive all the way around, especially given 9/11. What's coming up that could kick our ass in the next six months?"

"I think we're solid, Geoff. We've got the acquisition in Toledo, but that's not going to hit us until August or September. Our big ticket device – implantable automatic cardiac defibrillators, titanium hips and knees and such – contracts are nailed down and delivered until October. I think we are solid, I really do."

Boyer polished off the Chivas and leaned back, "So for the year, our contribution to margin should be on target?"

"Bingo! Just north of $70 million and best ever for HHC."

"Outstanding work," Ralph.

"Kudos to you, my man. You did it."

Boyer paused and cleared his throat, "Thanks, but I'm still not satisfied – and keep an absolute lid on this, Ralph – I'm sending out a 'dire straits memo' leveraging this 9/11 economy bullshit into numbers that will knock the shareholders' socks off. Besides, I want our lazy ass hospital CEOs to get serious about contribution to margin. And Ralph, hear this. Do not share the profit and loss statement you just gave me with anyone. Not *anyone*. Instead, I want you to create a bogus P & L that establishes for everyone – I mean everyone – the mindset that we're in for a grim year at Humanitarian."

"Gotcha'. No problem. Easy enough. And you can rest assured, Geoff – mum's the word," Appleton promised.

"That's why *you're* my Chief Financial Officer. Hey, you and Suzy want to have dinner with us at Del Frisco's Saturday?"

"Del Frisco's! Filet mignon drizzled in hot butter? I'll confirm with Suzy, but I'm in."

Boyer hung up and went back to his calculator. At 10% of contribution to margin, his July *bonus* would exceed $7 million plus stock options. Not bad, he thought, but it could, and *would,* be better.

He twirled around in his chair and faced the windows. The day, now black as night, drew light from the surrounding skyscrapers. Boyer often wondered what everyone did in those well-lit offices after dark. "Probably like me, looking to bang their secretaries," he answered and chuckled out loud.

Conversation 18
Los Angeles County Health District
Thursday, January 24, 2002; 5:45 a.m.

A fine drizzle fell from the dark morning sky. A brisk breeze out of the north deepened the winter chill. The streets were quiet; the city still slept. Paco pulled his pickup to the curb at Pinkerton Pathology Laboratories, got out, and took his mattock pick and shovel from the truck. A sidewalk streetlamp illuminated the space between the structures and lit the falling raindrops like Cinco de Mayo sparklers.

Paco turned his Dodger cap so the bill faced backwards, lifted the mattock pick and swung into the dirt. The earth pushed back with a thud. He swung again; hit the same spot, penetrating the crust. With the mattock turned chisel end down, Paco swung once more. He levered the handle forward and turned up a 6-inch clump. He swung again – thud. Swing. Lever. Shovel. Swing. Thud. Swing. Lever. Shovel. Swing. Thud. Swing. Lever. Shovel. Rotating the pick and chisel ends of the mattock, over and over, bit by bit, the trench began to take definition.

He decided to cut the trench 8 inches wide by 3 feet deep for two reasons. The ditch needed only to accommodate a 4 inch conduit. Second, he needed convenient space to put the dirt. A narrow trench created sufficient room for Paco to shovel the earth along the edges of the trench rather than wheelbarrow load after load down the line only to wheel it back later to refill the trench after the conduit was laid. He also understood that by laying the conduit in tandem with the ditch, he could bury 8 foot segments at a time, reducing the need to move the dirt any farther or any more often than necessary. Swing. Thud. Swing. Lever.

Shovel. Swing. Thud. Swing. Lever. Shovel – over and over, again and again.

Shortly after Paco's seventh birthday, his father died and, with little other recourse, Mamacita leaned on her brother Raphael to prop up a family devastated by her husband's accident. Uncle Raphael was neither married, nor did he have children, and to Mamacita he seemed the perfect surrogate. Her four children – Paco, Emilio, Jesus and Margarita – needed emotional support and took to Uncle Raphael immediately; and although Raphael tried to hide it, Paco soon became his favorite.

Raphael made his living as a brick mason; in his pastime he smoked cigarettes, flirted with all the women and drank tequila. Paco dismissed Raphael's rough edges and looked up to him for his funny jokes, mild manner, and love of baseball. On summer weekends, Raphael took Paco to Mexican League games to watch the Charros de Jalisco. Paco learned early that Mexicans forgot their troubles and their struggles at these games. Baseball and summer life went together in Mexico.

Swing. Thud. Swing. Lever. Shovel. Sweat ran down Paco's face dripping into the trench. Swing. Thud. Swing. Lever. Shovel.

On Paco's 14th birthday, Raphael came to Mamacita. He explained to her that he wanted to move to the United States, "to set up life, where I can find work every day and shed the burden of poverty. Paco must come with me," he said. "He is like my son. I make him a good man like his father. Perhaps in the United States there is a doctor who can fix the brown spider bite. I make for sure he goes to school, learns English and someday I can teach him the mason's trade. When he gets a little older and we are established, you can come too, Mamacita, and bring Emilio, Jesus and Margarita."

Swing. Thud. Swing. Lever. Shovel.

"Three, maybe four years, no more." Raphael had said.

"Can you find a doctor that will fix the brown spider bite, Raphael? I pray you find a doctor for Paco. Then I can let him go."

Raphael promised. So with a tear in her eye and a kiss on the forehead, Mamacita set her firstborn free. Raphael and Paco moved to the United States in 1988.

Swing. Thud. Swing. Lever. Shovel.

Paco laid the mattock pick to the side, stretched his back, and wiped his brow. He looked at his watch – 8:20 a.m. No Mr. Scarantino. The trench stretched 7 feet and measured 3 feet deep along its reach. It surprised Paco that Scarantino hadn't arrived. Mr. Pinkerton seemed rushed. "Mañana, mañana," he said out loud, picked up the pick and went back to the ditch.

At 8:45, Scarantino showed up out of breath. "The guy that agreed to help you didn't show, but I brought the conduit, it's in my truck, 80 feet of it, 10 8-ft pieces, 4 inches in diameter – say, you're making real progress, Paco."

"It goes okay."

"All right. How about this? I'll drive around back, unload the conduit at that end, and you can work from there. Sound good?"

"No problema, Mr. Scarantino. If you can bring me the cement and the connectors and the cable, I can do this without nobody."

"Run the cable too?" he paused, and then exclaimed. "I knew it, Paco. Gotcha' covered already. Everything is in the truck. I will lay it out for you, around back."

Conversation 19
City Centre, Los Angeles
Thursday, January 24, 2002; 8:16 a.m.

While Paco Sánchez labored over Pinkerton's ditch, seven miles distant in the heart of the financial district Chief Executive Officer Geoff Boyer reached over his desk and picked up the Dictaphone. Turning to his skyscraper view of the outer world, he dictated the following:

"Kathy, this is a letter to all of our hospital CEOs. Copy Ralph Appleton and mark it highly confidential. And Kathy, set up a meeting with Appleton ASAP. I want to discuss this strategy with him in person, face to face. Here's the letter."

Gentlemen:

JAMES LENHART

Humanitarian's Chief Financial Officer Ralph Appleton and I have reviewed HHC's consolidated profit and loss statement for the first six months of fiscal year 2002. To say I have anxiety would be a misnomer and understates my concerns for our company. While certain units have performed admirably, overall our projections for the year suggest corporate contribution to margin may be slim to none. As you all know, the impact of September 11 devastates this economy. Nonetheless, as president and CEO of Humanitarian Hospital Corporation, I hold a fiduciary responsibility to our employees, patients and stockholders to ensure the viability of the corporation and a healthy return on investment, while maintaining the "quality of care" reputation HHC enjoys. Therefore, effective immediately, all units must institute the following:

1. Increase Staffing Ratios: Our current staffing ratio is 8.41 patients to every nurse. Mr. Appleton informs me that the industry standard nationally hovers near 8.21 to 1. Going forward, adjust ratios to 10 patients for every nurse on all medical-surgical units except intensive care. In addition, and effective immediately, compensation for overtime must cease.

2. Reduce Supply Costs: You all understand that medical devices such as internal automatic cardiac defibrillators and titanium joints drop directly to our bottom line. No patient – not a single one – may have an implantable device placed without prior authorization from their insurance company and a signed commitment to pay any and all implantable device co-pays. Finally, all candidates for such procedures must authorize a credit check prior to implantation procedures. Patients with poor or marginal credit must place a refundable deposit to cover the cost of implantable devices prior to surgery.

3. Reduce Uncompensated Care: HHC must shift the financial burden of uncompensated care to the public sector. Going forward, individuals without a third party payer source must be referred to public facilities for follow-up care. Patients with past due accounts will not be treated and must be referred to an alternate facility when it is determined their presenting illness is neither emergent nor life-threatening.

Please maintain this correspondence in the strictest confidence and implement the described measures immediately. No exceptions.

Very truly yours,

Geoffrey M. Boyer
President and CEO
Humanitarian Hospital Corporation

Conversation 20
Los Angeles County Health District
Friday, January 25, 2002; 5:18 p.m.

The day turned to dusk when Paco, lying prone in the dirt, reached into the trench to pull the last of the cable through the conduit and cemented the final piece of PVC pipe into place. Locking the conduit end to end, he looked up to the sound of footsteps. It was Pinkerton and his lab director, Richard Steinberg.

"Señor Sánchez," bellowed Pinkerton. "¿Que pasa?"

"I am almost finished. I just shovel this little bit of dirt back into the ditch."

Pinkerton flashed an ear to ear grin, "Well I'm happy. Looks good to me. What do you say, Richard?"

"Fabulous, great, good. Thank you, Paco. Hard work."

Paco crawled onto his knees and stood up. "It is not too bad. The digging it is hard, but I made the trench so the dirt is not falling back, so it is a little easier."

Pinkerton reached into his wallet and pushed three crisp $100 bills at Paco. "Here you go, Mr. Sánchez."

Paco looked at the money, embarrassed, "I no have change, Mr. Pinkerton."

"Here, take it, Paco. You did a good job, completed it on time and you laid the conduit too. The extra $50 pays you for that."

Paco smiled, accepted the money and said, "Thank you."

"What's the ribbon for?" Steinberg asked.

"I tied a red ribbon to the cable at the end of the chase, bring it out of the ground, and then I put the dirt back. You know where the cable is by this red ribbon."

"Fabulous, great, good," Steinberg said again. "And, oh, good luck with that baby, Paco."

"Thank you, Mr. Richard. I finish now and go?"

"Yeah, finish and go," Pinkerton said.

They watched Paco tie the red ribbon to the cable, pull it to the surface and shovel the last of the dirt back into the hole over a coil of CAT-5. Dusting off his hands and clothing, Paco picked up the mattock pick and his shovel, "I think it is done. I go now."

"Looks like it. Get out of here before the traffic gets worse."

Paco laid the tools in the back of the truck and glanced at his watch. 5:35. He climbed into the cab, started the pickup and headed for Humanitarian Hospital. Sarita had called at 4:00 p.m. relating she was well into labor. "Maybe she has not delivered yet," he whispered to himself and stepped on the gas.

Paco moved through five o'clock traffic at a snail's pace. When he finally parked his truck in Humanitarian Hospital's Emergency Room lot and charged into the foyer of the hospital, the wall clock read 6:37 p.m. The receptionist gave Paco Sarita's room number and directions to the elevators, which he found straightaway. When the doors opened on the Labor & Delivery floor, he hurried down the corridor to labor, delivery and recovery room 333.

Paco found Sarita sitting up in bed holding their newborn. The moment she saw his face Sarita broke out in a flood of tears. "Oh, Paco! You are-are h-h-he-here," she sobbed. "I c-c-could not tell-l-l you this on the ph-ph-phone," she wailed.

"What? You have the baby already?"

"No it is n-n-not that," she said looking away from Paco. "It is her lip," she said turning the baby to face Paco and then broke out in tears all over again.

Conversation 21
Rancho Palos Verdes
Saturday, January 26, 2002; 6:19 a.m.

Geoff Boyer pulled his BMW 650i convertible to the curb in front of Jack MacDougall's home and honked. He glanced at his Rolex, six-nineteen. When he saw Jack heading out the door he rolled down the passenger window and said, "Throw your briefcase in the back, Jack."

MacDougall did what he was told, got in, shut the door and they were off.

"Nice place," Boyer commented.

"Thanks. We like it. What time are we supposed to be there?"

"I told Dean to meet us at the hangar at 6:30. We're a little late but no big deal. One of the advantages of corporate jets," Boyer smiled.

"I guess so," MacDougall agreed. "Airport security has been a major pain in the ass since 9/11."

Boyer angled the BMW into the commuter lane heading toward Burbank, stepped on the accelerator and asked, "Have you spent much time in Phoenix?"

"Actually, I've never been."

"Really? Great city – at least I like it," Boyer said dodging in front of a semi-tractor trailer and swerving back into the commuter lane. "We've had multi-specialty clinics in Phoenix since the mid nineties. As I told you, I'm thinking of replicating them here and want your advice. You can benefit by taking a look at what we've done in Arizona."

At 6:42 they exited the freeway and made their way to Million Air. When they reached the hangar, Dean Stubblefield waved Boyer into the cavernous building and signaled him to park along the wall to the left. Boyer shut the vehicle down, popped the trunk open for his grip, and got out.

"Hey, Mr. Boyer," the pilot smiled. "Let me get your things and we'll be on our way. Looks like a great ride all the way – oh, leave the keys in the ignition in case they have to move her."

"I did. Is it okay there?"

"Perfect. Just right." his pilot replied.

"Dean Stubblefield, meet Dr. Jack MacDougall. Jack, my pilot Dean. Dean flew for Delta almost twenty years. When he got tired of all the bullshit, he came to work for me."

The two shook hands, and then the three of them walked out of the hangar. Boyer strode on the tarmac behind the pilot, but ahead of Mac-Dougall.

"Your plane is beautiful, Geoff. What is it?"

"Gulfstream GIV-SP. Best corporate jet in the business. Gorgeous, huh?" Boyer answered, looking up at the aircraft.

"Awesome."

"Thanks," Boyer responded, but then paused. The words on the fuselage – *Humanitarian Hospital Corporation Giving ~ Sharing ~ Loving ~ Caring* – stuck out like a sore thumb and caught him off guard. Flaunting like a jet setter ran counter to his new corporate austerity program. "I'd better fix *that*," he whispered.

Stubblefield loaded the luggage in the aft bay, locked it down, and helped the two men onto the staircase. "Watch your head up there, doctor," he warned MacDougall. "When you get in, go ahead and buckle up. The flight attendant should be right with you."

The pilot inspected the landing gear and examined the tires one more time, checked the door on the luggage bay again, climbed the stairs and pulled the cabin door tight behind him. He looked toward his two passengers and said, rubbing his hands together, "Okay, gents. I'm heading up to the cockpit. If you need anything from me or have any questions, ask Melissa. Otherwise, have a nice flight. As I said, it should be a great ride."

MacDougall surveyed the cabin – cushy leather seats wide enough for a football lineman, soft loopy carpet, walnut inserts all around, burnished stainless steel trim, a flat panel TV, stereo sound. Nothing missing. Whisper quiet. Nice. "Boy. This *is* a beauty, Geoff."

"Way better than Southwest Airlines, huh?" Boyer snickered.

"What does something like this cost – fourteen, fifteen million?"

"Put it this way, Jack my man. If you have to ask, you can't afford it. Besides, I don't have to pay for it!"

MacDougall shook his head and glanced toward the galley, "Is that your flight attendant?"

"Bingo!" Boyer whispered. "Knockout, huh?"

MacDougall leaned closer to Boyer, maintaining a fixed gaze on the young woman, "Jesus, I guess. What does she serve besides Johnnie Walker? Cock Tales?" he smirked from the corner of his mouth.

"You bastard, MacDougall," Boyer snorted. "Hold on a second."

Boyer pulled a cell phone from his vest pocket and dialed. After several rings, a voice picked up, "This is Kathleen Carrier executive assistant to Mr. Geoff Boyer, President and CEO of Humanitarian Hospital Corporation. I can't take your call at the moment, but if you'll leave your name, number and a brief message at the beep, I'll get back with you as soon as possible."

He waited for the tone, then said, "Hey Kathy, Geoff Boyer here. Remind me to call Jasperson about re-painting the plane. Thanks. Have a great weekend. See you Monday."

"Okay. How about something to drink?" he said signaling the attendant.

Momentarily she made her way back carrying a tray of toasted English muffins, orange marmalade, fresh papáya, melon and assorted berries. "Good morning, Mr. Boyer. I brought your favorites," she smiled.

"Hi, Melissa. Fantastic. Orange marmalade I hope. Oh! This is my friend and business associate, Dr. Jack MacDougall."

The attendant nodded, "Yes, sir. Orange marmalade. Good morning, Dr. MacDougall. Nice to meet you."

"Nice to meet you, Melissa," MacDougall winked.

"Bloody Mary, mimosa or coffee, Mr. Boyer?"

"Coffee on this leg. Business today. Maybe something alcoholic on the way back. What about you, Jack?"

"Coffee is perfect. And some water."

"Would either of you care for scrambled eggs or an omelet after take-off?"

"Fix me one of your fantastic gruyere cheese and mushroom omelets," Boyer said as the plane pushed forward. "How about you, Jack?"

"Sounds good," he winked at the attendant again.

"Yes, sir. Let me get your coffees real quick before I have to buckle up. Feels like Dean has us under way," she said heading back to the galley.

MacDougall leaned into Boyer, "Nice legs."
"Uh-huh," Boyer smiled. "Very nice."

At 37,000 feet MacDougall finished the last bite of the omelet and washed it down with Melissa's fresh brewed Starbucks. Wiping his mouth with a warm, moist towel he looked out the window and down at the austere desert landscape. In the far distance, a winding river led to a glimmering lake. Hmmm? "What's a lake doing out here?" he wondered. Beyond the river, mountains rose up to meet lacey clouds. Something contrary, yet beautiful, about the desert he decided.

Boyer broke MacDougall's train of thought. "So, Jack. As I explained, I want to build a multi-specialty clinic that feeds our hospital. Some primary care, but mostly sub-specialties – cardiology, gastroenterology, surgery, neurology, pulmonology – the works."

"Why just one? Are you strapped for cash?"

"Humanitarian Hospital Corporation? Not hardly. It's recruiting and maintaining all the human resource to run them that bothers me. Besides, I don't want it to compete like I'm trying to put the medical school and University Hospital out of business. I worry about the reaction of the private practitioners too."

"Uh-huh," MacDougall pondered, then asked. "How are the Phoenix clinics set up?"

"You mean the physical layout or their locations?"

"Both."

"There are two of them. Strategically located geographically – at least I think. Other than that, pretty typical layouts. Waiting room, receptionist, medical records, twenty-four exam and two procedure rooms."

"Serving the purpose?"

"The usual problems. Wait times for appointments, wait times in clinics. Keeping staff expenses down. Keeping physician expectations up."

"You thinking new construction or leased and build-to-suit layouts?"

"Could be either. Want some more coffee?"

"Sure. Thanks."

Boyer held up his cup catching the attendant's attention. She re-filled them both and looked at MacDougall. "Anyone ever tell you that you look like William Hurt?" she asked.

"They have," he frowned. "I'd rather they thought Kevin Costner or Dennis Quaid. You're a little young for William Hurt, aren't you?"

"Maybe. I like him all right. My mother loved him in *Kiss of the Spider Woman*. She bought it and watched it over and over, like a little kid. I think she had a crush on him. Of course she was never telling *me* that. Anything else for you, gentlemen?"

"Thanks, Melissa. I think we're good," Boyer answered.

"Okay. Just give me the high sign," she said heading back to the galley and her magazine.

MacDougall leaned into Boyer, cleared his throat and asked, "Don't you love those eyes? Wow!"

"Crystal blue aren't they?"

MacDougall laid his head back and after several moments sat forward, "So Geoff, pretend money is no object. I know it is – it always is. But pretend for a moment it's not. Second, screw the University and the privates. Given the same opportunity and the capital, they'd take you on from the front and the rear – believe me.

"Once you get comfortable with 'damn the torpedoes full speed ahead' and money's no never mind, here's what I'd propose."

While MacDougall detailed his concepts, up in the cockpit Dean Stubblefield pointed the nose of the aircraft down for the descent into Phoenix. When MacDougall finished his proposal, Boyer leaned back, cogitating. He thought for a long time. MacDougall took another drink of coffee, ogling the flight attendant – legs crossed, turning the pages of her magazine – and wondered if maybe he leaned ever so little to his left, he might be able to see up her skirt. Boyer finally responded, inter-rupting MacDougall's fantasy, "Now, I know why you're my consult-ant, Jack. That's creative. Novel. Cutting edge. I like it," he said lean-ing forward.

"I thought you would," MacDougall countered. Then he closed his eyes, fell into reverie and whispered to himself, "Now, how about we analyze your flight attendant? Holy shit is she gorgeous."

JAMES LENHART

Conversation 22
Humanitarian Hospital, Los Angeles
Saturday, January 26, 2002; 9:11 a.m.

Cleft lips serve chilling evidence that human reproduction can go awry. Their cause remains a mystery, although some things are known. During early embryonic stages, humans come into being as two dimensional cellular plates. Under normal circumstances – as development progresses – the outer edges of the plates roll forward and fuse in the midline, giving the fetus its three dimensional form.

*Defect*s in fusion, however, manifest in several ways at birth – the open abdominal cavity called gastroschisis; the patent spinal canal or spina bifida; and the cleft palate, with various developmental abnormalities in the upper lip, nasal passages and palate. Depending on the extent and severity of the cleft, complications in feeding and speech are early manifestations of cleft palate with the psychological impact coming later in early childhood.

Although the cause of cleft palate is not understood, American Indians, Asians and Latinos are more likely to be affected than Caucasians and African Americans. Environmental factors like smoking and alcohol consumption during pregnancy and folic acid deficiency may be predisposing factors. Paco and Sarita possessed none of these, except of course, their Latino origins.

The morning after her delivery, Paco paced the hospital floor. Sarita rocked their newborn and encouraged her to suckle.

"It is more hard for her than José and Miguel. When she gets on, right away she comes off. Maybe if I burp her," she whispered covering her breast and repositioning the baby over her chest and shoulder. "What should we name her, Paco?"

Paco eyes darted about the room, but drew no comfort from the flowered draperies, framed pastoral landscapes or the portrait of a mother comforting her idyllic, cherubic child. "I cannot tell you. I do not know."

"I am thinking Angelina."

"Angelina it means little angel," Paco retorted.

61

Sarita hesitated patting and massaging the newborn's back. Tears formed around her eye lashes and cascaded down her cheeks. "She is our angel, Paco. Why do you act this way? What she have, she cannot help."

"I am acting no way," he growled "What way am I acting? What do you want me to do, Sarita? How do you expect me to *act*, Sarita?"

"You act mad. You act like-like-like you-you-you do not love our b-b-baby," Sarita sobbed.

"So what do you want me to do?" Paco shouted. "Do you want me to pretend I do not see what I see?"

"Please, Paco, do not yell at me. I cannot help this."

"I cannot help my yelling! When I look at her, I cannot see the beautiful hair you have given her – or her eyes and skin – so pretty that you have given her. I can only see the monstruoso lip that I have given to her! I cannot look at her face, for when I do I only see the faces of the other children when they call her Caracortada. I cannot touch her, for when I do I can only feel what it is she feels when the people they stare. I cannot listen to her cry knowing that the others will laugh and tease when she talks. How do I tell her she is so beautiful when she looks in the mirror, and *knows* she is not? How, Sarita? You tell me. How?"

Conversation 23
University Quadrangle, Los Angeles
Saturday, March 16, 2002; 8:57 a.m.

The day felt very much like winter when Professor Peter Dornwyler took long strides across the quadrangle and mounted the stairs to Falkner Hall. In his right hand he carried a well-worn copy of Engelhardt's *The Foundations of Bioethics*. His left hand held a folder of manuscripts; under his left arm nestled a thermos of fresh coffee. Despite the chill, an uncharacteristic bright morning sun cast radiant light through his red beard, slowly growing grey.

Dornwyler freely admitted his addiction to caffeine and considered himself a home-roasting artisan. In general, he made his brews strictly from Ethiopian beans – "It's the origin of coffee for God's sake" he argued – but he also possessed a fondness for Sumatran coffees, which he blended with Guatemalan roasts to even out the edge of Sumatran's earthy overtones.

He entered room 131 marked Small Conference, set Engelhardt and the folder on the table and looked around the room. "Hmmm. Eleven eager faces. Where's the twelfth?" he asked himself.

Before uttering a word, Dornwyler divided the manuscripts evenly, passed them out and uncorked the thermos. He poured a cup and held it to his nose. The rich aroma filled his nostrils, settling his nerves. He took a sip, smiled and said, "Ahh ... that's better," and continued.

"Good morning and welcome to seminar 641, *The Ethical and Social Aspects of Healthcare*. I'm Dr. Peter Dornwyler. This is the first of eight medical ethics seminars the University has found the time to cram into your medical school curriculum. I grumble and whine to Dean Zuckerman that eight hours of ethics in a four year course of study short changes the importance of the discipline. Alas, it falls on his deaf ears, *and* he has the gall to schedule them on Saturdays after Friday nights of too much good gin," he smirked. "None-the-less, in the time we spend together, the discourse shall include the principles of medical ethics – concepts such as truth telling, autonomy, malfeasance, justice and the like."

Dornwyler paused, took another drink from his coffee and went on, "The seminars conclude with a robust dialogue on surrogate decision making, euthanasia and, finally, physician behavior. And while I'm on the concept of physician behavior, let me briefly provide my perspective. Not a one of you in this seminar or your entire medical school class lacks the ability to acquire the medical knowledge to deliver on the promise of extraordinary care. You are, after all, the best and the brightest. Don't let it fool you. It is deviation and disregard for the principles taught in these seminars that derails the careers of even the most brilliant practitioners of the art. More on that later.

"Any questions?" he paused and looked about the room. "Good. By the way. Who is missing? There should be twelve of you ..."

Dornwyler turned to the interruption of the door opening and closing and Amy Fligner tiptoeing to the only vacant seat. The professor looked at his wristwatch. "Interfering with your morning?" he asked.

"I'm sorry sir. Too many daiquiris last night," she blushed.

63

"Well I hope you took some Excedrin. And what's your name?"

"Amy Fligner."

"Nice to make your acquaintance, Ms. Fligner," Dornwyler frowned. "Please. Settle in."

He finished off his coffee and poured another cup. "Before we launch into today's discourse let me refer to those of you interested in medical ethics to the classic texts of Beauchamp's *Principles of Bio-medical Ethics* and Pellegrino's *The Virtues in Medical Practice.* Either dissertation is worthy reference for all that can be said on the subject. Of course, if you want to blow smoke up my backside, you'll choose Dornwyler's *Medical Ethics in Modern Medicine,*" he smirked.

"Okay. What I handed out – and what you have before you – is a current day translation of the Hippocratic Oath. Let's see … Amy Fligner. Who was Hippocrates and what single lasting contribution did he make to medicine?"

Fligner squirmed in her seat, feigned a cough and looked around the faces of her classmates, hoping for help. Seeing none, she sputtered, "Hippocrates was an ancient Greek physician to whom is credited the Hippocratic Oath."

"Right. Hippocrates wrote the Hippocratic Oath – I'll give you that – but why is *it* of significance?"

Fligner hesitated and blushed again, "I'm not certain sir. I didn't …"

"Read the preparatory assignment."

"No sir."

"Ms. Fligner, before you came in late and disrupted my seminar, I commented to the class that each and every one of you possesses the ability to acquire the knowledge to practice medicine. But what sepa-rates the good from the great – indeed what separates the good from the bad – is behavior. Qualities like the discipline for life-long learning for instance." Dornwyler paused, ran his fingers through his beard and car-ried on.

"I suggest you get up and take leave of this morning's seminar us-ing the free hour you have just earned to write a twenty-five hundred word, well referenced work on the history of medical ethics, which will

64

be due in my office no later than Monday afternoon, or risk an unpleasant conversation with Dean Zuckerman. Is that clear?"

Fligner gathered her stuff, rose from the chair and headed out the door, "Yes, sir. That's clear."

Dornwyler picked up the seminar roster and walked around the remaining students, taking sips of his coffee as he pondered where to pick up from where he left off. Finally, he said, "My apologies for Ms. Fligner's rude interruptions. Let's continue – let's see – Mr. Sutherland? Can you answer my question for the benefit of the class?"

Justin Sutherland looked up from the table and replied, "Yes, sir. Hippocrates is credited with writing the original code of medical ethics and memorializing the concept of 'first do no harm.'"

"Correct. Very good. Anyone else care to comment or embellish Mr. Sutherland's answer?"

"No?" he asked looking over his nose at the class. "Going once, going twice ... good. Let's go on and discover what he meant by 'first do no harm.'"

Conversation 24
Bellflower
Monday, March 18, 2002; 10:12 a.m.

Two months after his daughter's birth, reality finally set in for Paco Sánchez. Sleepless nights and misdirected anger could not fix Angelina's birth defect. So he picked up the telephone and dialed. After three rings, the receptionist answered. "Good morning. University Plastic Surgery & Reconstructive Consultants. How may I help you?"

"My name is Paco Sánchez. I have been a patient of Dr. Alexandre. My daughter she has what you call it – a cleft lip? I want to make an appointment."

"With Dr. Alexandre?"

"Yes. Only Dr. Alexandre."

"I'm sorry, Mr. Sánchez. Dr. Alexandre is on sabbatical teaching at the University of Bologna in Italy. He won't return until June. Are you certain one of our other doctors can't help you?"

"No I only want her to see Dr. Alexandre. She have to wait."

"He is booked solid when he returns ... you've been a patient in the past?"

"Yes. Many years ago ... in 1993."

"I see. Well, Dr. Alexandre asks us to always accommodate returning patients, Mr. Sánchez. You say your daughter has a cleft lip?"

"Yes. That is right."

"Let me see. Here we go. How about Thursday, June 6th at two o'clock?"

"We will be very happy to see you then," Paco answered.

"And what is her name?"

"Her name it is Angelina Sarita Sánchez."

SPRING 2002
Conversation 25
Bellflower
Friday, March 22, 2002; 7:53 p.m.

"Come with me, José. Papá is going to tell us the story of El Toro!" Miguel exclaimed pulling at his brother's pajamas.

The two boys scrambled onto Paco's lap and he began. "Fernando Valenzuela was born in Navojoa, Méjico ..."

"Like you, Papá?" José asked.

"Yes like me, but I was born in Guadalajara."

"Stop interrupting, José," Miguel protested. "Papá is telling the story."

"When Mr. Fernando was just seventeen years old he becomes a professional in the Mexican Baseball League playing for the Guanajuato Tuzos. But then in 1980 he becomes a pitcher for the Los Angeles Dodgers ..."

"The Dodgers?" Miguel asked wide-eyed.

"Yes, and he becomes the Dodgers best pitcher. He strikes out all the batters with a very mean screwball that no one can hit."

José wrinkled-up his nose. "Papá? What is a screwball?"

"It is a pitch that comes at you spinning very fast and jumps all over so you cannot see where to swing at the ball. So good is Fernando all of the baseball fans love him and they give him the name, El Toro!"

"El Toro! The bull!" exclaimed Miguel waving his arms.

As the story continued, José looked up staring into Paco's nose. "Papá?" he asked pointing at Paco's right nostril, "What happened to *your* nose?"

Paco abruptly curtailed his story telling. José's question left him speechless. His heart pounded and the hairs on his arms and on the back of his neck stood straight up. How do you tell a four year old that in the middle of the night a spider crawled into your nose, took a bite and injected its venom? Or how ugly you became to look like a monster from the spider's bite? Or the surgeries it took to fix the grotesque scar? The answer for Paco was, "You do not," so after pondering the question for several seconds, he fabricated his answer.

"When I am a little boy," he stammered, "I am playing on the rocks and I slip. I cannot catch my balance and I fall against the rocks and I cut my face very bad. We have no money and no doctor and it have to heal on its own."

"Did it hurt," Miguel asked.

"Very much, but I now almost forget about it."

"Is that what happened to Angelina's nose, Papá?"

Tears flooded Paco's eyes as he stumbled on this question as well. So he didn't answer it. Instead he suppressed his emotions and said, "It is late my little niños. You must go off to bed. Tomorrow we finish the story of El Toro."

Conversation 26
Los Angeles
Friday, March 22, 2002; 10:17 p.m.

Justin Sutherland shaped a half pound of ground chuck into a patty, sprinkled it with McCormick's Grill Mate and threw it on his George Foreman grill. He spread equal parts of Dijon mustard, ketchup and mayonnaise on a toasted bun and layered on red onion, some romaine lettuce and a slice of dill. When the meat looked medium well, he finished the assembly and sat down with a bottle of Budweiser and the question for the morning's ethics class.

Professor Dornwyler's assignment read: "Critically evaluate the Health and Human Services document a 'Patients' Bill of Rights,' which is attached. Come to Saturday's medical ethics seminar prepared to comment on its relevance in today's healthcare environment."

Sutherland munched on his burger while he read through the document. Several statements stood out – the "right" to understandable health information; the "right" to choose your doctor; the "right" to fully participate in all decisions related to a patient's care; the "right" to emergency medical services; the "right" to healthcare without discrimination; the "right" to speedy dispute resolution; the "right" to privacy in healthcare information and, finally, a broad statement regarding the patient's responsibility for maintaining good health.

Sutherland licked his fingers and took another drink from the Budweiser. "Hmmm. Should make for lively discussion," he said out loud while turning the page.

Conversation 27
Bellflower
Friday, March 22, 2002; 10:32 p.m.

Before preparing for bed Paco penned two advertisements for the classified section. The first solicited handyman work – "Reasonable rates, dependable, no job too small! I haul trash." The second promoted his masonry skills – "Masonry as Art! 12 years experience. Brick, natural stone, block walls. Call for free estimates!" Satisfied he had them right, he tucked the ads into an envelope for submission to the newspaper the following morning and let Muchi out to do her business. Then he undressed and snuggled in next to Sarita whose melodic breathing told him she was fast asleep.

Conversation 28
University Quadrangle, Los Angeles
Saturday, March 23, 2002; 8:54 a.m.

As he made his way across campus to Faulkner Hall, a blustery March wind blew through Dornwyler's beard pinning it back against his cheeks and parting it at his chin. Spring was late coming and Dornwyler detested winter. Trudging his way up the stairs he bent his head into the wind and said to himself, "Jesus, I need a cup of coffee."

He entered room 131 to the "good mornings" of twelve somber faces including that of Amy Fligner. Justin Sutherland sat at the table opposite her. Dornwyler poured coffee from his thermos, took a sip, sighed and said, "Now then, good morning to each of you as well."

Looking around the table, he spied in the center a flat box with a familiar green and red label. "Well, well. Krispy Kremes – 'Hot Now's!' I hope."

Dornwyler cleared his throat. "So, whoever is blowing smoke up my backside today ... I trust you brought a baker's dozen?" he declared flipping open the box and picking out the last doughnut. "Hmmm ... not bad," he said taking the first bite. "In point of fact, very good. Is it true too many of these will kill you?" he chuckled.

Dornwyler swallowed, handed a stack of blank cards to one of the students to pass around and went on, "This morning we're going to have a little fun – at least I hope – a mini debate if you will. While I start my heart with this delicious blend of Sumatran and Guatemalan coffees and, of course, gain my composure, I want each of you to write your names on one of these three by five cards and turn it face down. From the twelve cards I'll draw two names. One individual will argue the affirmative position and the other will argue the negative position.

"As you finish that little bit of work, let me begin this morning's discussion with the following. In 1998 President Bill Clinton directed Donna Shalala, the Secretary of Health and Human Services, to bring health programs into compliance with the U.S. Constitution's Bill of Rights.

"Clinton's goals," Dornwyler continued, "included the creation of a fair and responsive healthcare system. Clinton wanted reaffirmation of the importance of a strong doctor-patient relationship and finally a declarative statement regarding the critical role each and every individual plays in safeguarding their own health. As you know from your reading assignment, the HHS articulated a set of seven patient rights and one set of patient responsibilities in its final work product."

Dornwyler observed the students and poured another cup of coffee. "Looks like you are ready with the cards. Push them up to me. I'll shuffle and draw the names."

He took a sip, mixed the cards with a swirling motion over the table and drew from the pile. "Ahh-ha ... let me see here. Mr. Sutherland and ... Ms. Fligner," Dornwyler smirked, "Amy, it seems you can't escape me, nor can you, Mr. Sutherland ... Justin is it?"

"Yes, sir."

"Time – drat there's never enough of it is there?" the ethics professor went on, "Time does not permit us to dissect all seven rights. So for today's purposes our seminar focus will be limited to the right to care without discrimination. Justin, I want you to argue the affirmative, Amy, you tackle the negative."

Dornwyler paused and looked about the room popping the last bite of Krispy Kreme into his mouth. "When I was in graduate school, my girl friend called these things 'Hot Now! Yummy goo'. My, my, my-y-y-y – my, my! She was brilliant – at least on that one – how can anything so bad, be so good?" he chortled.

Dornwyler licked his fingers, dried them with a napkin and pointed at the class. "Okay. Before Amy and Justin begin, understand this as well, I'm not looking for a formal debate or anything like it. Amy, I want you to start with a statement that challenges the patients' right to care without discrimination. Justin you counter her argument. Following that I'll steer the discussion prompting participation from the entire class. Easy – at least for everyone except Amy and Justin," he grinned. "Make sense?"

The students nodded in affirmation. Dornwyler drank from his coffee and proceeded. "To refresh your memories, the Health and Human Services document makes this statement regarding care without discrimination: *'Care without Discrimination - Patients have the right to considerate, respectful care from all members of the health care industry at all times and under all circumstances. Patients must not be discriminated against in the marketing or enrollment or in the provision of health care services, consistent with the benefits covered in their policy and/or as required by law, based on race, ethnicity, national origin, religion, sex, age, current or anticipated mental or physical disability, sexual orientation, genetic information, or source of payment.'* Amy? You're on."

Fligner leaned forward staring at the document. With the index and long fingers of both hands, she pushed her bleached-blond hair behind her ears, twirling it between thumbs and forefingers. She feigned a deliberate cough and frowned, "Do you have any more of that coffee?"

"Sorry," Dornwyler smiled, "I just poured the last of it."

"Darn," she said looking up and pushing the hair in her face behind her ears once more. Sutherland could feel Fligner rap-tapping her foot. Finally she started.

"While the Health and Human Services statement of 'Care without Discrimination' conforms to the spirit of the U.S. Constitution, in our 21st century economic climate, care without discrimination makes promises impossible to keep. Most would agree that quote-unquote 'patients have the right to considerate, respectful care from all members of the health care industry at all times and under all circumstances.' However, limitless health care for illegal aliens crossing our borders; persons with mental disabilities including drug abusers and alcoholics; gays, who through indiscriminate and perverse sex acquire, and then spread, HIV disease; and persons with genetic disorders costing millions of dollars throughout a lifetime of care – opens financial floodgates that would spell financial ruin for hospitals, and disaster for the U.S. economy.

"Uh, let's see," she stammered looking back at the document. "Uh – darn I was thinking of something else," she said skimming down the page. "Okay. Let's see. Uhhh – yeah, okay. Yeah, I remember what I was going to say.

"Every person has the personal responsibility to find work that provides health insurance benefits or, alternatively, create rainy day savings for their expected and unexpected health care needs.

"In a perfect world care without discrimination feels warm and fuzzy; but it is fiscally irresponsible and not sustainable. 'Care without Discrimination' means those deserving care may go without care," Fligner set her pen down, flashed a sardonic grin and leaned back.

"Whoa. Very good, Ms. Fligner. Very good. Pungent in point of fact. Mr. Sutherland you've got your work cut out for you.

"Oh! By-the-way, tomorrow night's the Academy Awards – I love movies – don't you?" Dornwyler said combing his beard back and forth with the fingers of both hands. "What do you think? For my money Sean Penn's performance in *I Am Sam* eclipsed Russell Crowe's, but I'm betting *A Beautiful Mind* gets Best Picture."

"Well, that's off the subject, isn't it?" Dornwyler chuckled, "Don't anyone answer. Mr. Sutherland will never get his chance for rebuttal. Go ahead, sir."

Sutherland looked across at Fligner's black eyes darting under the table, arms folded across her abdomen, just under her pancake breasts; a smug expression on her face that didn't belie the pride she took in her soliloquy. She revered it.

"Actually it is not off our subject," Sutherland asserted. "The subtext in both movies strikes at the core of health care without discrimination. In one – *I Am Sam* – the main character struggles for custody of his child in a world indifferent and unresponsive to cognitive handicaps. In the other – *A Beautiful Mind* – the resources to treat psychiatric illness are eclipsed by years – maybe centuries – of disregard for the intricate biochemistry that drives the phenomenon of mental disorders.

"Morphed by social Darwinism, our culture tolerates little in the way of human frailty, marginalizing those less capable or those perceived to be weak or unable to quote-unquote 'pull themselves up by the bootstraps.' Clinton's hope for 'Care without Discrimination' speaks to those who, like Scrooge in Dickens' *A Christmas Carol*, would 'rid the world of excess population.' Healthcare cannot – or should not – be reduced to harsh, inhumane economic calculations ..."

"Economic *realities*," Fligner interrupted.

Dornwyler paced the room absorbing Sutherland's remarks, waiting for him to finish. Outside a winter-like wind bent lifeless trees. Grey, overcast skies portended torrential rain. The professor shook his head, "Any of the months but January, February or March," he said to himself.

"Disease," Sutherland concluded, "*disease* has value in America. Insurance companies handsomely reimburse oncologists treating cancer, yet refuse to pay primary care doctors for preventing it ..."

"Thank you, Mr. Sutherland," Dornwyler interjected. "Very good. Both of you."

Dornwyler scratched his head, "Your father's a physician, Ms. Fligner?"

"Yes, sir. A gastroenterologist."

"What about your father, Sutherland?"

"Postal clerk. Mail carrier. My parents never went to college."

"Interesting … very interesting. Permit me to interject a moment. The World Health Organization developed its mantra 'Health for All' over a forty year period beginning just after World War II, concluding with the dissemination of their policies in 1986 at the Ottawa Conference. I suggest all of you read them at some point.

"Unlike the U.S., most European countries view, and provide, healthcare as human right. The United Kingdom's National Health Service represents one of the most extensive …"

"But I read England's health system is in shambles. Patients wait in line forever," a voice at the end of the table chimed in.

"It's true that the NHS is undergoing reformation," Dornwyler countered. "None-the-less, countries in Europe, including the U.K., spend far less per capita on health care than the U.S. and enjoy much better health outcomes."

Fligner placed her hand over her heart and sat forward. She had a pug nose and it was hard to avoid those nostrils from any angle. "Are you proposing we adopt *socialized* medicine in America?" she gasped.

"If that's the 'dirty commie plot' *you* prefer to label it, Ms. Fligner – yes," Dornwyler grinned.

Conversation 29
City Centre, Los Angeles
Tuesday, April 9, 2002; 10:22 a.m.

Jack? Geoff Boyer here. I'm scheduling a meeting with the architects to begin planning for the Humanitarian Hospital outpatient clinics. The concepts you laid out on our trip to Phoenix fascinated me. The Innovations Group out of Denver lead the initiative, but I want to retain you as a clinical consultant on the project. I'm prepared to pay three-hundred an hour plus expenses along with $10,000 upfront to bring you on. Interested? Excellent! We can schedule meetings that fit your schedule. I'll have Kathy call you with the details and contractual arrangements. What say we get together for a beer and discuss it further? Okay! Talk soon. Oh! I almost forgot. If you haven't purchased Humanitarian Hospital Corporation stock you really should consider adding it to your portfolio.

Conversation 30
Santa Monica
Saturday, June 1, 2002; 6:42 p.m.

Paco took Sarita's hand and helped her down the stairs and onto the beach. Walking with her tucked under his arm, they approached the water's edge, removed their sandals, and walked toward Matteo's Restauranté. An almost summer sun set behind them, casting scarlet hues through drifting clouds, and splashing their long evening shadows across the wet sand. Provoked by the cool ocean breeze, Sarita pulled her sweater up and over her bare shoulders.

Shaking his head Paco spoke, "Seven years, Sarita. *Seven years*, it went by so fast."

Sarita glanced up at Paco, "Remember how hard it is at first? When you asked for me to come to the United States, leave mi madre and mi padre, I did not know. I was so scared. Guadalajara is my home. I only know one thing; I love you and have to be with you. Then I came here and everything is okay."

A sand piper darted in front of them; three seagulls fought over the remains of a washed up fish; a receding wave rolled over their feet. Paco looked down and said, "I love you, Sarita."

"Do you ever wonder about your love for me, Paco?"

"Never, never, never. I love you more than ever. What makes you ask?"

"Sometimes there is no time. I just wonder. But I know I love you, Paco," she said staring into the sand.

Near Matteo's, the music and patrons' voices competed with the sound of the rolling surf. "It looks like the restaurant is busy," Paco said, "It is good you make a reservation."

They sat on the restaurant's outdoor balcony at a table for two facing each other. Mariachi music played overhead. The distant surf rolled

74

over hard-packed sand, and the sunset threw evening light across Sarita's face. A forties something woman came up to them. "Good evening. My name is Adrianna. Welcome to Matteo's. I will be your server tonight. Something to drink?"

Paco looked up at the waitress and smiled, "Buenas noches Adrianna. I want Sarita to have something special. What do you have for her?"

"Make the Calypso Tequila Colada with Patrón Silver and I think you've got the best there is, if she likes tequila."

Paco looked at Sarita, "You like that, Sarita?"

Sarita looked up at the waitress, "It sound very good."

"So Sarita will have what you call it with Patrón and I will have Modelo Especial," Paco said.

"Good choices," the waitress smiled. "I'll get those for you and go over our specials when I come back."

"Can you bring chips, guacamole, and salsa too?" Paco asked.

"You bet. Coming right up," the waitress said as she disappeared.

Sarita turned and looked out at the last vestiges of sunlight as the uppermost edge of sun sank below the horizon. Ribbons of rolling surf caught the fading rays of sun like slivers of lightning, then in a wink disappeared below the horizon. She pushed the unlit candle toward the center of the table, reached over and took Paco's hands. "Happy anniversary."

"Happy anniversary, my princess," he paused. "I wish this restaurant is more fancy, a real special place. You deserve more."

"What do you mean? I love Matteo's. It is my favorite. You know that."

"It would be nice …"

"Here's your Modelo and your Calypso Tequila Colada," Adrianna interrupted. "Special occasion?"

Paco smiled, "Anniversary."

"Really, which one?"

"Número siete," Sarita beamed.

"Yeah? You two look too much in love for seven years. Me and my old man, no way," she hesitated. "Oh well. I'll get your chips and salsa," she sighed.

"Gracias," Paco said as the waitress trailed away, then raised his beer and said, "Happy anniversary, Sarita."

Sarita lifted her drink, tilted it toward Paco's, smiled and said, "Happy anniversary."

Paco set his beer on the table, reached into his jacket pocket, produced a small box, and handed it to Sarita. "This is for you."

She removed the gift wrap and from a plain, unmarked box produced a silver bracelet laced with seven tiny sapphires. Tears welled up in her eyes. "Oh, Paco, you should not have done this. We have no money ..." she insisted, "but it is so beautiful. Thank you. I love it always. Thank you," she said again wiping her eyes and slipping the bracelet onto her wrist.

Paco reached into his pocket again and withdrew a greeting card, "I am happy you like it," he smiled. "And this is for you too," he said extending the card across the table.

Sarita wiped her eyes with the back of her hands, opened the envelope and pulled the card from it. On the outside, printed in sepia tones, a young boy crowned with a fedora and dressed in a Sunday suit looked under the hood of a red Radio Flyer. Adorned with a flowered bonnet, and sitting in the driver's seat, his cherubic girl friend peered around the steering wheel and the open hood with a fanciful look, oblivious to the conundrum, but confident in her hero's ability to diagnose *and* repair the car's problem. "The picture looks like you and me," she smiled and opened the card.

Inside, Sarita read Paco's handwritten message.

My dear Sarita,
Deep in my heart,
There, lives my soul.
And when we met
I brought you in.
So you live there too,
Giving it the reason
to beat.
Every second,
Of every minute,
Of every hour,

Of every day.
My love always,
Happy anniversary, Paco

Holding the card to her chest with both hands Sarita looked up at Paco, tears streaming down her face. "You wrote something like this?"

Tears came to Paco's eyes too, "You like it, Sarita?"

"I love it ... and I love you, Paco," she said putting the card down and reaching across the table for Paco's hands. "I love you ... so much," she whispered.

Paco reached across the table with his napkin and dried her tears. "I love you too. Don't cry, Sarita."

Adrianna appeared with the chips, salsa and guacamole, "Did he hurt you?!"

Catching her tears and laughing, Sarita wiped her eyes a final time. "Look what Paco gave to me," she beamed, extending her wrist toward the waitress.

Adrianna took Sarita's hand. "It's beautiful. Where did you find this guy?" she asked winking at Paco. "Are you giving lessons?"

"No lessons, only one princess," Paco grinned.

"Yeah, yeah, so I get the bum's rush," the waitress frowned, looked out toward the ocean and sighed. "Oh, well! Let me tell you about our specials. Tonight, we've got a Baja-style lobster taco and shrimp enchiladas smothered in a green chili salsa. That comes with rice and beans for $15.95. Then, we've got grilled marinated carne asada and shrimp, sautéed with a tequila lime reduction, served with Mexican rice and rancho beans. That's $17.95."

"How is the Burrito del Mar?" Paco asked.

"If you like shrimp and lobster, it's fantastic," she answered. "I'll give you a few minutes to look things over, munch on those chips ... love and celebrate some more, and be right back. Any questions?"

"Thank you ... no," Paco said. "Oh, wait! Could you light our candle?"

Conversation 31
Rancho Palos Verdes
Monday, June 3, 2002; 7:12 a.m.

Jack MacDougall finished packing his suitcase and zipped it closed. Carolyn MacDougall rinsed her mouth with Listerine, spit into the sink, wiped her lips and asked, "When are you coming back?"

"The meetings are over late Thursday. I fly back early Friday. I think the flight gets in around 10:00 a.m."

"Are you presenting?"

"Actually, I am."

"What?"

MacDougall stared into the mirror, primped his hair one last time and answered, "Acute phase reactants in Guillain-Barré syndrome."

"Sounds esoteric."

"Oh, I wouldn't go so far as to say that. I'm reporting on the past twenty years in the trenches. It's a way to keep my academic credentials up and stay published. The entire symposium, and my paper, will go to print as a supplement in *The Annals of Neurology*. I'm sitting on the expert's panel as well, so it's a pretty good splash."

"Need me to do anything while you're gone?"

"Don't think so. Actually haven't thought about it."

Looking away from Carolyn, he drew an envelope from his sport coat pocket. "Oh, here, sorry I forgot. Happy anniversary. After 23 years it's hard to remember."

"Ahhh ... Neiman Marcus. Thanks. Don't fret, I forgot too," she frowned. "Maybe I can use this to get you something."

"Maybe" he sighed, kissing her cheek. "Better go, I'll miss my flight."

MacDougall picked up his suitcase, folded the garment bag over his arm and headed toward the door.

"Yeah, okay, can I help you carry ...?"

"No, I've got it" he interrupted. "I'll see you Friday."

Following him down the hall she said, "Okay. Ciao, see you Friday. Fly safe."

"I'll call you when I get a chance," he promised.

"That would be nice," she sighed.

Jack MacDougall closed the door behind him with his free hand and was off.

Carolyn MacDougall stood, arms folded across her chest, staring at the closed door. "Every day it's the same. Up early. Jack gone. No connection," she said to herself.

She took a deep breath and walked back to the kitchen where she poured a cup of coffee and spread out the newspaper. The headlines dramatized Saddam Hussein's evil doings on pages one, two, four and nine, and the implication that his direct involvement in terrorism brought the World Trade Center to its knees. A related article quoted President Bush ready to invade Iraq if the genocidal Saddam didn't surrender his dictatorship. On page three the economic slowdown related to the 9/11 attacks spilled out across the print – the GNP down 5.4% year to date – construction particularly hard hit. She shook her head and wondered where it all would lead. "Thank God Jack's a doctor," she said out loud.

She leafed through the remaining pages and pushed the paper aside. Too depressing. The coffee tasted fresh across her lips, so she poured another cup and picked a family photo off the shelf. There stood little John, holding mommy's hand, decked out in snorkel gear complete with boogie board. Alyssa grasped her daddy with an arm wrapped about his leg. In her free hand she carried a sand bucket and shovel. The annual family Hawaiian vacation – those were better times she thought.

Young John left for Duke University in 1999, enrolled in pre-law and, like his father, joined Sigma Alpha Epsilon fraternity. For John, Jr. life was a cabaret. He never wrote and rarely called – except when he needed more money. Carolyn labeled it "empty nest number one" and filled the void with Alyssa's soccer matches and doctor appointments for an ill defined stomach disorder and nonstop trichotillomania that plagued Alyssa during her junior and senior years of high school.

Jack MacDougall's indifference to Alyssa's medical problems irked his wife and, in fact, Carolyn developed the belief that the maladies took root in response to her husband's indifference to his entire family. Except, of course, his insistence on perfect grades, perfect soccer, perfect complexion and perfect, perfect, perfect. When Alyssa accepted a full ride soccer scholarship to University of Southern California, Carolyn declared life "empty nest, complete." That Alyssa's symptoms disappeared when she left for college, served to support Carolyn's contention that her bastard of a husband was indeed the cause.

She wiped away a tear, set the photograph back in its place, took a final drink of coffee and reviewed the week's to do list. Go to the cleaners, call the window washers, appointment with Dr. Alexandre, lunch with the Auxiliary, find a better pool service. She added Neiman Marcus – Jack's anniversary gift. "I guess I'm up to those tasks," she sighed.

Then she poured a glass of Rombauer chardonnay, just to be certain the day got started right.

Conversation 32
University Hospital Clinics, Los Angeles
Thursday, June 6, 2002; 2:00 p.m.

Dr. George Alexandre knocked on the exam room door and entered. "Well, well, well. Paco Sánchez! It's great to see you," he said shaking Paco's hand and looking toward Sarita. "And you must be Paco's bride."

"I am Sarita and this is Angelina," she blushed.

Paco cleared his throat, "Sarita, this is the great Dr. Alexandre who I have told you so much about."

"It's nice to finally meet you, Sarita. She's beautiful, Paco," Alexandre smiled. "And, Paco, how are you doing?" he asked peering into Paco's moustache and scrutinizing his nose. "My, my … everything looks good."

Paco gave Alexandre a brief recap of the events since he had last seen him in 1993 – marriage to Sarita, moving Mamacita and Emilio to the United States, Margarita and Jesus staying behind in Guadalajara, Paco's unemployment since the catastrophe of 9/11, the births of their three children – especially Angelina.

Alexandre listened intently, acknowledged Paco's story and then got down to business. "All right," he said turning away from Paco and taking Angelina from Sarita's arms. "So this must be our patient. Aren't you a sweetheart? Would you look at those eyes? How old is she?" he asked.

"She is over 4 months."

80

Alexandre laid Angelina on the exam table, took a penlight and tongue depressor from his jacket pocket and said, "Let's have a look. How is she feeding? She looks healthy."

"At first I have trouble with her. I tell Paco it is not like Miguel and José. Now she can take the breast more better."

Paco and Sarita anxiously gathered around the exam table as Alexandre completed his examination. He carefully inspected her nostrils, the cleft lip, her dental ridges, tongue and palate. Finally, he raised up, lifted Angelina back into Sarita's arms and said, "Have a seat."

"So here's my take on this," he began. "Actually it's not so bad. As you can see the cleft barely intrudes into her right nostril and only slightly extends to the dental ridge. If the defect were any more extensive, she couldn't feed and might suffer from failure to thrive. As it is, she is lucky. The issues are significant, but mainly cosmetic ..."

"Can you fix? You have to fix," Paco pleaded.

"Absolutely."

"You can fix her as good as you fix me?"

"It's a different set of circumstances ..."

"How can you fix?" Paco interrupted.

Alexandre surveyed Paco searching for the right words, which in this circumstance escaped him. Finally, he cleared his throat and blurted, "The chart says you are self-insured. You don't have insurance, Paco?"

"As I say to you, construction have been very slow so I lose my job and the insurance goes with it. How much does this cost?"

The surgeon looked away, fumbling for the answer. Alexandre could think of no worthwhile purpose in minimizing the expense, so he just came out with it. "My fee is typically $7500. Then there's the hospital, surgical suite, the anesthesiologist and the additional costs for revisions as necessary. The total bill could be over $30,000. Maybe more. I can reduce my fees somewhat – which you can pay in installments – but the hospital won't take this on without a substantial upfront deposit to cover their costs."

Paco got up from his chair and paced the room. His stomach tied in knots as he recollected again the nightmare of children taunting him after the brown recluse bite. The thought that Angelina would endure such rants chilled him, so he let down his pride.

"Like with me could we do this on the research?"

"The funds for my research grants are committed through June 30th," Alexandre sighed. "With the economy in such a funk, the National Institutes of Health has warned us to be ready for cuts next year. The short answer is I can't say just yet. My applications of course have been submitted. I'll know more in July."

Sarita squirmed in her chair, cleared her throat and blushed with embarrassment, "What about the Medicaid?"

"Not for certain," the surgeon scowled. "If you lived in Hawai'i or Iowa or Massachusetts – the Feds let every state set eligibility – Medicaid would most likely cover this in a heartbeat. Since it does not interfere with feeding the bureaucrats in this state may consider it cosmetic and, therefore, not medically necessary. In other words, as grotesque as a cleft lip might be, if it does not impact an essential function like feeding, it may not be covered, not an eligible benefit. I'll submit it and we'll see. None-the-less, the decision may take months."

Paco bit his lip, pacing the floor, shaking his head back and forth, mumbling. The thought of children teasing Angelina to tears obsessed him. Then like a sunset turning scarlet, his face transformed from flesh colored to bright red, "Jesus Christ!" he burst out, "Jesus Christ!"

"Paco!" Sarita exclaimed, "Do not use such words!"

"I cannot help it. There is nothing else I can do! Angelina will have to live with this!?" he shouted slamming his fists on the examination table and sinking to the floor.

CONVERSATIONS FOR PACO

PART III

"The social determinants of health are the circumstances in which people are born, grow up, live, work, and age, as well as the systems put in place to deal with illness. These circumstances are in turn shaped by a wider set of forces: economics, social policies, and politics."

~ Centers for Disease Control and Prevention, 2011

SUMMER 2002
Conversation 33
Bellflower
Friday, July 12, 2002; 4:15 p.m.

Several sleepless nights later, Paco Sánchez burst through the door yelling, "Sarita! Sarita! I got the job!"

Sarita came to him from the kitchen. "You what?"

"I got the job, Sarita, I got the job!"

"You kid me?"

"No!" he said, taking her into his arms. "I not kid you. I got the job!"

"Oh! Pray to Jesus, Paco, when? Where?"

"Monday! I start on Monday," he said spinning her around like a top. "First thing on Monday."

"Through the Union?"

Paco halted his dance and looked away. While driving home he churned over and over in his mind how he would break the news. He knew Sarita would object. But there was no choice and in the end he would need to make a clean break of it no matter how he explained it. It was what it was. So he said, "No, not quite ... but I got the job, Sarita."

Sarita angled her head to make eye contact, "Well who? Who hires bricklayers?"

"Well, it is not brickwork, Sarita."

"What then, if not brickwork? What?" Sarita pleaded, shaking him by the arms.

Paco hesitated, "Republic Waste."

"What they doing hiring bricklayers?"

"They are not." Paco explained, lowering his head.

"What then?" she asked, and then it came to her. "Oh, no. Oh, no, Paco. You are not garbage man. You are a bricklayer," she insisted.

"Just until construction picks up. We need the money. We have got the bills. We have got the children, and the house and the hospital. Especially there is Angelina. I must make the money and get the insurance to fix Angelina's lip. In my prayers I promise her like I promise you."

Sarita imagined Paco in the hot sun, surrounded by the stench of trash, lifting can after can, dumping them into the truck, wiping his sweat, moving to the next house. "To hell with that hospital, Paco. Angelina she have to wait. You are not a garbage man. You lay bricks. I won't …"

"We have no choice."

"We have a choice. I can go back to the hotel. Angelina she no longer needs my milk."

"You cannot go back to the hotel. It does not pay for nothing. Who will take care of the children?"

Vivid visions of uncollected trash strewn about the streets of Guadalajara fueled Sarita's discontent. She saw hungry children sifting through garbage, digging for left-over scraps of something, anything, to eat. She smelled the feculent putrefaction from bags thrown against walls and in out-of-the-way corners, left to rot at the whim of the cobradors. Her stomach turned. "Mamacita took care of you. She can take care of our children. Angelina does not need my breast. I can work the hotel. You are a bricklayer; you are not basurero, Paco!"

"It have to be the way it is," Paco protested. "Miguel and José and Angelina need their mamá. We have bills. I must get the money for the surgery before Angelina she gets too old. And with Republic there is insurance that will maybe cover. I took the job. It is final."

"But you did not even tell me."

"I tell you now, and it is final, Sarita. There is no more talking."

Sarita buried her face in her hands and sank into the chair. "Paco, oh my dear, Paco."

Paco brushed away his own tears, walked across the room, picked up Angelina and cradled her in his arms. "It is just until construction picks up, Angelina. Papá promises."

Conversation 34
Bellflower
Friday, July 12, 2002; 5:12 p.m.

Sarita set out the simple meal of pinto beans, rice, flour tortillas, and iced tea. They ate in silence. She breastfed Angelina over her left arm and helped José when he needed it. Frustration and worry riddled her appetite. She couldn't look in Paco's direction, let alone talk with him. "Like he said," she whispered. "The talk is over. Garbage man? Paco he *is not* a garbage man."

Paco scooped up the last grains of rice between a tortilla, finished it with a single motion, and left the table. "The Dodgers are playing. I think I will go watch."

Sarita finished her meal, sitting in silence. When they were done, she shooed José and Miguel off to play and cleaned up the dishes. Then she carried Angelina on her hip out into the backyard, watching the sunset over the laundry hanging on her clothesline and between adjacent rooftops. Next door she heard the laughter of children's playful voices. As she stood there, the day turned to twilight. The children's voices faded, muffled by her thoughts. She wiped away a tear as it rolled down her cheek and went back into the house to sit with Paco. Odalis Perez was pitching in the bottom of the fourth and the Dodgers led the Giants 3 to 2.

Conversation 35
Rancho Palos Verdes
Friday, July 12, 2002; 4:49 p.m.

That same evening, Jack MacDougall threw his overnight bag behind the driver's seat of the Mercedes, got in behind the wheel and started down the driveway. He glanced at the dashboard clock, 4:49. "Shit. Late again," he mumbled to himself. The tires squealed coming onto the street. He slowed for a speed bump, took a right at Caliente, then a left on Del Dio Rios, exited the guard gate, and they were on their way.

"What time is our flight?" he asked.

"Six-thirty. If traffic's bad we might miss it."

"We could, but I'll get us there. Don't worry."

"I hate always being late and rushed. It is not good for you."

"It's the way I live, Carolyn."

"It's not good for you. And *I* don't like rushing."

MacDougall cleared his throat. "You never complain when the money is coming in."

"Oh, for Christ sakes, Jack, if it's going to be this way all week-end, I don't want to go. This conversation is not about money and I don't want to argue."

He angled the Mercedes into the commuter lane, stepped on the accelerator and asked, "Argue? Who's arguing? I'm stating facts."

"Jack, what's the matter?"

"Nothing. I don't want to talk about it."

Carolyn MacDougall rubbed her forehead, "Is it something I did or said?"

"No. Of course not. And why does it always have to be about you? I said I didn't want to talk about it," he chided, dodging right, passing the car in front of him and swerving back into the commuter lane.

At 5:42 they exited the freeway and made their way to valet park-ing. MacDougall grabbed their luggage and broke out ahead of Car-olyn. Walking in high heels, she lost her balance and nearly stumbled trying to keep up with his long, rapid strides. He looked over his shoul-der and asked, "You coming?"

"Go on ahead. I'll meet you at security," she puffed.

At 6:17 they took their seats in first class. The flight attendant, a well groomed woman near Carolyn's age, approached them.

"Good evening. I see you made it. Would you like some cham-pagne?"

"Mmmm, yum," answered Carolyn. "What is ...?"

"Sweet doesn't sound good to me. Got any Chivas Regal or John-nie Walker Black?" MacDougall horned in.

"Johnnie Walker Red. No Chivas. On the rocks?"

"On the rocks. That'll be great."

"And you?" she asked, looking back to Carolyn.

"What's the champagne?"

"Mumm's Brut. Not Dom Pérignon, but not bad," she smiled.

"I'll have that. And do you have an InStyle magazine?"

"Sure. I'll be right back. Secure your seatbelts. We're about to take off."

Jack leaned into Carolyn, "Remember when stewardesses were babes?"

"They still are. Just aged babes. And they're flight attendants, not stewardesses. You're showing your age too," she scowled.

Buckling his seat belt MacDougall asked, "You going to read the whole way? I thought maybe we could talk."

"Talk? About what? I don't care to 'talk' when you're in one of your moods," she whispered.

"It's never enough, is it?"

"You said that, Jack, I didn't. And you know what I would like to know? I would like to know where this deep seated, but right-on-the-surface anger comes from," she retorted looking away and out the window.

"Fuck you, Carolyn MacDougall. *Fuck* you. Where's my drink?"

At 31,000 feet and well into her second flute of Mumm's, Carolyn MacDougall grew weary of the chilly silence. She set the magazine aside and took her husband's hand. "You look nice in that shirt, Jack. Teal is a great color on you."

He looked down. "Thanks. Where did you get it?"

"Nordstrom silly, where else? It's Assam-Muga silk. Beautiful isn't it?"

She took a drink of champagne and continued, "I made reservations at *Prime* for 8:30."

MacDougall glanced at his wristwatch, "Should be about right. We're staying at the Bellagio?"

"Uh-huh. I got us a Jacuzzi suite. A limo is picking us up."

MacDougall took another drink of the Johnnie Walker and reclined back. "Thanks Carolyn. I needed this. The office has been the pits. Maybe I'll get a massage while we're there. What are you going to play tonight?"

"I don't know. Maybe video poker, maybe the slots, maybe Pai Gow. I kind of had fun with that last time. You?"

"Craps," he said taking in the last of the scotch.

"Need I ask?" she smiled, squeezing his hand.

Conversation 36
Bellflower
Friday, July 12, 2002; 10:03 p.m.

With the children put to bed, Sarita undressed, slipped on her nightgown and slid in next to Paco.

"Paco? Are you awake?"

"Yes."

"I love you," she said.

He rolled toward her, drawing her close, and looking into her eyes, "And I love you."

"Tell me construction picks up."

"It will," he said kissing her on the forehead. "It has to."

"When do you think?"

"Soon I guess."

"I hate to have you do such an awful job."

"I do not like it either but we have no other way. It is okay."

Kissing him, she said again, "I love you so much, Paco. You are my everything."

"And I love you too."

"You want to see how much I love you?" she simpered.

"How much?" he grinned. "You trying to start something?"

"Maybe," she blushed.

Moonlight crept into the room, glistening off their faces. Avoiding Paco's gaze, Sarita pulled her nightgown up, straddled him between the soft skin of her thighs, and said, "I love you this much my brave one." Then she guided their bodies together and slipped Paco's stiff penis into the moist lips between her legs.

"Mmmm. You love me so much," he groaned.

"I do love you," she smiled. "But do not go too fast, Paco – when I have you in my arms like this – I want you here forever."

And then they kissed. A deep, thoroughly wet kiss. When Sarita came up from their tangled arms, she caught her breath, let it out and dove back for more.

Their bodies rocked. As they kissed. Together. In slow, so slow, then quicker, faster, then slower. Rhythmic. Unison.

Conversation 37
Bellflower
Saturday, July 13, 2002; 7:09 a.m.

The nightmare and a squawking crow outside their window wrestled Paco from his sleep. He rolled to his side and pushed away the hallucinations from the never, never land between unconsciousness and reality, but the distortions wouldn't budge. In dark, twilight sleep, he saw scores of workers sorting through mounds of waste with bloodied, bare hands. Sweat ran down their faces and drenched their clothing. Green containers strapped to their chests like shields caught their vomit when the stench overwhelmed them. Then Paco realized he was one of them, sweat pouring off his face, the green container catching his puke. Seagulls circled overhead, diving into the garbage when the workers uncovered discarded morsels. Big, black African-American superintendents walked in a line behind the men growling orders. "I said metal in metal, paper in paper, and glass in glass. And I don't give a rat's motherfucking ass what you do with the food some rich bitch threw out. Take it home for all I care, you miserable Mexican cocksuckers. Now get moving. I ain't got all day!"

As the dream unfolded, the straw-boss stuck his face into Paco's. What teeth he had were stained mocha brown, and his eyes were fully bloodshot. The man's breath reeked of cigarettes, the morning's coffee and last night's whiskey. "Now what the fuck we got here, Jasper? Ain't you the ugliest son-of-a-motherfucker I ever did lay my eyes on. *Je-e-e*-sus Christ boys. Get your lazy asses over here. This one's hardly got any nose. You can see clear down to his asshole and half the way up his brain – that is if he's got one!" he roared. "Let's call him double ugly or better yet, Mex the mother-fucking Monster! Son-of-a-bitch. I ain't never seen such ugly. Never, ever in my whole God-damn life."

Paco sat up with a jolt. Sweat rolled down his face and onto his chest. He reached for his nose and felt for his moustache. Certain they were still there, he took several deep breaths to clear the images. Eventually, he lay back, pulling the covers over his shoulders, burying his head in his pillow and curling into a ball. He shivered again, took another deep breath, and after some time blinked his eyes open.

Unlike Paco, Sarita lay quiet, still in deep, peaceful morning sleep. He examined her sleep filled face – rich, brown skin; dark, silken hair; upturned lips, pointed nose – the hint of a smile despite deep slumber.

He felt his muscles loosen and the ugly hallucinations fade. Like in life, Sarita's peace brought Paco peace.

Finally, her eyes opened, then shut, then opened again. "Buenos días," she yawned. "You are already awake?"

"Buenos días. I am awake."

"You are all sweaty. You slept okay?"

"Uh-huh. I have a dream, but now I am okay. And I have been thinking Sarita, maybe we should take the kids and Mamacita to the beach today."

"That sounds nice," she yawned again. Then she remembered that Paco started his garbage man job on Monday. The thought turned her stomach. She couldn't imagine Paco holding on for dear life behind a smelly truck in the hot sun. But he was right about one thing. They had bills to pay. And Angelina needed surgery.

"How did you sleep?"

"Our love helps me to sleep at first," she smiled. "Then I wake up and cannot sleep for a long time, then I go back to sleep."

Sarita cleared her throat and asked, "Paco?"

"Yes."

"I could not tell you."

"Tell what?"

"I could not tell you, and I could not sleep, so I have to tell."

"What? What?"

"The woman – Mrs. Mimi at the hospital – she calls again."

"What did she say?"

"She asks when we are going to pay the bill."

"What did you tell her?"

"I tell her that you are still out of work. I tell her you are a good man. You work hard every day you can find work. I tell her that we have to have the house for the family and that Miguel and José and Angelina come first. She not even care, Paco. She say she is going to send us to collection if we cannot make a payment."

Paco winced and blurted, "Shit."

"Don't be mad."

Paco sat upright, circling his arms about his knees, "I am not mad, it is just …"

"Just what?" she interjected.

"I thought when I came to the United States I would never have it like this," he said shaking his head.

Sarita reached up and placed her hand on Paco's shoulder, "At least in the United States there is hope that it will get better."

"That has to be true … I guess."

"Paco, I could not tell you something else."

"Tell what?"

"I could not tell you, and every night I could not sleep, so I have to tell."

"What, Sarita? What do you not want to tell me?" he frowned.

She reached for his hand and said, "Come back here a minute. Promise me not to be mad."

Paco turned to her and laid on his side, propped up by his elbow, "What?"

"We could not pay for the birth control pills. They are so expensive, Paco. I cross my fingers and pray that maybe the breast feeding will be enough. You say that Republic have insurance?"

"Not at first. I think it is in ninety days. Why?"

She took his hand again and placed it on the soft skin of her abdomen and said, "That is good," she said smiling. "The test it turns blue, Paco. I am pregnant again."

Conversation 38
Hermosa Beach
Saturday, July 13, 2002; 2:26 p.m.

They sat on a blanket outspread on the sand. The sun shone brightly, reflecting the glittering sea toward them. Sarita held Angelina under a beach umbrella, sheltering her from the ultraviolet rays. Paco lathered José and Miguel with sun screen and applied generous dollops to his arms and neck as well. The crowded beach rang with a cacophonic medley of laughter, playful screams, and boom box music. Paco pulled a can of Modelo from the cooler and asked, "Hey, Miguel and José, you want to build a sandcastle?"

"Yes, Papá, yes!" they cried, grabbing their shovels and buckets and running toward better sand. Paco followed, and they began to dig.

"Papá, can we build Pancho Villa's hideout?" Miguel asked.

"Pancho's hideout again?" he laughed. "Of course, you can build whatever you want. But you make sure Pancho is very safe and he has a place to ambush Carranza, okay?"

"Pancho will be very safe," Miguel promised.

As his children dug and molded the walls of the fortress, Paco drank from the Modelo and thought of his father making bricks day in, day out in the hot Mexican sun on the banks of the Santiago River. It was the summer of 1981. Paco had just turned eight; Papá asked Mamacita if he could help. She said yes, as long as he remembered that in the fall, Paco would begin school. Papá reassured Mamacita that education was "muy importante" but he needed the help. So Paco became their "poco aprendiz" or little apprentice. He learned how the men tied bandannas about their heads to keep incessant sweat from their eyes, smoked cigarettes and rhythmically turned the river bank silt. Paco watched them mix the mud – 10 shovels silt, two shovels manure, one of cut straw and just enough water to scoop the heavy slag into molds, level it with a screed and leave the bricks to set-up in the sun. Later, at what seemed just the right moment, they released the bricks from the molds and stacked them crisscross twenty-four high, eleven wide and five deep. When completed, the latticed stack made a pallet four feet by four feet by four feet with sufficient space between each brick to finish the cure and ready for the kiln. Paco took the men fresh water and at noon helped Mamacita with lunch. During high heat, he brought the workers salt tablets to take with cool water. The work dragged endlessly, but on a good day they counted four to five hundred new bricks. Made in silence. There was nothing to sing about. Paco admired his papá's work and wondered if some day he might wear a bright bandana, smoke cigarettes and learn the trade.

On a rainy day after school that same autumn, Mamacita ran home to the children screaming and crying. "¡Su papito ha muerto! ¡Su papito ha muerto! Se ha caido al río. Como no sabe nadar, la corriente se lo llevó y se nos ha ahogado. Nadie lo vio caer en el agua. ¡Ay, Dios mío! ¡Ay, Dios mío! ¿Qué vamos a hacer, mis niños?"

Mamacita's hysteria made it difficult to understand what meaning hid behind the clamor of her emotions, but soon it became clear. Papá had slipped on the bank of the Santiago, lost his balance, got swept away in the currents and drowned. Mamacita had warned Paco about the river and its dangers. He now understood why. Paco remembered the faces of his brothers and sisters huddled together, tears streaming down their faces, and stunned by disbelief. Paco wondered too. What would become of them without Papá?

"Papá make bricks, I lay bricks," Paco Sánchez whispered, shook his head and drank the rest of his Modelo.

Within an hour, the fortress stood tall and mighty, complete with gunnery and stable. Paco agreed with his sons – it was a fitting monument to Pancho Villa. "You build a very good hideout for Pancho," he told them.

Sarita walked up behind Paco and her sand-covered children. "Having fun my little niños?"

There was no answer. They were too busy building the secret passage. "Paco, get between the boys, I want to take the fotographia."

Paco crawled on all fours around the sandcastle and between Miguel and José. "Stop for a minute. Mama takes our picture," he said putting an arm around each of them and drawing them close. "You have to make a big smile."

"Everyone says fotographia," Sarita said. "Good. One more. Say fotographia. Perfecto," she smiled. "All finished."

Miguel and José resumed their project. Paco crawled back to Sarita and sat next to her, legs bent, his arms folded just below his kneecaps, "It is a good idea to come here today."

"Everyone always seem happy at the beach. It takes away the problems ... how are you doing?" she asked.

"The sun feels good. Miguel and José they are having fun," he said, then reached over and placed his hand on the soft skin of Sarita's bare, pregnant belly, "How long?"

"Three months. Dr. Rodríguez say December 27th. Maybe sooner."

"Christmas baby?"

"Maybe," she blushed. "And you are okay with this?"

The words to vent his immutable fear – that this baby, like Angelina, could also be born with a cleft palate – eluded him. Besides what good would it do to upset Sarita? She could not change what was. So

94

instead, he answered her question with a question, "Did Dr. Rodríguez say a boy or girl?"

"He could not tell for sure, but he thinks it is a boy."

Paco smiled. "More castles in the sand, Sarita?"

"More castles in the sand, Paco."

Conversation 39
Bellflower
Friday, July 26, 2002; 7:37 p.m.

Two weeks later Sarita helped Paco into the Caravan. Easing him into the front passenger seat she asked, "Are you in?"

"Uh-huh."

She walked around, got in behind the wheel, and drove away from the curb. "When did this start, Paco?"

"Yesterday I think, but I thought it was the heat and I did not have enough to drink."

"It is the garbage, Paco; the people's la basura you pick up."

"I do not think so, Sarita. I just have a very bad cold or something. The doctors can fix me."

Sarita drove across 8th Street to Lancaster and dodged in and out of traffic along the Interstate heading to the hospital. In the distance, the letters *HUMANITARIAN*, backlit in blue, struck out across each parapet of the 7 story edifice and lifted her confidence.

She found a space in the Patients Only lot next to the Emergency Department, parked the car and got out. A cool summer breeze momentarily refreshed her. Looking to the right she read the monument sign's bold letters.

HUMANITARIAN HOSPITAL
Over 50 years of Giving~Sharing~Loving~Caring

A young child skipping between the hands of her parents exited the double door entrance singing "Oh, I wish I were an Oscar Mayer Weiner! Oh, I wish I were an Oscar Mayer Weiner!" Sarita breathed a sigh of relief, walked around and helped Paco from the car.

Fini Dobyns, the receptionist, looked up staring through big bug-eye lenses, too large even for her pudgy face. A video solitaire game on the computer monitor in front of Fini reflected off her glasses and back at Sarita. "Name?" she yawned.

"Mine or Paco's?" Sarita asked.

"Patient's," she retorted through her chewing gum.

"Paco Sánchez."

"Does he have a middle initial?"

"Paco Raphael Sánchez," Sarita stated.

"So the middle initial is 'R'?"

Sarita prickled, "Yes, 'R' like Raphael. R-A-P-H-A-E-L. Raphael."

"Date of birth?" Fini asked, looking up, then down, changing computer screens and tapping in Paco R. Sánchez.

"September 21, 1973," Paco answered.

"Equinox baby, huh? Bet you were a handful," she blew a bubble, popped it and typed in 09211973.

"Equinox baby?" Sarita asked.

"Oh, never mind. It's a thing with me. Been here before Mr. Sánchez? Hmmm ..." she said scrolling down the Sánchez list. "Doesn't look like it."

"Just for our babies," Sarita answered. "Not for Paco."

The receptionist shoved a clipboard toward Sarita and said, "Fill this out, bring it back to me completed in its entirety. He signs here," she said circling the Patient's Signature line, looking away and turning back to the video solitaire on her monitor.

Sarita led Paco back to a quiet corner and completed the forms. "It seems strange to fill these out for you, Paco. It is me who have to be seeing the doctor all the time. What do I put down for insurance?"

Paco shivered, "None I guess, we do not have any."

Sarita left the answer blank and asked, "It says chief complaint, Paco. What do you want me to write?"

Paco wiped the moisture from his forehead, "Sore throat, fever ... ache all over."

"What about the headache?"

The pain started above both eyes, spread across his forehead, pierced his brain at the base of his skull and throbbed like an accordion at his temples. Moving his head made it worse and stirred up a well of nausea. "Yes, you have to put that too." he mumbled.

Sarita completed the form, walked back to bubble gumming Fini Dobyns, and handed her the clip board.

Dobyns reached up, took the chart without looking and said "Done? Take a seat. The nurse will call you in a few minutes."

Sarita and Paco sat in a corner watching CNN News. The coverage included a passenger train catastrophe in Belgium and concern that terrorists might have instigated the carnage. Twenty-seven passengers dead, scores injured. Sarita shook her head at the news. Paco lay slumped in the chair, eyes shut, warding off the fluorescent light. Except for the television, the waiting room was quiet. No kids. No loud conversation. Sarita held Paco's hand and reassured him he would get better after he got some medicine. Paco nodded, but sat silent.

"Mrs. Sánchez?"

Sarita looked up. It was Fini. "Yes."

"I need to ask you some questions."

Managing a smile, Sarita got up and walked over to the receptionist.

"Mrs. Sánchez," she paused, cleared her throat and whispered. "Our records indicate your account is quite past due."

"I know. But Paco is very sick."

"I'm sorry, Mrs. Sánchez, it is Humanitarian policy … we have to refer you to County Hospital."

"What?" Sarita asked. "You cannot treat Paco?"

"I'm afraid …"

"But he is very sick. He have a fever!" Sarita interrupted.

"Mrs. Sánchez …"

"Do not Mrs. Sánchez to me. Paco he is very sick. He needs a doctor very bad. He cannot leave until he gets to be seen. I want to talk to your supervisor!"

"Please, Mrs. Sánchez. Keep your voice down – it won't do any good to see my supervisor. I have my directives."

"You can throw your 'directives' or whatever you have to call them into the Sea of Baja, Ms. Fini Dobyns. Humanitarian Hospital is our family hospital. This is where Miguel and José and Angelina are born. Now my Paco needs treatment and you are refusing?" she blurted. "If you will not let me talk to your boss, who will?" she asked, and then shouted. "Paco cannot leave without treatment!"

"I asked you to keep your voice down," the receptionist glared back, then said, "One moment, Mrs. Sánchez."

Fini stood up and turned away harrumphing. "Some people," she mumbled under her breath and disappeared through a set of double doors marked "Restricted Access. Authorized Personnel Only!" When she returned, she had in tow an anorexic, clipboard-toting woman dressed in white. Her nametag read Ms. Linda Adderley, Charge Nurse.

Adderley spoke first, managing the hint of a smile that highlighted lipstick slithering into the crevice-like wrinkles encircling her lips, "What can I do for you, Mrs. Sánchez?" she sighed.

"It's my husband Paco. He is very sick. His temperature is 102 degrees. He needs to see a doctor. This person says you cannot treat him because we owe you money."

"It's Humanitarian's policy ..."

"It may be your policy, but it is not – how do you say – human?" Sarita blurted out and burst into tears.

Nurse Adderley paused searching for comforting words. Mrs. Sánchez was right, she thought to herself, the policy is not humane. Taking a deep breath, she reached over the counter and placed her boney hand on Sarita's wrist. "Okay. Okay, I'll call the hospital administrator and see what we can do."

Conversation 40
Los Angeles
Friday, July 26, 2002; 8:11 p.m.

Waiters and waitresses scurried about delivering chocolate mousse to the guests, when the president of the County Medical Society, Dr. Jack MacDougall, returned to the podium.

"Ladies and gentlemen ... ladies and gentlemen. Ladies and gentlemen, may I have your attention ... ladies and gentlemen, may I have your attention, *please* ..."

When the drone of the crowd finally subsided, MacDougall continued.

"Ladies and gentlemen, honored guests. As most of you realize, this 73rd annual Medical Society dinner and fundraiser reveres past successes, celebrates current honorees and – much to my chagrin – witnesses passing of the gavel to the president elect.

"As many of you also know," MacDougall went on, "it is a well established tradition that the final act – the swan song if you will – of the outgoing president is presentation of the Society's Physician of the Year Award. It is my distinct pleasure to do so at this time.

"This year's recipient stands in distinction amongst his colleagues for several compelling reasons. *First,* and of course foremost, distinguished medical service. This year's Physician of the Year has faithfully and diligently provided extraordinary medical care to our community for the better part of fifteen years. This year's Physician of the Year re-engineered laboratory services at County Hospital to the degree that ever escalating laboratory costs stabilized, providing reliable relief to County Hospital's all too wobbly bottom line.

Second, national distinction among his specialty peers. This year's Physician of the Year serves on the editorial board of the esteemed *American Journal of Pathology,* lending an extraordinary scholarly dimension to his well rounded contributions in the healthcare of our citizens."

MacDougall took a drink of water and continued, *"Third,* leadership in medical education. When the Accreditation Council for Graduate Medical Education cited the University for insufficient autopsy examinations in 2000, this year's recipient worked hand-in-hand with the medical school faculty to rectify the issues and cure this important academic deficiency. In this day of high tech imaging, no small task, I might add.

"Finally, and perhaps most notably, this year's Physician of the Year is remarkable *not* for his face to face care of patients, but the superb behind-the-scenes clinical support he provides each and every one

of us that work tirelessly in the trenches day in and day out, ministering to the sick, and delivering on our promise of best in class patient care."

MacDougall cleared his throat, paused and then went on, "As a past recipient of this award and your immediate past president – well almost immediate past president," he frowned, "permit me to digress a moment."

"This year's recipient and I first met in medical school at Johns Hopkins University. Many nights we studied together mastering the Kreb's cycle, studying subjects like neuroanatomy and pharmacology and yes, when time permitted, drinking a few brewskis," MacDougall chuckled.

"As fate would have it, we continued on together at the Peter Bent Brigham and Massachusetts General Hospitals, as well as Washington University for our residencies and fellowships. Ed married his lovely wife, Judi; I married Carolyn. And as couples, we became fast friends. Now we practice the art of medicine – although in different specialties – side by side, day in and day out, in the same wonderful community.

"So it probably comes as no surprise to anyone here tonight that I nominated this year's recipient for physician of the year. But may I assure you, he receives this award after the careful scrutiny, deliberation *and* the vote of our *entire* Board.

"Ladies and gentlemen. Physicians. Members of the healthcare profession. Husbands and wives – it brings me great pleasure, and it is my honor this evening, to present to you this year's Physician of the Year, Dr. Edmund M. Pinkerton."

Conversation 41
Humanitarian Hospital, Los Angeles
Friday, July 26, 2002; 10:19 p.m.

Humanitarian Hospital intern Dr. Jerome Spivey entered the cubicle walled off and separated by curtains from the adjacent spaces. Paco held his head, shielding his eyes from the fluorescents. Sarita stood at the gurney by his side. She glanced at her watch and looked back at the doctor. Two day's beard stubble dotted his face. He wore green surgical scrubs and a white, short waistcoat in need of a laundry. A stethoscope dangled around his neck like a caduceus. Sarita noticed his fingernails. They needed scrubbing too.

"What's going on?" grumbled the intern, looking down at Paco's clipboard.

"We have waited three hours," Sarita scowled.

Spivey, short on sleep but shorter on patience, glared at Sarita. "Emergencies come first, ma'am."

"But we have waited three hours. Paco *is* an emergency."

"Ms. Sánchez, I don't much like gettin' rude. But I'll say this. About two hours ago a little four year old came in here from a motor vehicle crash. Mom and dad didn't have him buckled in. He went through the windshield and banged his head up right much. Got his arm nearly tore off at the elbow too. Little kid so scared he pooped all over his self," he paused. "Now that's an emergency."

Sarita thought of Miguel and José and turned scarlet, "I'm sorry doctor. I ... how did *that* happen?"

"It goes something like this, ma'am. People have what we call a defecation reflex. When they get frightened or real excited or anxious – they get a big adrenalin rush – and they do one of two things. Cramp up and get all constipated. Or, mostly, have a right much urge to defecate," Spivey explained. "Sometimes it can be explosive. Uncontrollable. That's what happened to the little boy."

"No, I mean how did the accident happen?" Sarita asked.

Spivey blushed and cleared his throat, "Oh, the accident. I'm sorry. I thought you were asking how he pooped on himself. Don't know about the crash. Going too fast. Lost control. There could have been alcohol. Something like that," he hesitated and turned back to Paco.

"So you have a sore throat, Mr. Sánchez?" Spivey continued in his Deep South drawl that came out mushy backwoods, straight from Uncle Remus.

"Uh-huh."

"How long?"

"Two days. But today it kill me."

"What else?"

"Fever. I have fever."

Spivey began his exam, sliding a tongue depressor over Paco's tongue, "Say ah," he instructed and then flexed Paco's neck while simultaneously feeling for swollen glands. "How about chills?" the intern asked removing the stethoscope from its perch around his neck and sticking the tips into his ears.

"No, no chills."

"Take a deep breath. Good. Again. Once more. Okay. What else?" he asked passing the stethoscope over Paco's chest.

"You said you have a headache, Paco," Sarita interjected.

"Please. I'll ask the questions, Ms. Sánchez," Spivey directed. "Do you have a headache, Mr. Sánchez?"

"Yes. Very bad. Right here," Paco pointed between his eyes.

Spivey pushed on Paco's abdomen and felt for enlarged lymph nodes under Paco's arms and in his groin. "Well, you've got no lymph nodes and your spleen's not big. This looks right much like a virus, but I want to get some tests to be sure. The nurse will be right in to get those and I'll be back."

"How much longer?" Sarita asked.

"Right away ... I think," the intern said and disappeared.

Sarita looked first at Paco, then away at the floor and up at the ceiling, then back at Paco. "I hate hospitals."

Paco covered his eyes, took a deep breath and mumbled, "Me too, Sarita."

Conversation 42
Humanitarian Hospital, Los Angeles
Friday, July 26, 2002; 10:44 p.m.

Spivey stood at the end of the gurney only half listening to Paco's past medical history and the description of the brown recluse spider bite, its devastating destruction and the two year ordeal to repair the consequences. Nurse Adderley's words in response to the tests he needed to make Paco's diagnosis unglued and roiled him, *"Can't Spivey, unless it is life-threatening. He's category 3. New Humanitarian policy since February. Patients with bills past due over 120 days get treated and streeted. No tests unless it's an absolute, life threatening emergency. Pretend this is a Monopoly game. Take a Chance card. By the way, did you get a past medical history? Medical records will bounce the chart back if you didn't. It's another new rule. Administration wants complete past medical histories on everyone – improves reimbursement – and believe me, around here most often it's all about the money."*

"Is medicine *just* about the money? Who *does* wield the power to make it an entrepreneurial hoax?" he asked himself over and over, while intermittently nodding and mindlessly grunting, "Uh-huh. What happened next?" in response to Paco's story. When he decided he had enough information to satisfy hospital administration and complete the Emergency Department form, he excused himself and shuffled back to the nursing station.

Spivey sat in a cubicle, shoulders slumped, recording the details of Paco's present illness, his review of systems and past medical history. He felt utterly isolated, all alone and distracted. He missed the comfortable surroundings of home. "What have I gotten myself into," he wondered and then recalled the images and ministrations of his mentor Dr. Bacon back in Chapel Hill.

Pontificating through coffee breath and a snarly beard, Bacon's words welled up in Spivey's mind. "Son, ninety per cent of the diagnosis is in the history. Always take a good one. 'Ya hear me? Y'all can't go wrong that way. *Then* the physical and the labs go along with what you already know. Do 'ya see? And know your differential diagnosis, boy, so you'll order the right tests every time and you don't go gettin' a bunch of cockamamie ones you aren't never going to need and that cost the patients a bunch of money they don't have. 'Ya hear me? Do 'ya see? Lord knows medicine is right much expensive the way it is."

Spivey remembered too how Bacon would look around, make certain no one stood in ear shot, give a wry chuckle and whisper, "And, Spivey, recollect a nigger 'ill put his dick in just about anything all day long, so don't go forgetting that syphilis and the clap mimic every disease known to man – I think God put them on earth to punish whoring niggers, don't you? – some people 'ud think that's a racist talkin', Spivey. Well they can go and shove it up their backside. All as I'm saying is don't go forgetting that syphilis and the clap mimic every disease on God's green earth. And you had better treat them for every sex-ually transmitted disease known to medicine when you suspect them. 'Ya hear me son? Even if you don't have the tests for it. Y'all can't go wrong that way. Do 'ya see?"

Finally, Spivey shook off his reverie and pulled the Palm Pilot from his white waist coat again and re-checked the recommendations in eProcrates. *"Untreated complications of Streptococcal infection include rheumatic heart disease and kidney failure. Penicillins are the preferential therapies. If gonorrhea is suspected treat with intramuscular Rocephin 250 milligrams stat."* He slid the Palm back into its case, began writing and motioned to nurse Adderley, "So give Mr. Sánchez two-fifty of Rocephin IM and let's get him out of here."

"I can get him out of here," the nurse countered. "But I *can't* give him the Rocephin. Part of Category 3. Too expensive. You'll have to prescribe him something he can take by mouth that covers whatever you're diagnosing, and that he can get at a pharmacy. And Spivey. Don't forget to tell them about follow-up at County."

Spivey shook his head, turned away from her in disgust and headed back to Paco's cubicle. Nearly tripping over an untied shoe lace he mumbled, *"Category 3?* What kind of fucking humanitarian hospital is this?"

Conversation 43
Humanitarian Hospital, Los Angeles
Friday, July 26, 2002; 10:57 p.m.

The intern pulled back the emergency bay curtains, "Mr. Sánchez?"

"Uh-huh?"

"You've got Strep throat. I'm going to give you some antibiotics and send you home."

"What about the tests?" Sarita asked.

"Well, there is really no need for them," Spivey lied. "They would take forever and you look exhausted. He has fever, swollen glands, and his throat is bright red and has exudates ..."

"Exudates? What are those?" Sarita asked.

"Pus. He has pus on the back of his throat. It's Strep," Spivey apologized, handing Sarita the paperwork and prescriptions for Keflex and Lortab. "I am giving him a strong antibiotic – that's the Keflex – to cover everything just in case it's something other than Strep. There's a prescription there for the pain too. Make sure he drinks lots of fluids."

"So, we can go?"

"Yes, you can go," Spivey said, looking down at the clipboard. "Oh, in case he does need follow up, he will have to go to County Hospital."

Sarita's heart sank for the third time that day. First, Paco's peculiar illness, then Fini Dobyns telling her they couldn't treat her husband, and now the intern declaring they would have to go the County Hospital if Paco didn't get better. But it was near midnight; she was exhausted, and just didn't have the energy to defy the doctor's order.

"What do I watch for?" Sarita frowned.

The intern shrugged and turned away, "Worsening of symptoms – vicious headache, vomiting. Things like that."

Conversation 44
Marina del Rey, California
Friday, July 26, 2002; 11:11 p.m.

That same night and dressed in nothing but undershorts, Dr. Edmund M. Pinkerton tiptoed to the master bedroom and peeked in. Judi laid there in bed, curled-up, captured by deep, sonorous sleep. He turned and quietly made his way back down the hall. A yawn that came from deep inside hindered him momentarily; the Medical Society banquet and his acceptance speech for Physician of the Year left him exhausted. Pinkerton didn't revel in the public limelight.

At the landing he pushed his bald, aging body up the spiral staircase to his crow's nest, a sanctuary he designed, built and decorated for his "personal" use on the third story of their home. Judi Pinkerton sardonically referred to it as his "man cave."

When he reached the upper level, his breath came in deep, prolonged wheezes. "Jesus Christ, I have got to lose some of this weight," he puffed.

The good doctor rested his pounding heart on the banister, and when he finally caught his wind, waddled over to the bar. He took down a glass, poured three fingers of Tanqueray Ten and filled the remaining space with a fistful of cubes from the icemaker. He swirled the gin, took a long drink and refilled it.

Pinkerton set the glass next to his Lazy-Boy, rummaged through several DVDs in the credenza and loaded his choice into the player. The title words, *Devil and Miss Jones,* lit up the Pioneer Elite plasma screen. Satisfied, he sank into the chair and drank once more from his gin.

The pornographic classic filmed in the 1970s still ranked as his favorite. Although the quality of the reformatted video, shot 30 years before, did not match the resolution of his high definition technology, he watched it over and over.

Pinkerton cleared his throat and took another drink. He hit the fast forward to get beyond the credits; crunched gin soaked ice between his teeth and reflected on what fascinated him with the film.

First, there was Georgina Spelvin. The way her sucking and fucking came to life on the big screen gave any man a hard-on. To Ed Pinkerton, Spelvin's sexual prowess made her the all-time queen of porn. Then there was the tale of Miss Jones. Her free fall from Puritan ways into sexual debauchery allured him. Her insatiable appetite for sordid sex and orgasm fed the primal urge in his loins. "Why couldn't more women fuck like that," he wondered. He delighted in her demise as well – ending empty and in hell, unable to masturbate to orgasm. "Serves the cunt right," he often said to himself.

Pinkerton had the walls and ceiling of the crow's nest papered with Penthouse Pets from a collection he started in college. His eyes drifted from Spelvin's rollicking in the newfound pleasures of fellatio and back to his favorite pet, Ms. Nikie St. Gilles. Plastered on the ceiling above him, Pinkerton was certain she was looking him straight in the eyes, smiling, urging him on. Spreading her lips so he could look deep inside.

He took a long drink, reached below his fat belly, found his penis under his undershorts and began jerking off. Pinkerton watched Spelvin work her man's bone until she got him to come. His eyes darted back and forth from the video to the tits and pussies papered on his ceiling. Spelvin was taking it from the rear and the allure of Ms. Nikie St.

Gilles impelled him on. I can still get a good stiff one he thought as he jerked. "And it feels so damn good," he whimpered.

Dr. Edmund M. Pinkerton jerked faster and harder until he too came, and then realized in disgust that he had forgotten the tissues.

Conversation 45
Bellflower
Friday, July 26, 2002; 11:52 p.m.

"The card didn't go through, ma'am."

"It did not? It should be okay," she declared. "I make a payment."

"Let me try once more." The pharmacist swiped the card and waited, "I'm sorry it declined it again."

Sarita dug through her purse. "How much is the prescriptions?"

"They come to $63.92; $47.33 for the Keflex and $16.59 for the Lortab."

Counting what money she had, Sarita thought about groceries and school clothes. "I have only $55.00 and a little change. Have you the generic?"

The pharmacist didn't carry generics so he fibbed, "Keflex doesn't come in generic."

"What is it for?"

"Keflex? Antibiotic ... for infection."

"What is the other one?"

"Lortab? That's for pain. It comes as a generic, but I don't have it tonight, just the brand name."

Sarita gripped the dollar bills between her fingers, "What else could he take for pain?"

"Aspirin. Tylenol. Advil. Whatever ... whatever you have at home for things like headache and menstrual," the pharmacist explained.

Sarita looked over her shoulder and out to the parking lot. Paco sat slumped in the car seat, head against the window, eyes closed, face grimaced. "I have never seen him like this. He hurt so much," she said, thrusting the money toward the pharmacist. "Give me the antibiotics. I have got some aspirin at home."

Conversation 46
Los Angeles
Saturday, July 27, 2002; 8:35 a.m.

MacDougall and Pinkerton boarded United flight 6752 and took their seats in first class. They each ordered a drink, Johnny Walker Red on the rocks for MacDougall; Tanqueray straight-up for Pinkerton. The flight attendant brought Pinkerton a seatbelt extension, and before long, they were off. At 32,000 feet MacDougall nudged Pinkerton, "So, what's the itinerary Ed?"

"Itinerary?"

"You know," he winked, "the game plan. You're the social secretary on this one."

Pinkerton smiled, "Ah, yes, the social secretary!" he chuckled polishing off the Tanqueray and signaling the flight attendant for another one.

"Okay, we arrive in San Francisco at 10:05. I say we grab a cab to the Hyatt Regency from the airport, check in, grab a little lunch at the Taddich Grill and take the Muni Metro to Pac Bell Ballpark around 12:30, maybe we'll see a little batting practice, maybe not. The game is at 1:30."

"Have a few brewskis?" MacDougall toasted.

"Have a few brewskis! I figure the game is over 4:00 - 4:30."

"Great, what's next? Get down to the good stuff, Ed," MacDougall demanded, smiling and taking another sip from the Johnny Walker.

Pinkerton swirled his beverage and laughed, "Oh! The good stuff. You mean this little weekend sojourn's not about the Cardinals and the Giants? You are a shameless prick, Jack MacDougall."

"Come on. Get on with it. No sarcasm asshole."

"Okay. Okay," Pinkerton laughed again. "I looked up San Francisco strip clubs on the internet. Boy, was that ever neat. Near the Hyatt I found three – the Gold Club, Crazy Horse, and Larry Flynt's Hustler."

MacDougall smiled, "See anything you like, one over the other?"

Pinkerton smirked, "What the fuck do you think, Jack? They all look good to a fat bastard like me!"

JAMES LENHART

Conversation 47
University Quadrangle, Los Angeles
Saturday, July 27, 2002; 9:03 a.m.

Professor Dornwyler looked over the class, twirling a pen between the index finger and thumb of his right hand. He looked at his watch, shook his head, turning to the sound of Amy Fligner entering the room, "Too many daiquiris again, Ms. Fligner?"

"No sir, my car wouldn't start. Dead battery. I took a cab. I'm sorry, sir."

For some people there's always an excuse Dornwyler thought – of course it's never their fault – so he bit his tongue and said, "Take your seat, so we can get started."

Dornwyler strolled about the conference table, "The reading assignment for today, an article I got published in the British Medical Journal – by the way, the Brits do know their bioethics – centers on a discussion regarding four principles of medical ethics: autonomy, beneficence, non-malfeasance, and justice. In large measure, these four principles intertwine and work together.

"The principle of autonomy literally means 'rule by self,' and establishes the patient's right to make healthcare decisions and the physician's obligation to respect and abide by them, providing of course the patient is informed and has the capacity to understand the consequences of his decision. Make sense?"

Dornwyler drank from his coffee and looked over the table, scratching his head, "What? No Krispy Kreme 'Hot Nows!' You guys are dead," he smirked. "You are ... definitely dead."

"Beneficence and malfeasance," Dornwyler said picking up the class roster, "Beneficence and malfeasance – let's throttle someone else on this one – let's see, let's see, Mr. Bradbury. Discuss beneficence and malfeasance."

Bradbury, a wily, spectacled youth, not yet rid of adolescent acne, answered directly, "Beneficence commands physicians to do what is right – a moral obligation, if not a mandate. Malfeasance, as I understand it, trumps beneficence. In a sense it instructs physicians to con-

109

duct themselves professionally for the purpose of inflicting no harm either intentionally or unintentionally ..."

"Very good, very good, for now. We'll come back to that," Dornwyler interjected. "Okay. Who wants to take a stab at justice? Let's see," he said looking at the student list through the reading glasses perched on his nose. "Ahh-ha! Ms. Ayres, define justice for the group."

Kathryn Ayres picked up the journal article and flipped the page, coming to the segment on justice. "Well, according to Dornwyler," she looked up and grinned, "Justice is synonymous with social equity. Dornwyler also asserts there are three categories of justice – fair distribution of resources, respect for patient's rights, and respect for the standards of medical practice."

Dornwyler chuckled, "Brilliant, Ms. Ayers, truly brilliant. All right, put the article down and listen for a moment," he said, wandering about the class.

"Pretend you are a physician in an emergency ward and in cubicle nine you encounter a 42-year-old homeless, disheveled derelict who smells heavily of alcohol; Rescue One found him under a bridge, semiconscious, and brought him into the Emergency Department.

"When you examine him, he is lucid enough to tell you his name and date of birth as well as the day's date, but for the most part is indifferent to your questioning. He says he wants to go home.

"In addition to filthy dirty and smelling badly, you discover what appears to be an enlarged liver. His blood sugar is 413, and his liver enzymes are compatible with alcoholic liver disease. His blood alcohol is 1.7.

"When you explain the results, and your concerns to him, he shrugs his shoulders and says, 'What the fuck is new, doc?' and reasserts his desire to be discharged. What do you do?"

Amy Fligner's hand shot in the air, "Can we assume he has no apparent life-threatening circumstances – he is just intoxicated and homeless?"

"For the purposes of this discussion, yes ... if you want."

"Then let him sleep it off in the ED and discharge him in the morning," Fligner said.

"But what about his blood sugar and his liver disease?"

Fligner harrumphed and said, "Isn't that the crux of autonomy and justice – respecting his wishes? If he doesn't care, why should we care and exhaust scarce resources that can be reserved for someone more deserving?"

Bradbury raised his hand, "Does he have insurance or even Medicaid?"

"Why? What does that matter Mr. Bradbury?" Dornwyler asked.

"He might be covered for rehab at West Haven or Brookington."

"Uhhh," Fligner interjected. "This guy is not going to stay dry. Even if he stayed in rehab a month – which he likely wouldn't – he'd be back out on the streets, under the bridge, drinking Ripple. His problem is self-inflicted. Medicaid is for people who deserve it."

"We'll come back to that too. What about his liver and his blood sugar, Sutherland?" Dornwyler asked.

"He has at least three serious problems: diabetes, cirrhosis, and alcoholism. In the face of the alcoholism, it is difficult – if not impossible – to treat the other two," Sutherland said. "Amy is correct, resources are scarce. In terms of beneficence and non-malfeasance, we have been entrusted with an ethical responsibility to do what is right for patients, even if their disease is self-inflicted."

"Say he's got no insurance, Medicare, or Medicaid," Dornwyler countered.

"That's a problem," Sutherland said. "Our society doesn't provide for the impoverished or ..."

"It shouldn't provide for dereliction," Fligner interrupted.

Dornwyler chuckled, "Sutherland has you going again, Ms. Fligner."

Dornwyler polished off his coffee and paced back and forth, head down, contemplating. "So," he finally said, "think about it for a moment – who are the deserving and, perhaps more importantly, who decides?"

"No one has to decide," Fligner asserted. "If you have a job, work hard, better yourself, and learn a trade, rewards are a natural consequence. Reaping what you sow, so to speak."

"So you don't view healthcare as a right?"

Fligner looked about the table examining the facial expressions of her classmates. With the fingers of both hands she pushed the hair dangling in her face behind both ears. Sutherland took notice smiling, then mumbled to himself, "My, my. Elephant ears."

Eventually Fligner responded to Dornwyler's question, "As long as you work for it, healthcare *is* a right."

"Ms. Fligner, answer this. Forty-four million hard-working Americans have jobs. Some have two jobs, yet they do not – I repeat – *do not* have health insurance. What about their right? Where is the justice in that? What have they earned?" Dornwyler asked.

Fligner flicked the hair behind her ears again, glanced around the room, and out the window, "Well, I'll have to think about that, I guess."

Conversation 48
Bellflower
Saturday, July 27, 2002; 5:16 p.m.

Paco lay on the couch, hugging his shoulders. Beads of perspiration dotted his forehead. A tooth-rattling chill shook him from head to toe. "I am so cold, Sarita."

Sarita wiped his brow and pulled the blanket over his shoulders.

"You do not look good, Paco. You sweat so much."

"I do not feel good, Sarita. The headache comes back and it is worse."

"I will get some aspirin and more Gatorade. The doctor said lots of fluids." She looked at her watch, "It is time for the antibiotics again. I will get those too, Paco."

Conversation 49
San Francisco, California
Saturday, July 27, 2002; 8:49 p.m.

"We'll have two more," MacDougall said to the cocktail waitress.

"Tanqueray Ten for your friend and Johnny Walker Black for you, right?"

112

"Right. Perfect. Thanks," MacDougall answered reaching for the Bolívar Belicosos Finos in his jacket pocket. "Okay if we smoke in here?"

"Cigarettes – no cigars," she smiled.

"No cigars? Shit," he muttered. "Bring us a pack of Marlboros then. When I'm at a joint like this, I need something to smoke."

The waitress turned and walked away. Pinkerton snorted, "I'll take one of those too!"

MacDougall smiled, "What a body, huh? Pretty skin too."

"Oh-oh! Oh-oh! Jack MacDougall's got the hots for poon tang. You like a little piece of that black ass, Jack?"

MacDougall chuckled, "Sounds like you wouldn't turn it down either, fat fuck. You goin' back for another VIP session, Ed?"

"Shit yes, I'm just waiting for Misty or whatever her name is to get off the stage. Look at her! Ain't she something, and those eyes? Jesus, the way she looks at you Jack, worth every bit of $200 for the VIP – uh, shall I say 'therapy'," Pinkerton chortled.

"Hey, Ed. What do you think Professor Petersdorf would say if he found us here?"

Pinkerton finished his drink, frowned, wagged his head and guffawed, "He'd say we should have gone into gynecology!"

When MacDougall finally finished howling, Pinkerton continued, "Really, you know what, Jack? Petersdorf can go fuck himself. That son-of-a-bitch is a gadfly if I ever met one. The cocksucker screwed me out of neurology into a career looking down a microscope and cutting up the dead and gone. I might as well be a God-damned necrophile. If the bastard walked through the door right now I'd give him the finger with both hands. Give him the royal dually big time. Then I'd shove my fist up his ass and pull out his motherfucking guts."

"Whoa. Sorry I brought it up, Ed. You've still got a lot of emotion."

"Yeah, well you made it Jack. Most don't. I didn't. Harry Rumsfeld didn't and he was smarter than both of us put together."

MacDougall set his glass back on the table and swallowed, "It wasn't smarts that got me through it. It was dumb luck. Petersdorf went on sabbatical. I slid through under the radar, right before his very eyes."

"Lucky you."

"What difference does it make? I hate neurology as much as you hate pathology."

Leaning over, the waitress disrupted their banter, setting the Tanqueray Ten, Johnny Walker and Marlboros in front of them, "That'll be $42.00 gentlemen."

Pinkerton stared at her cleavage, then dug out two twenties and a ten, stuffing them under her G-string, "Anybody ever tell you you've got a nice ass sweetie?"

"Once or twice," she smiled.

"Nice tits too honey, really nice."

"Thanks mister, and thanks for the tip. If you need anything else just holler," she said turning to go.

"Hey! What's your name?"

"Precious ... what's yours?"

"Boy, you got that right. Doesn't she Jack? Jeeee-zas! You going to dance for us, Precious?"

"I don't dance. Just cocktails."

"What about the VIP room?"

"Just cocktails mister. What's *your* name?" she asked again.

"Edmund M. Pinkerton. Edmund M. Pinkerton, M period D period," he slurred.

"You're a doctor?"

"Yup," Pinkerton laughed, "We both are. What? Don't we behave like it?"

"What kind of doctor," she countered.

Edmund M. Pinkerton, M period D period felt certain the pretty little bimbo standing in front him wouldn't know a liver from a kidney. That she would understand the term pathology was unfathomable. Besides, who gave a flittering fuck what she knew or thought? So he said: "Tonight? Tonight we're gynecologists!" he answered laughing and slapping his friend on the back. "Right, Jack?"

"Right," Jack scowled.

Precious glanced at MacDougall and glared back at Dr. Pinkerton, "I'm a second year student at University of California San Francisco."

"Second year what honey?" Pinkerton blurted.

114

"Medical student."

Dumfounded, Pinkerton took a drink from the Tanqueray Ten, chewed the ice and said. "No kiddin'. UCSF is no slouch. How did you get in?"

She wanted to tell Pinkerton by overcoming contemptuous pricks like you, but instead she answered: "Studying hard. Persistence."

"Persistent Precious. I like that," Pinkerton teased.

Pinkerton reminded Precious of Reginald Hornsby, the physician that interviewed her the first and second years she unsuccessfully applied to medical school. Overweight, overbearing, and *over* obnoxious. Hornsby's words rang in her ears. *"Medicine is, after all, applied science in its purest form, Ms. Thomas. Don't misunderstand me – uh, Precious. Altruism has its place. However, the study of medicine requires rigorous discipline and substantial intellect. The father of medicine, Hippocrates, said it best over 2500 years ago 'Primum non nocere' or 'first do no harm.' In the battlefield of patient care the vast cognitive capacity necessary to absorb, retain and apply medicine's principles boggles the finest minds. If we are first to do no harm, the science of medicine must be astutely studied and comprehended. Warm and fuzzy does have its place, but only until the higher measures have been satisfied."*

MacDougall lit a Marlboro and chimed in, "What are you doing working in here?"

"I need the money. The hours fit my schedules and the tips are great. I guess you 'gentlemen' know med school's not cheap. Besides, my parents have three other kids to watch out for."

MacDougall took a deep drag from the cigarette and asked, "Got a specialty in mind?"

She didn't hesitate, "Pediatrics in an inner-city clinic."

"Very good," MacDougall patronized. "Very good."

"You two need anything else?"

"No thanks. I think we're good. Right, Jack? And here's to you," Pinkerton said tipping the Tanqueray Ten in her direction. "Good luck in medical school. And, Precious, don't forget us. Keep the drinks coming."

While MacDougall and Pinkerton cavorted in Larry Flynt's Hustler Club, Paco Sánchez's dream carried him far from home, back to Guadalajara and a celebration in the Plaza de Armas. Bright sun warmed the cobblestone streets. Spring flowers draped the verandas. Scents from roses, gardenias and jasmine floated on a gentle breeze. A mariachi band, outfitted in silver studded regalia and wide-brimmed hats, sang Mexican ballads. Children, screaming in delight, whirled about breaking piñatas and swooping up the prizes. Fireworks popped; sparklers sizzled. A couple stood on the plaza portico with a priest reciting nuptial vows. The bride clutched a white rose bouquet. Sun danced off her silken hair and veiled, dark brown eyes. Paco knew her beauty. It was Sarita, and this was their wedding day.

Paco held her by his side; the priest proffered first the body, then the blood of Christ. They accepted the bread and drank the wine. Paco slipped a band of gold on Sarita's finger and she slid one on his. They kissed. And the ceremony was over.

Friends and family clapped and sang "Solamente Una Vez" and paraded arm-in-arm around and around the portico. When the music paused, they poured tequila, sucked limes, held their glasses high and tossed the liquor down. Taking turns, the old men danced with Sarita, stuffing 10 peso notes in the bodice of her gown. They danced and laughed and sang until the day grew gray, the vision dim.

A hawk swept in from the twilight sky, plucked the bouquet from Sarita's hands, and flew away. The mariachi band gave way to dissonant waves of resonating, cacophonic sounds. The twilight turned to night. Sarita disappeared – then reappeared, her wedding gown tattered and torn and splattered with mud and blood. "¡Paco, Paco!" she screamed. "¡Por ahí vienen, Paco!" (They are coming, Paco!).

"¿Quién viene, Sarita? ¿Quién, Sarita? ¿Quién?" (Who is coming, Sarita? Who, Sarita? Who?)

"¡La migra, Paco! ¡La migra, Paco! (The border police Paco! The border police!)

Then they came. Three (or were there four?) pink, puffy-faced, eagle eyed la migra dressed in olive drab. They flashed bright badges, toted clubs and brandished pistols. "No te preocupes, Sarita. Te voy a explicar. Ahora eres mi esposa. No va a haber ningún problema, ya verás." (Don't worry, Sarita. I will explain. You are now my wife. It will be all right, you will see).

Paco held her tight and tried to tell them. But they would not listen. He felt the tugging, then pulling. Pulling harder. He held her tighter and exclaimed "¡Sarita es mi esposa! ¡Sarita es mi esposa!" (Sarita is my wife! Sarita is my wife!). But la migra wouldn't listen. They wrenched her from his grip; tore her from his fingers and carried her away kicking and screaming. "Cut the crap you Mexican bitch," they warned her.

"Pero Paco es mi esposo, yo le pertenezco," Sarita sobbed. "¡Por favor! ¡Soy la esposa de Paco!" (But Paco is my husband. I belong to him. Please! I am Paco's bride!). Paco watched in horror her image shrink. Smaller, ever smaller, and then like morning vapor in a rising sun, she disappeared. Paco knew she was gone forever. The border police had taken her away!

Paco sat straight up in bed, drenched in sweat, mortified by the nightmare. He reached over and touched Sarita. Thank God. She *was* there. Fever racked his body; chills spread up and down, from head to toe. Pain pulsed like a dagger between his eyes, piercing through to the base of his skull. His mouth felt hot, his throat flushed. The well of nausea suppressed earlier, stirred full force. "Shit. I have to throw up," he mumbled.

Scrambling from bed, Paco lunged for the toilet, but came up short. Vomit projected from his mouth and nose, splashing on the walls and toilet and everything around it. "Motherfucker," he gasped. Then he sunk to his knees, threw his arms about the toilet, coughed and retched and puked again.

Conversation 51
San Francisco
Saturday July 27, 2002; 11:48 p.m.

"Where's that pretty little Precious, Jack? I need another Tanqueray. Hey, who won the ballgame?"

MacDougall stared at his friend. "Who won the game? Another one? If I drink one more I will die. The Cardinals 5 to 3. You can't remember?"

"That's right, Cardinals 5 to 3. Way to fucking go, Cardinals. Come on, Jack, one more. A nightcap so to speak. And one more lap dance!" Pinkerton urged.

MacDougall looked at his watch. "Caroline and Judi would shit if they knew we were here."

"So? Who cares? The last time I saw Judi's tits was on our wedding night, and 22 – 23 years later she still hasn't given me a decent blowjob."

MacDougall howled slapping Pinkerton's back, "No shit! You too? Hey Misty! My Friend needs another lap dance!"

"Then we're getting out of here, Ed. We've got another ball game tomorrow."

Conversation 52
Los Angeles County Hospital
Sunday, July 28, 2002; 12:13 a.m.

"Name?"

"My husband's or mine?" Sarita asked, thinking with more make-up, a little lipstick and bug-eyed glasses, the receptionist might pass for Fini Dobyns at Humanitarian Hospital.

"Patient's name."

"Paco Sánchez," Sarita pulled Paco close to her side. "Paco Raphael Sánchez."

"What's the problem?"

Sarita's eyes welled with tears, "Headache and vomiting. Humanitarian Hospital said to come to the County Hospital if he got a bad headache and vomiting."

"Humanitarian sent you here?" the receptionist huffed.

"Yes. They say if he gets worse to bring him to County Hospital."

The receptionist looked away from the monitor and stared at Paco, "He does look sick doesn't he?"

118

"He is. Paco never gets sick. I have never seen him like this."

"Uh, who's his employer?" the woman asked typing in Paco R. Sánchez.

"Republic Waste. I tell them he gets sick picking up other people's …"

"Sarita," Paco pleaded. "We have said that already. I have got to sit down."

The receptionist handed Sarita the clipboard, "Here, take the paperwork, fill it out and bring it back. We'll get him right in."

Head down, Paco shuffled back to the waiting area on Sarita's arm and sank into a well worn chair. Patients and patients' families overflowed the room, their faces a mix of boredom, anxiety, and distress. Illness filled the air and matched the gray, lifeless walls. Sarita completed the forms and returned them to the receptionist. To her surprise, in a few minutes they called Paco back.

A plump, Clairol-red haired woman in her late 50s entered the Emergency Department cubicle. "Mr. Sánchez?"

"Yes."

"Mr. Sánchez, I'm nurse Rachel," she said checking his armband. "What brings you here tonight?"

"Headache. Very bad headache," he winced.

"And vomiting," interrupted Sarita. "Humanitarian Emergency say to bring him to County Hospital if he gets worse headache or vomiting."

"You've already been to Humanitarian?"

"Yes. On Friday."

"What did they do?"

"Check him over, give him antibiotics."

"Any tests?"

"No. They say it is not necessary. The doctor there say he have something like Strep throat. He say the antibiotics would cover everything, but take him to the County if he gets a worse headache or vomiting."

"I see," Nurse Rachel frowned. "Let me take your vital signs, Mr. Sánchez," she continued, poking the thermometer through Paco's parched lips.

"You do look dehydrated, Mr. Sánchez. Hmmm, let me see. Heart rate is 88. Blood pressure is 148/90, respirations 18, and temp is 102.7. Not too bad, but you've got yourself a fever. Any chills?"

"Yes, mostly a very bad headache," Paco said.

"The doctor will be right with you. In the meantime, drink this," she said, handing him some water.

Conversation 53
San Francisco
Sunday July 28, 2002; 12:56 a.m.

The cab stopped at the Hyatt Regency. Pinkerton and MacDougall got out. They pub-crawled through the lobby, entered the elevator, rode to the 29th floor and got out. "Jesus, I haven't been this fucked up for a long time," MacDougall declared as the two men staggered down the hallway.

"You're out of shape, Jack. We need to do this more often," Pinkerton laughed.

MacDougall took the room key from his pocket. "Yeah? Maybe you. What I need is sleep. See you in the morning."

"What time?" Pinkerton asked.

"Shit, I don't know, Ed. Before the ball game. Call me when you get up," he said opening the door to room 2942.

Pinkerton continued down the corridor, "Sounds good. Hasta mañana, good buddy."

"Hasta mañana."

MacDougall shut the door behind him, threw his jacket on the chair and headed for the toilet. He had to pee. When he finished that, he washed his hands and splashed water on his face. The cool tap water refreshed him. "Whew! That's better," he said out loud.

The mini-frig door unlocked with a single twist of the key. Mac-Dougall removed a two once bottle of Johnnie Walker Red and checked for champagne. Between the beers he found a split of Mumm's Cuvee Napa. That should do he thought. Don't need to go overboard anyway. The ice cubes cracked easily from the freezer tray. He added them to a glass and poured in the whiskey. "Now let's see what this city has got –

some real action, so to speak. Enough of Pinkerton's prick teasing, lap dancing cunts."

He opened the desk drawer, pulled from it the Yellow Pages and flipped them to Entertainers. "Hmmm … Wild Vietnamese Twins. Beautiful Desperate Housewife Ready to be Naughty. Full Service Man Date. I don't think so – queer motherfuckers. Petite Brunette Jasmine Always Discreet. Direct-to-You! Hmmm. Maybe. Affordable College Cutie – no, too close to Alyssa. Busty & Voluptuous. Waiting for Your Call – I like big tits – what else? Sweet Dreams with Spicy Latina. Full Service Black Beauties. So much to choose from … so *much* to choose from!"

He took a drink, scrolled down the pages with his finger, flipped them back and found Jasmine again. "Okay. Let's see – 1-555-734-7827."

MacDougall's hands trembled and he had to dial the number over. It rang twice. When she answered her willowy voice whispered, "This is *Jasmine*. How may I be of *service*?"

"Are you – uh, ah – available?" MacDougall stammered.

"It depends. Who might I be speaking with?" she asked.

MacDougall fumbled for words; then said, "My name? Uh … it's, uh Ed … Ed Pinkerton."

"And where are you staying, Ed – do you mind if I call you Ed – where are you staying?"

"No. Ed is fine. Just fine. Perfect in fact. The Hyatt Regency Embarcadero."

The woman took a deep breath. "I can be available. What time did you have in mind, Mr. Pinkerton?" she asked.

MacDougall took another drink and looked at his watch. "Anytime. Really, right away would be best."

"I can be there in thirty minutes if you like," she answered.

Jack felt his guts squeeze. "Mind if I ask … what are your measurements?"

"I'm five-four and weigh 122. My hair is raven black. I'm 36-24-36, a C cup and, I might add, no enhancements. You won't be disappointed, Mr. Ed, I promise."

"And how much?"

"Well you do get down to business don't you, Mr. Ed? But I'm glad you asked. It all depends on what you want. $500 gets my clothes off. It goes up from there. I do kinky, but it will cost you."

MacDougall hesitated and said to himself, "I just want a little party, a good fuck and maybe some head. I can handle five-hundred and up."

"You there, Mr. Pinkerton?"

MacDougall cleared his throat and said. "Yeah. Sure. Sounds good."

"My price agrees with you?"

MacDougall grabbed a Kleenex on the night stand and wiped away the sweat on his face. "Sure. Like I said, it sounds good."

"So what's your room number?"

"2942."

"The Hyatt Regency Embarcadero – I'll see you in thirty minutes?"

Jack said, "You bet. Yes. See you in thirty minutes," hung up the phone and rushed for the toilet. Jack MacDougall – aka Ed Pinkerton – had to defecate.

Conversation 54
Los Angeles County Hospital
Sunday July 28, 2002; 1:24 a.m.

It seemed like hours, but eventually a tall, Ichabod Crane lookalike entered the cubicle pulling the curtains behind him.

Sarita liked him immediately. "He has trusting eyes and a kind face," she said to herself.

"Hi. I'm Dr. Nicholas Vanderjagt," he said extending his hand to Paco. "Mr. Sánchez?"

"Uh-huh."

"What brings you here tonight?"

"I already told the nurse. Very bad headache. And tonight I vomit," Paco muttered.

"Where's the headache?"

"Right here," Paco said, pointing at his forehead.

"And where does it go?"

122

"Back here," Paco pointed to the base of his skull.

"Okay. I see, and what does it feel like?"

"Throboom, throboom. Man, it is all over."

"You mean throbbing?"

"Yes, throbbing very bad."

"On a scale of 1 to 10, how much pain, 10 being the worst."

"Sometimes 7, maybe 8. But when I puke it is a ten."

"Uh-huh, I see." Vanderjagt made some notes and looked back at Paco. "So, what besides vomiting makes it worse?"

Paco hesitated, "Walking. Noise."

"Okay," the doctor responded making more notes. "And what makes it better?"

"Nothing. Nothing makes it better. Nothing. It is there all the time," Paco said covering his eyes and holding onto his head.

"Any other symptoms?"

"I have vomiting and a sore throat. The nurse say I have a fever."

"He looks very bad, doctor. I have never seen him like this," Sarita interjected.

"He does appear sick all right," Vanderjagt agreed. "Let me look him over."

The doctor examined his eyes, then his throat, moving next to his glands and neck. When he flexed his head, Paco groaned.

"That hurt?" Vanderjagt asked.

"Only just a little."

"Does it make the headache worse?"

Paco looked at Vanderjagt, "Not too much."

"Your pupils look okay; your throat is red as a beet, your glands are swollen. Let's have a listen to your chest." Vanderjagt took out his stethoscope, listening first to his lungs and then his heart. His stethoscope slid down to Paco's abdomen where he listened again. "Any trouble with your digestion? Diarrhea? Constipation?"

"No, I have nothing like that," Paco said.

"How many times have you vomited?" the doctor asked pressing over and around Paco's stomach.

"Just the once or twice, and then I have … how do you say? The dry heaves."

"Well your heart and lungs are okay. Your belly seems all right too. Did you feel any better after you threw up?"

"Maybe a little bit. It is the headache mostly."

Dr. Vanderjagt laid his hand on Paco's knee, "Listen, I don't think this is anything serious, probably bad Strep throat just like they said over at Humanitarian. But you are a little dehydrated, and I can give you something for the pain. I'm going to order some x-rays of your sinuses, get a CBC and some electrolytes. I'll cover you with IV antibiotics, and give you some IV fluids, too. Okay?"

"Thank you doctor, thank you for doing something. Thank you. At Humanitarian they do nothing, nothing," Sarita scowled, then smiled and said, "See Paco, you're going to be better." Then she placed her hand over her pregnant abdomen and wondered what she would do without Paco. Who would love her? Who would love and care for their children? Then she whispered, "Those are stupid thoughts."

Dr. Vanderjagt left, but nurse Rachel soon came back, drew some blood, started an IV of dextrose and saline, and hung a gram of Cefizox with military precision. Next she pushed IV Dilaudid, Toradol, and Zofran for the headache and nausea. Then she popped 500 mg of Zithromax and some Tylenol into Paco's mouth saying, "Here, swallow these with some water."

Paco obliged, but winced with pain.

"You'll be better in no time," she reassured, smiled, and left the cubicle.

Paco laid back. The Dilaudid took over and he fell fast asleep; Sarita nodded off too.

"Mr. Sánchez?" It was Dr. Vanderjagt. "Mr. Sánchez?"

Paco rolled over on the gurney. Sarita sat up, rubbing her eyes.

"Sorry to disturb you. How are you feeling?"

"Better I think. I have been sleeping."

"What do you think, Mrs. Sánchez?"

Sarita pulled the blanket down and yawned, "I have been sleeping too." She looked at Paco, "Yes, better I think. Thank you."

"Okay. Look, I am sending you home. I am switching the antibiotics they gave you at Humanitarian to Augmentin. I want you to stop the

124

Keflex. Drink lots of fluids. Here's a prescription for Vicodin for the headaches. And of course, get back here if you are worse or not getting better. Do you have a family doctor?"

"Dr. Rodríguez," Sarita answered.

"Miguel Rodríguez?"

"Yes."

"Great. Miguel's terrific. You can take Paco to him for follow-up if you like."

"What do you think this is?" Sarita asked.

"I'm calling it a bad case of Strep, maybe mononucleosis or an early sinus infection. Don't worry; he's going to be just fine. His blood count didn't show a serious infection and his electrolytes were normal. Sinus x-rays were okay too."

Paco shivered and looked down and over to Sarita.

"I hope so," Sarita said.

"Of course you do. So do we, Mrs. Sánchez. Rachel will help you get discharged," Vanderjagt smiled. "Anymore questions?"

"No, I guess not," Sarita said.

Conversation 55
Bellflower
Sunday, July 28, 2002; 7:03 a.m.

Sarita helped Paco from the car and arm-in-arm walked him to the side door and into the house.

"Papá, Papá!" screamed José running to his father.

"Miguel, José. Help Papá to bed, I have to feed Angelina."

Sarita gave Paco over to the children and went to the kitchen where she found Angelina and Paco's mother.

"¿Como está Paco?" (Is Paco okay?) Mamacita asked.

"Mejor Mamacita pero todavía anda muy enfermo," (Better Mamacita but he is still very sick) she said, taking Angelina and putting the child to her engorged, swollen breast.

"He gave Paco another prescription but it costs $89.00. I could not get it and the pain medicine."

"¿Y entonces que has hecho?" (What did you do?).

125

"I did my best Mamacita," she said. "What can I do? Paco needs the pain medicine. His headache kills him it is so bad. He has already the antibiotics Humanitarian give him. Oh, Mamacita he feels so sick," she frowned.

"¿Cuando le pagan a Paco?" (When does Paco get paid?).

"Every two weeks and that will not be until Friday, Mamacita," she said switching breasts.

Conversation 56
Los Angeles County Hospital
Monday, July 29, 2002; 12:36 a.m.

"He's back," nurse Rachel declared, handing off the clipboard to Dr. Vanderjagt.

"Who's back?"

"Mr. Sánchez."

"From yesterday?" Vanderjagt frowned, "What now?"

"Worse headaches, but I think I've got this figured out. He's trying to get out of work. You know … like all Mexicans."

"What do you mean by that?"

"Well, his wife told – boy is she something – his wife told me he couldn't get work as a bricklayer, so he took a job with Republic Waste. Two weeks ago. Even asked if you could write a doctor's note for his visit here *and* from his visit at Humanitarian. She's got the nerve. And by the way, she didn't get the Augmentin. Like I said, Dr. Vanderjagt, I really don't think he is that sick; just getting an excuse to get out of work."

Vanderjagt looked at the nurse straight on, "I'm not writing one from Humanitarian, yesterday is okay."

"Want me to write it?"

"Sure, where is he?"

"Number seven."

Vanderjagt shuffled over to bay seven. Swinging the curtains to the side he asked, "What's up, Mr. Sánchez?"

"My head it hurts so bad, and my neck it is killing me."

"He's throwing up more too," Sarita chimed in.

Vanderjagt peeled open a tongue depressor. "Open your mouth. Throat still hurt?"

"Uh-huh," Paco uttered through the tongue blade.

Vanderjagt flexed his neck, "Jesus!" Paco squirmed. "What are you doing?"

"My apologies, just examining for something," the doctor answered.

Paco grew pale, then ashen, and rolled to his side. He grabbed the emesis basin, but it was too late. His vomitus sprayed over the bedrails and onto the floor just missing Vanderjagt.

"See, what have I told you?!" Sarita cried.

Paco coughed between dry heaves and truncated breaths. Finally, he wiped his mouth, and fell back on the gurney.

Vanderjagt stepped around the vomit and apologized, "I'm sorry. I didn't mean to cause that."

Paco blew his nose to clear the debris from his nostrils and accepted a Styrofoam cup of water from Sarita. When he finished drinking he said, "It is okay. I have been doing that for all day."

Vanderjagt placed his hand on Paco's arm, "We'll get more tests. I'll give you a liter of IV fluid, something for the pain and nausea, and call housekeeping to clean up the mess. Okay?"

Paco managed a smile and whispered, "Okay. Thank you doctor."

Conversation 57
Los Angeles County Hospital
Monday, July 29, 2002; 3:16 a.m.

Dr. Vanderjagt pulled the curtains back disturbing Paco's sleep. "Mrs. Sánchez? I've got good news. The repeat tests look okay. Paco's white count is 18,000, mostly lymphs. Feeling any better Mr. Sánchez?"

"Some. A little, maybe ..."

Sarita interrupted, "He has not thrown up again. What do you mean – I think you say 'mostly lymphs' Dr. Vanderjagt?"

"Lymphs are what's in the blood with a viral infection. *Another* kind of cell, called polys, indicate bacterial. So the lymphs tell us he has a viral infection, not a bacterial one, and that's good."

"So what is this he have?"

"Well quite frankly, Mrs. Sánchez, and don't be alarmed – given Paco's symptoms – I think this is meningitis."

"Meningitis! Meningitis?! I have heard that meningitis it is very bad!" Sarita blurted.

"No, no. It sounds horrid, but that's the bacterial kind. We see viral meningitis in the summer routinely. In fact, we just had another case in here yesterday. It comes in epidemics. Paco is young and strong. He will have a complete recovery. It just takes time."

"How long?"

"Two, three, four days – it's hard to tell for certain," Vanderjagt reassured her.

"I want him in the hospital. He cannot go home like this," Sarita said.

Vanderjagt sighed, then cleared his throat. "I thought about that, Mrs. Sánchez, but the hospital is full and he really doesn't need admission. Just fluids and something for the pain and nausea … and, of course, what I call tincture of time."

"But I want him in the hospital."

Sarita's insistence chilled Vanderjagt. He remembered how, as an emergency medicine resident, he and his fellow classmates made a contest out of who could turn away the sickest admissions. He remembered how, in the end, that the 'Katie bar the door' high stakes game they played became a mockery – how he had sent a young woman with abdominal pain home, only to come back two days later in her husband's arms – cyanotic and nearly dead from a ruptured ectopic pregnancy.

The painful memory, and Sarita's resolve did not, however, deter Vanderjagt. "Mrs. Sánchez, we can't admit everyone with a virus. Besides, he's better at home where he won't be exposed to hospital germs. Is he taking the Augmentin?"

Sarita looked away, down at the floor and back to Vanderjagt. "I could not buy it. It cost more than $80.00. We do not have the money."

"So, what are you doing?"

"I give him the medicine Humanitarian Hospital prescribes him," she blushed.

"The Keflex?"

"I think that is what you call it."

"Look, I'll tank him up with another liter of IV fluid and some additional intravenous antibiotics just to be safe. And I'll write him a prescription for the nausea to take with the Keflex at home. You can bring him back if you need to. Okay?"

"I guess that you give us no choice, Dr. Vanderjagt," Sarita frowned.

Nurse Rachel walked up behind Vanderjagt at the nursing station. "So, what's the verdict, doctor?" she asked.

"I think he's got viral meningitis."

"Really? Another one, huh? You going to tap him?"

"I don't think so," he said, not looking up from his paper work. "I'm way behind and Rescue One just called. They're bringing in an acute coronary syndrome. Sánchez's CBC shows a white count of 18,000, mostly lymphs. He has the signs and symptoms to go along with viral meningitis. Give him another liter of normal saline, 500 milligrams of Cefizox, some Zofran and get him out of here. His wife asks too many questions and is driving me nuts. Give him this for the nausea too," he said, handing off a prescription for promethazine.

"If it's viral, why more antibiotics?"

"If I'm wrong, and this is bacterial, I want him covered," Vanderjagt declared.

Conversation 58
Rancho Palos Verdes
Monday, July 29, 2002; 7:10 a.m.

Caroline MacDougall squatted, pushed a fresh tampon into her vagina, rinsed her hands, and asked, "So? How was San Francisco?"

Jack MacDougall continued clipping his nails, and without looking up said, "Great. Fabulous in fact. The Cardinals won both games and the weather was good – at least for San Francisco. Pac Bell is a beautiful ballpark."

"Was you flight delayed? You got in late last night."

"You mean this morning – it was nearly 1:00 a.m. Something about the connecting flight that left late out of Seattle."

Leaning into the mirror, Caroline MacDougall painted her lashes with mascara and asked, "Where did you eat?"

"The waterfront one night. And we went to the Taddich Grill. Pinkerton eats like a pig."

She pushed the mascara brush back into the tube and screwed it shut. "I thought you were going to call me?"

"I did."

"When?"

"Saturday night, last night," he lied. "Why?"

"Well, it's nice to know you are alive. How you're doing. Maybe find out how I am, or what I'm up to."

"Look, I called you. You didn't answer."

"The phone's memory didn't pick up any received calls from you. I checked."

MacDougall knew she had him. "Well, I called. Maybe it's not working. You know electronics – they're fickle. My calls are probably out there someplace darting through cyberspace or San Francisco's fog. Do I need to show you the 'sent calls' on my cell phone?"

"No, of course not. I just missed you," she retreated. "Do anything at night?"

MacDougall thought first of the strip clubs, then raven haired Jasmine. The perfume wasn't cheap, and neither were her clothes. Make-up didn't plaster her face and she applied just enough mascara to highlight those radiant, emerald eyes. Jasmine was right. He wasn't disappointed. In fact, she had an aura of innocence, which MacDougall found disconcerting and he wondered if the woman he talked with on the phone was one and the same. But in no time Jasmine took charge, asking if he had anything for her to drink and what kind of party he had in mind. When he handed her the Mumm's she winked, said thanks, sat on the edge of the bed and invited him to join her. "Nothing kinky," MacDougall remembered saying. "And don't hurry. I need some nice, slow sex. You know ... let it come naturally. Maybe you can pretend it's my first time and you are showing me the ropes. Yeah, I'd like that. In fact, I'd like that a lot."

What happened next with the hooker flooded MacDougall with guilt. So avoiding eye contact, he swallowed the lump in his throat and said to his wife: "Dinner. Nothing much. I was tired. Must be the air up there or something. I just about finished Karl Rove's book though. What a dynamo. The Democrats only wish they had his balls." Then he glanced at his watch, "Holy shit. I'm late for rounds. I'll see you later," he said, pecking her on the cheek and dashing out the door.

Conversation 59
Bellflower
Monday, July 29, 2002; 11:09 a.m.

Sarita hurried to the phone, answering it on the fourth ring.

"Is this the Sánchez residence?"

"Yes, this is Sarita Sánchez."

"Hi, Mrs. Sánchez. This is Theresa at University Plastic Surgery. Please hold for Dr. Alexandre."

Sarita cradled Angelina on her hip waiting for Alexandre to pick up. Finally, he came on. "Sarita, good morning. Dr. Alexandre here. Listen. I've got good news. The NIH has approved my research grant for three additional years. We'll be able to proceed with Angelina's reconstruction."

Sarita could not believe her ears. The news left her speechless. When she caught her wits she said, "Oh! That is very good. Paco he have been very sick. What you tell us will make him more better I know!"

"Paco's sick? What's wrong?"

"The doctors in the emergency say he have meningitis."

"Meningitis ...?"

"Yes. They say it is caused by virus or something like that and he will get better. But I am so worried. I have never seen Paco like this."

"Where is he?"

"He is home. He is sleeping. Should he be in the hospital? The doctor said he did not need to be."

Alexandre didn't answer immediately. Out of his residency over twenty years, it seemed like centuries since he'd treated patients for life threatening infections and, to say the least, he was not up on the medical literature in infectious diseases. "I'm not a qualified expert on this, Sarita," he eventually said, "but the last I knew, viral meningitis made you sick as a dog for a few days, and then – bingo! Complete recovery."

Tears welled into Sarita's eyes. Although Alexandre's opinion reassured her, she found it hard to catch her breath. "Paco have to be happy you say these things," she blurted. "He trusts you so much and when he is better we will bring Angelina to you right away."

"So here's the other piece," Alexandre stammered. "These government grants are strange birds. The NIH approved the application but won't fund it until January of 2003, which means I can't begin Angelina's reconstruction until next year. The University strictly forbids research activities until the money is in the bank and locked down – too many surprises in the past that left them holding the bag."

"But then you can do it?"

"Ninety-eight percent certain of it."

"Then we have hope," she sniffled.

Conversation 60
City Center, Los Angeles
Monday, July 29, 2002; 5:22 p.m.

Geoff Boyer opened the Chivas Regal 18 and drizzled 2 oz. over fresh ice. The liquor's abundant nose drifted up from the glass infiltrating his nostrils. "Wow!" he said to himself. "This stuff should be as good as MacDougall says it is."

He swirled the glass, took a sip and held it in his mouth, experiencing it linger over his taste buds. When he finally swallowed, he discovered what Chivas advertised: Velvety dark chocolate, elegant floral notes and a wisp of sweet mellow smokiness. "Um-hmm," he said again. "Good shit."

He walked over to the windows and looked out over the traffic. The interstate moved at a snail's pace. Not time to leave yet, he thought. He turned back to his desk and clicked his remote to NBC News with Brian Williams. "On Wall Street today, Goldman Sachs revealed that investors expect to be jolted by earnings reports for Humanitarian Hospital Corporation next week, when it releases year-end results. Citing the economic downturn, rising expenses and increasing demands for uncompensated care, the nation's largest for-profit hospital chain may report bottom line declines as much as $2.59 per share. Amid speculation that the healthcare giant's financial picture for the fiscal year looks gloomy, investors bid down the stock from it's all time high of $47 in January. On the New York Stock Exchange today HHC closed at $23.33 per share."

Boyer took another sip of the Chivas, leaned back in his chair and skimmed the pages of Luxury Estates International. Villa Mira Mar Cortez in Cabo San Lucas caught his eye again. *"Water front refined, tropical luxury. Private two and three bedroom villas. Choose from 2,232 to 2869 square feet of extraordinary comfort. Breathtaking views of the Sea of Cortez and Land's End over your own infinity edged pools. Spa, golf, tennis. Luxury homes by the sea."*

"Cindy and the kids deserve something like this," he whispered.

Boyer closed his eyes and smiled. He wondered if he should call his Chief Financial Officer, but then thought better of it. Next week would be soon enough to drink Chivas 18 with Ralph Appleton.

Conversation 61
Los Angeles
Monday, July 29, 2002; 11:14 p.m.

The torrential downpour that flooded streets earlier, eased to a fine mist falling from the summer night sky. Sarita gutted through the traffic intent only on her destination. Paco sat in the seat next to her hugging a bucket, and suppressing another urge to vomit. A yellow Ryder truck cut Sarita off in the far right lane, and sprayed her windshield with a slurry of muddy water that momentarily blinded her vision. Perturbed, but in control, she turned her washer-wipers on high and slowed down to separate her Caravan from the truck's wind and water draft.

"We are almost there, Paco," she reassured him.

"Good, Sarita. Sarita?" he paused staring into the bucket. "Are my little niños okay?"

"Mamacita have our children taken care of. Remember? She take such good care of you and Emilio and the others? She is doing the same for Miguel, José and Angelina."

"I only wonder. Does Miguel understand why I missed the t-ball game?" he whispered.

"I already told him many times, Paco, I tell him you are very sick. He understands."

"And Dr. Alexandre say he can fix Angelina? He have the research?"

"Yes, Paco. I have told you over and over. Don't you remember? It cannot be until January."

Paco sighed struggling to keep from vomiting, "All that matters is he can make Angelina more better. If he can do that, I am happy."

In the County Hospital parking lot Sarita spied an abandoned wheel chair and parked next to it. Paco slid from the seat. Sarita eased him into the chair, handed him the bucket and headed toward the Emergency entrance. The automatic doors to County Hospital swung wide.

Sarita pushed Paco through, ignoring the security guard. "Help! I need help! He vomits again! The headache it is worse and he does not know where he is some of the time!" she screamed steering the wheelchair toward emergency receiving.

The receptionist looked away from her computer monitor and gave Sarita a dumb-founded stare. "Hey, whoa! Why all the commotion? What's wrong *now*, Mrs. Sánchez?"

"Paco he is worse. He still vomits," she panted. "He says his head it want to explode and he becomes confused! He cannot remember anything I tell him! Sometimes he does not know where he is!"

The receptionist looked down at Paco slumped in the wheelchair holding his head and the bucket half filled with vomit. "I see. Well, he looks about the same to me," she fudged. "But I'll get the nurse. You can fill out the paperwork in the back."

Conversation 62
Los Angeles County Hospital
Tuesday, July 30, 2002; 12:16 a.m.

A sophomoric face peered into the cubical, "Mr. and Mrs. Sánchez?"

"Yes, this is Mr. Paco Sánchez," Sarita answered.

"Good. Well, hello. It's nice to meet you. My name is Justin Sutherland; I'm a 4ᵗʰ year medical student here to see, Mr. Sánchez."

Sarita stared in disbelief but bit her tongue. *Paco is sick like this and they are sending a student?*

Sutherland sensed Sarita's displeasure. He understood patients often bristled at the notion of students and interns caring for them. Despite the off balance moment, Sutherland moved toward Paco's wheelchair and pressed on. "So what brings you here tonight?" he asked.

When Paco didn't respond Sarita sighed and interjected, "This is our 3ʳᵈ or 4ᵗʰ time. I cannot remember how many times. Paco he is so sick. Throwing up. Headaches, and now he does not know who he is."

Sutherland glanced at Paco and back to Sarita, "Uh-huh … when did this start?"

"Maybe four, maybe five days ago. Friday we took him to Humanitarian," she answered.

"What did they diagnose?"

"They say he have some kind of sore throat, maybe Strep."

"And he's worse?"

"Yes. That is why we are back."

"I see … did they give him antibiotics?"

"Yes, they give him antibiotics and he takes them, but he is only worse. He starts to throwing up Sunday. I bring him here. They change the antibiotics, but I could not pay for them. He does not know where he is. I could not help it. I could not pay for the antibiotics," Sarita cringed and burst into tears.

Sutherland gave Sarita time to check her emotions while reflecting on Professor Dornwyler's' *The Ethical and Social Aspects of Healthcare* seminars. Dornwyler made a compelling case for what he labeled "health for all" arguing that the financial burden of uninsured healthcare cost society far greater sums on the back end due to costs for delay in care, lost worker productivity, the medical complications of untreated chronic disease and freefall into the abyss of poverty. "The extraordinary costs of U.S. medical care can rocket a family into bankruptcy. Indeed, pay me now … or pay me later," Dornwyler argued, "Most Americans are one health crisis away from financial ruin."

Sutherland bought Dornwyler's arguments hook, line and sinker, while many classmates – like Amy Fligner – labeled Dornwyler's perspective socialistic, dismissed his arguments as liberal jibber-jabber and, over too many Budweiser's, nicknamed the professor Peter 'Karl off the Marx' Dornwyler. Sutherland, on the other hand, understood that Mr. and Mrs. Sánchez represented the America Dornwyler depicted.

"That's okay, Mrs. Sánchez," he comforted her. "A different antibiotic probably wouldn't have made any difference. He will be okay. Here's a tissue. Let's get him onto the gurney. I'll get the nurse to help."

Sutherland reappeared with Nurse Rachel who acknowledged Sarita with a nod and helped ease Paco onto the gurney, "So you're back again," Rachel stated. "He's worse?" she asked without looking at Sarita.

"Yes, and he is ... how do you say? Confused?"

"I see. Let me get his vitals."

Sutherland took Paco's bucket, emptied it, rinsed it out, and gave it back to him. By the time he fluffed Paco's pillow and covered him with a blanket, Rachel had his vital signs.

"Here we go: Temp's 101.7, respirations 20, heart rate 88, BP 130/90. Not too ..."

"I need posturals," Sutherland declared.

"What? Why?" the nurse challenged the student.

"I want to see if his pressure drops. I want to see if he is dehydrated."

"I can tell he is dehydrated just looking at him," the nurse defied Sutherland.

"You're probably right, but if I don't have his posturals, the attending will chew my butt out – chew it out good. I have to get posturals."

Sarita stood at the end of the gurney. She watched them ease Paco flat, take his blood pressure, sit him up and take it again. Changing positions precipitated more vomiting, followed by spasms of gagging and heaving. Sarita grabbed a wet cloth, wiped his mouth and forehead, rinsed the cloth and placed it over his brow.

136

Rachel spoke first, "It's hard to hear his BP when he is vomiting, but I got 132/86 supine and 120/68 sitting."

"Thanks, Rachel. That's a substantial drop," Sutherland declared, moving over to Paco's right and asking, "Mr. Sánchez? Where are you?"

"Hospital?"

"That's right. What month is it?"

Paco looked up, thought for a moment and then asked, "April?"

Conversation 63
Los Angeles County Hospital
Tuesday, July 30, 2002; 3:32 a.m.

Dr. Michael Mack poured another cup of coffee and sank into the threadbare chair next to Sutherland. "Okay, go ahead."

Sutherland cleared his throat and proceeded, "Mr. Sánchez is a 29 year-old Hispanic male with a 5-day history of sore throat, headache, nausea, and vomiting. He comes in this morning with his wife who states he is confused, that the headache is worse and the vomiting persistent ... oh, she also says he has terrific fever. She is really concerned and thinks he should be admitted. Actually, she is pretty pushy. She says she refuses to go home until we admit him."

"What do you think?" Mack asked sipping at his coffee.

"Well, he looks pretty sick. Maybe we should admit. Let me see what you think."

"Okay, go on. Sorry for interrupting."

"That's okay. Where was I?"

"History of present illness."

"Yeah. Okay. His past medical history is remarkable ..."

"Wait. Hold it. Finish the history of present illness."

"I thought I did."

"No, you didn't. Tell me what happened between the onset of his illness and now. Dr. Vanderjagt saw this guy either Saturday or Sunday. There's a lot more."

Sutherland's face turned a shade close to scarlet and admitted, "Oops! Yeah. Sorry."

"That's okay. No need to apologize. That's why I'm sitting where I'm sitting, and you're sitting where you're sitting. Go back."

"They examined him Friday at Humanitarian, treated with Keflex, and sent him home. His wife said they diagnosed Strep. She also told me, that they told her, she would have to bring him here if he didn't get better or needed follow-up."

"Figures. Must not have insurance. Bastards."

"What?" Sutherland interjected.

"Just think of them as oxymoronic humanitarians and leave it at that," Mack protested. "Go on."

"She said they've got a big unpaid bill at Humanitarian from her last pregnancy," Sutherland continued. "Anyway, he came here on Sunday and Monday. Dr. Vanderjagt saw him, did some more labs, diagnosed viral meningitis, switched to Augmentin – which they couldn't afford – and sent him home. He came back in again yesterday and his wife brings him in again tonight. She says he is confused. He is oriented to person and place, although he thinks the month is April."

Mack drank from his coffee and said, "All right. Go to the past medical history."

"Except for a spider bite that required surgical reconstruction of his lip and nose, his past medical history is unremarkable. He doesn't smoke, abuse alcohol, or do drugs. He is a bricklayer by trade, but with the construction meltdown he works as a garbage collector for Republic Waste. He is married and has 3 children, ages 6, 4, and 7 months. His wife says she is pregnant again. His family ..."

"Hold it a second. What's this about a spider bite?"

"Well, as I got the story from his wife, when he was a little kid a spider crawled up his nose and bit him. The venom apparently ate through the tissue in his nostril and the skin above his lip – creating what sounds like a fistulous tract running from his nostril into his mouth."

"A spider up his nose? Fistula? You're pulling my leg?"

"No and get this. Sometime after he came to the United States, Dr. Alexandre at the medical school took two years reconstructing it."

"Must have been a species of the brown recluse – nasty little critters. We had a guy in here once that was sleeping on an old couch in the garage. A *reclusa* crawled up his undershorts and bit him on his balls. The venom destroyed the scrotal skin covering his whole left testicle and the base of his penis. Sloughed so bad he needed skin grafting – but up your nose? Gives me the willies just thinking about it. Eight claws crawling up your nose?" Mack mused. "I think I'd crap my pants. Alexandre's terrific though. Go on."

"Family history is unremarkable. He has no allergies. Review of systems is negative ..."

"Wait, wait, wait! You've got to give me pertinent positives and negatives. Presenting a patient is like good story telling Sutherland. You've hooked me. I'm on the edge of my seat. I want to hear the grisly details. So tell me. Any visual disturbances?"

"No."

"What's the character of the vomit?"

"Bilious. No blood."

"Any diarrhea?"

"No."

"What about his balance? Can he walk?"

A lump caught Sutherland's throat, "I think so."

"Think so ...? Did you ask?"

Sutherland flushed and said, "No."

"Mr. Sutherland, this guy has headache, confusion, and vomiting. I don't give a good God damn if you didn't ask him if he has had ingrown toenails, but your review of systems should include a comprehensive inquiry and discourse of his neurologic and gastrointestinal symptoms."

"I am sorry."

"Don't be sorry. Think. As much as we'd like the public to see us as a bunch of Einsteins, medicine is ninety per cent methodical data gathering and common sense, not rocket science. But you've got to ask the right questions – get a thorough history. Understand?"

"Yes, sir."

"Good. Go on."

"On physical examination, he is moderately ill-appearing and distressed. His temperature is 101.7, respirations 20, heart rate 88, blood pressure 130/86 supine, 120/68 sitting ..."

"Good. You did posturals. Great. I'd have wrapped your knuckles if you hadn't. Keep going."

"His optic fundi are clear. No hemorrhages. Ears are unremarkable. Mucous membranes dry. Throat is erythematous but no pus. When I flexed his neck, he cried out in pain, so he's got meningismus. His skin is clear. No rashes. No jaundice. Lungs and heart are clear to auscultation; no murmurs. His abdomen is benign. I didn't do a genital or rectal exam.

"On neurologic exam, cranial nerves two through twelve are intact. I thought maybe I saw some nystagmus – can't be certain – I would like you to check. Reflexes are two plus and symmetric. Sensation and motor are intact and symmetric. His Glasgow coma scale is 13."

"Romberg?"

"I didn't check it. When he tries to stand up he gets dizzy and starts to puke again."

"Anything else?"

"Labs ..."

"Hold it, hold it Justin. Did *you* find him to be confused?"

"His wife thinks so. I think he seems more lethargic and ill, than confused. He knows his name and where he is. But, as I said, he thinks it's April.

"So his labs: white count not bad – 15,700 – predominately lymphs. Hematocrit and hemoglobin normal – 46 and 15.3. Metabolic panel – sodium 148, potassium 4.8, creatinine 1.2, BUN 23."

"So what's your diagnosis?"

"Viral meningitis, moderate dehydration."

"How do you know it's not the more vicious form of meningitis – bacterial?"

"I don't."

"Good. You're right. You don't," Mack concurred.

Conversation 64
Los Angeles County Hospital
Tuesday, July 30, 2002; 4:23 a.m.

Paco lay on the gurney sleeping, when Mack and Sutherland parted the curtains. "Mr. Sánchez? Mrs. Sánchez? I'm Dr. Michael Mack," he said extending his hand. "I apologize for taking so long. Sutherland and I have been discussing Paco's case. As Dr. Vanderjagt told you, this looks like viral meningitis. But we can't be certain and we have to rule out bacterial. He needs to be admitted and ..."

"What you say confuse me. What do you mean bacterial?" Sarita interrupted.

"Well, he's not getting better. We need to do more tests. Sedimentation rate, cold agglutinins, spinal tap. Things like that."

"Spinal what?" Sarita asked.

"Spinal tap. Long needle carefully inserted into the spinal canal at the base of his back. We take some fluid and analyze it for bacteria."

Sarita pushed back her emotions and asked, "Will this spinal tap hurt him?"

Mack cleared his throat, "Maybe a little. Usually not at all. We numb up the spot with local anesthesia. He's well developed and slim. He should have good landmarks. Worst part will be rolling him into a good fetal position to open up the spine so we can slip right in, get the fluid, and get out."

"Is that the only way? There must be ..."

"It's the only way to be sure Mrs. Sánchez. And we've got to be certain this time."

Sarita crossed her chest with her arms, shivered and stared at Paco. "I guess you have to do this. Just do not hurt him," she pleaded. "Just do not hurt him."

Conversation 65
Los Angeles County Hospital
Tuesday, July 30, 2002; 4:44 a.m.

Sutherland followed Mack back to the supply room, "How many of these have you done?" the attending asked.

"Three. Four if you count the one I flubbed."

Mack scrutinized his pupil. "The most important person is the holder. You've got to hold them down, hold them tight, and curl them into a ball, head and all. Kissing their bellies so to speak. Knees to his chest. Roll a man so tight he could give himself a blow job. Ever do a cannonball, Sutherland? Curl patients up just like that … that'll be my task. You'll go after the fluid."

"Yes, sir."

"And one more thing, Sutherland. Impeccable sterile technique. Understand?"

"Yes, sir."

Paco lay motionless, shielding his eyes from the fluorescent glare with his right arm. Mack spoke.

"You understand what we're going to do, Mr. Sánchez?"

Paco opened his eyes, looking in the direction of Sutherland, "Yes, I think so."

"Did you sign the permit?"

Paco deliberated, "I think so …"

"He tried, but he couldn't," Sutherland interjected. "Mrs. Sánchez signed for him."

"Good. Let's get on with it," Mack responded placing his hand on Paco's shoulder. "Listen to me, Mr. Sánchez. This should take only a few minutes. Follow my directions and we'll be done in no time. The first thing I want you to do is roll on your left side, grasp your knees with both arms and roll into a tight ball, chin to chest. I'll help you while Sutherland does the procedure. Okay?"

Paco stared at Mack, "Yes."

"So go ahead, grab your knees and roll into a ball," Mack ordered, nudging Paco to his left side.

Sarita sat in a chair in the corner, examining her nails and picking at them. She looked up at Sutherland. "He wants me to be in here."

Sutherland looked toward Mack who declared, "I've got no problem with that, why don't you bring the chair over here at the end of the gurney. Look away, head down, sitting only. You can comfort him by holding his foot but touch nothing else. *Nothing else.* Is that clear?"

"Yes, doctor," she said sliding the chair across the floor. "I have got you, Paco."

Sutherland donned the surgical gloves, opened the lumbar puncture tray, set out the collection tubes and methodically arranged the instruments, careful to maintain the sterile field. Nurse Rachel helped him draw up 3cc of 1% Xylocaine anesthesia. As the syringe filled, he remembered the first time he performed this procedure. The patient was a delirious, overweight woman unable to comprehend instructions. She resisted positioning and her adiposity obscured the important boney landmarks. After three frustrating attempts, he gave up and turned the procedure over to his mentor who, of course, got the fluid on the first attempt. "You'll do better next time," the attending physician consoled him afterwards, "She was tough."

But Mack had Paco Sánchez in a tight ball and every anatomical part on Paco's lean, muscular back stood out in clear definition. Sutherland painted Paco's back with Betadine, identified the sweet spot between the fourth and fifth vertebrae and draped his target. He anesthetized the area, prepared the shiny, 6-inch needle, gave Mack the sign, and in one fluid, uninterrupted motion slipped the needle between the spinous processes and into the canal. Sarita felt Paco flinch for a flash. Sutherland heard the characteristic pop. Crystal clear fluid oozed from the needle. He was in.

Conversation 66
Los Angeles County Hospital
Tuesday, July 30, 2002; 5:36 a.m.

Mack released Paco and climbed off the gurney. Stripping his latex gloves he said, "Good news, Mr. and Mrs. Sánchez. The fluid is clear. The lab still needs to run the tests, but I think they will point to viral."

"Thank god! Do you hear that, Paco?"

Eyes shut tight, Paco nodded.

"We are still going to admit him though. I want him observed. He needs IV fluids and while we're at it, we'll quiet the vomiting and treat his headaches."

"So, what is wrong with him?" Sarita asked.

"Viral meningitis. Dehydration. The way I put it together it started with a viral sore throat four or five days ago and progressed into this. It's the way meningitis often presents," he asserted.

"Is he going to be okay?"

"I think so. In fact, he should be better in no time. Oh, who's his doctor?"

"Dr. Rodríguez," Sarita answered.

"Miguel Rodríguez?"

"Yes, Miguel. He delivers our babies. He is our family doctor, the kids, me, Paco. He is our doctor for this one too," she blushed, proudly rubbing her pregnant belly.

"Another one? Congratulations," Mack smiled. "Rodríguez is a good man, and a darn good doctor. Make sure you put Rodríguez on as attending in the orders, Sutherland."

"Yes, sir."

Mack parted the curtains to leave. "Oh. And by the way, Sutherland, nice workup, good tap."

"Thank you, Dr. Mack," Sutherland beamed.

Conversation 67
Los Angeles County Hospital
Tuesday, July 30, 2002; 11:36 a.m.

Later that same morning, Dr. Charles Overstreet bent over Holly Peerbhoy's foot and looked down into the ulcer, "How long has it been like this?"

"I can't really say. It never really hurt all that much. Then one day about a week ago it exploded and all this smelly pus came out," she said.

Overstreet agreed. The odor turned his stomach. Deep in the ulcer bed, pus oozed from open flesh. It reminded Overstreet of cauliflower marinated in red wine. The margins of the wound blanched white, and then slowly back to red.

"Does this hurt?" he asked, pressing on the edge of the wound and over the ball of her foot.

"No, I can't say it does, doctor," Holly Peerbhoy confessed.

"Has anyone ever told you that you have diabetic neuropathy?"

"Diabetes, yes, but not that – why, what is it?"

"Diabetics get it. Causes the nerves in the feet to go numb. Patients suffer, but can't feel a thing. Now you've got an ulcer and the bone is probably infected too – osteomyelitis."

144

"Oh my goodness. That sounds awful doctor, uh – what's your name again?"

"Dr. Overstreet. Dr. Charles Overstreet. I'm an infectious disease specialist," he answered handing Peerbhoy his business card.

Holly Peerbhoy smiled, looked down at her foot, hesitated, then frowned, "Oh my Lord … what can be done?"

"I need to take a specimen, examine it under the microscope and start some strong antibiotics. It just takes a minute or two to do the tests …"

"Really?" she interjected. "Well, do what you have to do doctor. I've got to get back to work."

"First, I put on sterile gloves," Overstreet continued, "stick a Q-tip-like swab down into the bed of the ulcer to take a culture and do what we call a gram strain. When that's done, I'll come talk and explain everything."

"Like I said Dr. Overstreet, do what you have to do."

Four types of organisms – bacteria, viruses, fungi and parasites – make up and inhabit the germ microcosm. Charles Overstreet paid reverence to every one of them. Why shouldn't he? Fascinating science aside, Overstreet made an audacious income doing battle day in and day out with them.

Like his colleague Ed Pinkerton, Overstreet garnered his substantial largesse not from patient care – "Medicare makes certain of that," he often grumbled – but rather his Infusion Center, which provided outpatient therapy for long term treatments for infections like osteomyelitis, Clostridium difficile colitis and methicillin resistant Staphylococcal cellulitis. Insurance companies respected entrepreneurs like Charles Overstreet. And why shouldn't they? In 2002 a hospital bed cost more than two-thousand per day – just for the bed. Dr. Overstreet's outpatient enterprise provided the opportunity for early hospital discharge and saved them plenty.

When he got to the lab, Overstreet prepared Holly Peerbhoy's specimen, adjusted the lens and gazed through the microscope. On forty power he saw nothing more than amorphous purple and red speckles.

Switching to oil emersion brought the tiny dots to life. "Hmm ... gram-positive cocci and gram-negative rods – darn," he muttered.

He pulled his eyes away from the scope, reached into his shirt pocket and removed a small black book. In it he wrote, *Holly Peerbhoy: acute osteomyelitis, gram-positive cocci and gram-negative rods. Probable staph aureus and pseudomonas. Begin vancomycin and piperacillin. Order MRI to rule out osteomyelitis. Schedule infusion therapy. ICD-9: 730.0.*

Ms. Peerbhoy heard Overstreet whistling as he made his way down the corridor and turned into her room.

"Well, I got a good specimen," he asserted. "And, as I suspected, my preliminary diagnosis – osteomyelitis or bone infection – looks to be correct. That's the good news. The bad news, Mrs. Peerbhoy – two potent germs – what we call staph aureus and pseudomonas, have invaded your tissues ..."

"Oh my goodness *gracious*," she whimpered, "that sounds *terrible.*"

"To be quite blunt, Mrs. Peerbhoy, it's not good. Coupled with the diabetes, healing this will be tough. At least six weeks of antibiotics called vancomycin and piperacillin, limited walking on that foot, blood tests, office visits – intense, very intense."

"Do I have to stay in the hospital?"

"No, in fact we can do all of this in my Infusion Center. I'll get you started here and finish you up at the Center."

"When can I go back to work?"

"Not until it's healed and your diabetes shows improvement."

"But you said at least six weeks. I can't. I'll lose my job."

Overstreet shrugged his shoulders. "Like I said, Mrs. Peerbhoy, this is not good. I'm sorry to say it's either that or risk an amputation ..." he hesitated. "Look, I've got to get over to University Hospital. Write down all of your questions and I'll answer them in the morning. Okie-dokie?"

She stared out the window, numbed by the diagnosis and the prognosis. Okie-dokie she thought, then whispered, "Amputation? Yes, okay. Tomorrow."

Overstreet pulled the door open, "Good morning then?"

146

"I guess, Dr. Overstreet. Yes, good morning," she frowned.

Overstreet turned the ignition on his Acura RL and pressed the speed dial on his cell phone. It rang twice. The automated intercept picked up. "Hi. This is Kelly, Dr. Charles Overstreet's nurse. We are closed for lunch and will return at 1:30. Please leave a message at the beep and I will call you back just as soon as possible. If this is an emergency, please hang up and dial 911."

"Hey Kelly, Dr. Overstreet here. Book the following beginning Friday. Book Mrs. Holly Peerbhoy – that's Peerbhoy, P-E-E-R-B-H-O-Y – at the Infusion Center. Date of Birth: September 15, 1946. Diagnosis: Diabetes, ICD-9: 250.6 and Osteomyelitis ICD-9: 730.0. Staph and pseudo. Vancomycin and piperacillin IV daily for six weeks. Oh, I almost forgot. She has great insurance – Aetna Plus – so we should have no problem there."

Conversation 68
The Grove Mall, La Brea, California
Tuesday, July 30, 2002; 12:32 p.m.

Carolyn MacDougall and Judi Pinkerton sat on the veranda of La Fleur sipping lemon drop martinis. A gentle breeze cooled the humid sun. Skylarks hopped along the wrought iron railing hoping for a handout.

"I hate those things. It's the only thing I don't care for out here," Carolyn MacDougall complained.

"What *things*, what *are* you talking about?" Judi asked.

"Birds. Birds and restaurants. They're *so* dirty, yuk," Carolyn frowned.

"Carolyn, in my life birds are nothing," Judi stated taking another drink. "What are you going to eat?"

Carolyn looked over the menu, finished off her martini and said, "Another martini."

"No food?"

"Don't know. Right now another martini," she laughed. "You?"

"What the hell, another martini. Food just fats you up anyway. Can we smoke out here?"

"I thought you quit."

"I did – for the most part, but a good cigarette is still one of life's simple pleasures and Lord knows there are not enough of those," she laughed, reaching into her handbag, coming up with a Virginia Slim and lighting up. She blew smoke over the railing's edge away from her friend. "So, Carolyn, tell me, if you don't mind me asking. What's your secret? What keeps your boobs so perky?"

"Boobs? Perky?"

"Yes, perky. Look at you, nice cleavage, boobs that look like 17."

Carolyn smiled, signaled the waitress for two more lemon drops, leaned forward and whispered, "Liposuction."

"Liposuction?"

"Liposuction. Jack said my breasts were a mess – which I did not particularly appreciate – in fact, I said, 'Go fuck yourself you bastard. You didn't have to have babies.' And he said, 'Go see George Alexandre. He's done the definitive research on a new procedure.' And Voila! Liposuction," she declared extending her arms and trumpeting her chest.

Judi Pinkerton smiled, "I didn't know you breastfed."

"I didn't – God, I wouldn't for the life of me – but after two kids and 45 years, I must admit they looked pretty droopy."

The waitress brought the fresh martinis and set them on the table. "So, have you decided on lunch, Mrs. MacDougall?"

Carolyn looked up into the sun at the waitress's face, "Yes, Crystal I have. Lemon drop martinis!" she snickered.

"Sounds delicious," the waitress chuckled. "If you change your mind, just let me know. I am here all day. We've got some specials; I can tell you about them when you are ready," she turned and disappeared.

Judi Pinkerton took a long drag from her cigarette, blew the smoke skyward and asked, "So, what's with the liposuction?"

"Really, it's pretty neat. Alexandre suctioned fat from my ham hocks – God knows I could use less of those – and injected it back into each breast."

"No kidding? Really! And I'll bet there's no scar or the sensation of the implants."

"Not one, not a bit. It's great," Carolyn said taking a drink from the lemon drop.

"Painful?"

"Hardly. Alexandre is excellent, Judi. Stanford graduate. Chief of Plastics here at University Hospital. National Institutes of Health research grants. Humanitarian awards for charity work for the underserved and, I might add," she said pointing to her breasts, "a fabulous plastic surgeon!"

"Expensive?"

"Of course!"

"How much?"

"Close to fifteen grand for the whole thing – body sculpting, ham hocks and boobs!"

"That's not bad."

"Jack thought so. First he complains about my tits. I get them done at his whining insistence, and then he bitches about the bill."

"They look great. Can I touch them?" Judi asked.

"Not here! But buy me a third martini, take me home and you can look, and touch, and feel the whole enchilada," she winked. "By the way. You got another cigarette?"

Conversation 69
Los Angeles County Hospital
Tuesday, July 30, 2002; 12:47 p.m.

"Dr. Rodríguez! Thank God you are here. Paco he is so bad. He have been so sick!" Sarita exclaimed.

Dr. Miguel Rodríguez took Sarita's hand and held it. "What's going on?"

"It is like I said. He have been so sick. It started Friday. We went to the Humanitarian. They say he have Strep throat or something like that. They give him antibiotics and he has only gotten worse. At first it was just a sore throat and fever. Then he start to have the headaches and he vomit. He cannot keep nothing down, not even a little bit. Humanitarian Hospital tell us we have to come here if he did not get better. Then we came here. I cannot even count how many times we have been back to the Emergency Room. Last night, they finally admit him. I am so worried. Look at my Paco. He is so sick. Look at him. He cannot hardly talk and he is confused or something. Tell me he is going to be better. Please tell me, Dr. Rodríguez," she pleaded.

"He's going to be okay, Sarita. Don't worry. Viral meningitis works this way. Makes you very sick for a few days then – mucho mejor!"

"But look at him, he is so bad."

"Well, there's some good news," he said looking away from Sarita and over to Paco. "The blood cultures from the Emergency Department are negative and the preliminary results of the spinal fluid point to a viral infection all the way. Let me look him over."

Rodríguez took out his stethoscope, said "Good morning, Paco" and began listening to his heart and lungs. Next he flashed a penlight in Paco's eyes, looked in his throat, and felt his glands. When Rodríguez flexed his neck Paco emitted an abrupt groan, but otherwise laid still as the doctor finished the exam with reflexes, the abdomen, and skin. "Has he had a rash, Sarita?"

"No, no rashes, just what I told you."

Rodríguez placed his hands on Paco's shoulders and shook him "Paco? Paco?"

"Uh-huh."

"Paco? Where are you?" he shook him again.

"Uh-huh."

"Paco, where are you?" Rodríguez repeated.

"Uh-huh."

"See? See what I mean? Nothing, Dr. Rodríguez. Nothing! He is worse even since they admit him!"

"It's okay, don't worry," he reassured her. "This is viral and Paco is going to get better."

"But when?"

"Tomorrow. Wednesday or Thursday. Soon. You'll see."

"I believe you, Dr. Rodríguez, but I am so scared. He is my only Paco. He is the papá to my niños."

"I know, Sarita, I know. Look, I'll get the infectious disease doctor to look in on him just to make sure we're covering all bases. Tomorrow he'll be better. Okay?"

"Okay," she said, sinking into the bedside chair. "You promise?"

"I'm 99% certain."

Conversation 70
Los Angeles County Hospital
Tuesday, July 30, 2002; 1:24 p.m.

Sarita knelt on the floor next to Paco's bed. She clutched her rosary beads, she bowed her head and she began to pray. "Our Father, who art in Heaven, hallowed be Thy name; Thy kingdom come; Thy will be done on earth as it is in Heaven. Give us this day our daily bread; and forgive us our trespasses, as we forgive those who trespass against us; and lead us not into temptation, but deliver us from evil. Amen.

"Hail Mary, full of grace! The Lord is with thee; blessed are thou among women, and blessed is the fruit of thy womb, Jesus. Holy Mary, Mother of God, pray for us sinners now and at the hour of our death. Amen. Glory be to the Father, and to the Son, and to the Holy Spirit. As it was in the beginning, is now, and ever shall be, world without end. Amen."

One, after another, after another, the beads slipped through her fingers. Tears dripping from her eyes, she repeated over and over, "Hail Mary, full of grace! The Lord is with thee; blessed are thou among women, and blessed is the fruit of thy womb, Jesus. Holy Mary, Mother of God, pray for us sinners now and at the hour of our death. Amen."

Sarita looked up and out the window toward the heavens pleading, "God, please watch over Paco. Take this evil sickness from his body. I pray for Paco's doctors that they feel your power and through the wisdom you have to give to them, to heal Paco's sickness. Whatever this may be, make it go away. Paco he is a good man. Paco he is a good father to our children. Paco he is a good husband. Dear God, Paco he is my very best friend. Please, please dear Lord, make my Paco better. Make my Paco better, Lord. Amen."

Conversation 71
Los Angeles County Hospital
Tuesday, July 30, 2002; 1:33 p.m.

"This is Charles Overstreet."

"Hey Charlie, Miguel Rodríguez. Thanks for taking my call. The ER admitted a patient. Name is Paco Sánchez. I'm the attending. He's a 29 year-old Mexican male with what appears to be viral meningitis. He has been in and out of the ER since Friday and he's no better. They thought it was Strep, and gave him antibiotics. Something about this worries me though. I've known Paco and his wife for some time. He's sick and I don't think we really know why. I need your help."

"Has he had fever?"

"On and off. Hundred and one, hundred and two, something like that. What worries me most is the lethargy and his altered mental status."

"Does he have meningismus?"

"He apparently had it. At least they recorded it in the Emergency Room. Now he's limp as a dish rag. Doesn't respond much to anything. Merely groaned when I flexed his neck."

"Where is he?"

"4-South, room 413."

"I'll see him straight away and call you."

"Thanks, I'll be on my cell phone."

"Speed dial?"

"You bet. Thanks, Charlie."

"No problem. Oh, Rodríguez. What's his insurance?"

"Doesn't have any. He's been laid off for six months or more and just two weeks ago went to work collecting garbage for Republic Waste."

"Uh-huh," Dr. Overstreet frowned. "Okay, well I'll see him when I can get to him."

"And call me?" Rodríguez scowled wondering if Overstreet confessed to the medical school admissions committee that he would short shrift patients who had no health insurance, when he made his application to medical school.

"Yes. You bet," Overstreet answered.

Conversation 72
Humanitarian Hospital, Los Angeles
Tuesday, July 30, 2002; 2:32 p.m.

Ms. Mimi Martin toiled as the collections manager for Humanitarian Hospital. She ascended to the position in 1989 and actually relished it. Days were never long enough. She arrived before seven and never left before six. Sometimes she stayed until 10:00 p.m., or even ten-thirty. Why not? Three meowing cats were all she had to go home to. Mimi had the face of a bulldog and a pair of meatloaf saddlebags for a derrière. She dressed in drab monotones and too seldom shampooed her hair. Appearance made no difference to Mimi; she directed her minions from the dismal dregs of Humanitarian's subterranean spaces, adjacent to building maintenance and behind medical records. Each morning began with a disposable plastic container of Kellogg's All-Bran, six ounces of acidophilus yogurt and the funny papers, which she read while she ate at her desk; life provided few other pleasures, except, of course, running her shop with an iron fist and harassing delinquent patients as if she were wringing blood out of desiccated turnips. Above her desk she hung a sign – *The Squeaky Wheel gets the Grease. Fear is a Righteous Tool.* She smirked every time she read it.

Sarita hurried across the room, reached into her handbag and answered her cell phone on the 5th ring. "Hello."

"Mrs. Sánchez?"

"Yes."

"This is Mimi Martin calling again from Humanitarian Hospital."

"Yes."

"I am calling about your bill. Remember I called last month?"

Sarita caught her breath. "Yes, I am sorry. I am at the County Hospital. Paco he have been admitted."

"Really, I see. Well anyway I am calling about your bill – *again.*"

Sarita stood holding the phone in disbelief wondering how things could get any worse. "Paco, he is very sick. He …"

"As I said, your bill is *several* months past due."

"I know Mrs. Martin. It is like I told you, Paco he have been out of work. We would not be in this if Paco have not lost his job," Sarita pleaded.

"Well, I'm sure of that Mrs. Sánchez, but you promised to make a payment …"

"I know …"

"Last month and there has been nothing," the collector interrupted.

"I try, but the kids have to come first. I am sure you understand that whatever, you have got to take care of the kids. And the house payment. We must have a place to live."

"Mrs. Sánchez, the bill amounts to over $5000 *plus* interest. Humanitarian Hospital has tried to work with you. But we have not had a payment."

"It is like I say, and like I have said, Paco he is sick. He just get a job with the Republic Waste two weeks ago and now he is sick. Before he have only odd jobs and work at the Union. We lose the insurance when Paco lose his job, just when Angelina is born."

"Mrs. Sánchez. You should have thought of that before *you* got pregnant. Humanitarian Hospital cannot absorb the cost of poor planning and indiscriminant pregnancies."

Sarita looked over at Paco and began to cry. She choked back the tears and asked, "Mrs. Martin could you hold a minute?"

"Certainly."

Sarita set the telephone down, blew her nose and wiped her eyes. Martin's persistence and the heavy, stolid air in Paco's ward enveloped her like a steamy blanket. She had no idea what indiscriminant meant, but the context of the call coupled with the grating, insistent whine of Mimi Martin's voice insulted and left her cold. In Guadalajara the midwife delivered your baby and you went a la casa. In a few days they sent the doula to check on you. The doula helped you breast feed and taught you baby care. And neither the hospital nor the doula sent a bill. She took a deep breath and picked up the phone, "Mrs. Martin?"

"Yes."

"I do not understand what you mean by this word 'indiscrimin' or whatever you call me, my baby or Paco or my children. But Paco is a good husband and a good father. He work very hard every time he have a chance. He try so hard to find a job he takes one picking up what you call the garbage. Angelina and José and Miguel are my beautiful children. *Everyday* Paco he worries how we will get the money to fix Angelina's lip. *Everyday* Paco he worries about the money and he says to me we have to pay the bills. I say I know. And all we can do is shake our heads.

"Everybody say that since the planes flew into the Towers that there is no work. Well let me tell you something Mrs. Mimi, Paco did not fly those planes into the buildings. First he takes a Green Card, then he becomes a citizen. I have a Green Card. Someday soon I become a citizen. We are both what *you* call legal. Paco works everyday he can. He is not criminal."

"Mrs. Sánchez, I did not imply your husband was a criminal," Martin replied.

"You said he was 'indiscrimin'. It sounds like criminal to me."

"Mrs. Sánchez?" the collector asked, *"Mrs. Sánchez?"* she asked again. "Maybe I could talk to ..."

"Paco is sick. He cannot talk. He is vomiting all over and he does not know where he is," Sarita blurted, forcing back more tears. "When he is better I can talk to Paco. That is all I can do."

"Mrs. Sánchez if we don't receive a payment by next Friday ... *if we don't receive a payment by next Friday*, I am afraid I am going to send you to collection."

"Send us to collection or whatever you call it. What can we do?"

Martin persisted. *"And don't forget. It's like I told you before Mrs. Sánchez.* Until you settle your account with the hospital Angelina cannot have her surgery at *any* of our facilities. Do you understand that you fit a Category 3 profile according to our administrative protocols?"

Sarita shrugged her shoulders. "You have to have your rules, this I do know. Paco have his rules too and he is very strong. When he is better he will find a way. For now all I can say is goodbye, Mrs. Mimi," she choked and hung up.

Conversation 73
Los Angeles County Hospital
Tuesday, July 30, 2002; 3:16 p.m.

Charles Overstreet entered Paco's room and asked, "Mrs. Sánchez?"

Sarita stood up from the side of Paco's bed. "Yes?"

"Hi. I'm Dr. Overstreet. And you must be, Mr. Sánchez?" he said, he toward Paco.

"It is nice to meet you, Dr. Overstreet," Sarita answered. "Paco has been so sick. He just now wake up and he is much better. When we came into the hospital this morning he was vomiting and confused and now, how do you say – suddenly? He is better!"

"Hmmm? Excellent. What's the reason?"

"I do not know. The doctors they give him the fluids and the antibiotics. And I prayed so hard. I think Jesus answered my prayers. What do you think? I am so thankful."

Overstreet ignored her question. Religious hocus-pocus had no place in modern medicine. "How's the headache, Mr. Sánchez?"

"Better. I tell you I have never felt so bad."

Overstreet looked down at an empty bedside tray. "Appetite's back I see."

"Yes. I am very hungry."

"All he has been doing is throwing up," Sarita added. "It is no wonder."

"Has he been exposed to anything or anybody with a similar illness?" Overstreet asked.

Sarita looked away then down to the floor.

"Paco? Mrs. Sánchez?"

Sarita spoke first. "He is picking up other people's garbage. It is so dirty. He come home smelling every night, clothes all ..." she persisted. "Paco is a bricklayer, not a garbage man."

Overstreet looked over at Paco, "I see. Garbage collection must be rough work."

"It is very hard. Like Sarita say it is not very much good, but I have a job and it makes the money. It is okay," he said shrugging his shoulders. "The construction has been very bad."

Overstreet moved closer to Paco and examined him, taking some notes and grumbling, "Uh-huh," from time to time. When he was finished he said, "Well I think you've seen the worst of this Mr. Sánchez. Viral meningitis acts weird. Comes on with a vengeance and then you get better. Your temperature is 98.7, which is normal. Your appetite is obviously back. I don't see anything on exam either. What do you think Mrs. Sánchez?"

Sarita beamed from ear to ear. "Thank God, Paco you are going to be okay!"

"Look, I'll call Dr. Rodríguez, tell him what I think. I'll see Paco again tomorrow. If everything is okay, we'll send him home. Oh, we'll be able to remove the isolation precautions so you don't have to wear that silly gown and mask."

"What about the gloves, Dr. Overstreet?"

"Those won't be necessary either," he smiled. "I'll see you tomorrow."

Conversation 74
Los Angeles County Hospital
Tuesday, July 30, 2002; 3:31 p.m.

"Rodríguez?" Dr. Charles Overstreet asked into the phone.

"Yes."

"Charlie Overstreet, here. I saw your man, what's his name? Uh … let's see. Sánchez? Yeah, Sánchez. Wife says he looks a lot better. He was sitting up eating. I looked him over pretty good. I didn't see anything. The cerebral spinal fluid showed 89 lymphs and no growth thus far. His white count from this morning is normal. So, *I'm* calling this viral meningitis too. But the dumb bastards in the ER didn't do a spinal tap before giving him all the antibiotics. I think we should continue the ceftriaxone until he is afebrile for 24 hours and the cultures are no growth for three days. I took him off the isolation. Boy, his wife sure doesn't like him collecting garbage."

"Can't say I blame her."

"Ugh. That's for sure. Pardon the pun – it must be a shitty job."

"Worse thing is he's one hell of a brick layer. I had him do some work for me. The guy is unbelievable."

"Hopefully for him – for all of us for that matter – the economy will turn around."

"Agreed … hey, thanks for seeing him, Charlie. I can't believe he's so much better. He was sick as a dog this morning."

"Mrs. Sánchez can't either. When I asked her what was different, she said she prayed and prayed! I didn't say anything."

"Well, he's better and that's all that matters, isn't it?"

Conversation 75
Medical Arts Plaza, Los Angeles
Tuesday, July 30, 2002; 3:42 p.m.

Dr. Jack MacDougall gripped the exam room doorknob hoping to escape the conversation with Velma Richardson's daughter, who chattered incessantly about Velma's behavior – undressing in the middle of the day, walking out of doors, dancing naked in the street. She started the dialogue the same each visit, "Mama graduated summa cum laude from Duke, she taught philosophy at UC Berkeley – Dr. MacDougall Mama wrote the book on critical thinking. Now look at her. She can't manage her own toilet! There must something you can do for her ... *something.*"

Velma's daughter had two chins. A mole with a hair in the center garnished the upper one, while the lower jowl – a protuberant doughnut of flesh extending from ear to ear – framed a scowl etched in permanently around her lips. The composite made it difficult – no, nearly impossible – for MacDougall to look at her, let alone discuss Velma's disorder.

"Her Alzheimer's is very advanced, Jean," he reiterated. "I wish there were something else I could do. We've tried everything – even experimental drugs. This is an unfortunate and devastating disease. Alzheimer's spares no one Jean. Your dear mother is living proof."

"Well then, what's next?"

"Her exam is unchanged today. Actually she's been at this baseline for some time," he yawned. "Have you given any more thought to custodial care?"

The words "custodial care" bristled the hair on Jean Richardson's neck. She stood up, walked over to her mother, slid her flabby arm around her mother's waist and said, "After all she has given me, been there for me my whole life, I can't do it. I've told you that before, doctor. Can I Mama?"

Velma's vacant eyes stared out into space. She pursed her lips, rolled her fingers, grunted a throaty utterance, but did not speak.

"See?" her daughter frowned. "Dr. MacDougall, I just can't bring myself to that. You know as well as me. Just as soon as I do, Yale or Harvard or Duke will find a cure. Where would that put us?"

A knock on the door disrupted the discussion. MacDougall pulled it open.

Stephanie, his dowdy, reverent office nurse, stood there, "Dr. MacDougall, Steve Wasserman is on the phone."

"Oh, terrific. I'm done here. Refill Velma's Aricept and schedule her back in six weeks ... and Stephanie, get Jean enrolled in the Care Giver Support group," he said turning to Velma's daughter. "I promise you will like it, Jean. Good people. I'll see Velma back here in six weeks. And call if your mother needs anything. Anything at all, understand?"

"What? No further testing?" Jean Richardson asked.

MacDougall pondered her question. At Velma's advanced stages of dementia, the diagnostics were complete; no amount of testing would alter her fate. On the other hand MacDougall knew Medicare would likely reimburse only $43 dollars of today's $170 office visit. If he ordered a study through his neuro analytics lab he could bill $1800 and be reimbursed $1400. Jean's question opened the door and he liked the suggestion, "Of course. I almost forgot. Let's get a sleep study, Stephanie."

"Another one?" Velma's daughter countered. "She just had one in May."

"I know, Jean. But not with CPAP titration. A new study suggests Alzheimer's patients may benefit from CPAP even if their sleep apnea is mild to moderate. Let's see what it does for your mother."

"Oh, Dr. MacDougall," Jean Richardson beamed. "I knew you would come up with something. Thank you. Did you hear that, Mama? You're getting a CPAP test," she declared as MacDougall turned to go.

The good doctor did not want to talk to Wasserman – what could that stupid cocksucker want anyway? But he did need extrication from Jean Richardson, and his stockbroker's call gave him the out. He looked at his watch. Nearly four o'clock and done with patients for the day. He breathed a sigh of relief and picked up the receiver in his office. "Dr. MacDougall."

"Hey Jack. Steve Wasserman here. I understand you're busy, but listen. Our analyst thinks he's got a livewire. A can't miss opportunity. You know Google?"

"Google the internet search engine?"

"That's the one."

"What about it?"

"Google is privately held by its Silicon Valley co-founders. They have never floated an Initial Public Offering – apparently the IPO is a year or two off – but the word on the street says these guys will own the internet in three to five years …"

"Steve, get to the point. I've got patients," MacDougall lied.

Wasserman harrumphed and continued, "Our venture capital arm aims to float a junk bond issue to raise twenty-five million for Google's software development management. Their strategy converts the bonds to stock when the IPO goes live. Investors who weigh in on the junk bonds, cash out on a five for one opportunity when it's all said and done."

"If this is another of your harum-scarum ideas forget it. If it's not, get on with it. Translate."

Wasserman knew MacDougall gave him little credit, if any, for amassing his $22 million portfolio. From the stockbroker's estimates, at least half of it resulted from his strategic management and he had long ago tired of MacDougall's sarcasm and hubris. So he seized this moment to counter it, "It's not calculus, Jack. In fact, it's barely arith-metic. Say the Initial Public Offering goes for a hundred bucks a share, your cost per share – if, and when, you convert the junk bonds to pre-ferred stock – is twenty dollars per share. Hell of a deal, really."

"What if the whole thing goes tits-up? What if Microsoft comes in asses and elbows and vaporizes Google? Then what?"

Wasserman wanted to say, "You'll blame me, you pretentious prick" but bit his tongue and said, "You lose your shirt. But that ain't gonna' happen. Our analysts have got this one pegged. Google will dominate the search engine enterprise in ways that will make Microsoft drool. Our info tech analysts called Microsoft back in the eighties. They're calling Google now."

"I say it's risky."

"No pain, no gain, Jack."

"Easy for you to say, Wasserman. It's not your money."

"I thought you had balls, Jack. You're not going to get risk averse on me are you?"

Suddenly, blood swirled in MacDougall's viscera and spread to his loins. His penis stiffened. Swallowing the lump in his throat he asked, "How much?"

Wasserman knew he had the good doctor hooked. Now to reel him in. "$50,000 minimum, but if it were my money – to cash in big-time – takes guts. I'd go higher."

MacDougall's mind inexplicably flip-flopped and flashed back to the Hyatt Regency three nights before and the image of raven-haired Jasmine slowly, and oh so carefully, massaging and licking his throbbing dick. Then he did the math. A hundred thousand investment converted to a cool $500,000. It takes it, to make it. No pain, no gain, Jack. I like *that* … but I *love* Jasmine. Jesus, she has beautiful tits. And that ass, holy shit! The way she pampered my prick. Looking at it. No, examining it – like she'd never seen or held one before. Exploring it like it was the ninth wonder of the world. Lying against my thigh. Rubbing it good and slow. Staring down on it and smiling. Then sucking on it … just a little bit. Getting it nice and wet, taking it from her mouth and rolling the tip of it against her nipple. Looking up at me, straight in the eyes, grinning. Oooh. Makes me shiver. God damn I'd like to fuck her again. Next time I should probably wear a condom though – just to keep it safe – but bareback feels so much sweeter. I'll tell Carolyn I have to speak at a conference. Fly to San Francisco. Just for the night. Fuck Jasmine's pretty little pussy from behind.

"Jack? You there?"

MacDougall squirmed, suppressing the sudden urge to defecate, "Yeah. I'm here. Just calculating … so sell enough of my Microsoft to float it, Wasserman. I'm in for two-hundred grand."

"Fabulous, Jack, Fabulous. I'll place the order right …"

But MacDougall cut Wasserman off, hung up the receiver and hustled off to the john. "Jesus, I've got to take a dump," he mumbled.

Conversation 76
Los Angeles County Hospital
Tuesday, July 30, 2002; 5:56 p.m.

The sun shone hot and bright, but dark clouds loomed to the east that same afternoon when Justin Sutherland knocked on Paco's hospital room door and entered. Sarita sat at Paco's bedside holding his hand, and watching a rerun of *Los Ricos También Lloran* on the Spanish television network.

"Mrs. Sánchez?"

"Yes."

"I'm Justin Sutherland."

"Yes, I remember, from the Emergency Room," she said.

"Dr. Rodríguez and Dr. Overstreet said it would be okay for me to look in on Paco if it was all right with you."

"Yes, of course, he is so much better, thanks to you and Dr. what is his name?"

"Mack?"

"Yes, Dr. Mack. He has finally stopped vomiting and he ate something for lunch."

Sutherland stuck out his hand and shook Paco's. "I'm Justin Sutherland. I'm a fourth year medical student. I did your spinal tap last night."

Paco managed a smile, "I do not remember."

"You were pretty out of it, Mr. Sánchez. It's good to see you feeling better. Viral meningitis knocks you for a loop."

"The headache," Paco explained. "I never feel anything like that before."

"It's better?"

"Much better. My neck still hurts but not so much now."

"Dr. Overstreet said he could go home tomorrow," Sarita smiled.

"That's great. Anything I can do?"

"Can I ask you a question?"

"Yes, of course. Shoot."

"My children they are all at home. I am breastfeeding Angelina. Would it be okay to leave Paco to check on the children and feed her? Mamacita have them all to herself, and I must check on them."

Sutherland looked over at Paco, "What do you think, Mr. Sánchez, you okay alone?"

"No problema. You can go home to the children. I will be okay. The hospital takes good care of me," he stated.

Conversation 77
Los Angeles
Tuesday, July 30, 2002; 6:34 p.m.

The rain from the thunder burst finally stopped when Jack Mac-Dougall valet parked his Mercedes and entered O'Doul's Sports Bar & Grill. At the moment he swung the door open, the crowd roared. Manny Ramirez had just hit a two run shot off Matt Morris over the Green Monster in deep left center field. The blast tied the score at two runs apiece.

"Fucking-a-right, *Manny*," MacDougall cheered under his breath.

Luckily, he found a prime spot at the bar and settled in to watch the rubber match of the St. Louis Cardinals-Boston Red Sox interleague series.

An attractive redhead with a broad smile and green eyes approached MacDougall. She floated down a napkin and asked, "What can I get for you, mister?"

The sparkle in her face and splash of freckles across her cheeks underscored her Irish ancestry. He guessed her to be twenty-five, maybe twenty-six. Beautiful smile. White teeth. Wow. Not much older than my daughter. What's the difference he wondered? "I'll take a 20 oz. Foster's and a double shot of Johnnie Walker Black," he answered. Reaching for a Bolívar Belicosos Finos he asked, "Can I smoke in here?"

"Cigarettes – no cigars," she frowned.

"No cigars?"

"Sorry. Not since the election. When the state law passes, no cigarettes either. I'll get the Foster's and Johnnie Walker."

"Thanks," MacDougall retorted, glancing up at the big screen and grumbling as Jason Varitek grounded out to short to end the bottom of the seventh.

Growing up, MacDougall's father forced him to play baseball. Despite his dad's insistence, or because of it, Jack developed little enthusiasm for the game preferring instead individual sports like golf and tennis. "What fun is it to play your heart out, hit a double or a triple and the teammates that follow can't bring you home?" he complained.

Nevertheless, during residency at the Peter Bent Brigham and the Massachusetts General, MacDougall fell in love with baseball. Distant from the influence of his father's badgering and awed by the electricity of Fenway Park, the game took on new meaning. In Boston baseball *was* life. It didn't hurt that his best friend from Johns Hopkins – Ed Pinkerton – loved the game as well, and MacDougall became a dyed-in-the-wool Red Sox fan.

Despite Red Sox worship, as a multiple sclerosis fellow at Washington University, the St. Louis Cardinals and the atmosphere at Busch Stadium sucked him in as well. By the time MacDougall left St. Louis, he claimed the Cardinals his National League team and the Red Sox his American Leaguers. All the better, "Dad loves the Dodgers and Yankees. How can he? Ugh! Oh, well. Something else to give my old man shit about."

Derek Lowe took the mound for Boston in the top of the eighth. MacDougall wondered why Grady Little didn't pull him. But when Lowe got Edgar Renteria to ground out to Nomar Garciaparra, MacDougall agreed with Little; Lowe still had fire in his arm even after seven full innings. Jim Edmonds came up next.

Edmonds' good looks and chiseled jaw triggered MacDougall's childhood memories. He recollected vividly at age six looking up at his father in awe, hoping he too would be as big someday. At 6' 1" and 190 pounds Edmonds and his father were built much alike, but his dad's squared off chin and sharp jaw beat Edmonds by a hair. Picture perfect, all-American men MacDougall sighed, while wondering at the same time if Edmonds, like his dad, vied for the Prick-of-the-Century award too.

Lowe got Edmonds to foul tip the first pitch, and a fastball in the dirt evened the count at one ball, one strike.

Escaping his father's insistence on playing baseball proved easy compared to his dad's obsession with medicine as a career for his son. "As if it were his life," mumbled MacDougall when Lowe threw the third pitch high and outside. "God dammit, Lowe. Get it over the *fucking* plate. And why for Christ's sake am I thinking about my father?"

The bartender brought MacDougall the Foster's and a 2 oz. shot of Johnnie Walker Black. Before she could give him his total, he threw down the shot, winced for a split second and washed the scotch away with a good slug of beer. "Want me to start a tab?" she asked when he came up for air.

"Yeah, sure. Hey? Have you got an extra cigarette back there?"

"I do, but they're Marlboro Lights."

"No matter. I'll take one. By the way, what's your name?"

She handed him the pack. MacDougall took one and gave it back. "Caitlin."

"Caitlin? Pretty."

"Thanks," she smiled extending her lighter.

MacDougall steadied her hand, inhaled and lit the cigarette. "Not a Belicosos Finos," he winked, "but it will do. Thanks Caitlin."

Edmonds hit Lowe's next pitch foul down the 3rd base line. "Strike the bastard out, Lowe," MacDougall frowned.

He unsuccessfully applied to Berkeley and UCLA for college – where his high school academics didn't cut it – so his father pulled strings at Stanford that got him in. During fall rush he pledged Sigma Alpha Epsilon based on ΣAE's solid reputation as a party house *and* the knowledge the fraternity possessed the most complete pre-med test file of all the fraternities on campus. ΣAE pledged Jack for his decent looks and acerbic wit, but most of all a golf handicap, that promised the fraternity would rule the links for the next four years to come.

MacDougall took a deep drag off the cigarette and asked Caitlin for another double shot of Johnnie Walker. Edmonds hit Lowe's 2-2 pitch into the right field corner for a double. One on, one out, the go ahead run on second. "I told you to take the son-of-a-bitch out, Little," MacDougall blurted. "His arm is done for today."

He reached into his pocket, extracted his cell phone and dialed Ed Pinkerton's number. When Pinkerton answered MacDougall said, "You coming? It's the top of the eighth for Christ's sake."

"Can't, Jack. The coroner and three detectives just rolled in with a double homicide-suicide. And get this. Looks like the perp tied the victims up, drilled out her cunt with a two-inch spade bit and cut off her lover's dick with a serrated bread knife. All that before he stuck the gun in their mouths, shot and killed them ... and then put revolver to his own head."

MacDougall cringed at the image, "So-o-o ... put them in the cooler, come over here for the final two innings and go back after the game?"

"Nope. This one's high profile. Certain to shake the local political world. I can't take a chance on botching the evidence."

"Shit. This is a good game too. Tied top of the eighth. Lowe's pitching."

"Have fun, good buddy."

"Catch you tomorrow," MacDougall sighed and hung up his phone.

J. D. Drew came to the plate next. Lowe got him to ground out to second on the first pitch. MacDougall exhaled smoke, took a long drink from his Foster's and downed the Johnnie Walker. "All right, Derek. Atta' boy ... s-h-h-hit Pujols is next. You better take him out, Grady – come on. Let's have a fresh arm."

Despite its academic reputation, Stanford gave students like Mac-Dougall sufficient opportunity to party. Between the fraternity test file and well-developed in-exam crib notes, MacDougall managed a 3.8 GPA. With a knack for taking standardized tests, he aced the medical school admissions exam and got accepted to his father's medical school alma mater, Johns Hopkins University. "That's my boy, Jack," his father beamed; MacDougall knew he had finally got something right.

Pujols swung and missed Lowe's first two pitches. His next pitch came in low and outside. With the count one ball and two strikes Pujols stepped out of the box, adjusted his helmet and batting gloves and stepped back in. Lowe checked the runner and threw a ninety-four mile an hour fast ball straight down the middle. Pujols didn't hesitate. He drilled Lowe's pitch deep into the right center field bleachers driving in Edmonds. St. Louis Cardinals 4, Boston Red Sox 2. "SON-OF-A-MOTHREFUCKING BITCH," Jack MacDougall shouted. "GRADY, I TOLD YOU TO TAKE HIM OUT GOD-DAMN IT."

MacDougall felt a tap on his shoulder. He turned to the touch and looked up to O'Doul's six-foot-six bouncer. "Hey mister. Check your language. Some of the patrons are complaining."

"Language? Complaining? This is baseball and this is a sports bar for Christ's sake," MacDougall hissed.

"Yeah, I get it, but the ladies at the table behind us asked me to ask you to watch your mouth. Not so loud, okay?"

MacDougall looked over the bouncer's shoulder. "If they can't take the heat, they should get out of the kitchen," he whispered. "This is no place or no sport for prissy bitches," he said turning back to the big screen.

"I understand that and you know that. But keep it down, all right?" the bouncer warned and walked away.

MacDougall rubbed his eyes in long, circular motions. To the patron sitting next to him he said, "Grady Little is a stupid cocksucker. Lowe's thrown 98 pitches. You've got a two-two tie, a runner on second and you let Lowe pitch to Pujols. I don't fucking get it."

"Doesn't bother me," the man chuckled. "I'm rooting for the Cardinals."

MacDougall took another drag off the Marlboro Light. Grady Little left the dugout and strode out to the mound, signaling to the bullpen for Alan Embree and taking the ball from Derek Lowe. "It's about fucking time," he blurted looking over his shoulder to see if the prissy bitches were listening and the bouncer was in earshot.

From the first anatomy class MacDougall secretly wondered when, what, how, where but mostly *why* he had landed in medical school. The smell of bodies pickled in formaldehyde gagged him.

Memorizing the Krebs cycle bored him. He cared less about the pharmacodynamics of angiotensin converting enzyme inhibitors. So MacDougall did what any prodigal son would do – drank scotch and played golf – and cheated on bioscience exams when he did too much of both. When he entered the third and fourth years MacDougall leveraged his country club swagger to overcome his indifference to medical education, but because Johns Hopkins taught to the National Boards, he still scored in the 90th percentile on both parts I and II of the U.S. medical licensing exam.

Embree's first pitch to Tino Martinez drifted low and inside. Martinez swung and missed on Embree's second pitch – a ninety-seven mile an hour fastball.

The bartender slid a bowl of popcorn in MacDougall's direction. "You like the Bosox, huh?"

Without looking away from the screen MacDougall answered, "I did my residency in Boston and my fellowship in St. Louis. I like them both – but at the end of the day, the Red Sox are my team. Popcorn's good," he chortled chewing on a fistful with his mouth open.

"Most people around here are Dodger fans ... you're a doctor?" the bartender asked.

"That's me."

"What kind?"

"Neurology – strokes, dementia, multiple sclerosis – stuff like that."

"Sounds interesting. I'd like to be a doctor someday."

"Really? Want some advice? Don't," MacDougall grumbled taking another sip of beer.

Conversation 78
Los Angeles County Hospital
Tuesday, July 30, 2002; 7:07 p.m.

Back at County Hospital Paco woke from fitful sleep and rubbed his eyes. Sarita dozed in the bedside chair; curled up, a blanket covered her shoulders.

The urge to urinate spread like a spear from his bladder into his erect penis. Careful not to disturb Sarita, he covered his crotch, slid

168

from bed and made his way to the bathroom. He felt wobbly and his feet tingled. So he paused to steady his balance with the IV pole and examined the soles of his feet. Seeing nothing, he gained his bearings and continued toward the restroom.

Paco closed the bathroom door, planted his feet wide apart and leaned spread eagle against the wall in front of him, bracing his body with his left arm and hand. He found his penis, and bending it against its will, aimed its stiff trajectory downward toward the toilet. His urine dribbled at first, gradually picked up steam and hit the water full force. Relieved, he rinsed his hands and returned to bed.

Sarita stirred in the chair and looked up at her husband. "I get ready to go home and then I fall asleep," she yawned.

"Me too," he grimaced. "I did not want to wake you."

"What is the matter, Paco? You are sweating."

"My feet feel like I am walking on buzzers."

"Buzzers?"

"Yes, like many bugs are crawling on the bottom of my feet. It feels like buzzing. It make me very nervous. I looked. There are no bugs. I do not like bugs Sarita."

"You have only been in bed too long, Paco," she reassured him. "How is the headache?"

"Right now *it* is okay."

Sarita stretched, laid her face against the back of the chair and closed her eyes. "I am *so* tired Paco. For you to be in the hospital makes me tired – I feel like I can sleep forever, but I have to go home and feed Angelina. My breasts they are so swollen."

Paco sat on the edge of the bed wiggling his toes and massaging the soles of his feet. "Maybe I get to go home tomorrow," he sighed.

"The doctors say so," Sarita yawned although in the back of her mind she couldn't help worrying what the sensation of bugs crawling on the soles of his feet forecast.

Conversation 79
Los Angeles
Tuesday, July 30, 2002; 7:26 p.m.

The barmaid at O'Doul's busied herself between orders washing beer mugs and cleaning the bar in circular motions with a damp towel, "You should loosen your tie."

"What?"

"You should loosen your tie. You'd be more comfortable," she smiled.

MacDougall stuck his index finger between the tie and his shirt, tugged at the knot, undid the button and loosened his shirt. "You're right. That *is* better."

"Another cigarette?"

"Sure. Thanks for offering."

She shook one from the pack and handed MacDougall her lighter. "Doctors should know better not to smoke."

"Yeah, yeah, yeah," MacDougall snorted lighting the Marlboro and taking in the smoke. "Who cares anyway?"

On Embree's next pitch Johnny Damon made a diving, acrobatic catch in short, left center field to end the top of the eighth. Cardinals 4, Red Sox 2.

The distance created by college and medical school softened the tension between Jack MacDougall and his father. But in the senior year of his medical studies, the perennial conflict resurfaced full bloom. Jack's father wanted him to follow his footsteps and specialize in orthopedics. The sight of blood turned MacDougall's stomach. Observing the orthopedist's drill spinning off bits of bone, bone marrow and blood left him woozy.

Tony LaRussa brought right hander Mike Crudale in to pitch the bottom of the eighth. Crudale threw seven pitches and retired the Red Sox in short order, 1-2-3. "Son-of-a-God-damn bitch," MacDougall exclaimed.

MacDougall pushed in another handful of popcorn remembering vividly the arguments with his father. "First off, I'm twenty-five and hardly a little kid living under your thumb. Second, I'm more a scientist than a carpenter – you've got to admit that chisels and drills and hammers and screws are mechanical ..."

"Hold it. Hold it one God-damn second buckaroo," his father interjected. "Describing orthopedics as carpentry insults the hell out of me and, quite honestly, pisses me off, *Jack*. I've made a good living working my butt off my whole fucking life for this family. And you? *You* never complained about having new cars and attending the best colleges money could buy – on *my* free ride, I might add."

"Wait a second. I didn't mean that. Let me explain. Neurology is heady. Its mysteries intellectually challenge me. Most of my classmates don't even begin to comprehend nervous system function. *I do*. And I marvel at the hand-eye coordination it took for Reggie Jackson to be Mr. October and Willie Randolph to win gold gloves. I wonder – how is it Carl Sagan can understand the complexities of outer space on one hand and make it come alive for the rest of us on the other? Why is it the brain deteriorates, yet the heart beats strong leaving the living in the dark shadows of a persistent vegetative state? I'm sorry; I don't want to follow your footsteps on this one. Let me pursue a career that stirs my intellectual curiosity and intuitive passions."

"Oh, fuck it, Jack. That's mumbo-jumbo horseshit," his father said walking away. "Do what you want. This fucked-up conversation is going nowhere and I, for one, am happy to say is over."

Dr. Jack MacDougall matched for neurology at the Massachusetts General Hospital and the Peter Bent Brigham in March of his senior year at Johns Hopkins.

MacDougall munched on the last of the popcorn and ordered another Foster's. Grady Little sent Ugueth Urbina in to pitch the top of the ninth. Urbina retired the Cardinals in order thanks to another extra-base-saving catch by centerfielder Johnny Damon to end the inning. Jason Isringhausen took the mound for the Cardinals in the bottom of the ninth.

Caitlin slid the beer toward MacDougall and nodded. "See the woman at the end of the bar?"

MacDougall looked to his left, "The one with the Cardinal's cap and pony tail?"

"That's the one … she wants to know if you're William Hurt."

"I've been asked that before," he sighed. "I wish I were. Got some more popcorn?"

Trot Nixon fouled the first pitch – a slow roller – down the right field line. The video cam zeroed in on the ball girl retrieving Nixon's foul. Her turned up nose, blond ponytail and enchanting smile bore a striking resemblance to Carolyn twenty years earlier, before she and MacDougall got married.

Nixon drove Isringhausen's next pitch into the left field corner for a standup double.

MacDougall stood up, thrust both arms in the air, nearly knocking the patrons to his left and right off their stools, and yelled over the other whoops and hollers, "YES! YES! FUCKING-A-YES!" One on. Nobody out.

Jack met Carolyn in the neuroscience research lab in Boston where she toiled as a lab technician while working toward a doctoral degree in neurophysiology. Her intellectual curiosity, drop-dead good looks and outrageous body graced Carolyn with a sexual inveiglement Jack found irresistible. Jack's edged wit put Carolyn off at first, but his blue eyes, charming smile and athleticism in bed won her over. They married during his second year of residency.

Isringhausen walked Ricky Henderson pinch hitting in Urbina's spot. Runners on first and second. Nobody out. Johnny Damon came up next. MacDougall downed the last of the Foster's, ordered another and shouted, "COME ON! DRIVE THE MOTHERFUCKING BALL WHERE THE SUN DON'T SHINE, JOHNNY!"

Carolyn MacDougall tired of Jack's sarcasm, unexplained indifference to their life and insistence on foreplay-less sex within the first year of their marriage. Before they tied the knot, she actually enjoyed fellatio. But Jack pushing the back of her head toward his penis graveled her. "What? You just sucked on it to trap me? What? I'm not good enough? What? You don't like my looks? My cock's not big enough? Oh, fuck you Carolyn *MacDougall* or whatever you call yourself."

Damon lined Isringhausen's next pitch into the gap driving Nixon home and Henderson to third.

"YES! YES! FUCKING-A-YES!" MacDougall shouted again.

St. Louis 4, Boston 3. Runners on first and third. Nobody out.

MacDougall turned to the tap on his shoulder and looked up at the bouncer. "Forget what I asked?" he said.

"No," MacDougall grinned.

"What? What then didn't you understand? You hard of hearing?"

"What?" MacDougall asked cupping his hand behind his ear. "What?" he chortled again.

"Are you hard of hearing?"

"No, I'm not hard of hearing and I understood just fine?"

"Then keep it down mister. The women behind you aren't happy. It's my job to keep *everyone* happy. No trouble. Okay?" he said walking away.

MacDougall turned back to the bar and eyed Caitlin delivering his next Foster's.

"How's the Johnnie Walker?" she asked.

"Unless you're driving," MacDougall winked, "no more."

"Sorry, *I'm* not driving," she quipped.

"Why not? We could have a little fun," he slurred. "Oh, what the hell. Give me another Johnnie."

Despite their early marital spats Carolyn got pregnant and, bing-bang, first John, and then Alyssa came into the world. Carolyn dropped her doctoral studies and Jack turned his attention to residency – then fellowship – then back home to private practice *and* an academic appointment at the medical school. The MacDougall's – one big happy all-American family.

Isringhausen struck out the next two hitters bringing up Nomar Garciaparra batting .310 with Manny Ramirez to follow at .349. Isringhausen had no choice but to pitch to Garciaparra.

The bartender slid the Johnnie Walker and another bowl of popcorn in front of MacDougall. He slammed down the scotch and took a long drink of Foster's as Garciaparra stepped in. Garciaparra hit a little blooper to shallow right that dropped in for a single, scoring Henderson. Game tied 4 runs apiece. Garciaparra on first. Damon on third. Two out.

"ALL FUCKING-A-RIGHT! WAY TO GO NOMAR!" MacDougall shouted and clapped his hands.

Caitlin delivered a drink to another patron, walked down the bar and back to MacDougall. "Hey, doctor *please* keep it down. You heard what Bouncer said. He'll throw you out."

"What? You too? Stop what?"

"Swearing."

"SWEARING? FUCK YOU. I'M DR. JACK MACDOUGALL! I'LL DO AND SAY WHATEVER THE FUCK I PLEASE!"

"This way mister," Bouncer's voice came from behind.

"What? Fuck you. I'm going nowhere."

"You heard me. This way. The lady said pipe down and I've warned you twice. Let's go," he said taking MacDougall by the arm.

MacDougall pulled away, "I'm watching the game."

"No – you *were* watching the game. Let's go."

"Fuck you asshole!" MacDougall mumbled.

"Let's go or we call the cops."

MacDougall turned, downed his beer, yelled "FUCK YOU" again and staggered out the door.

Heading toward the valet he heard the roar from inside. Manny Ramirez hit Isringhausen's fast ball into deep center field for a walk off home run. Game over Boston Red Sox 7, St. Louis Cardinals 4.

Conversation 80
Bellflower
Tuesday, July 30, 2002; 8:36 p.m.

Sarita sat in the rocker, staring at the wall. Angelina sucked from her breast in deep, desperate gulps. Miguel and José built a Lego fortress on the kitchen floor. Mamacita crocheted, pulling yarn in rhythmic cycles, looking up at Sarita and back to her task.

"Paco a la casa mañana, Mamacita. At least Dr. Rodríguez thinks so."

"Muy bien, Sarita. Mucho inferma es muy mal. Paco es mejor?"

"Si, Mamacita, Paco mucho better," Sarita said, switching breasts and wiping a tear from her cheek. "You should have seen him. He is so sick and now he is better. I pray and pray and pray. I pray the rosary,

174

too. And God, he answers my prayers. Before I left, Paco asked me to call Raphael and Emilio to tell them he is better."

"Mal de ojo, Sarita?" Mamacita grumbled under her breath, working the crochet.

"Stop, Mamacita! To think the evil eye comes can only make Paco worse. Do not talk or even think of the mal de ojo! Please, Mamacita! Please!"

Conversation 81
Los Angeles County Hospital
Tuesday, July 30, 2002; 9:58 p.m.

The sapid purr of Vin Scully's voice broadcasting the Athletics-Dodger interleague play by play, nudged Paco into trance-like sleep until Jeremy Giambi's 430 foot home run drove in Carlos Peña, woke up the crowd and abruptly brought Paco back to reality. Shielding his eyes from the glare of the television, he reached for his water, nearly knocking it to the floor before readjusting his grip and taking a drink. Half asleep, the television images were blurred. Nevertheless, as he rose to full consciousness, he made out that the Dodgers led the Oakland Athletics in the bottom of the thirteenth inning 5 to 4. But with two out, Oakland was battling back.

Oakland's Cody McKay came to the plate pinch hitting for Jim Mecir. The Dodger's new pitcher, Paul Quantrill, wound up and delivered his first pitch to McKay, a high inside fastball for a strike.

The images on the TV were still blurred and Paco blinked several times to bring the projection into focus. When that didn't help, he wiped his eyes with the bed sheets, yet that was no better – the players were still fuzzy. He looked away from the television, massaged his eyes again and looked back. Except for the umpires dressed in black, magenta halos outlined the players. The lights on the center field scoreboard shined like so many star bursts, the numerals merging into an array of meaningless light.

Paco looked about his room and out the window. In the dark of night everything appeared normal. Reassured the halos were but an artifact of the aging County Hospital television, he laid his head back, watched Quantrill strike out Cody McKay and fell fast asleep consoled by the Dodgers winning over Oakland 5 to 4.

Conversation 82
Marina del Rey
Wednesday, July 31, 2002; 12:14 a.m.

Dr. Edmund M. Pinkerton tiptoed down the hallway and climbed the spiral stairs to his sanctum sanctorum. The homicide-suicide post-mortems left him sapped; worst yet he'd missed the ball game with MacDougall. "Wait until I tell Jack that the perp jacked off in the victims' bloodied faces before he took his own life," he chuckled as he poured Tanqueray Ten over ice.

Pinkerton flipped through his video collection not certain what debauchery might satisfy his carnal appetite this night. Finally, he selected Anal Lust III, inserted it into his DVD player, grabbed two or three tissues and settled back. "Ahh. Prurient pleasures, prurient pleasures" he snickered, taking a drink and fast forwarding to the good parts.

Conversation 83
Los Angeles County Hospital
Wednesday, July 31, 2002; 8:09 a.m.

A thorough night's sleep and the knowledge that Paco was to be discharged home propelled Sarita's mirthful mood. She skipped down the corridor humming "Solamente Una Vez" and stopped at the nurses' station.

A late forty-something woman dressed in starched whites, looked up and asked, "May I help you?"

"Paco is going home? Dr. Rodríguez is to discharge him?"

Her name badge read: Ms. Priscilla Collins, Charge Nurse, 4-South. "You mean, Mr. Sánchez? Well we don't have orders yet. I can't discharge him without orders," she scowled.

"Well, he's going home and I'm taking him as soon as you have to get your orders," Sarita turned and disappeared down the hall.

"She's got some attitude," Collins mumbled under her breath and went back to her paperwork.

JAMES LENHART

Conversation 84
Los Angeles County Hospital
Wednesday, July 31, 2002; 8:36 a.m.

Nurse Collins glanced up from the computer screen staring blankly at Sarita. Finally, she acknowledged her, "Yes, Mrs. Sánchez?"

"He cannot walk right. I try to get him up to get dressed and he cannot walk! And his eyes, they are all funny and twitching or something," Sarita blurted.

"I'm sure it's nothing if, as you claim, Dr. Rodríguez said he is okay to go home. He has been at bed rest a long time, probably just postural hypotension."

"Postu, postu – what?" Sarita frowned.

"Postural hypotension. If you lie in bed a long time, you get low blood pressure. Makes you dizzy and lightheaded when you try to stand up. All kinds of things. Let's go look," Collins sighed, rising from her stool.

Paco sat in the bedside chair, staring forward. Sarita and Collins approached.

"*Good morning,* Mr. Sánchez," she chirped. "How are we today?"

"I try to walk, but I cannot," he frowned.

"Well let's see. Stand up and walk for me," the nurse commanded, taking his arm and pulling him to his feet. "Come on. Let's see how you do."

Paco stood and wobbled forward, his head arching back, then to the left, and then right – his torso straddled on broad-based, rubbery legs. Weaving ahead, he reminded Collins of a scarecrow.

"And look at his eyes," Sarita said.

Collins halted Paco's tilted gait, cradled his chin and gazed into his eyes. They flittered rhythmically side to side. "Hmm, I see what you mean …" she deliberated. "Well, like I said, this is probably just postural hypotension. Stand up straight, Mr. Sánchez. Keep walking until it feels normal. There ya' go. One step at a time."

"Dr. Rodríguez, Priscilla Collins on 4-South calling. Were you going to write discharge orders on Mr. Sánchez?"

"Yes. I already did and left his chart in the orders rack. I'm sending him home. Why?"

"Really? I didn't see them ... anyway, Mrs. Sánchez just had me take a look. She's all anxious he can't walk. I think it's just postural hypotension, but I would like you to check him before we discharge. Besides, I think he may have nystagmus and he says he is having some trouble with his vision."

"Nystagmus? Hmmm. Funny. He didn't have it earlier this morning. I actually didn't watch him walk though, and he didn't say anything about his vision. I'm up on 5-North. I'll come down after I finish here. It shouldn't be but a few minutes."

"Do you think this all could be malingering, just faking it?"

"Not if he's got nystagmus, can't fake that, why?"

"Intuition I guess ... and the nightshift nurse said he was talking about how his wife hates him collecting garbage."

Rodríguez frowned and shook his head. "Can't say I blame her. And I know Paco. I seriously doubt he's faking it. I'll be right down," he said and hung up the phone.

Conversation 85
Los Angeles County Hospital
Wednesday, July 31, 2002; 9:12 a.m.

Rodríguez scratched his head, "When did you first notice his trouble walking, Sarita?"

"When I get him up to get him dressed. Do you know what is it?"

"Well, I'm not certain. It could be many things. Paco, do you see anything strange? Are you seeing double?"

Paco cleared his throat and shook his head, "No ... some flickers but nothing else. Last night when I am watching the Dodgers, the players they seem very blurry and they have purple lines around them."

"How's the headache?" Rodríguez asked.

"It come and go. Right now it is better," Paco answered.

"Do you feel weak all over or just your legs?"

"My legs. And I did not know until I get up to go to the bathroom this morning and then again when Sarita try to get me up."

"You should have told me that earlier, Paco. I need to have the details," Rodríguez stated and then asked, "What about numbness or tingling in your legs?"

"Maybe a little. Yes," Paco answered rubbing first the back of his neck then his thighs. "Last night I begin to feel like I am walking on many bugs. Even if I rub my feet it does not go away."

"Really? Why didn't you tell me these things earlier, when I came in to discharge you?"

"I want to go home. Hospitals and doctors make me very nervous" Paco answered. Beads of sweat appeared on his forehead, "If you let me go home, it means that I am better."

"I can't discharge you until it is safe, Paco. How is your urine?"

Paco looked up at Rodriguez and the glare of the fluorescent lights. Wincing, he shielded his eyes and answered, "The urine is all right, I get up by myself during the night and this morning. Everything seem okay then."

"You walked to the bathroom and peed on your own?"

"Si."

"No trouble starting or stopping it?" the doctor asked.

"No problema, I tell you if I did, Dr. Rodríguez," Paco reassured him looking away.

Rodríguez took out a penlight and examined Paco's eyes. Except for the rhythmic, side-to-side flickers consistent with nystagmus and sensitivity to light, they appeared normal. "Stand up. Let me see you walk."

Paco slid down the side of the bed, put his feet on the floor, and stood holding the bedrail. Rodríguez watched Paco wobble forward. First one, then two steps, then three, then four.

"Okay. Turn around and come back."

Fixed in place, both feet planted, Paco said, "I cannot."

"What do you mean?"

"I cannot. That is all. I cannot. If I try to turn around, I am afraid I will fall. Something does not feel right."

Rodríguez extended his hands. "Let me help," he said taking Paco's arm with one hand, slipping the other around his waist, leading him back to the edge of the bed and helping him get in.

Sarita asked, "So what is it, Dr. Rodríguez?"

Rodríguez hesitated, recalling the patient he cared for during residency. Several weeks before her admission, the 71 year-old woman had received Swine flu vaccine, a public health misadventure that resulted in more deaths in the US from the vaccine than all the spontaneous cases of Swine flu combined. In 1977, Rodríguez's patient dodged the bullet of death, but spent months in a rehab ward recovering from the paralysis caused by the vaccine and the consequences of a paralytic illness called Guillain-Barré syndrome. Furthermore, she never fully recovered her ability to walk. Except for his age and gender, Paco's presentation mimicked hers to a tee. How could he tell Paco and Sarita he might *never* walk again, let alone lay another brick? He couldn't. So he said instead.

"I can't be certain – but it acts like an unusual condition caused from severe viral infections. We call it Guillain-Barré syndrome. I'll get Dr. Overstreet back in here and I'm going to call in a neurologist to take a look."

"Another doctor?" Sarita asked. "Who?"

"Jack MacDougall. He's excellent – well trained. Very smart. National reputation. Actually he's the Chief of Neurology at County Hospital and has an academic appointment at the medical school."

"Whatever you think. I have my trust in you. But you will still be his doctor?"

"Of course. Dr. MacDougall just comes in to consult and help me with Paco's case. Makes certain we're doing everything we can for him."

"Does this mean Paco cannot go home?" she asked.

"I'm afraid he can't, Sarita, not until we know more. He could get worse. Let me get the orders written," he said turning to go.

Sarita walked back to Paco, took his hand and looked into his flickering eyes. She pushed back her tears remembering what Mamacita said about Paco and the mal de ojo. Then she opened her cell phone and called Paco's uncle Raphael and his twin brother Emilio.

Conversation 86
Medical Arts Plaza, Los Angeles
Wednesday, July 31, 2002; 10:11 a.m.

Nurturing a pounding headache that sprang from too much John-nie Walker and too little restraint at O'Doul's the night before, Mac-Dougall carefully unlocked his private office entrance and crept in. His emotions reeled, thinking that the bouncer had tossed him just before Manny Ramirez hit the walk-off home run. "No way to treat a good customer," he growled again under his breath. "See if I ever go back there, you stupid bastard."

He looked up to the sound of Stephanie's footsteps and her voice, "Good morning, Dr. MacDougall," she smiled. "A doctor from Boston called. Said his name – I think Venkatesh? He asked me to give you this letter and call him as soon as you can after you read it. He empha-sized the importance at least three times," she said handing off the let-ter. "Here you go. I opened it for you already."

MacDougall cleared his throat, extracted the letter and read.

July 29, 2002

Dear Dr. MacDougall:

As president of the American Neurological Society it is my distinct pleasure to inform you that you have been chosen as the 2002 James Lawrence Wilson visiting professor in neurology. Nominated by your esteemed colleagues nationwide, your outstanding academic accom-plishments as well as unwavering commitment to the clinical practice of neurology established the basis for your selection.

The recipient of the award receives a stipend of up to $25,000 to travel to the nation's top academic medical centers during the year to interact with medical students and residents throughout the United States to stimulate the pursuit of careers in neurologic medicine. As the Wilson visiting professor, you shall role model your accomplishments as a practicing academic neurologist, effectively demonstrating the translational interface between basic and clinical neuroscience. Fur-thermore, you shall emulate the mission, vision and values of the Amer-ican Neurological Society which, as you well know, are to disseminate knowledge about the nervous system and its diseases, promote research into the causes of neurological disorders and promulgate policies that support the goals of academic neurology.

Your selection as this year's recipient will be publically acknowledged at the 127th annual American Neurological Society symposium to be held in Seattle, Washington October 6-7, 2002.

The Wilson professorship honors the life and considerable contributions of James L. Wilson, M.D. whose career exemplified extraordinary achievement as a person, physician, teacher, researcher and citizen. Your selection is indeed an honor and testament to your professional accomplishments. Let me again express my warmest congratulations.

Sincerely,

Ajay Venkatesh, MD, FACN
President of the American Neurological Society

Massaging his forehead MacDougall turned and slowly made the way back to his desk re-reading the letter, "Son-of-a-bitch," he muttered. "The Society finally got something right." Then his cell phone rang. It was Dr. Miguel Rodríguez.

Conversation 87
Rancho Palos Verdes
Wednesday, July 31, 2002; 11:16 a.m.

That same morning Judi Pinkerton sat on a chaise lounge flipping through the pages of *Vogue*. She looked up, gazing beyond the glimmer of the infinity edged pool and into the deep ravine below. Carolyn MacDougall lathered her skin with Coppertone #30 SPF. A gentle breeze out of the northwest cooled the bright summer sun piercing the azure sky. Judi lit a cigarette and broke the silence.

"You have the greatest backyard, Carolyn. The view. The privacy. It's spectacular. Just perfect."

"We like it. When Jack and I built this place Jack insisted – I mean insisted – on this location. I wanted to be closer to the schools and shopping. The price was absurd. But up high like this is wonderful and I'm with you, the privacy makes it. Nikon binoculars couldn't see in.

It's nice to sunbathe nude like this isn't it?" she chuckled. "Are you ready for another margarita?"

Carolyn's friend took a long drag from the Virginia Slim and said, "Sure, might as well. You want a cigarette?"

"Not yet. I'm smoking too much. You'll get me hooked again. Give me your glass. I'll be right back."

Judi handed her the empty glass, went back to her *Vogue*, nodded her head and said, "Like I confessed, Carolyn, smoking is one of life's simple pleasures. Lord knows being married to Edmund Pinkerton isn't one of them."

Carolyn returned with two margaritas, one in each hand. Judi looked up to the sound of her flip-flops flapping against the Kool Deck and closed her magazine. Carolyn handed off the refilled concoction, set hers on the end table and sat back on her lounge.

Judi exhaled the last smoke of her cigarette and snuffed it out, "I made an appointment with Alexandre."

"Really? When?"

"The twenty-third I think. Something like that. I figured I better do something before these puppies head any further south. Can I tell him I want beautiful boobs just like yours?"

Carolyn MacDougall frowned, "First off, Judi, you are beautiful just the way *you are* – I wish you would stop putting yourself down – but tell him anything you want. Did you know his name is really Alexander? Jack thinks he must have changed it to convey panache."

"How did you find out?"

"Easy. The degrees on the walls in his office. They all say 'Alexander' with an '-er' not a '-re.' He went to Stanford too," she reminded her. "Hey, I'll take that cigarette now."

Judi handed her the Virginia Slims and her lighter and took the first sip from margarita number three. Between the summer sun and the agave, she felt a nice buzz. Another of life's simple pleasures she thought. "What's in a name, Carolyn? If he can reproduce on me what you've got, I'm happy."

"Thanks. You'll like him I promise. Ed will too," she said exhaling the smoke.

"Baloney. If I get a pair of those they won't be for Edmund M. Pinkerton. Not to look, not to touch, not to kiss, not to feel. When he was in medical school I thought he was so cute. Now? I know it sounds awful, and it's terrible to admit, but the fat bastard turns my stomach. Pink and puffy. He's bald and got so much weight I can hardly be with him and you know what else? This is really awful ... he smells half the time," she pushed back her tears. "I can't stand it. He breathes so heavy, too."

"Sounds like you're considering an exit strategy."

Judi lit another cigarette and took a long drink from the margarita "Believe me, I would if I could, Carolyn," she shook her head. "I would if I could," she said again, looking up and staring out over the infinity edge.

"Why not? Golden handcuffs?"

Carolyn's friend hesitated, "Maybe. Possibly ... probably."

"That's bullshit, Judi. A lawyer's brief cuts like a surgeon's scalpel. Razor sharp words slice through anything. And a good lawyer works like a great plastic surgeon – you never know it happened. I've thought about leaving Jack a hundred times – except for the kids. He is such a prick," she said looking at Judi over the rim of her sunglasses and licking the salt off the edge of her glass.

A gust of wind whipped the pages of Judi's *Vogue* and blew Carolyn's sun visor off her head. She jumped up and retrieved it from somersaulting across the pool deck. Pulling the visor over her brow, she returned, sat back on the lounge and asked, "Could you rub some Coppertone on my back? I feel the sun."

Judi reached for the suntan lotion, squirted a dollop in her hand and said. "Sure. Roll over Beethoven and scoot to the other side of the lounge."

Carolyn dragged from the cigarette, put it out and turned onto her stomach. Judi moved to the edge of Carolyn's lounge and began slowly massaging the lotion over her shoulders and onto her back. The gentle touch and cool lotion soothed Carolyn's hot skin. "Umm. That feels good. When you're done there put some on the back of my legs too."

"So you and Jack fight a lot?" Judi asked.

"Fight? No, we never talk. He works, comes home from the hospital – if he doesn't have a meeting, which he frequently does – we have dinner and I watch Jeopardy. He sniffs cognac and smokes Cuban cigars out on our balcony. I go to bed. Sometime later he follows."

Judi finished her margarita and continued with the Coppertone. "What about sex?"

Carolyn snickered, "That would be *never*. Jack lost interest eons ago. In the last five or six years – actually God knows how long – if we do have it, I'm the one to initiate it. I thought getting my boobs done would perk things up, but it didn't. It takes me forever to get Jack up, and then – bingo! – he loses it. I sometimes wonder if he's not got real problems with erectile dysfunction and maneuvers in every way he can to avoid confronting it."

"Really, how fascinating. You're so beautiful. I'd think he would be all over you."

"Thanks, but not hardly. Too much marital history I guess. From what I read it's not unique."

"Well, if it's any consolation, me and Ed too. Not for a long time. But like I said he's gotten so big. Ugh! Sometimes I miss it – not with Ed – I miss having *sex*" she said, then asked. "You ready for your legs?"

"I am. This feels nice. You're a natural Judi … being touched is important – I think – don't you? Maybe we should find us a gigolo," she laughed and continued. "I've been reading this fabulous book – *Touch for Life* – Sabrina Szczerbiak. She's a neuro-endocrinologist or something like that. In fact, she was on Oprah with Dr. Phil. Anyway, she researched white guinea pigs. She touch deprived what she labeled the control group and touch enhanced the experimental group – she called them 'touch rich'. The touch *deprived* guineas ate more, gained weight, developed high blood pressure *and* diabetes. The touch rich group ate less, maintained their pre-study weight and consistently mated."

Judi applied the Coppertone with light, linear strokes over the length of Carolyn's thighs and smirked "Really? Interesting. No wonder I can't lose this weight."

"Well *it is* interesting. There's more. Szczerbiak of course wondered what her research meant for humans, so she randomly selected two groups and labeled one as touch deprived – made no change in usual routines or lifestyles – and the other touch rich. The touch rich group received Tantric massage by the same certified therapist twice weekly. Like the white guineas, the touch deprived humans gained weight, developed high blood pressure, diabetes *and* – listen to this – the men more often reported erectile dysfunction and women more often reported anorgasmia."

"Serious?"

"Serious. The touch deprived men couldn't get it up; the touch deprived women couldn't get it off!"

"Wow."

"I know. The touch rich group *lost* weight, reported greater satisfaction with their partners, had enhanced quality of life and less depression. She also demonstrated higher levels of testosterone, estrogen, human growth hormone and endorphin production in the touch rich group."

"That's amazing," Judi said taking a drink from Carolyn's margarita. "Want me to rub some lotion on your bottom?" Judi asked squeezing more Coppertone from the bottle and spreading it on her friend's buttocks before she had time to answer.

"Why not? Ummm ... feels really nice there," Carolyn giggled. "Let's forget shopping and just stay here all day. Jack's likely got some meeting tonight and won't be home for dinner anyway."

"If I drink any more margaritas I'll need to take a cab home," Judi whispered. "So you like this?"

"Um-hmm. I do. I like it a lot," Carolyn sighed.

Judi felt her pulse quicken, a surge between her legs and fullness in her throat. Carolyn's skin felt so soft; so supple. Could this be another of life's simple pleasures, she wondered? Her trembling thumbs nudged at the space between Carolyn's thighs. Hoping Carolyn wouldn't resist, she probed ever so slightly, drawing concentric circles near the deeper, delicate tissues. When Carolyn cleared her throat, arched her pelvis and spread her legs, Judi's heart jumped. Not once, but twice. Everything was visible and Carolyn was wet. "Oh my goodness gracious," a voice in her head said.

Although she could hardly breathe, Judi's fluttering fingers slid closer, ever so nearer Carolyn's labia. "Is this okay?" her voice quivered.

"Shhhh – don't talk – do," Carolyn groaned.

So Judi Pinkerton, wife of Dr. Edmund M. Pinkerton, took a deep breath, placed the fingers of both hands on Carolyn's buttocks and with trembling thumbs spread her friend wide. Carolyn did not resist. In fact, Judi thought she heard her moan.

Splayed open, the delicate folds of Carolyn's labia minora were red hot and swollen. Although from nursing school Judi knew the parts by heart, now, for the very first time, she studied them – the generous labia majora, its adjacent minora, the introitus, Carolyn's urethral opening, and of course her clitoris – drenched in succulent, sexual sweat.

Like dew on a summer's rose.

Judi's heart raced. Mesmerized, she couldn't take her eyes off of it. Like this, it was the most exciting – if not the most enticing – thing she had ever seen. Then, without warning, her thumbs began to move. "Oh ... my ... God" she whimpered. But she couldn't stop. And as her thumbs rolled toward Carolyn's clitoris she panted, "I think I need ... another ... margarita."

"What?"

She cleared her throat, caught her breath and whispered again, "I need another margarita."

"What? Why now? I like this," Carolyn whispered.

Embarrassed, Judi Pinkerton dillydallied. She didn't dare admit it, but instinct told her. Carolyn's nectar and Patrón tequila would pair well together. "I just need one. That's all," she shrugged.

Conversation 88
Los Angeles County Hospital
Wednesday, July 31, 2002; 1:09 p.m.

Paco was sleeping like a baby when Dr. Jack MacDougall pushed through the door without knocking, "Hello, I'm Dr. MacDougall. Chief of Neurology at County Hospital and Director of the University's Neurology Institute. Dr. Rodríguez asked me to evaluate your ... you are, Mrs. Sánchez?"

The unannounced intrusion startled Sarita, but she regained her composure and said, "Yes, I am Paco's wife. And what is your name?"

"I'm Dr. MacDougall. Dr. Rodríguez wanted me to evaluate your husband."

MacDougall looked over at Paco and approached the bedside. Paco rubbed the sleep from his eyes, yawned and stretched his arms above his head, "I am sorry. I was sleeping. It feel very good," he yawned again.

"No problem. Sleep is the best medicine for most illness. Let's take a look. Follow my fingers, Mr. Sánchez. Boy, Rodríguez is right. You do have full-blown nystagmus. Let's get you up and check for ataxia too."

"For what?" Sarita asked.

"Ataxia. Means unsteady gait. Up, up, up, Mr. Sánchez," he commanded, pulling Paco to sitting, feet dangling at the edge of the bed. "Stand up."

Paco slid down the side of the mattress and tried to stand but couldn't.

"Try it again. Slower this time. Hold both my hands, let's go."

MacDougall held Paco's hand walking backwards, urging Paco forward, "Can you lift your feet?"

"Come on Paco, lift your feet," Sarita coaxed.

Try as he might Paco could at best manage a wide-based shuffle. Bent at the waist, tilted forward, sliding his feet herky-jerky, he looked decrepit – the caricature of a hunched up, little old man.

"That's enough," MacDougall declared.

Helping Paco back to bed, he completed his exam and spoke again, "What kind of work do you do, Mr. Sánchez?"

"I'm a brick mason ..."

"But there is no work and he is picking up the garbage," Sarita interrupted wiping her eyes.

"Garbage man? Hmmm. I see. Anyone else at work sick?" MacDougall asked, simultaneously making notations in Paco's chart.

"Not that I know," Paco answered.

"Okay, here's how I put this together. Post-infectious polyneuropathy secondary to viral meningitis. It's quite common actually. Sometimes comes in epidemics. In medical school we studied the Swine flu vaccination disaster of 1977 or '78 – I can't remember which – I wasn't there. Big deal nationally though. People up in arms over flu shots and such. Of course, from a healthcare standpoint, vaccinations represent one of the major advances of the 20th Century. No doubt about that ... Mr. Sánchez, any immunizations recently?"

"No."

"What do you mean post-infected poly whatever?" Sarita asked.

"Oh, it's the same thing as Rodríguez told you – Guillain-Barré syndrome. I am certain of it. Look. I graduated from Johns Hopkins, did an Internal Medicine residency at Harvard – the Mass General to be exact – and a neurology fellowship at Washington University. We saw this stuff all the time."

The educational pedigree MacDougall boasted meant nothing to Sarita, "That is very good but how do you treat this thing you call Guillain-Barré?"

"Well just to make absolutely certain of the diagnosis, I need to run some more tests first, another spinal fluid, an MRI to rule out reversible posterior leukoencephalopathic syndrome and I want Dr. Overstreet to come back and see him once more," he smiled. "Then again, if it is Guillain-Barré syndrome not much we can do but wait it out. Used to use plasmapheresis – still do in severe cases – but I don't like it; too many possible complications. I don't think we'll need it here. Any questions?" he asked moving toward the door.

Dumfounded by his jargon and hubris, Sarita stared through MacDougall, "What about his vision? He cannot ..."

"Okay. Good," Dr. Jack MacDougall broke in. "I'll be back later, Mr. Sánchez," he promised, and disappeared.

Conversation 89
Los Angeles County Hospital
Wednesday, July 31, 2002; 3:44 p.m.

Jack MacDougall cradled the cell phone in the palm of his hand, looking around impatiently while it rang. When a voice finally came on

189

he said, "Overstreet, Jack MacDougall here. I tried to call Rodríguez, but couldn't get him. I saw your patient Sánchez. Complicated history. After talking with Priscilla Collins, I thought he could be malingering too, but the nystagmus rules that out. Nobody can fake nystagmus. Besides the ataxia is reproducible.

"Listen, in addition to the post-viral polyneuropathy, I worry the virus could be herpes. Obviously, I can't rule it out until we do another spinal tap and culture for it. In the meantime, I am going to get an MRI and start acyclovir if that is okay with you."

Overstreet paused, then said, "Well, sure, you're the expert on this Jack."

"Well, you're the infectious disease guru. I wanted to run it by you. Could you dose the acyclovir and order it. I don't like that stuff."

"No problem. Easy. 70 kilogram man, 20 milligrams per meter squared, peak and trough acyclovir levels. I can do that blind folded."

"Excellent. Thanks, Charlie."

"Hey, listen," Overstreet interjected, "I thought post-viral polyneuropathy didn't manifest for two or three weeks after the acute episode?"

"It usually doesn't, but I have seen it like this too. At the Mass General, we saw everything. My mentor Petersdorf wrote the book on this," MacDougall boasted.

"Okay. Charge ahead, Jack." Overstreet said. "Oh, by-the-way, will you call Rodríguez again?"

"Sure, why?"

"When I finished my exam this morning, Mrs. Sánchez went off on this harangue about so many tests, too many doctors, blah, blah, blah. Then she says they have some sort of special relationship with Rodríguez. Says he is their family doctor and wants him in on everything."

"The warm and fuzzy family doc … okay, whatever."

"Yeah, right. Will you call him?" Overstreet asked again.

"Sure, I'll call him. Mrs. Sánchez needs to understand who calls the shots and who writes the orders. Too many cooks spoil the proverbial broth, Charlie. I'll take care of it," MacDougall assured his colleague.

Conversation 90
Los Angeles County Hospital
Wednesday, July 31, 2002; 4:12 p.m.

MacDougall dialed the phone. It rang twice. "Rodríguez, Dr. Jack MacDougall here. I saw your man Sánchez. Very sick guy. This could be herpes encephalitis with superimposed post-viral polyneuropathy."

"Guillain-Barré."

"Exactly. Listen this is getting pretty complicated and I don't want everyone and his brother writing orders. So for the acute phase, I would like you to leave the management to Charlie Overstreet and me."

Rodríguez winced, looked up at the ceiling and then down to the floor. "Sounds like Lidocaine."

"Lidocaine?"

"Yeah, Lidocaine. When I was a resident, my hotshot medical professors busted my balls if I didn't bolus a hundred of Lidocaine and hang a four milligram drip on every patient with chest pain. Twenty years, and thousands of patients later, that dogma went down the toilet. Went down the proverbial toilet when we discovered Lidocaine improved the rhythm strip but killed the patient. We treated the sign, not the patient, Jack."

MacDougall couldn't believe his ears. Cocky little Mexican motherfucker. "Lidocaine not-with-standing, I need control of the patient, Dr. Rodríguez."

"But he is *my* patient. I'm *their* family doctor. I deliver their babies. I take care of them – and their kids – when they are well and when they are sick," Rodríguez scowled.

"I'm sure. That's nice, but this is serious and I don't want the left hand not knowing the right hand."

"Serious? Who says I don't treat serious?" Rodríguez said to himself. He wanted to tell MacDougall to go fuck himself but deliberated, thought better of it and said instead, "How about this. Any orders I write, I'll ask them to call you for agreement."

"That can work."

"And keep me in the loop for any changes," Rodríguez insisted.

MacDougall pondered, then acquiesced, "Sounds good."

"What an asshole," Rodríguez thought, then changed the direction of the conversation. "By-the-way, do you think this could be some unusual strain of E. coli?"

"E. coli? Why?"

"The course is unusual."

"What do you mean?" MacDougall asked.

"Guillain-Barré usually comes two to three weeks after the acute infection. He is still febrile. Besides, as a garbage man, he must to be exposed to some bizarre strains of bacteria."

"I've seen it all over the place. At the Massachusetts General, we saw everything. Petersdorf was my mentor. As you must have learned, he wrote the book. Besides, the cultures didn't show any bacteria."

"I know. Just wondering. Just thinking. Something here is not two plus two equals four."

"Well don't you worry about it, Rodríguez. We'll get this thing straightened out," MacDougall patronized. "In the meantime Miguel, why don't you leave the thinking to the specialists?"

Conversation 91
Los Angeles County Hospital
Wednesday, July 31, 2002; 4:17 p.m.

"Dr. Charles Overstreet speaking."

"Charlie? Good. Jack MacDougall here. So I got Rodríguez straightened out. Sometimes I wonder. Hey listen. I was just thinking. Do you suppose Sánchez could have some sort of bazaar strain of E. coli?"

"E. coli? The cultures are no growth. This all points to viral, Jack."

MacDougall scratched his forehead, "Just trying to think of everything. You know – a complete differential diagnosis. As a garbage man he must be exposed to some pretty wild microbes."

"Good thought but ..."

"How about I add polymerase chain reaction to E. coli on the spinal fluid?" MacDougall suggested.

"That's fine. Might as well add for Herpes, Cytomegalovirus and Streptococcus too. Along with the E. Coli that should cover everything infectious."

"Good. Great. Thanks, Charlie. As always I appreciate your help. Listen. I've gotta' run. I thought I'd get to Sanchez's spinal tap this afternoon, but if I do I'll be late for a special executive council meeting," he fibbed.

"It would be nice to have the tap done today. But he's covered for everything so I guess it won't hurt to wait until tomorrow."

"I appreciate that. You've dealt with Pierpoint. He'll cut my nuts off if I'm late. You got the acyclovir ordered?"

"I did. All buttoned up."

Conversation 92
Los Angeles
Wednesday, July 31, 2002; 4:33 p.m.

MacDougall slipped behind the wheel of his Mercedes S600. After a year, the leather interior still smelled new. Better than a Bolívar Belicosos Finos he thought. With the July temperature at 97 degrees and the late afternoon sun penetrating the windshield, the heat in the sedan's cabin suffocated him. He loosened his tie and turned the ignition on the V-12 bi-turbo. The engine came to life, as did the air conditioning, and Jack felt instantly relieved.

He took out his cell phone, scrolled to speed dial, found the letter X and punched it. After three rings the voice answered.

"Well, hello," she whispered.

"Xenia? You knew it was me?"

"Of course. It's been two weeks, it's Wednesday and – here's the kicker that establishes my genius – your number came up on my phone. I should know *your* number by now. It's not ESP after all."

Hearing her voice aroused MacDougall. It had a hard-to-describe, sultry edge he found captivating. "You got time for me?" his voice quivered.

"I always have time for you, Dr. Ed. What time were you thinking?"

Dr. Jack cleared his throat, looked at his watch and said, "Say an hour – 5:30 or so?"

"That should work. You sound anxious or nervous or something. Anything wrong?"

193

What is it about this woman Jack wondered? She may not have ESP – she's really nothing but a high-class whore – yet she can tell by my voice my very mood, my every emotion. Carolyn just wants my money and her lifestyle – and the kids of course – selfish bitch. No time for Jack. Carolyn wouldn't know if I felt anxious or nervous or depressed if she were standing in front of me. Nor would she care. She'd look right past it. *She* didn't have to slave over anatomy and physiology and biochemistry in medical school. Oh, yeah. She supported me through residency, but *she* wasn't on call every third night, drunk out of her mind for lack of sleep. Sure, she loves the money. Who wouldn't? But no time for old Jack. Not even a decent blowjob once in a blue moon. No time for Jack. After Johns Hopkins, Harvard and Washington University, I deserve more. No time for Jack. No time to understand what it's like to treat complex patients day in, day out. Put up with their incessant whining and demands. Get up early. Sit and listen to the never-ending, God-almighty depressing stories of worn-out Alzheimer's caregivers. Come home late. Go back to the hospital in the middle of the night. Then run an office. Coddle the nurses' antagonism toward the receptionists and the receptionists' acrimony toward the nurses. Deal with absenteeism. Fight to get money in the door. Make pay-roll every two weeks. Keep expenses in check. Battle with Medicare and the insurance companies to get a fair shake on reimbursement. Re-negotiate the lease. On and on. What the fuck does Carolyn know ... or care? Selfish bitch. A life like this deserves – no, is entitled to – some relief. Carolyn-my-bitch-wife just doesn't get it.

This woman does.

"Dr. Ed?"

"Oops! I'm sorry. Daydreaming I guess. Can you get Henri to come over too?" he stammered.

"Whoa! That's pushing it. I don't even know if he's available. Am I enough if he isn't?" she asked.

"Of course, you know that," he apologized. "He just adds another dimension to the tryst. Spices it up so to speak ..."

"You probably want candles and a movie too," she laughed. "Tell you what. Be here at 5:30. I'll call Henri and we'll go from there. How does that sound?"

"Perfect. See you at 5:30," he said pushing the shifter into drive and heading back to the office to freshen up with a quick shower.

Conversation 93
Los Angeles County Hospital
Wednesday, July 31, 2002; 4:36 p.m.

Sarita sat drumming her fingers on the arm of the chair, staring out the window. Her nerves had the better of her appetite. She knew she needed to eat even if she wasn't hungry, but Dr. MacDougall said he was coming back to do the spinal tap and she didn't want to miss him. She looked at her wristwatch again and wondered what could possibly be keeping him.

Conversation 94
Los Angeles
Wednesday, July 31, 2002; 4:39 p.m.

At the next red light MacDougall lifted his cell phone off its cradle and speed dialed his wife, Carolyn.

"Hello."

"It's me."

"I know. Your number came up on the phone. How are you?"

"Busy day as usual. Tired actually. I've got a sick guy in the hospital. He's only 27 or 28 or something. Looks like he has Guillain-Barré."

"That's not good. Is it a bad case?"

"They're all bad. What are your plans for dinner?" Dr. Jack Mac-Dougall retorted.

Is that what I'm good for Carolyn wondered? She wanted to say "bumps on a log" or "hot dogs and potato chips" or "Chef Boyardee" but instead answered, "I haven't decided yet. Judi Pinkerton has been here all afternoon. We've had a fabulous day together. *What time will you be home?*"

MacDougall took a breath, "Pierpoint called a special medical executive committee meeting for six o'clock."

"Again? This is ridiculous," she bristled.

"You read the papers Carolyn," he snapped. "The hospital's financial situation is dire. It's the medical staff's responsibility to help the CEO dig it out of the hole. They could close the place if we don't come up with a solid strategic plan."

"There's always something," she countered. "So when will you be home?"

"Probably around eight or so."

Carolyn looked at her watch, calculated and spoke, "Well that gives me some time. Lasagna sounds good to me. I'll get that together and have it ready when you get here. I bought a nice Bordeaux at Marché Bacchus yesterday. We can have that, some salad and a hard-crusted Italian loaf."

"Hmmm ... what Bordeaux?"

"Château La Gaffelière? I'd never heard of it, but the owner said it literally grabbed his palate when he traveled to France last year. It's a Saint Emillion 2000 Premier Grand Cru Classé – 65% Merlot, 20% Cabernet Franc and 15% Cabernet Sauvignon – he had some open for tasting. Trust me; you'll like it ... so how does lasagna sound?"

"Fabulous," Jack said pulling into his office parking lot. "Look, I'm at the hospital. I want to see my patient with Guillain-Barré again before the meeting," he lied. "I'll call you on my way home."

"Okay, see you soon," she said.

"See you soon," he said and hung up.

As MacDougall stepped from his car, a limerick written in his honor by a fraternity brother popped into his head and he began humming, "Oh, where? Oh, where? Could Jackie boy be? Oh, where? Oh, where could he be? With his eyes bugging out and his pecker so stout. Oh, where? Oh, where could he be?!"

Conversation 95
Los Angeles County Hospital
Wednesday, July 31, 2002; 5:19 p.m.

Sutherland knocked and poked his head through the door. "Mrs. Sánchez? Mr. Sánchez?"

Sarita looked up. "Hi! Come in, doctor."

"Not doctor yet," Sutherland corrected.

"Doctor to me," Sarita insisted.

"Thank you. That's nice. Someday," he paused. "How are you, Mr. Sánchez?"

Paco started to speak but Sarita interrupted.

"He is much worse. This morning I came to take him home but when I get here it is too hard for him to walk. He has to hold on just to stand up."

"I heard. Dr. Rodríguez told me he may have Guillain-Barré."

"Paco and me just do not understand this thing you call Guillain-Barré," Sarita countered. "First the doctors say he have Strep throat, then meningitis. Some say it is a virus. Then they say he does not have a bacterial. Now this Guillain-Barré."

Sutherland pulled a chair over to Paco's bed, sat down, motioned for Sarita to do the same, and said, "Let me explain, at least if I can."

The student adjusted his glasses, loosened his necktie and began, "Paco has a *viral* infection ..."

"What do you mean viral?" Paco interjected.

"Viruses are germs, Paco. They cause many infections. Viruses cause colds. A certain virus causes chicken pox. Usually viral infections make you feel bad for a few days, the body fights them off, and bingo! You're better. Sometimes they cause other effects, longer lasting effects. Have you heard of hepatitis?"

Sarita gasped, "Yes. Hepatitis is muy peligroso. *Does Paco have hepatitis?*"

"No, no, not at all, I apologize. I didn't mean to confuse you, but hepatitis is an example of a viral infection that doesn't go away, at least right away."

"Yes, I see."

"So, we think that the virus that's causing the meningitis is making the nerves in Paco's legs to go numb and his muscles to be weak. We call it Guillain-Barré syndrome, named for the doctors that first described it. We also call it post-viral polyneuropathy, which better defines it medically – 'post' meaning after, 'poly' meaning many, 'neuro' meaning nerves and 'pathy' meaning sickness. When you put it altogether, it means a condition affecting many nerves, caused by the viral infection that came before it."

Sarita frowned and hesitated.

When she didn't respond, Sutherland asked, "Doesn't make sense?"

"No, I think I understand … I think? But how long will it last? Paco's legs they are like jelly."

"We don't know. Sometimes it takes weeks to recover, then rehab."

"So what can be done? How do you treat?"

"That's not exact. Actually, we don't really know. Dr. Overstreet refuses to use steroids – he worries they might make the infection worse – but he ordered acyclovir to fight the infection, kill the virus. Dr. MacDougall rejects plasmapheresis except in the most severe cases. There is …"

"I have to have work," Paco frowned, interrupting the medical student, "I have to work. I have Sarita, Mamacita, and my children to take care of. I can fight this what-ever-you-call it, but I have to have something to make me more better."

A twitter-tweep, twitter-tweep from Sutherland's pager disrupted the conversation and cut short his explanation. "Look, I understand this is difficult," he said checking his message. "It's never easy. I'm sorry, Mr. and Mrs. Sánchez. The Emergency Room is paging me. I have to go. We can talk more later. I'll come back."

Conversation 96
Los Angeles
Wednesday, July 31, 2002; 5:21 p.m.

Jack MacDougall entered the Interstate at the 8th Avenue on ramp and pressed the accelerator. The V-12 sprang to life pulling him effortlessly to 85 mph. Heading west toward La Brea, he veered into the commuter lane, backed off the pedal and set the cruise control. Leasing this extraordinary machine ranks as one of my bright ideas he thought. Never mind it gets eleven miles to the gallon. This is heaven. And I've earned it. He turned off his cell phone, punched in Black Sabbath's "Paranoid" CD, smiled and settled back.

When he reached his destination, he parked the Mercedes, retrieved a bottle of Hanae Mori *HM* from the console, sprayed three wisps about his neck, rubbed it in and exited the vehicle. His watch read 5:33 p.m. "I wonder what she'll be wearing?" he pondered under his breath.

The doorbell rang with an alto-bass ding-dong – dong-ding. A Bichon Frise on the other side chased the sound barking incessantly. Behind the door MacDougall heard a voice, "Quincy, stop it. It's Dr. Ed. You know, Dr. Ed. He won't hurt you."

Bullshit MacDougall thought. I'd just as soon squish him as look at him.

The door swung open and there she stood – all 5 foot 11 inches of ecstasy – blond hair flowing to her shoulders, diamond earrings. She wore a black serpentine-fishnet body stocking, V-ed at the neck and open at the crotch. High heels accentuated a svelte, linear frame. Her breasts protruded through the fishnet. Now those are tits – real tits, he thought. She was the most beautiful woman he had ever seen, "Holy Christ, I'm hard already," he said to himself.

"Well, hi there," she smiled welcoming him above Quincy's barking. "Quincy, be still. Come on in."

MacDougall shoved his hands in his pockets and stepped over the threshold, restraining the deep urge to kick the white yip-yapping fur ball that danced around his legs. "Hi Xenia. How are you?" he asked.

"Good. I'm good. It's been busy. Quincy, stop it – he doesn't do this with anybody else – Quincy, be still. You're somber. Something wrong?"

MacDougall felt a pang of jealousy, "It's been busy?" he said to himself, wondering who her other johns were.

Finally, he answered, "Nothing's wrong. Same old BS. Just tired I guess. Stressful day."

Xenia led him through the foyer, down the hall and said over her shoulder, "I called Henri. He can be here at 6:45 or 7:00 if that's okay? I thought we might take a candle light Jacuzzi and drink some Perrier-Jouët before he gets here. How does that sound?"

MacDougall glanced at his watch. He told Carolyn eight o'clock. This cuts it close and I don't want to hurry. I hate to hurry. Carolyn hurries. He looked back at the woman and melted. Jesus you are gorgeous, he thought. And then said to himself, "So what the hell, the Châ-teau La Gaffelière will just have to open up a little longer."

"Dr. Ed?"

"Yeah, no. Yes. That will be good," his voice quivered.

"Boy you *are* on edge today," she declared moving so close he could smell Dominique Ropion's *Carnal Flower*. "But we can fix that," she whispered. "Oooh ... *you're* hard," she smiled. "Put a thousand on the counter for me and $500 for Henri. Go to the spa, get undressed and hop in while I'm pouring the champagne. I'll call Henri and be right with you."

Conversation 97
Los Angeles County Hospital
Wednesday, July 31, 2002; 7:08 p.m.

Sarita stayed with Paco, massaging his legs and wiping his fore-head, hoping Dr. MacDougall would return to perform the spinal tap and Sutherland would come back to finish his explanation. When nei-ther showed up, and her breasts could no longer take the engorgement, she tucked Paco in and kissed him goodnight.

On her way out, the atmosphere of hospital illness engulfed her like a shroud. The elevator car and long corridors squeezed her claus-trophobic, like a cave with no end. Gray paint everywhere. Gurneys, respirators, and portable x-ray machines parked in the hallway like stal-agmites blocked her path and escape to freedom. Finally, she found the exit and pushed it open to the out-of-doors and fresh air.

Conversation 98
Marina del Rey
Wednesday, July 31, 2002; 7:32 p.m.

As Sarita Sánchez dodged in and out of traffic frantic with worry, Judi Pinkerton slid into a teal silk bathrobe. The delicate fibers of the natural fabric cooled her simmering skin. Grinning from ear to ear, she rehearsed the events of the day. Was it real, or just a reverie? It came so natural. And it felt *so heavenly*. So why am I still blushing? I can't get it – or Carolyn – out of my mind. Then again, why would I want to? At long last, *I'm alive!*

Carolyn liked it too, Judi knew. They had played all day like voracious virgin nymphs – exploring, touching, smelling, tasting, moaning – and then Jack called, pissing Carolyn off and spoiling everything. But there would be more times. Judi knew that too. The door was cracked and opened wide.

She thought about taking a bath, but blushing, reconsidered. Carolyn's sex lingered over all of her body, down into her pores and she liked it there. No, she adored it *there*. No, not tonight. Tomorrow would be soon enough for bathing.

She crawled into bed, thinking. With a friend like Carolyn MacDougall, maybe I could put up with being married to the fat bastard Ed Pinkerton. Maybe I wouldn't need that lawyer with the sharp as a razor legal brief. We *have* been through a lot together, Ed and I. I like his money. What's more with a friend like Carolyn, I don't have to be – what had she called it – touch deprived?

It wasn't infidelity.

"Or was it?" she wondered.

And then, Judi Pinkerton fell fast asleep contemplating what Sabrina Szczerbiak, author of *Touch for Life*, would say about that?

Conversation 99
Bellflower
Wednesday, July 31, 2002; 7:43 p.m.

"Mamacita, Paco cannot walk. He cannot walk. Today he knows where he is, but now he cannot walk. Everyday something different! Yesterday he does not know where he is! Today he knows where he is, but he cannot walk! Oh, Mamacita, I'm so worried, he *cannot* walk," Sarita exclaimed, sinking into the chair, opening her blouse, and exposing an engorged breast for Angelina.

Mamacita merely grunted. To be sure, Paco's inability to walk troubled her. It *was* not good, but what of his eyes? Was he seeing things? If he was, what was he seeing? Were the colors vivid and bright or were they gray, turning black? Were there multiple images or just a single vision? Did they move around him, or toward him? Did they talk to Paco or were they silent? Mamacita knew that *how* the mal de ojo swarmed over Paco's sickbed prophesized the lurking danger and foretold if evil spirits wanted her son. But Sarita had admonished her the evening before and, actually, Mamacita didn't want to hear the answers, so she avoided the questions. Instead, she looked askance, shook her head and handed Angelina off to Sarita.

Angelina suckled hard, not letting up until she emptied her mother's swollen breast. Sarita watched Angelina gain vitality and strength from the milk. "What a miracle," she whispered. "If only I could bring Paco back to life like this. If only it was so simple."

On the second breast, Sarita and Angelina fell fast asleep. At nearly mid-night she woke up, fed Angelina one last time, and then trudged off to bed for the night. For the life of her, she didn't have the heart to tell Mamacita that Paco was seeing things.

Conversation 100
Los Angeles County Hospital
Thursday, August 1, 2002; 8:27 a.m.

At the very moment Dr. Charles Overstreet entered the room, Paco reached for the water on his bedside table, knocked it off and spilled the entire pitcher on the bed, the linens and the floor.

"MOTHERFUCKER!" he shouted.

"Paco, do not use those words. I will clean it up and get more. Do not worry, it is okay," Sarita said.

"Motherfucker," Paco said again, pushing the wet linens to the side.

"Paco!"

"Sarita, I cannot help it. I have got no strength. I cannot walk. My motherfucking head it is pounding again."

Overstreet steered the conversation in a different direction, "Did they give you something for the pain?"

"Yes, but whatever it is, it does hardly nothing."

Overstreet approached Paco's bedside avoiding the spilled water. He put his stethoscope to Paco's chest, and said, "Take a deep breath,

Mr. Sánchez. Good. Again. Once more," he said, moving the device across his skin.

"So the headache's bad again?" Overstreet asked.

"It gets worse again in the night. The nurse she gave me something but it does not go away, no matter what. It hurts so very bad."

"Where does it hurt?"

"Mostly here," Paco said pointing to his forehead, just between his eyes.

"What does this do?" Overstreet asked, placing his hand behind Paco's head and flexing it forward.

"Son-of-a-bitch," Paco exclaimed, pushing Overstreet's hands away. "That hurts like a motherfucker."

Sarita shook her head, "Paco! Please! I ask you not to use those words."

Overstreet deflected Paco's comment and instead whispered, "Hmmm ... strange. What's going on here?"

"What?" Sarita asked him.

"Nothing, really. Just thinking out loud," Overstreet answered. "I do it all the time. It's a fault of mine I guess."

Overstreet stood erect, rubbing his chin, "How about your vision, Paco?"

Paco squinted at the objects in the room, then out the window and back at the television, "Today it is more better ... but the light it hurts my eyes."

Overstreet made some notes in Paco's chart and then finished his exam, testing Paco's reflexes, vision, and sensation, "So. Can you walk for me?"

"I cannot. I try this morning. I try this morning, but I cannot walk. I even have to use the piss bottle. I cannot get to the bathroom."

Overstreet glanced out the window and sighed, "Okay. Well look. You have this meningitis-encephalitis thing. We have you covered with antibiotics and antivirals. Dr. MacDougall and I want to get another spinal fluid and you're going down for an MRI this morning. Actually, the nystagmus looks to be a little less, and you think your vision is better, so that's good. All in all, I think you are improving. I will order something stronger for the headache …," he said looking back at Paco. "Any questions?"

"They already did the MRI," Sarita interjected.

"When?"

"I go down this morning," Paco said.

"Great. Then we'll have the results. Any other questions?"

"But he cannot walk at all today. He got out of bed yesterday. Today he cannot do nothing. I do not see how you say he is improving …"

"Sarita, please," Paco interrupted.

"Well how is it that you are better, Paco!" she shouted.

Overstreet cleared his throat and interjected, "Subtle clues, experience. His fever is down. The cultures are negative. The other tests are coming back normal. He looks better. I understand how you feel. Don't be alarmed. I'm certain Dr. MacDougall will be in to confirm my opinions as well."

Conversation 101
Los Angeles County Hospital
Thursday, August 1, 2002; 9:02 a.m.

Overstreet dropped Paco's chart on the nursing station counter and sighed, "What an ordeal. This guy is a mess."

"Are you sure? I understand he has nystagmus and all but, I'm still not certain he's not faking the walking symptoms to get disability," Priscilla Collins incriminated, then leaned over and whispered in Overstreet's ear, "Of course I would never say this to Dr. Rodríguez, but I've seen it before with these good-for-nothing Mexicans. You know how they live, always looking for some welfare or a hand out. And she's pregnant again!"

"You're kidding me?"

"No I'm not – you know how Mexicans are."

"Maybe you're right. Nothing fits. It's too bizarre. See what you can dig up for me."

Conversation 102
Los Angeles County Hospital
Thursday, August 1, 2002; 9:34 a.m.

Dr. Rodríguez entered hospital room 413. "Good morning, Sarita. Good morning, Paco. How are you feeling today?"

Paco looked up, squinting at Rodríguez. "The headache it is very bad."

"And look, Dr. Rodríguez, I just noticed he have this rash," Sarita said, pulling back Paco's bedclothes.

Rodríguez took out a penlight and moving his fingers across his skin, examined the red blotches on Paco's chest, arms and legs. "When did you first see this?"

"Just now. I was washing him. He did not have it when Dr. Overstreet examine him earlier."

Rodríguez pressed on the spots and lifted his finger observing the color changes. "Hmmm. Well, your fever is down, Paco. What about walking?"

"I cannot. I try to get up to go to the toilet this morning, but I have to use the piss bottle."

"Dr. Rodríguez, he cannot get out of bed. Not at all," Sarita said.

"Bend your knees, Paco, and push against my hand."

Try as he might, Paco couldn't satisfy either request.

"Try this. Push your toes against my hand."

Nothing.

Rodríguez lightly walked his fingers across Paco's foot, "Do you feel this?"

Paco looked down, "No. It is all numb. I feel nothing. Before it felt like many bugs. Now I feel nothing."

Rodríguez took a safety pin from his pocket and opened it. "Close your eyes, Paco. I am going to test your response to pinprick."

Paco closed his eyes. Dr. Rodríguez gently poked the pin up and down Paco's legs. Paco neither winced nor moved. For good measure, Dr. Rodríguez jabbed the pin hard enough on the sole of Paco's left foot to draw blood. Paco neither flinched nor withdrew his leg.

Rodríguez pulled the covers back and said, "Hmm. Impressive. Any trouble breathing?"

"No."

"Dr. Rodríguez. Do you think Paco could get something like this at work, some kind of germ or something from the garbage?"

"Interesting that you would ask, Sarita. Actually, yes I do. I talked with Dr. Overstreet and Dr. MacDougall. At first they thought it a stretch, especially MacDougall, but then he agreed too. They've ordered studies for unusual bacterial strains in the blood and the spinal fluid."

"When are they going to do the spinal?"

"This morning. I saw MacDougall before I came in here. He is going to get more blood at the same time as the spinal tap and take Paco down immediately after for the MRI."

"They already did the MRI, didn't they Paco?"

"The boom, boom, clang, clang in the tube X-ray? Yes. I have that this morning. I thought with all that noise my head would explode and I feel so closed in."

"I understand it's pretty noisy and claustrophobic," Rodríguez frowned. "I'll get the results and be back later. Oh, by-the-way. Tomorrow's my last day. I'm leaving on vacation."

"What?" Sarita frowned. "What about Paco?"

"Don't worry. He will have coverage. Besides MacDougall and Overstreet are all over this. By the time I'm back, Paco will be up and about and home again."

"Dr. Rodríguez, I don't like this Dr. MacDougall."

"Uh? Oh? Why not?"

"He thinks he is some kind of big shot," Sarita answered.

"Well, he does have a national reputation, Sarita."

"Maybe he have. But not with Paco and me."

Rodríguez walked back to the nurses' station, set the chart on the counter, and began writing. Charge Nurse Collins walked up, flashed a sarcastic grin and asked, "Well what you think of our man Sánchez, Dr. Rodríguez? Pretty good actor, huh?"

"Good actor?"

"Dr. Overstreet and I were talking this morning," she said from the corner of her mouth. "This just doesn't fit. We think this is all a put-on to get disability."

"A put-on?" Rodríguez said, signing off on his note.

"Yeah, a put-on. Too many inconsistencies. Oh, he has fever and a headache, but not able to walk? Give me a break. What do you think?"

Thunderstruck by her accusations, Rodríguez slid Paco's chart into the physician's order rack, looked Collins eyeball to eyeball and countered in a whisper, "If you want my medical opinion, Priscilla Collins, I think you're full of shit."

Conversation 103
Los Angeles County Hospital
Thursday, August 1, 2002; 10:15 a.m.

MacDougall sauntered down the corridor toward Paco's room whistling Black Sabbath's "Ironman." He walked into Paco's room without knocking, carrying a spinal puncture tray and sterile gloves. His uncharacteristic bright mood lightened the gloomy atmosphere. Last night's tryst erased the dark cloud that had hung over him for days. Besides, he'd gotten home in time to enjoy the Château La Gaffelière and Carolyn's lasagna.

"Good morning, Mr. and Mrs. Sánchez. How's our Paco today?"

"Not better. He cannot walk. Not one step. And the headache is more worse."

"Is that true, Mr. Sánchez?" MacDougall asked avoiding Sarita's gaze.

"It is true. I had to use the piss bottle this morning and the headache it is very bad again."

MacDougall sighed. He had no time for this. Stephanie from the office had just called. Velma Richardson's daughter needed to talk with him *again*; his first patients were in the exam rooms. Waiting.

"Uh-huh. Well," he said glancing at his watch, "I've got to get some spinal fluid for more analysis."

"What's that?" Paco asked.

"Same as in the Emergency Room, take fluid from your back."

"He does not remember," Sarita reminded MacDougall. "He have a very high fever and he was out of it."

"Well, okay. Only takes a minute. I roll you on your side, and zip, zip, needle in, fluid out. Did you sign the consent?"

"The nurse have it already," Sarita answered.

"Good. Great. Paco roll to your side. I'll get the nurse to assist me and we'll be done in no time."

Conversation 104
Bellflower
Thursday, August 1, 2002; 11:36 a.m.

Mamacita looked at her watch and answered the telephone, "Buenas días."

"Mrs. Sánchez?"

"Si."

"Mrs. Sánchez. This is Mimi Martin telephoning *again* from Humanitarian Hospital. I am calling you about your bill. Are you going to make a payment tomorrow or am I sending you to collection?"

"Si?"

"Mrs. Sánchez, I'm calling about your bill. Do you remember I called on Tuesday?"

"No comprendo." (I do not understand).

"Is this Mrs. Sánchez?"

"Soy la madre de Paco Sánchez." (I am Paco Sánchez's mother).

"So you are not Sarita Sánchez?" Mimi Martin drummed her fingers, twirled her pen like a pinwheel, sighed and continued.

"Is Sarita Sánchez home?"

"No, no sé. Quizás si, quizás no. No sé." (No. I do not know. Maybe, maybe not. I do not know).

"I'll call back, Mrs. Sánchez," Mimi Martin winced and slammed down the phone. "Stupid flipping Mexicans. They shouldn't be allowed in *our* country unless they learn the language. If they don't or won't or can't, we should send them all back to Mexico. Every damn one of them. What difference would it make anyway? Oh, the hell with it. I need a cup of coffee," she stood up grumbling. Then she waddled her saddlebag derrière down the corridor toward the break room.

Conversation 105
Los Angeles County Hospital
Thursday, August 1, 2002; 12:19 p.m.

When Charles Overstreet returned, Sarita sat at Paco's bedside working her way through a March 1999 *People* magazine she'd stumbled upon in the hospital lobby that morning.

"Good afternoon, Mr. Sánchez. How are you feeling?"

"Not so good."

"What's bothering you?"

Paco scowled and rubbed his forehead. "The headache. The fever it ..."

"Actually, your temperature is down. Only 99 this afternoon," Overstreet reassured them. "That's a good sign – but what's this about a rash? Dr. Rodríguez and I spoke. He asked me to check it."

"It came on this morning. Dr. Rodríguez say it may have come from something on the garbage truck. Some kind of bad germ or something. Look," Sarita asserted pulling back Paco's bed clothes and pointing at his skin.

Overstreet leaned in, frowned and said, "Hmmm ... very interesting. Flat, purplish hues. Hmmm ..."

"And he still cannot walk doctor," Sarita declared. "He cannot even get out of bed."

"Still can't? Huh. Was Dr. MacDougall in?" Overstreet asked placing his stethoscope to his patient's heart, then examining his reflexes and checking his pupils.

"What's this?" Overstreet continued, palpating Paco's abdomen.

"Have you been going to the bathroom – I mean urinating?"

"I have to use that piss bottle thing."

"You mean the urinal?"

Paco scowled, "Yes, whatever it is you call it."

"When did you last pee?" Overstreet inquired.

"When, Paco, this morning?" Sarita asked.

"I do not remember," Paco said, rubbing his forehead again. "Why?"

"Well – as I examine your abdomen – I detect a full, distended bladder. You don't feel like you have to pee? This doesn't cause discomfort?" Overstreet asked, further probing Paco's abdomen.

"No, not really. I can feel nothing."

Overstreet glanced at Sarita, looked back to Paco and said, "We'll have to drain it then."

"Drain it? What do you mean, Dr. Overstreet?" Sarita asked.

"Put a catheter in his penis, let the urine out."

"Wait! No fucking way man," Paco bristled. "I have had enough. And nobody is sticking something up there."

"Paco!"

"No *fucking* way, Sarita! I am tired of something new every few minutes. You know how this has been for me with all the doctors. My head it hurts so very bad. Give me a chance. I know that I can go."

"Does it have to stay in?" Sarita asked.

"We can just do an in and out, see if this is just a matter of a temporary reflex sympathetic dystrophy or true paralysis ..."

"Reflex sympathy? What you call it?" Sarita shook her head.

"Reflex sympathetic dystrophy. It's kind of hard to explain in layman's terms. In these cases, sometimes the nerves that trigger the bladder to empty don't fire. The urine fills up; can't empty. Often just draining it once is all that we need to get it working again. Okay, Paco?"

"I say no way. I can pee on my own," he said shaking his head.

"Just slip it in, drain it, and take it out?" Overstreet deliberated summing up the situation. "In point of fact, I don't recommend waiting, Paco. This could make the infection worse. Your bladder could even burst," Overstreet warned. "Besides with the paralysis in your legs I doubt you will even feel it."

"Paco, you have better let them."

"No way. Let me do it on my own," he pleaded.

"Paco," Sarita began to cry. "Please, I cannot stand this. Please do what Dr. Overstreet ask."

Paco looked over at Sarita. Tears running down her cheeks.

"Okay, okay. But only the motherfucker in and the motherfucker out! I do not want to have it left in. You are not going to leave it in. No fucking way."

"Paco!" Sarita sobbed, "Please. They have to do what they have to do."

Conversation 106
Los Angeles County Hospital
Thursday, August 1, 2002; 1:00 p.m.

Dr. Rodríguez sat writing his note when Overstreet, sitting in a nearby chair, wheeled next him.

"So what do you think, Charlie?" Rodríguez asked.

"Collins had me believing the preposterous idea he was scamming us to get disability. But his bladder is distended almost to his umbilicus, his temperatures are all over the map and guess what? He looks sick; actually he looks sicker. Breaks out in sweats. Even smells sick."

"Collins laid that one on me too. I told her she was full of shit," Rodríguez growled. "So what are you calling this?"

"Well, the blood cultures and spinal fluid results are okay. There could be something in the first spinal tap, though we won't get the polymerase chain reactions back for another day or two. They've been sent to a lab in Nashville, Tennessee. The only thing that fits is viral meningoencephalitis with Guillain-Barré sequelae. That's the one single diagnosis that explains the headaches, neck stiffness, his eye movements, the fluctuating symptoms ..."

"Confusion, inability to walk, and now the rash *and* bladder paralysis?" interrupted Rodríguez.

"You got it."

"So you're the infectious disease expert. Anything to my idea of this being a bizarre strain of E. coli or some other pathogen picked up on the garbage truck?"

"It's a prudent concern, Miguel. Those studies went off to Nashville too. Maybe we will know tomorrow or Monday. In any case, he is covered for most bacteria ... at least the strains we usually deal with."

"What about the Guillain-Barré? The paralysis seems to be moving up, worsening," Rodríguez inquired.

"That's up to MacDougall. He is against plasmapheresis unless it's severe. I think he is going to start intravenous immunoglobulin though," Overstreet said.

"Hey, listen, Charlie," Rodríguez asked changing the subject, "tomorrow is my last day before vacation. Can you cover for me while I'm gone? I hate to bring in another primary when this is so complicated."

"No problem. But you know how MacDougall is. You better tell him and ask for his coverage too. I don't need him in one of his moods on this. Where are you headed?"

Rodríguez smiled, "Glacier Park up in Montana. Fly to Kalispell. Rent a car. Just 10 days, but we can't wait. It's been way too long since my last vacation. I need a break and we've never been to Montana."

"Wow! It's beautiful up there. Are you camping?"

"Oh hell no, staying at the resort on Lake McDonald. We'll do an overnight hike to Granite Falls Lodge, but no camping, my wife hates it."

"Mine too," Overstreet chuckled. "Actually I don't much like it either, especially getting my hands dirty – anyway, your time away sounds great. Don't worry. Have fun. I'll cover. But don't neglect to tell Jack you're heading out. Hopefully Sánchez will be home before you get back."

"Hopefully ... hey Charlie?"

"Yeah?" Overstreet said, signing off on his progress note.

"I'm really worried about him."

"You know what, Miguel?" he said looking up. "Me too. And somehow I don't think we've seen the last of this."

Conversation 107
Los Angeles County Hospital
Thursday, August 1, 2002; 1:56 p.m.

MacDougall pushed the door open and flew in unannounced, "Well, the MRI is normal and the repeat spinal fluid confirms that it's viral. How do you feel, Mr. Sánchez?"

"Maybe he is better," Sarita answered. "He have the catheter in and out. He say he feels a little better. Right, Paco?"

MacDougall cut Sarita off, "Mrs. Sánchez, I must ask you to let Paco speak for himself. I need to discover how he thinks he feels, not what you think or want him to feel."

Then he turned back to Paco, "So, Mr. Sánchez, what do you think?"

"Like Sarita say, I am better after the catheter, but I still have the headache and I am so weak and I have to sweat all of the time."

"Well, even though you can't walk or pee, I am encouraged by the tests. Probably sounds contradictory I realize. We saw cases like this all the time at Massachusetts General, even Wash U. Any questions?" he said grasping the doorknob.

"Oh, I started some intravenous IG for the Guillain-Barré. Should help to get things going; get the Guillain-Barré cleared up. Well, if there aren't any questions, I'm out of here. Office full of waiting patients. Okay? See you tomorrow."

And he was out the door.

Sarita took Paco's hand and slumped into the chair. She looked into Paco's eyes and squeezed his hand, "I love you."

"I love you too, Sarita," he said shaking his head.

Conversation 108
Los Angeles
Thursday, August 1, 2002; 2:38 p.m.

Sarita turned off the television and tiptoed to Paco's bedside. Looking down, she realized again how sick he was, how helpless he looked. How could it be, she wondered? Paco is so strong. Tears welled up in her eyes. When he opened his eyes she asked, "How are you feeling, Paco?"

"I do not feel so good. I think I feel more better after the catheter but I am so weak and so tired. I do not feel the bugs on my feet. But the fever and headache come back and do not go away. Do not worry, Sarita," he reassured her. "For many years I have to have surgery for when the spider it bit me. Every time it is very hard. Then one day it is over. It have to be that way with this too. I promise."

She wiped his forehead and neck with a moist washcloth, "Soon you will be home."

"How are the little niños? Have Dr. Alexandre called?"

"No. He did not call. Remember I told you we have to wait until January when he have the research money? Miguel and José, they are okay. Mamacita too. She is with them. It is just Angelina. She have trouble with the bottles and my breasts they get so full."

"They look it," Paco smiled.

"Oh, Paco, just like you. Never too sick to notice my tetas," she blushed.

"Never. You are so beautiful."

213

"And you are silly," she said folding Paco's hands between her hands.

"I am not silly. God he makes you the most beautiful woman I have ever seen. And God he gives you a beautiful heart. You are my princess and I am very lucky."

"Thank you," she blushed again. "Can I lay next to you?"

"Of course," Paco smiled.

There was little room on the narrow hospital bed. Nevertheless, she propped up his pillow and slipped in next to him, one leg dangling from the mattress. She put her arm around his shoulders and soothed his hair, humming over and over the verses to "Solamente Una Vez". As she sang, she laid her head back and closed her eyes. The peaceful melody and romantic lyrics soothed her frazzled nerves. This was the best she'd felt for days.

And then it came to her.

In a single motion, she swung her leg over Paco, straddled his hips, opened her blouse, pulled down her bra and gave Paco her dangling, swollen breast. "Take it, Paco," she blushed. "Do not ask questions. Take it. Maybe it can make you more better."

The milk ran over her fingers and down her abdomen. Paco looked into her eyes and back at her breast. At first, he licked, suckled briefly, and then, like Angelina, latched on and rhythmically drew in her milk. His sucking kindled a torrid heat that spread from her breasts, through her abdomen and down into her pelvis. She blushed again – this time from the sexual urge between her legs. "Oh, Paco," she groaned.

But guilt – fueled by twenty-six years of Catholic dogma – swarmed Sarita, suppressed the uninvited desire and she whimpered, "That's right, Paco. You take it, Paco, take it all. Take what I have to give you my dear, sweet, Paco. Take what I have and you can be more better."

Conversation 109
Marina del Rey
Thursday, August 1, 2002; 2:44 p.m.

Judi Pinkerton worried. In fact, she worried a lot. Judi Pinkerton worried when there was nothing to worry about – a character flaw she detested. Today Judi worried more than most. She'd called Carolyn MacDougall three times and left messages three times. Still Carolyn had not returned her call. Wasn't yesterday the consummation of our friendship? Didn't we bridge our bond?

She sat at the kitchen table drumming her fingers. That didn't help, so she paced the floor. Pacing was no better than drumming, so she disinfected the kitchen counter tops. When that didn't improve her frame of mind, she opened a wine cooler and smoked a cigarette. She was smoking too much. That worried her too.

Finally the phone rang. She lunged for it, flipped it open and blurted, "Carolyn?" No, wrong number.

"Shit." The agony was worse than being seventeen and waiting on drop-dead gorgeous, love of my life – I gave you my virginity for Christ's sake – boyfriend to call.

She needed some air.

Out on the patio she pondered the situation. Was Carolyn pissed off? Too penitent for words? Couldn't face the blaring trumpets of their new found pleasures? Or was she disgusted, offended, repulsed by what they had discovered? What if that's it? "Maybe she never wants to lay eyes on me again," she whispered. A tear rolled up in Judi Pinkerton's eye. She couldn't bear the anguish of that.

"Why doesn't she call?" she asked for the 400th time.

Conversation 110
Los Angeles County Hospital
Thursday, August 1, 2002; 2:48 p.m.

"Holy crap!" red faced Priscilla Collins blurted out, throwing Paco's chart on the desk. "Now I've seen it all. I go into Sánchez' room and there they are in bed together and he's sucking on her tits."

"You've never caught couples doing that before?" the ward clerk countered, "I thought you knew. Patients have sex in their rooms all the time."

"This wasn't sex. It was as if she was breastfeeding him! And she had the where-with-all to tell me to leave. She is too much. I swear. Get the social worker on this case and get those two the hell out of here. I have no tolerance for that kind of monkey business on my floor."

CONVERSATIONS FOR PACO

Conversation 111
Los Angeles County Hospital
Thursday, August 1, 2002; 2:53 p.m.

Sarita rolled off the bed, wiped her nipples dry and pulled Paco's covers over him. A skylark, swooping in from above, overshot the landing, hitting the window just above the sill. Sarita jumped and turned to the noise. Concerned that it might be injured, she watched the dazed bird regain its bearings while she rearranged her clothing. Then she cleared her throat, fluffed Paco's pillow, and knelt on the floor beside his bed.

First, she recited the Lord's Prayer and the Rosary. Then she closed her eyes tight and asked of God, "Dear Lord, please, I beg of you, to make my Paco better. I mean no thing bad or disrespect to you feeding Paco with my milk. Something has got to make him better. Something has got to rid him of the mal de ojo I see in his eyes. The doctors try, I know. But nothing seems to work. So I give him my milk. God, he is so sick. Please, please rush the milk from my breasts to his brain and his nerves to fight this awful sickness, just as you do with the blood and body of Christ in our communion. Dear God, make my milk the miracle that heals Paco, just as you resurrected your only begotten Son. Please, dear God, please," she pleaded signing a cross over her heart.

"In the name of the Father, and of the Son and of the Holy Ghost amen ... oh! Dear God, I pray to you for Dr. Overstreet and Dr. Rodríguez ... and Dr. MacDougall that you give to them the wisdom and the strength to make Paco better. In the name of the Father, and of the Son and of the Holy Ghost, amen."

When Sarita stood up, she found Paco. Fast asleep.

Conversation 112
Medical Arts Plaza, Los Angeles
Thursday, August 1, 2002; 3:47 p.m.

Carolyn MacDougall's appointment at the gynecologist's frazzled her nerves and consumed the entire afternoon. First, the doctor was late returning to the office from a difficult delivery and then some sort of

216

office procedure increased the delay. Carolyn sat waiting, tapping her foot and flipping through a tattered copy of Martha Stewart's *Living*. She thought about calling Judi Pinkerton, but detested people talking on cell phones in public places. Finally, the nurse called her back to the examination area.

To make matters worse, the doctor "Found a little something" on her pelvic exam that he wanted to check with the ultrasound and before she could say Kalamazoo, he had the probe stuck up her vagina, rolling it around and then back and forth saying "Hmmm ... Okay ... Hmmm."

Humiliated. Violated. Defiled.

She looked at her watch while he finished his business and asked herself again, "Why hadn't Judi called?" Then she felt the probe slip out of her orifice and heard the doctor say, "Everything's all right. Just a little fibroid. Nothing at all to worry," as he retreated from the exam room.

The gynecologist's nonchalance unglued her. The hair stood on the back of her neck; a scowl formed over the corners of her mouth. She wanted to say to the assistant, "I sat in his miserable fucking waiting room for nearly two hours, he takes three minutes to do my exam, sticks that dildo up *my whatchamacallit* with hardly a word – let alone my permission – and tells me it's just a little fibroid. 'Nothing to worry your pretty little head about, sweetheart' and then leaves without further discussion."

Pure bullshit. No different than rape.

Instead, Carolyn backed off, requested Kleenex to wipe up his mess, got dressed and left without reconciling her account.

She huffed and puffed all the way down the elevator, but on the way to her car she reflected again on the day before and began to rebound. She wondered again why Judi hadn't called. In afterthought, was Judi disgusted with their tryst? She seemed delirious before she left. So why hadn't she called? Wasn't what they shared more than sexual frolic? Then again, who was to know? Jack had called stifling everything, and Judi scampered out without much more than a blasé "Goodbye".

Carolyn got in her car, started it and with trembling hands dug through her purse reaching for her cell phone. "Why hasn't she called?

Does she never want to see me again?" When she opened the phone she breathed a sigh of mixed relief. She had forgotten to charge her cell phone. The damn thing was dead.

Conversation 113
Los Angeles County Hospital
Friday, August 2, 2002; 7:42 a.m.

When she entered County Hospital room 413 on Friday morning, Sarita discovered Paco sitting up in bed, eating scrambled eggs.

"Buenos días, Sarita."

"Buenos días," she beamed feeling certain that her breast milk had made a difference. "You are feeling better?"

"Better yes, better no. The headache is gone and my neck is not so bad, but they had to put the cath thing back in."

Sarita's shoulders sagged and the smile left her face, "The what? The catheter? Why, Paco?"

"I could not pee, and I worry what Dr. Overstreet have to say that my bladder can explode."

She looked down at the urine-filled bag dangling from the bedside. "And they left it in, Paco?"

"I asked them to. I am so worried."

Tears filled Sarita's eyes. She wiped them away and sniffled, "But you are hungry?"

"The food it tastes pretty good."

She bent over and kissed him on the forehead. "I love you, Paco."

He looked up at her and smiled, "I love you too, Sarita."

"Miguel and José say to me when I leave this morning, 'Where is Papá? When is he coming home?' I tell them soon. Miguel he say to me, 'Mama I want to read to Papá. I have for him a special goodnight story.' I laugh and say 'Papá he would like that.' You are to be so proud, Paco. They are such fine boys and they love their Papá so mucho."

Paco sighed, "Maybe tomorrow or the next day I can get out of here and I go a la casa. What about Angelina?"

"She is fine. Did you try walking?"

He shook his head, "I cannot lift my legs. The nurse had to help me sit up. I cannot walk, Sarita."

Dr. Rodríguez knocked and entered the room as Sarita finished helping Paco with his breakfast. "Good morning, Sarita. Good morning, Paco. How are you feeling?"

"I think I am finally better," Paco said.

"Excellent," Rodríguez smiled, "And I have good news. All the tests have come back pretty much negative ..."

"Negative?" Sarita broke in.

"What I mean is normal. All good. None of the bad germs like herpes, toxoplasmosis or cytomegalovirus. Your temperature has stayed below 101 for 24 hours. And the MRI, as Dr. MacDougall told you, is normal."

"So I have to keep asking what is this illness Paco have?" Sarita asked.

"The best explanation is viral meningitis with Guillain-Barré overlay, what we've thought all along. Just couldn't say for certain until today."

"Dr. Overstreet he say yesterday he have meningitis *and* encephalitis. Nobody ever say anything about this encephalitis. He left in such a hurry. I do not understand."

"It is a mixed picture, Sarita. To some extent they are very similar. The persistent headache and visual disturbances make you think encephalitis or inflammation of the brain. The neck stiffness and pain speaks more toward meningitis – inflammation of the nervous system's protective coverings. The important thing today – Paco is getting better."

"What about a germ from the garbage truck?" Sarita asked.

"Well, I talked with Dr. Overstreet about that too. Some of the E. coli tests are still out but ..."

"So it still could be?"

"Yes, it could be, but we don't think so. This isn't acting like that. Dr. Overstreet thinks we should know for certain by tomorrow or Monday."

Sarita took Paco's hand and rubbed the back of it with both thumbs. She looked down at Paco and back to Dr. Rodríguez. "And this

219

Guillain-Barré, when will Paco be able to walk? Today he cannot even lift his legs."

"Usually it peaks at two to three weeks then slowly resolves. Given he is finally feeling better; I don't see it going beyond that. He has been in bed a long time though. I am going to order physical therapy two to three times per day to help keep his joints loose and his muscles working."

"What if he does not get better?"

"He will, Sarita, I am certain. We are going to give him what we call intravenous immunoglobulin or IVIG. Dr. MacDougall only wants to use plasmapheresis if the Guillain-Barré goes up to his lungs."

Sarita frowned, "Lungs?"

"I'm sorry," he apologized. "Sometimes the paralysis can spread up as far as the diaphragm making it difficult for patients to breathe."

Eyes opened wide, Sarita wrapped her left arm around her chest, massaged the furrows in her forehead with the fingers of her right hand and asked, "You are going to wait until he cannot *breathe*?"

"No, no, no. Not at all. Plasmapheresis has complications though. Dr. MacDougall doesn't want to use it unless it is absolutely necessary. And Paco is better. Look, the nystagmus is almost gone. The headaches are better ..."

"But ..."

"If he gets any shortness of breath whatsoever, we will start the plasmapheresis immediately. Everyone is watching him very closely, Sarita. Don't worry."

"I have to worry. He is my only Paco."

"I understand and I empathize. But this takes time," Rodríguez hesitated and looked away. "Also, remember what I said. I'm leaving for vacation today ... I've signed out to Drs. Overstreet and MacDougall; they'll take great care of him until I return. And like I said, he'll be home by then."

Rodríguez answered the rest of Sarita's questions to the best of his ability. When she seemed satisfied with his answers, he bid them both farewell, reassuring them when he returned, he would follow-up with Paco. Then he made his way out of the hospital with his words ringing in his ears, *"I've signed out to Drs. Overstreet and MacDougall; they'll take great care of him until I get back. And like I said, he'll be home by then, Sarita."*

"At least I think so," he muttered to himself.

Conversation 114
Los Angeles County Hospital
Friday, August 2, 2002; 9:19 a.m.

"Well, well! Dr. Rodríguez says you are better, Mr. Sánchez. Good morning, Mrs. Sánchez," Dr. Overstreet beamed. "Finally turning the corner, eh?"

"I am better but I could not pee last night, so they put the cath thing back in."

"Let's have a look," Overstreet said bending over to examine Paco's eyes. Then rocking Paco's head back and forth he asked, "Hurt when I do this?"

Paco winced, "A little. But it is not as bad as it have been."

Overstreet straightened up, "Well, the nystagmus *is* better and your neck is less stiff and less painful. All good signs – just like Dr. Rodríguez reported."

He then reached for the stethoscope hanging around his neck and said, "Let me have a listen."

Sarita fidgeted and then impatiently declared, "He still cannot get out of bed or walk."

Overstreet put an index finger over his lips and whispered, "Shhhh. Just a second, I've got to hear."

Sarita stood patiently with her arms crossed just above her pregnant abdomen drumming her elbows with the fingers of both hands. When Overstreet removed his stethoscope, she said again, "He still cannot get out of bed."

"Well, he's so much better today. What we have is the meningoencephalitis resolving while its sequelae – the Guillain-Barré – takes hold. Nonetheless I think we will see progress with that as well in a day or two. Right, Paco?" Overstreet said patting Paco's thigh.

Paco shrugged his shoulders, "I hope so. I have to believe whatever you think. You are the doctor."

Overstreet looked at Paco, "Well I'm stopping the acyclovir, and if you're better tomorrow we will d/c the ceftriaxone. I want to get that Foley out too."

"The cath thing?" asked Paco.

"Yes, the catheter. Foleys can cause urinary tract infections, not a problem that we need and that's for sure."

Paco frowned, "If I cannot pee, and you say I can explode?"

"Not to worry, Paco," Overstreet reassured. "We'll leave it in for just another day. We'll retrain your bladder today – open and close the catheter so your bladder 'learns' to contract again. Then out it goes tomorrow. Deal?"

Paco choked. The mere thought of a stranger grasping his penis and threading a catheter up it and into his bladder again left him short of breath. But what were his options? At last he agreed, "Deal – I guess okay."

"Excellent," Overstreet reaffirmed as he turned to make his way out, "Oh, Rodríguez is going on vacation for a week or so and asked Dr. MacDougall and me to cover for him. Is that okay?"

"Of course," Sarita frowned. "What choice have we? Dr. Rodríguez have to have rest too."

Conversation 115
City Centre, Los Angeles
Friday, August 2, 2002; 12:07 p.m.

Humanitarian Hospital CEO Geoff Boyer introduced Jack Mac-Dougall as his project clinical consultant to the members of the Innovations Group. MacDougall learned that Peter Jacoby was the lead, while Frederick Donahue, James Speer, Mike Rigglesgood and Nancy Milligan played critical supporting roles in design development, architecture, construction and land acquisition. Boyer spared not a single accolade in acquainting the Innovations Group to MacDougall – medical school at Duke, Harvard residency, sub-specialization in neurology at Washington University, Chief of the Medical Staff, immediate past president of the Medical Society, esteemed member of the medical community, and former medical director of the largest multispecialty group in the city. Boyer explained that he was – of course – deeply grateful that Dr. MacDougall had taken time from his demanding patient care schedule to lend his expertise to the project. The CEO had a way with words. The members of the Innovations Group were sitting forward, listening.

"In late January or early February, Jack and I flew to Phoenix. I wanted him to see the Arizona operation, analyze and critique it. We discussed my vision and several details including the business plan. I told him I wanted a foolproof, cutting edge strategy that didn't offend the University or the private medical community. Today you will discover what he came up with … Jack."

MacDougall rose, buttoned his suit coat, pursed his lips, but didn't skip a beat. After thanking Boyer, making small talk deferent to the Innovations Group and urging them to interrupt at any time, he began.

"So on the Phoenix trip, I said to Mr. Boyer, pretend money is no object. I realize it is – it always is. But pretend for a moment it's not. Second – and please pardon the expression – screw the medical school and the privates. Given the same opportunity and the capital, they'd take Humanitarian Hospital on from the front and the rear – believe me."

The lead for the Innovations Group, Peter Jacoby smirked and leaned into MacDougall's words thinking to himself, "I like this guy. He's got balls."

MacDougall paused, took a quick sip of water and continued, "My recommendations call for four medical office buildings exact same design, built from the ground up. You can't get what you want any other way. They're located for easy freeway access and situated within each quadrant of the city no more than seven or eight miles from the hospital.

"Each building has a foot print of twenty to twenty-two thousand square feet," he continued. "The main entrance foyer serves the upper floors, but does not serve – it may sound crazy, but stay with me here – does not serve the Humanitarian Hospital multispecialty clinics.

"Adjacent to the main foyer and around the perimeter, you build three clinic clusters – one on each side and one in the rear – each with cluster designated parking, a separate entrance and reception area, each with six exam rooms served by two medical assistants and a receptionist per two doctors – three exam rooms per doc. In the center you connect the clusters with a core of support services. Billing, special procedures, radiology, lab, telecommunications, electronic health record, scheduling, phone triage, info-tech, doctor offices, conference rooms – the whole wazoo ..."

"No main reception area for the entire clinic?"

"No. Absolutely not. That tired out, unimaginative design creates nothing but bottlenecks at the beginning – and the end – of every clinic. It's crazy. Staff hate it and you all know how patients go nuts with the lineup.

"Two clusters per complex serve primary and urgent care functions ..."

"So what's in the third?"

MacDougall smiled. He had them hooked. Boyer looked satisfied too. So he continued.

"The two primary care clusters feed the money making sub-specialists, which occupy the third. And here lies the real beauty of this plan – the sub-specialists rotate from geographic location to geographic location to cover the need but avoiding the hassle – and expense – of recruiting and hiring sub-specialists for every specialty and every clinic."

Jacoby broke in, "So far I like what I hear, but I'm troubled with the main foyer concept. New patients will be drawn into the main entrance and confused when they can't find their doctor."

"Form follows function," MacDougall countered. "In the center of each main entrance foyer an attractive, well groomed receptionist meets and greets visitors, directs traffic. It's consistent with the concept. After all, hospitality and hospital are derived from the same word root. The layout I propose is consistent with Humanitarian Hospital Corporation's tag line – *Giving~Sharing~Loving~Caring.*"

Conversation 116
Los Angeles County Hospital
Friday, August 2, 2002; 3:36 p.m.

Justin Sutherland knocked and poked his head in, "Mrs. Sánchez?"

His greeting did not disturb Paco's deep sleep; Sarita looked up from the aged *People* magazine, "Buenas tardes, Dr. Sutherland!" she whispered.

Sutherland walked over to where she sat and said, "I understand Paco is better."

"Dr. Rodríguez said maybe he can go home, but I do not see how if he cannot walk. We have steps."

"Has he had any shortness of breath?"

Sarita looked over at Paco. His breathing came in deep, dream-like crescendos and decrescendos, "He has not complain of any. I do not think so."

"Listen. From everything I gather it seems that the Guillain-Barré has leveled off, and as I understand it, it is not uncommon to see recovery of its effects immediately after it stabilizes. Hopefully, in two to three days, he will be up and around."

Sarita looked over at Paco, down at the floor and back to Sutherland. Reflecting on the day before when Nurse Collins burst into his room and caught her breast feeding Paco, she blushed, cleared her throat and asked, "Dr. Sutherland, how do you get privacy here? Nurses and doctors come in and out without knocking; they just push their way in."

"Why, what do you need?"

"Nothing" her face reddened again. "I need nothing. It would just be nice if everyone have to knock like you," she responded.

"I can fix that," Sutherland declared, "I'll be right back."

When he returned, he carried a fresh sheet of pink paper, a thick point Sharpie Marks-A-Lot and some Scotch tape. On the paper he wrote: PLEASE KNOCK BEFORE ENTERING! He re-capped the pen, picked up the paper and taped it to the door. "That should help. Anything else?"

"No. I guess not. Thank you."

"Well, I've got to get back to the Emergency Department, but I'll come by again tomorrow."

"Tomorrow is Saturday."

"I'm on call. I'll be here."

"Muy bueno, Dr. Sutherland. It will be nice to see you," she said. "Adiós."

"Adiós," he smiled and was gone.

Sarita sat staring at the door and the four gray walls wishing the doctors could all be like Justin Sutherland. Then she wiped a tear from her eye, blew her nose and went back to the *People* magazine.

Conversation 117
Los Angeles County Hospital
Friday, August 2, 2002; 4:17 p.m.

Sarita walked to the nurse's station and asked, "Is the nurse Collins here?"

"Nope, went home right after her shift at three," the ward clerk responded without making eye contact or interrupting her computer tasks. "She's punched the clock."

"Oh, okay. I was just checking."

The ward clerk looked up, "Can someone else help?"

"No ... that is all right, I will find her tomorrow," Sarita said turning to walk back to Paco's room.

"She'll be here at seven," the receptionist muttered. "No, wait! Tomorrow is Saturday. She won't be in again until Monday. Are you certain someone else can't help you?"

Sarita Sánchez looked back over her shoulder. "I'm certain," she smiled and continued down the corridor.

With the back of her thumbnail she rubbed the edges of the adhesive securing Sutherland's PLEASE KNOCK BEFORE ENTERING entreaty taped on the door of room number 413. "I do not want this to fall off," she whispered. Then she entered Paco's room and secured the door behind her. She pulled Paco's privacy curtains around them, slid in next to Paco and mounted him. "Take my milk again, Paco," she urged, exposing her breast and offering it to him. "It is the only thing that makes you better."

Conversation 118
Bellflower
Friday, August 2, 2002; 9:14 p.m.

226

Much later that same evening, Sarita kissed her children, tucked them in and said goodnight to Mamacita. "Finally," she whispered to herself, "some peace and quiet." Walking back to the kitchen, she felt the baby kick for the first time. She smiled and asked herself again, "Is this el niño y la niña?" She hadn't a clue – without health insurance or the money to pay for it – she couldn't get prenatal care. And Medicaid hadn't approved her yet either.

She entered the kitchen, opened the refrigerator and took from it a bottle of Mandarin Jarritos before retreating to bed. She settled back on her pillow, flipping through a current edition of the Jalisco Banderas News to unwind. She sighed, took a sip of the Jarritos, and turned the pages. Paco's absence rattled her, but it felt good to be in bed.

The first and second telephone rings rattled her as well.

Sarita picked up the receiver, "Hello."

"Mrs. Sánchez?"

"Yes?"

"*Sarita* Sánchez?"

"Yes. This is Sarita."

"This is Elizabeth Newton calling from MasterCard."

"Yes."

"Mrs. Sánchez, I'm calling about your past due account."

"Yes."

"You're over your limit and we haven't had a payment since May."

Sarita looked at her watch and bristled. "It is 9:30 at night; why are you calling me at this late hour?"

"We *have* called. Several times during the day, you're never home."

"Paco is in the hospital. He is …"

"I'm sorry to hear that, Mrs. Sánchez, but your MasterCard …"

"Please. He is *very* sick."

"Like I said, I'm sorry to hear that Mrs. Sánchez, but your Mas-terCard – if we don't receive a minimum payment in 48 hours …"

"We do not have a minimum payment. Paco he is in the hospital. He cannot work for almost two weeks," Sarita interrupted.

"I'm sure that is hard, but this is not the first time we've warned you, Mrs. Sánchez."

Tears rolled down Sarita's cheeks and fell into her lap, "I know! But now he is sick. Do not you understand?"

"Of course MasterCard understands, but your husband's illness ... well, quite frankly, it's not our problem. To be quite blunt, Mrs. Sánchez, if we don't receive a payment in 48 hours, I will have to cancel it."

"Then you will have to cancel it," she sobbed wiping away the torrent of tears. "We uh, we uh, I ..." she gulped, "I-I-I-I uh ... do not have no money."

Conversation 119
Los Angeles County Hospital
Saturday, August 3, 2002; 9:12 a.m.

On Saturday morning Sarita hurried down the hallway with Mamacita, Miguel and José in tow. José clutched his teddy bear Maximo; Miguel carried a cluster of roses picked from home – one Dream Weaver, two Morning Magics, and a Blaze of Glory. Mamacita brought up the rear.

"Everyone. Get on the elevator; hold tight to Maximo, José. Miguel, show José what button he have to push."

"What floor, mama?" Miguel asked.

"Four. Show José four. Here, this one. You know four."

Miguel took José's finger and touched it to the button labeled 4. The number lit, the door closed. José gasped and then giggled.

"Where's Papá?" Miguel asked.

"Up here. In room 413."

"Will he remember me?" José asked.

"Of course he will," Sarita reassured as the door opened onto the fourth floor. "Come on, let's go. This is his floor."

Sarita led them down the corridor and past the nurse's station. Priscilla Collins looked up. "Mrs. Sánchez?"

Sarita turned to her left and sighted the scowling Head Nurse. The ward clerk said she wasn't working until Monday. "Yes?"

"How *old* is he?" she asked pointing at José.

"Five," Sarita fudged hoping against hope it might make a difference.

"He's too young. Children must be at least eight to visit."

"But he has not seen his father for over one week" Sarita pleaded.

"I'm sorry. Rules are rules. Infection control."

José looked up at Collins. She was big and she was mean and she was ugly. Tears rolled down his cheeks. He squeezed Maximo with both arms and cried, "I want to see my papá."

"Please, Mrs. Collins, for just a moment. Please," Sarita pleaded.

Collins hesitated. Then sighed and relented, "Okay, but for just a few minutes, and they need to gown-up."

"Gown-up?"

"Yes, infection isolation. Dr. Overstreet ordered it this morning."

"What? Why?" Sarita asked in disbelief.

"Mr. Sánchez got confused last night … spiked another temp. You'll see, come with me," Collins stood and walked from behind the nurse's station. "Oh, and I took that sign off the door. We will not have just anybody, especially medical students, deciding this and that and making the policies around here. If you need privacy for something in particular … just let us know," she said marching toward Paco's room.

Paco stared catatonic at the ceiling, not moving. Sarita led the children to his bedside. Collins followed, taking her place on the opposite side.

"Paco? Look who is here!" Sarita said.

A hiccup from deep in Paco's chest shook him, but he held his gaze, fixed on the ceiling above him.

Miguel reached above the bed, squeezed his father's hand and said, "Papá, Papá. Look! I brought you roses."

Paco hiccupped again ignoring Miguel. Then, lifting his arms, swatted furiously at the air. "¡Maldita la araña!" he choked, "¡Maldita la araña!"

"Paco!" Sarita blurted out. "Paco! What is wrong!"

Terror gripped Paco's face, "¡Maldita la araña! ¡Maldita la araña!" he shouted.

Miguel dropped the flowers on Paco's bed, turned to Mamacita, threw his arms around her legs and buried his tears in her housedress.

José slumped to the floor, squeezed Maximo, slid a free thumb in his mouth and sucked frantically.

"He's been hiccupping since early this morning," Collins explained shaking her head. "Sometimes he is like this – in a trance – staring at the ceiling, flailing his arms in desperation, shouting. Then he changes, becomes alert and talks, but still seems confused and agitated. The night nurse said he didn't sleep well ... what's he saying?"

"He says there are spiders. He is seeing spiders. Paco he hates the spiders; he says they are wicked. When he is a little boy he have a very bad experience. Where are the doctors? They should be here caring for Paco. Have they been here to see him?"

Collins covered her mouth and feigned a cough, "No. Not yet. It's Saturday. Usually they come in a little later. I paged Dr. MacDougall. He hasn't called back. Dr. Overstreet is over at Humanitarian – said he'd be here shortly."

Sarita's expression grew stern and resolute, "Call them again. They must be here."

"I did, Mrs. Sánchez," Collins lied. "We're on top of everything."

Sarita looked down at the bulging bag of urine dangling from Paco's bed rail.

"His bag is full," she trembled pointing to the Foley catheter.

Collins shoulders stiffened and she retorted, "I *know*, Mrs. Sánchez. Please leave your husband's care to us. Like I said. *We're* on top of everything. You have nothing to be concerned about. I assure you."

Mamacita stood behind Sarita shaking her head whispering, "Mal de ojo. Mal de ojo."

Conversation 120
Rancho Palos Verdes
Saturday, August 3, 2002; 9:23 a.m.

While Sarita struggled with Paco's worsened condition and attempted to calm her bewildered family, Jack MacDougall, Geoff Boyer and Ed Pinkerton rolled up to the 7th hole of the Rolling Hills Country Club golf course and got out of the cart. Boyer teed up first. Adjusting his sunglasses, he took a few practice swings, and wacked the ball 220 yards, straight down the fairway.

"Nice shot," MacDougall applauded.

Pinkerton went next. He leaned forward over his enormous belly, grunted and pushed the tee into the turf. Wrapping his arms about his huge panniculus, he gripped the club, roared back and drove the shot 60 yards beyond Boyer's.

"Wow! *You* can still play this game, Ed. Nice. My turn." Mac-Dougall declared.

"Hey, Geoff?" MacDougall asked, teeing up his ball, "I heard on NBC Nightly News that Humanitarian Hospital Corporation is in for an upside down year financially. What's the what? You told me I should be buying up the stock."

"I heard that too," Boyer smirked.

MacDougall swung, slicing his ball left. It landed with a thud 180 yards down the fairway and rolled into the rough. He shook his head in disgust, "Son-of-a-bitch. Why do I play this stupid fucking game with you assholes anyway? Let's go."

They loaded their clubs and got back into the cart. Pinkerton boarded first. Boyer stood back watching the cart lurch, tip to the left and then right itself on Pinkerton's weight. When it seemed safe, Boyer cleared his throat and got in too. "How can anyone get so fat?" he asked himself. "I think I'd kill myself first."

Making their way to Jack's ball, MacDougall brought the subject up again. "So what's the deal with HHC Geoff? The stock has lost nearly half its value in the last six months. I thought you were on a roll."

"Why are you so interested? You thinking maybe it's a buy sign?"

"Maybe. Maybe not. As I told you, I don't have any HHC stock in my portfolio."

"Perhaps you should," Boyer grinned. "Look. You both know the situation with Medicare and Medicaid reimbursements. Right? The Feds are squeezing us big time. I mean big time. The days are long past when they pay a claim without scrutiny and without bouncing it back. Our Medicare rejected claims ratios have nearly doubled in the last twelve months. Bundled diagnostic related groups are bullshit.

"The nursing unions have us by the balls too. The recent benefits package they negotiated increased our expenses dramatically, eroding contribution to margin substantially. Plain and simple.

"And finally, we can't make margin by giving away care. Uncompensated care – the euphemistic self-pay patient – hits us like a hammer in this economy. You tell me, Jack? How can you run a practice if all you've got are patients with no payer source? You can't, can you? You've got to have revenue. Right?"

They pulled up to the spot where MacDougall's ball found the rough. He took out his nine iron, fanning it through the long grass until he came up with it. When he did, he picked it up, threw it on the fairway and said, "Right. You've got to have revenue. What do you think, Ed?"

Oblivious to the conversation, they caught Pinkerton picking his nose, inspecting the booger and wiping it under the dashboard of the golf cart. When he realized they were watching, he looked up and asked, "What?"

MacDougall winced, but ignoring what he had just seen, eyed his ball, whacked it with the nine iron toward the hole and repeated, "Yup. You've got to have revenue."

"Of course you've got to have revenue," Pinkerton echoed. "We have to make a decent living somehow for Christ's sake – besides no fucked up government program is taking care of me in my retirement."

When MacDougall got back in the cart, Boyer frowned and said, "I'm not up for discussing business out on the golf course – this is leisure time gentlemen – so I'm going to conclude this conversation by saying this. Our year-end financials will be reported next Wednesday and you are both mindless pricks if you don't listen to me and buy up as much HHC as you can get your hands on before August 7th."

"Really?" Ed Pinkerton hummed.

"Really," Boyer responded. "By the way, I'll deny on my deathbed and in a court of law I even hinted that."

MacDougall's stomach tightened, his face flushed and his palms grew wet with sweat. Then he smiled, took a deep breath, wiped his hands against his trousers and said, "Sounds like insider trading to me,

Mr. Geoff Boyer, President and CEO Humanitarian Hospital Corporation."

Geoff Boyer winked, "Insider trading? Bullshit. All I can say is you didn't hear it from me good buddy. You didn't hear it from me – let's play golf."

Conversation 121
Los Angeles County Hospital
Saturday, August 3, 2002; 10:43 a.m.

Sarita took Mamacita and the children home and sped back to the hospital. Discovering Paco was no better when she returned, Sarita went back to the nursing station. "He says he still he is seeing things."

"What?"

Sarita grimaced, "He is still seeing things – the 'la araña" he talk about when Miguel and José were in his room. He think there are many of them and he yell at me, and he push me away when I try to cover him. It is like he is mad. He swats at things and swears. And I do not see any spiders."

"Dr. Overstreet ordered some Thorazine for the hiccups. Maybe it's that."

"He spit it out," Sarita continued. "He spits out the medicine. Have you heard from Dr. MacDougall?"

"No, he hasn't called. I'll try him again. Dr. Overstreet did though. He is still tied up at Humanitarian. Let's go take a look."

Sarita followed Collins down the hall. When they entered, Paco glanced in their direction swatting at the air. "Motherfucking la araña! Jesus Christ, Sarita, you have to do something. There are more!" he cried.

Tears welled in Sarita's eyes. She wiped them away, pushed back her emotion and said, "Look, I brought the nurse, Paco."

"Mr. Sánchez, try to lie still. I'll get some medication."

"Huh? Get some bug spray and kill the little fuckers if you have to do something," he demanded.

"It's okay, all right, just lie still," Collins said.

Paco stared at her. "I cannot lie still. I see the spider and it hurts."

"Hurts? What hurts, Mr. Sánchez?"

Paco frowned, "Mi estómago."

Collins' face screwed into a fleshy gargoyle and she shook her head. She knew little Spanish and cared even less to learn any. "Mr. Sánchez, you'll have to speak in Eng ..."

"He says it is his stomach. It hurts," Sarita explained.

"Oh? I see," she apologized. "Well let me feel," she said pulling down the bed covers to examine Paco's abdomen.

When she palpated Paco's belly, he pushed her hand away. "Stop it. That do not feel good puta!"

"Paco!" Sarita exclaimed sinking into the chair and biting at her nails. The tears came back and rolled down her cheeks. Calling Priscilla Collins a whore didn't help, but the nurse seemed oblivious.

"Mr. Sánchez, when did you last go – you know – caca?"

"Not since he has been here," Sarita interjected. "Not for a long time I think. Paco when did you ..."

"I cannot take my shit for over one week. How can you shit if you cannot get out of bed, Sarita?" he swatted again. "Motherfucking la araña!"

Conversation 122
Rancho Palos Verdes
Saturday, August 3, 2002; 11:32 a.m.

MacDougall ordered a cheeseburger and an Anchor Steam. Boyer and Pinkerton got hot pastrami and Budweiser's.

"I thought you had to go in," Pinkerton stated.

"I do, one beer won't hurt. I've only got a couple of patients – both at County and neither with insurance. Complicated too – a lot of work for nothing. It's bullshit what's happened to healthcare. Then again, if people would get off their lazy asses and get a decent job," MacDougall huffed.

Boyer cleared his throat, changing the direction of the conversation. "Hey, how was your San Francisco trip?" he asked. "Good games?"

"Good games ... better dames," Pinkerton laughed. "Right, Jack?!"

"Good games, *great* dames!" MacDougall brightened.

"Gentlemen's Clubs, eh? Where did you go?"

"Larry Flynt's on Saturday night and Crazy Horse after the game on Sunday. In fact, the game was so out of reach, numb-nuts here dragged me out of PacBell Park before the 7th inning stretch," Mac-Dougall said.

"Jesus, Geoff. You should have seen the babes at Flynt's. Tits like you wouldn't believe – real too – and this one? Could she talk a line of sex trash in the VIP room? Whew! She had me real hard and very horny," Pinkerton said.

Jack chuckled, "I thought I'd never get him out of there. How much did you drop in the VIP room Ed, a couple of thousand bucks?"

"Fuck you, MacDougall – well actually – way more than that," he confessed taking a drink from his Budweiser. "Who gives a shit? Life is too short, and there is never enough fun. I earn it. I deserve it."

"She got you off?" Boyer asked.

Pinkerton reddened, and then he smiled, "Me to know, Geoff Boyer. Me to know."

"She got him off, Geoff. Trust me …" MacDougall frowned reaching for his cell phone. "Just a second guys, it's the fourth floor at County. I better answer. It's the third time they've called – Dr. Mac-Dougall."

"Oh, hi, Dr. MacDougall. It's Priscilla Collins. On 4 south? I'm calling about Mr. Sánchez. He's acting very strange. He didn't sleep well and this morning he's seeing spiders. Sometimes it's like he's catatonic and at others alert but confused and agitated – hallucinating. Swearing like a trooper and swatting at the air. I'm worried he might get violent."

"Give him some Thorazine."

"I did already. Dr. Overstreet ordered it. Can I restrain him?" she asked.

MacDougall sighed, "No. No, don't do that. Look. I'm about done over here at Humanitarian. I'll be in an hour or so. Okay?"

"Okay … but one other thing before you hang up. He says his belly hurts. I checked. He hasn't had a bowel movement since he's been here."

MacDougall shook his head, "So he's constipated. I'm a neurologist for Christ's sake. Remember? I don't do constipation, Collins. Call Rodríguez for that."

"He's not here. He's on vacation."

"Shit. That's right. He asked us to cover. Well, give him a Ducolax suppository," MacDougall growled. "I'll be there shortly," he promised, hung up, threw his cell phone to the table and said, "Stupid bitch."

When the sandwiches came MacDougall ordered another Anchor Steam. Boyer smeared Dijon mustard on his rye, took a bite and said, "Mmmm, good. Hey guys, we goin' hunting this year?"

"I'm in," MacDougall said. "You, Ed?"

"I'm up for it, but you guys aren't draggin' me to Montana and the Bob Marshall wilderness again. It's too much and I'm getting too old."

Boyer wanted to say, "You mean too fat, Pinkerton," but instead asked MacDougall, "Jack, you ever hunt bear?"

"No, hell no. Like to, but …"

"There's an area up near Glacier Park they opened up …"

"Glacier Park! Screw you cocksuckers. If I can't do the Bob Marshall wilderness, I sure as hell can't do Glacier Park," Pinkerton exclaimed. "No fucking way."

Conversation 123
Los Angeles County Hospital
Saturday, August 3, 2002; 2:16 p.m.

Jack MacDougall sat in a private corner adjacent to the nursing station reviewing the chart notes, labs and x-rays on Paco Sánchez. He burped and smelled the onions and the beer. He winced at the odor, scratched his head, leaned back, then forward, and began writing.

Subjective/Objective: Twenty-nine year-old Hispanic male vacillating in and out of confusion. Wife says he is not "with it" 70% of the time and is seeing things (spiders). Nurse Collins reports he has not had a BM for over one week. Last night he developed hiccups. Overstreet ordered Thorazine, but patient refused. He apparently slept poorly last night but was sleeping when I came in today. He is alert and appropriate at present, lying comfortably in bed. He indicates his upper extremities tingle but denies shortness of breath. Foley was out but had to replace because he couldn't void. He has hardly been out of bed since admission. Vital signs: heart rate = 78, respirations = 22, temperature = 99.8 with T-max 102.4 last night. Nystagmus is better, mostly rightwards. Hiccups on and off. Very ataxic. Unable to stand or walk. Heart and lungs clear. Reflexes are diminished in both lower extremities and sensation is absent. I think I feel stool in the left lower abdomen. He is unable to lift his legs. Blood counts and metabolic profiles are within normal limits.

Assessment: Meningoencephalitis – unstable. Intermittent cerebellar syndrome, Guillain-Barré superimposed. Abdominal discomfort secondary to constipation.

Plan: Continue supportive care. Antivirals and antibiotics per Dr. Overstreet. Enema for BM. Order physical therapy for range of motion and to help him ambulate. Thorazine for hiccups (told Mrs. Sánchez it may make confusion worse). Recheck labs in a.m. Conscious sedation for repeat MRI in a.m. if no change. Plasmapheresis if Guillain-Barré worsens (develops shortness of breath or difficulty breathing).

MacDougall closed the chart and leaned back twirling the pen between his fingers. "When did patients like Sánchez become such a pain in the ass? During residency? Five years ago? Last month? It's a blur," he mumbled to himself.

Staring into space, he calculated how much longer he had to be a slave to this horseshit. At forty-seven I have a nice portfolio he thought. At six percent I would have annual income of well over $600,000 if I parked just half of it in guaranteed interest bearing accounts. Not bad. Of course it would mean I would have to stick with Carolyn. She'd kick my financial ass big time in a divorce, and besides, the kids would go crazy. Not that that matters. They're grown ups. They understand the situation. They've known it for a long time. I guess the thing to do is get them launched – out of college – continue to build my portfolio, then make the move. I can decide about Carolyn when the time comes. Maybe I should shoot toward an administrative position at the medical school ... one that didn't obligate me to patient care. I bet I could work my way into becoming the Dean if I put my mind to it. I've got the pedigree – Johns Hopkins and all. Ugh. Every dean I've ever known is a shithead. A real shithead, and for that matter, a cocksucker to boot. Probably should get out of medicine altogether. How did I get into it in the first place?

MacDougall shook his head, leaned forward and looked at his watch. "Saturday, August 3rd. Let me see. That makes next Wednesday, August the 7th. Better make some calls," he whispered.

In one of the nursing station cabinets he found the Yellow Pages and flipped through them until he came to *Airlines – Commercial*. Scrolling down the list he found the number he wanted, opened his cell phone and dialed 1-800-Fly-United. A cheery voice came on after three rings.

"Thank you for calling the 'Friendly Skies.' Where are you traveling?"

"Uh, yes. This is Dr. Jack MacDougall. I'd like to book a flight to San Francisco leaving around noon on August the 7th, returning the early morning on August the 8th."

Conversation 124
Los Angeles County Hospital
Saturday, August 3, 2002; 2:39 p.m.

MacDougall checked to make certain he had ordered the labs, physical therapy and the enema and put Paco's chart in the order rack. Walking down the corridor to the family conference room, he entered and secured the door. "Ahh ... some peace and quiet," he sighed while opening his cell phone to place the next call.

An unexplained tremor made dialing the second call more difficult, but he finally got it right. MacDougall paced back and forth staring at the floor and then out the window, waiting anxiously for his call to be picked up. When no one answered, he left a message to return his call, flipped his phone closed and returned it to its holster in frustration.

An overstuffed chair invited him to sit, so he sank into it massaging his face with both hands until it tingled. A comfy soft spot on the back of the chair fit his head to perfection. He laid back, took a deep breath and closed his eyes. "Mmmm, good," he whispered.

When his cell phone rang he bolted straight up. "I must have dozed off," he mumbled reaching for his phone. He flipped it open and recognized the number, "Oh, good. She's calling back," he whispered.

"This is Ed Pinkerton," he answered.

"Hi, Mr. Pinkerton. This is Jasmine in San Francisco. I'm returning your call."

MacDougall squirmed in the chair, struggling for words. "Uh, hi, Jasmine. Thanks. I hope I didn't disturb you."

"Not at all. I've just settled in with a nice cup of hot tea. I was in the shower when you called."

MacDougall imagined showering with Jasmine – soaping her all over, feeling her slippery skin, touching her extraordinary breasts – just the thought of it made his penis swell. "Say listen," he said, "I'll be in San Francisco next Wednesday and wonder if you might be available."

Jasmine remembered how she suckered MacDougall and upped the ante with naughty talk. Last time she picked his knickers for thirteen bills. Certainly if she played her cards right, he was worth a lot more. She answered him in a wispy voice, "Mr. Pinkerton, you know I'm always available for you. What did you have in mind?"

He took a deep breath and exhaled, "My flight arrives at 3:35. I figure I'll be in my room at the Embarcadero by 4:30, no later than 5:00. Maybe we could have a light dinner somewhere, a few drinks, a little champagne, go to my suite after."

"Mmmm. That sounds nice, Mr. Pinkerton. How about this? I adore room service. It's so private, so sexy – eating in bed – don't you think? You can order up some chilled champagne and we can take a nice, slow bath together. After that we order dinner – maybe some more champagne – lay together naked feeding each other. See what happens from there. Do you like chocolate, Mr. Pinkerton?"

Jasmine's plan made MacDougall's penis throb, his guts churn and his sphincters tighten. "I-I-I love choc-chocolate," he stammered.

"Well then, we can do some fun things with chocolate. Chocolate and *me* go real good together, Mr. Pinkerton – if you know what I mean."

MacDougall was certain he did, but squirming in the chair, the cat got his tongue.

"So," Jasmine said breaking the silence, "you'll be in your room around five. Here's what you do. Call me to confirm Wednesday. Around noon should be good. When your plane arrives, and you're in your taxi, call again and we'll set up the appointment time. Of course I'll need your room number."

"Of course," MacDougall aka Pinkerton said. "I'll call you on Wednesday around noon."

"Perfect," she said and rang off.

MacDougall closed his phone, stood up and holding onto his abdomen scurried off to the men's room murmuring, "Boy, do I have to take a shit."

Conversation 125
Los Angeles County Hospital
Sunday, August 4, 2002; 8:56 a.m.

Sarita smiled, said "good morning" to Head Nurse Collins and Ward Clerk Natalie Savidge, continued past the station and walked toward room 413. She carried with her a bouquet of bright summer flowers and a framed 4" x 6" photograph of Miguel dressed in his T-ball outfit, posing with a bat in a hitter's stance.

Priscilla Collins ran her fingers through her hair and rubbed her eyes. She stared back at the chart in front of her, and tried to focus, but couldn't – the numbers blurred together. Seven days in a row and five more coming she reflected. It's too much. What the hell for? She leaned back and yawned, then sniffed at the air. "Natalie? What's that horrid stench? It smells like you know what."

Natalie blushed and covered her nose and mouth, "I don't know. It's awful though. Where is it coming from?"

"I have no idea. It smells like an outhouse."

Natalie turned, looked down the corridor and saw Sarita Sánchez running toward the nursing station, "Uh-oh. Looks like trouble, Priscilla."

Hell-fire eyes and bulging veins dramatized Sarita's raging torrent. Her face erupted pink, then scarlet and, finally, magenta. Twenty-five feet from the nurses' station she exploded like a grenade.

"What have been going on?!" She yelled. "I open the door to Paco's room hoping that maybe he will be better today and right away I smell it so bad I want to vomit and their he is, lying in his own caca!"

Flailing her arms and foaming at the mouth, she clenched her fists and spit out, "He is swatting at the spiders and wiping the shit all over himself! He have no idea what he is doing. Why have you not been taking care of him!? What have you been doing? You treat paco like he is an animal! He does not know where he is at. He cannot get up. You know he have been very sick, but you are paying no attention and he lies in the caca and wipes it all over everything! There is so much shit it now runs onto the floor. You think because we are from Mexico, *he is an animal*!?"

Collins jumped up when Sarita shouted animal. Wiping Sarita's flying saliva from her face she said, "Mrs. Sánchez! You *must* calm down. *We* have sick people here who need to get their rest."

Sarita fell to the floor, curled into a ball and wailed, "Paco! Oh, Paco," she sobbed, "I am so sorry. I will stay with you all of the time so they – uh, uh, uh – so they treat you right and nobody they – uh, uh, uh – they – uh, uh – they hurt you. Please forgive me, Paco. I am so sorry. Please – uh, uh, uh," she cried.

Conversation 126
Los Angeles County Hospital
Sunday, August 4, 2002; 10:36 a.m.

"See Sarita? See? It is crawling! It is crawling toward me!" Paco screamed.

"What, Paco?"

"The spider. Over there," he pointed.

"I do not see nothing, Paco. It have to be something else," she said running her fingers through his hair. "Don't worry."

"Sarita, it is not. It is there. See it ... see the little motherfucker. It's on the windowsill," Paco insisted waving his arms. "Kill it, Sarita, kill it!"

"There is no spider, Paco, I swear to Jesus. There is no spider!"

"There is Sarita. In the corner. On the windowsill. There! There is another one! They are all over! You have to kill them, Sarita. They are

241

coming for me," he panted. "They are coming for me! Stop them, Sarita!"

Sarita picked up the *People* magazine, rushed over to the window, and swatted at the sill. Whack! Whack! Whack! – Whack! Whack! Whack! Until the pages ripped and shards of celebrity photographs flew helter-skelter across the room.

"Did I get them, paco? Are they gone? Did I kill the little mother-fuckers, paco?" she cried, throwing the shredded magazine to the floor and rushing from the room.

Conversation 127
Los Angeles County Hospital
Sunday, August 4, 2002; 11:57 a.m.

Dr. Overstreet stood at the end of the bed staring at his patient, holding Paco's chart with both arms across his chest. Five milligrams of Haldol administered STAT an hour before Overstreet's arrival mollified Paco's hallucinations. Despite cleaning and copious air freshener, the room still smelled of feces and Overstreet's scowl dramatized his displeasure. Glade's Fresh Mountain Morning mixed with the odor of Paco's feces turned his stomach.

Suppressing the urge to vomit, Overstreet covered his nose and began, "We may have bad news, Mrs. Sánchez. Nashville is reporting a possible rare strain of E. coli. It's preliminary but I'm jumping on it now."

"From the garbage?"

"Possibly. We'll never know. Whatever it is, Paco is not getting better," he sighed. "I'm sorry ..."

"There they are, I see them, purple and yellow Sarita, purple and yellow and ... and brown Sarita," Paco broke in.

Tears welled up in Sarita's eyes, "It is the garbage truck ... I knew it."

"Here's the other part, Mrs. Sánchez. We don't know for certain how to treat it."

"What do you mean?"

"If that's what it is, it's a rare strain. We'll have to guess at the antibiotic and pick a strong one, hoping it works."

Sarita's shoulders sank in desperation, searching for hope. "Well, at least you have an idea what it is. And maybe we can treat it," she brightened. "We have to do something. This cannot go on. Paco he has never been like this. He has always been so strong."

"Mrs. Sánchez, we *are* doing everything we can. We've run lots of cultures so I can start the two strongest antibiotics I have in my armamentarium – Primaxin and vancomycin. I'll re-order the acyclovir and talk with Dr. MacDougall about something to tranquilize him and something to control his hallucinations. I understand he had a bowel movement?"

"Yes he did, and it make a big mess, and it is all over. I get so upset I embarrass myself, but Paco he does not have to lie in his caca. It is not right, doctor. I wish he could be at Humanitarian where we have our babies …"

"There they are. I see them, Sarita! See them? Purple and yellow, Sarita, purple and yellow. They are so beautiful. See them?" Paco interjected again.

Overstreet ignored Paco, looked back at Sarita and asked, "Has he been out of bed?"

She shook her head, "They have tried. He cannot stand and he does not walk."

"Okay … well, Dr. MacDougall and I are watching this Guillain-Barré thing very carefully of course. Has he had any trouble with his breathing as far as you can tell?"

"He has the hiccups, but I do not think he has any trouble breathing. Paco do you have trouble breathing?"

"See them, Sarita!? They are so beautiful the way they have to dance. Yellow and purple. But I see the brown spiders too, Sarita! Get them before them come for me! Get them, Sarita! *Please! Get them!*"

Conversation 128
Los Angeles County Hospital
Sunday, August 4, 2002; 12:32 p.m.

Jack MacDougall found Priscilla Collins in the medication closet preparing the pharmacy reconciliation. "How's Sánchez?"

"Sánchez? Oh he's just great," she scowled. "He had a bowel movement the size of Mount Vesuvius earlier – formed stool, loose stool, puréed stool – the whole shebang. It was everywhere. He was out of it, so he didn't know he was messing with it and spreading it all over ... Mrs. Sánchez went nuts on us too. It took forever to calm her down. I'll tell you. She's something. Are you ever going to get him out of here?"

"So he finally dumped, huh? Good. Diarrhea? I thought he was constipated?"

"Well he's not now. When the Fleets enema didn't work, I gave him a good old fashioned 'high hot and a hell of a lot' – serves me right I guess. You remember how it is. Behind all that pent up hard stool there's a bucket of liquid poop. I think this one may be my personal best, though. It was everywhere. Took over an hour to clean up. Housekeeping wasn't too happy either."

"What else?"

"His fever is up, respirations are up – hiccupping like crazy – he gulps for air sometimes. That just started this morning after Dr. Overstreet was in. And like I said, he continues to be in and out of it – hallucinating, seeing spiders. I was thinking. Any thoughts this could be alcohol withdrawal – the DTs? "

MacDougall fidgeted. He hadn't considered *that*. "Delirium tremens? Naw, well maybe," he dillydallied. "The history I got was negative for alcohol ..."

"Mine too," Collins interrupted. "But you know these Mexicans. Won't be straight with you on a blessed thing and most of them drink tequila like they're going to run out of agave. Besides he's got the other signs – increased temperature *and* increased respirations."

"Well you could be right," MacDougall confessed, "All in all though, this is most consistent with the pattern of meningoencephalitis. We saw this a lot at both the Mass General and Wash U. Hey, speaking of the Mass General, did you see the Red Sox swept the Yankees?"

Collins frowned, "You and the Mass General and your damned Boston Red Sox. Take a hike, Jack."

"Can't take the heat, can you, Collins?" MacDougall teased turning to go. "Better get out of the kitchen. I'll see you later," he laughed and then looked back. "And I'll check with Mrs. Sánchez on the alcohol thing. In the mean time, let's load him up with 2 milligrams of Ativan STAT and one milligram every 6-8 hours to cover him for the DTs. Give him some thiamine and folic acid too. She'll likely never confess the real deal on his alcohol abuse anyway."

Conversation 129
Los Angeles County Hospital
Sunday, August 4, 2002; 12:38 p.m.

She stood at Paco's bedside attempting to feed him when Dr. MacDougall pushed the door open and made his entrance. "Good morning – I mean afternoon, Mrs. Sánchez. How's our Paco today?"

Sarita hung her head staring at the bedside tray, "Our Paco?" she whispered. "He is not *our* Paco." Then she looked up and said, "Dr. Overstreet say they found a rare germ at the laboratory in Tennessee. I am more worried. He seems so – how do you say – out of it and he will not eat. He pushes me away and spits out his food."

"Rare germ? Really? Hmmm? Overstreet didn't call me … well, hospital food sucks. Especially in this place," MacDougall confessed. "What does he like?"

"He like Mexican mostly. Burritos. Tacos. Enchiladas. Could I bring him some of my burritos? Maybe he would eat them."

"What do you say, Paco? Some of Sarita's burritos sound good to you?" MacDougall asked.

Paco looked toward Sarita, then stared at MacDougall and grinned, "Uh-huh. See them. Yellow and purple …"

"Okay by me. I'll write an order that it's approved – can I check him over?"

"Of course," Sarita said, pulling the tray away.

MacDougall examined Paco, shining a penlight in his eyes, checking his reflexes, feeling his abdomen and listening to his heart and lungs. When he was finished he stood straight and said, "The MRI from yesterday looks okay. To some degree, the meningitis seems better although it's hard for me to tell whether the medicine to treat the hiccups is causing the hallucinations or if it's another manifestation of the meningitis."

Dr. Jack paused and then continued, "Let me show you something, if I can get him to do it. Paco, lift your arms … Paco, lift your arms. Like this. Okay. Good. Hold them real still. No, Paco, hold them still. See how they flap and flail – how he can hardly hold them up?"

MacDougall reached for Paco's arms and pushed them toward the bed, "You can put them down now, Mr. Sánchez. Put them down. Like that. Good. Okay.

"We call that ataxia."

"Yes?"

"Well that coupled with a slight increase in his respirations makes me think we should start plasmapheresis."

"Plasma what?" Sarita shook her head and frowned. "Tell me again what you mean this plasma?"

"I think I told you before. I really don't like it, but I feel it's necessary now. Plasmapheresis filters out the inflammatory particles in the blood that cause Guillain-Barré. Paco's syndrome appears to be progressing, although slowly, and in addition to the intravenous immunoglobulin, I intend to order plasmapheresis treatment."

"Will it hurt him?"

"No … no it doesn't hurt. We hook him up to a special machine for an hour or so twice a day. We have to put in a PICC line to run it – that's all."

Sarita wiped Paco's face with a moist towel and looked deep into her husband's eyes. "Just make him better. And don't hurt him," she pleaded.

MacDougall looked at his watch. Collins was right. Mr. Sánchez could have DTs. Indeed, he could even have Wernicke's syndrome, the most serious nervous system manifestation of alcohol abuse. But this visit was taking too much time for a Sunday afternoon. Delving into Paco's alcohol history would take forever. Besides. What difference would it make? If he was right, and Sarita lied to him, no matter what she said he'd treat for DTs anyway. "Don't worry. We won't hurt him, Mrs. Sánchez. In fact I've ordered a new medicine to calm him down; make him more comfortable. It's called Ativan. Should do wonders."

Conversation 130
Los Angeles
Sunday, August 4, 2002; 1:34 p.m.

Justin Sutherland candidly admitted what he knew of Guillain-Barré syndrome would fit into a thimble with room left over for a thumb and Paco's mysterious illness provoked him to discover more. The utility of plasmapheresis in Guillain-Barré gnawed at him – the disagreement he sensed among Paco's treating physicians disquieted his sixth sense. So he spent Sunday afternoon researching the disease. At first he consulted the 14th edition of Harrison's *Principle's of Internal Medicine*, which provided substantial background. But armed with the precept that medical textbooks were out of date even before they rolled off the press, he decided to search the recently published medical literature. He chose the National Library of Medicine's PubMed search engine which, according to his Medical Information Management seminars, provided the most comprehensive access to periodicals and publications pertaining to the health sciences. Seeking randomized controlled trials, systematic reviews or articles that leveraged metanalysis, he started with PubMed's Clinical Queries application. But with more than 3000 citations he recognized his results were too broad and too extensive. He decided to refine his search and chose a different, albeit more complex approach, utilizing Medical Subject Heading terms or the MeSH database. Sutherland knew PubMed's MeSH search strategies utilized Boolean logic, aiming to control the terminology used for indexing articles. He was certain MeSH would work to his advantage in the long run, despite the extra effort.

The term post-viral polyneuropathy was not in MeSH, so he switched his designation to Guillain-Barré and bingo! The search engine produced Guillain-Barré, Miller-Fisher syndrome and polyradiculoneuropathy among a list of five others. Delighted, Sutherland selected Guillain-Barré and sent it to the search box with the Boolean term AND. Next he searched MeSH for plasmapheresis, selected it and sent it to the search box with AND. The search box read "Guillain-Barré Syndrome" [MeSH] AND "Plasmapheresis" [MeSH]. Knowing that his search would still be too broad, he further narrowed

his strategy by clicking on the "limits" navigation tool where he selected "randomized controlled trials," "adults age 19-44," "humans," "English," "meta-analysis," and "core clinical journals". For good measure
he added "publications dated 1992-2002" and hit Search PubMed.
Much to his chagrin, his method produced "No results." Sutherland
scratched his head and leaned back. "Let's see," he mused.

Undaunted he leaned forward and tried again, this time reducing
the limits to "humans," "English," and "publications dated 1992-2002."
Double bingo! Thirty-five articles, a manageable number.

Sutherland stood up and stretched. His butt was sore from sitting
so long and he needed something to drink. On the way back from the
refrigerator with a diet Coke and a box of Snyder's sour dough pretzels,
he glanced out the window. He hoped Jennifer wanted to go out later.
When he finished his research, he'd give her a call.

Back at his computer he sat down and ran through the list of thirty-five articles. Two manuscripts – both Cochrane Database Systematic
Reviews caught his eye. By critically analyzing the combined results of
well designed randomized controlled trials, the Cochrane Collaboration
held international preeminence – amongst its peers there simply were
no equals; Sutherland proceeded, confident that what he found would
satisfy his curiosity.

He downloaded, printed and perused the two articles. Hughes and
others published "Intravenous immunoglobulin for Guillain-Barré syndrome" in 2001. *"Guillain-Barré syndrome is a potentially serious,
acute, paralyzing, probably autoimmune disease caused by inflammation of the peripheral nerves. Recovery has been shown to be speeded
by plasma exchange which replaces the patient's own plasma with a
plasma substitute. Intravenous immunoglobulin purified from donated
blood is beneficial ... . This study aims to determine the efficacy of intravenous immunoglobulin in comparison with no treatment or other
treatments for treating Guillain-Barré."* Sutherland continued reading,
dissecting and analyzing the data. Finally, he came to the author's conclusions. *"There are no adequate trials to determine whether intravenous immunoglobulin is more beneficial than placebo. Giving intravenous immunoglobulin after plasma exchange is not better than
plasmapheresis alone."*

"Hmmm," Sutherland pondered out loud. "This article suggests plasmapheresis is the *proved* therapy and IVIG is the *experimental* therapy. What the 'f'?"

He set the Hughes article to the side and picked up the second manuscript, authored by Raphaël and others which, like the Hughes dissertation was published in 2001. Entitled "Plasma exchange for Guillain-Barré syndrome", Sutherland devoured its contents. *"Guillain-Barré syndrome is an acute symmetric usually ascending and usually paralyzing illness due to inflammation of the peripheral nerves. It is thought to be caused by autoimmune factors, such as antibodies. Plasma exchange or plasmapheresis removes antibodies and other potentially injurious factors from the blood stream. It involves connecting the patient's blood circulation to a machine which exchanges the plasma for a substitute solution, usually albumin. Several studies have evaluated plasma exchange for Guillain-Barré syndrome. This study aims to establish the efficacy of plasmapheresis for treating Guillain-Barré."*

Sutherland took a drink from the diet Coke and resumed reading. *"Six eligible trials concerning 649 patients were identified, all comparing plasma exchange versus supportive treatment alone ... ."* Munching on his second pretzel he came at last to the authors' conclusions. *"Plasmapheresis is the first and only treatment that has been proven to be superior to supportive treatment alone in Guillain-Barré syndrome. Consequently, plasma exchange should be regarded as the treatment against which all new treatments, such as intravenous immunoglobulin, should be judged ... . Plasma exchange is more beneficial when started within seven days after disease onset rather than later, but is still efficacious in patients treated up to 30 days after onset of the disorder."*

Suddenly, Sutherland found it impossible to swallow the wad of pretzel in his mouth; what he read sucked his salivary glands dry like two aged prunes. "Holy shit," he groaned out loud. "Paco Sánchez is getting the wrong therapy."

Conversation 131
Los Angeles County Hospital
Sunday, August 4, 2002; 2:19 p.m.

Sarita looked down the hall checking the nursing station for Priscilla Collins. Satisfied the head nurse had gone home, she closed the door, pulled the curtains, straddled Paco and presented her breast. "Here, Paco. You have got to eat. *You* have got to eat."

Paco gazed over her shoulders, "You see them, Sarita. Over there. And up there," he pointed with his eyes.

"No. I don't see them, Paco," she said. "Here, Paco, drink. Please. Take my milk."

"Purple and yellow and brown! Look at them," he exclaimed, pushing Sarita away. "Purple and yellow and brown – *brown spiders!*"

Conversation 132
Los Angeles County Hospital
Sunday, August 4, 2002; 2:56 p.m.

When Paco's twin brother Emilio and his uncle Raphael entered hospital room 413, they found Sarita curled up in a blanket sleeping in the bedside chair. On the television, the Dodgers led the Diamondbacks 3 to 2 in the bottom of the 10th inning.

Sarita startled to the sound of shuffling feet. She rubbed the sleep from her eyes, pushed the blanket back and jumped up. "Oh! Raphael! Thank goodness you are here," she cried throwing her arms about his shoulders, "Paco he is so sick. Where have you been?"

Raphael glanced at Emilio and back to Sarita, "I do not know for Emilio, but I have to drive in the north last week for a job. I leave very early and get home very late. Working every day except Sunday. I cannot make it until today. I am sorry."

"I have been working too, Sarita," Emilio bullshitted her.

Sarita gave Emilio a perfunctory hug and said to Raphael, "I am so glad to see you. Paco he have been so sick. This morning he hiccups and hiccups and for two days he have been saying that he sees spiders. He want me to make them go away, and when I cannot, he gets very mad and shouts at me."

Paco opened his eyes, shook his head, smacked his lips and hiccupped. "Uh?" he uttered through his fog.

Raphael stepped toward Paco's bed and rested a hand on his leg, "Buenas tardes, Paco. How are you?"

Paco looked about the room and up at the ceiling, hiccupped twice and swatted at the air, "See them? See them? ... La araña! La araña!" he winced, "Kill them! Kill them! Please ... before there are more."

Conversation 133
Los Angeles County Hospital
Sunday, August 4, 2002; 4:37 p.m.

"Is there a library in the hospital?" Sarita asked the ward clerk.

Natalie Savidge looked up from the monitor in a stilted, day-dreaming haze and said, "Uh – yes there is, Mrs. Sánchez – it's mostly for doctors and nurses though."

"What about patients?" Sarita asked. "At Humanitarian Hospital they have one for the patients."

"Isn't Humanitarian nice? If I ever get sick, that's where I'm going and that's for sure. Not this place."

"I have my babies there. They have a library for patients," Sarita bragged.

"The library is on the first floor by the chapel. It's past 4:30 and it closes at 5:00. You had better hurry – wait, how is Mr. Sánchez doing?"

Sarita smiled and pushed back her emotion, "Everyday he has something new. I think he gets better and then how do you say – boom! – he gets worse. I tell Mamacita he is coming home. She worries and worries. The doctors they say he is improving one minute and he gets more sick the next. Then they change what he have. It seems like they cannot understand what makes him so sick. Now Dr. MacDougall say he is going to have that plasma something."

"I'm sorry," Natalie Savidge empathized. "My best girlfriend's brother went through something like this. It's awful. Hopefully the plasmapheresis will do the trick. It usually does – it did with my friend's brother anyway – well, you had better run if you want to get to the library before it closes."

"Thank you," Sarita said as she scurried down the hall.

"Guillain-Barré? Sure, let me see. We have the *Family Medical Encyclopedia* right over here," the librarian said, looking over her glasses and leading Sarita to the reference desk.

The woman pulled the book off the shelf and said, "Here you go."

"Can you look it up for me? I do not know how to spell it," Sarita confessed.

"Of course. I think it is spelled G-u-i-l-l-a-i-n-B-a-r-r-r-r-r," the woman said, walking down the index with a pointed index finger. "Yes G-u-i-l-l-a-i-n-B-a-r-r-e. Here it is. Pages 230 to 232. Let's see. Here we go. Guillain-Barré," she said sliding the book toward Sarita.

Sarita sat in front of the book and began reading. She fumbled over the medical jargon and terminology, struggling with the words. "I cannot understand this," she whispered.

So Sarita stood, walked over to the librarian and stared dumfounded.

"Is something wrong?" the librarian asked.

Sarita blushed. "Can you read it for me? I-I-I do not – cannot – read this very much. It is not like a newspaper," she whimpered.

The librarian paused for a moment, digesting Sarita's distress. "Medical words are difficult, aren't they? Let's go sit at that table," the librarian said, nodding toward the carousels.

Sarita took her place and leaned over the encyclopedia. "All right. What do we have here?" the librarian said as she began to read. *"No one knows why Guillain-Barré strikes some people and not others. Nor do doctors know exactly what sets the disease in motion. However, it is a syndrome classified as an autoimmune disorder. In autoimmune syndromes the patient's defense system attacks his own tissues. In the instance of Guillain-Barré, the peripheral nerves' myelin sheaths are degraded, resulting in inefficient transmission of electrical impulses along nerve pathways, which affects the ability of muscles to respond to commands emanating from the brain. Symptoms can be quite variable, but muscle weakness and vibratory sensations usually appear first in the feet and lower extremities and progress upwards. In the most severe cases the diaphragm may be affected, which results in difficulty breathing and the necessity for ventilation by artificial means."*

Sarita sat rubbing her hands together listening intently as the written words rolled off the librarian's tongue. Many of the encyclopedic terms confused her as much as the explanations from Dr. MacDougall and Dr. Overstreet. The final paragraph, however, seemed pretty clear.

"While treatments like plasmapheresis and immune globulin prove beneficial in treating the disease, doctors agree the most critical components of the treatment for Guillain-Barré syndrome are maintenance of body functions as the nervous system recovers. Patients usually require heart monitors, and as noted, in extreme cases respirator support for breathing impairment. The requirement for sophisticated technology and close observation are the reasons why Guillain-Barré syndrome patients are treated in hospitals, usually in intensive care wards. In the hospital, doctors can also look for and treat the many problems that can afflict any paralyzed patient – complications such as pneumonia, bed sores and muscle atrophy."

What the librarian read unsettled Sarita. She felt her heart pounding; she became short of breath. Then her heart skipped ... and skipped again. When the librarian finally paused, Sarita wiped the perspiration from her palms, grimaced and asked, "Is that all?"

"I'm afraid so. Is there anything else?"

"What is the name of the doctor who wrote what you have just read to me?" she panted.

"Let's see," she paused looking over the article. "Let's see ... well it doesn't list an author per se; however, it does credit the National Institute of Neurological Disorders and Stroke of the National Institutes of Health for the article's content ... so it's probably pretty accurate."

Sarita glanced at her wristwatch. It read 5:12 p.m. "I am sorry to have kept you here," she apologized. "Thank you. I can go now."

"Think nothing of it. I hope I have been helpful."

"Very helpful," Sarita Sánchez said, turning to go.

Conversation 134
Los Angeles County Hospital
Monday, August 5, 2002; 4:56 a.m.

In his dream, Paco drove Sarita in Emilio's aged Volkswagen Beetle along the winding road fronted by the Santiago River. He cradled her palm on the knob of the floor shifter, massaging the smooth skin on the back of her hand with the light touch of his work hardened fingers. Sarita's cameo profile and swirling hair sparkled in May's full moonlight. Outside, fireflies danced in the air flashing fluorescent yellow and purple sparklers through fragrant Night Jasmine growing wild along the roadside.

Around a steep bend, Paco steered the VW Bug right and turned off the road. "I want to show you something," he said.

The Volkswagen's dim headlights illuminated two dilapidated sheds, a stack of empty buckets, several neatly piled screeds and two pallets of carefully stacked bricks. The car bounced over the uneven surface until it reached one of the sheds where Paco parked the vehicle, walked around, let Sarita out and closed the door.

"Sarita, when I am a little boy I work here with my father and his men," he said picking up one of the bricks and showing it to her. "All day, working in the hot sun, they are smoking cigarettes and they make bricks like this," he continued and then set it back on the stack. "One day when Papá is working, he slips and falls into the river and he drowns. When he die it changes our lives. It is very bad for a very long time. Then one day when I am 14, uncle Raphael asks Mamacita if I can go with him to the United States to make a better life."

Sarita looked up into Paco's moonlit face and frowned, "You must have been very sad Paco ... to lose your papá."

"He teaches me so much, Sarita. Mi padre he is a very good man. He tells me to never say a bad word about no one. He says even if people they do something bad to you, you must understand that they not know why they do it. And every day, except Sunday, he comes here very early in the morning to make the bricks and he does not come home until the bricks are done.

"Many people in Guadalajara are very poor – and we are poor too – but Papá always have a few pesos and we always can have food. And he loves mi madre very much. When we eat at night, he always hold her hand, he says the prayers and he tells Mamacita how much he love her. Mamacita she loves him very much, too. When he dies, she cry so many days and so many nights – it is the only way she can go to sleep.

I think she never gets over it and she hates the river Santiago. She says it take away her whole life."

"Did she marry again?"

"No Mamacita says mi papá is her only love. She cannot love another. I tell her it is all right, but she shakes her head and says no, I love only Papá."

"She have to love him very much," Sarita smiled.

Paco walked back to the Volkswagen, opened the door, removed a blanket from the backseat and said, "She did, and Mamacita and all the children, we miss him."

Paco took Sarita's hand and led her to a knoll above the brick works. He spread the blanket on a soft grassy area overlooking the river and the gleaming lights of the city, shinning in the distance.

"Guadalajara it is pretty at night," she sighed.

Paco took her hand and helped her to sit. "It is," he said rolling onto his side next to her.

The full moon cascaded off the water lighting Sarita's face. "You are *so* beautiful," he whispered, then took her hand and asked, "Sarita?"

"Yes?"

"May I call you my princess?"

Sarita blushed, squeezed his hand, and said "Nobody have ever call me a princess. But yes, Paco", she kissed him on the cheek, "yes – *you* may call me your princess."

The yellow and purple fireflies danced along the river banks and nearby bushes, darting about, glowing in the night; the sweet smell of Night Jasmine permeated the air. When Sarita saw two fireflies kiss, she leaned into Paco and pushed him to the blanket. She slid the soft skin of her arm against the bare skin under his shirt, kissed his lips and whispered, "I love you, Paco."

Paco felt her soft breasts against his chest and his penis grew tight against his jeans. When he pulled her closer, and they kissed again, his erection throbbed. He wanted all of her – *so* much. But instead he sat up and said, "I love you too, Sarita. But we must not."

Sarita rolled onto her knees, looked into his eyes and smiled, "I love you, Paco. Do not worry."

"I am not worried."

"Good. Do not be," she said, reaching down, grasping the edges of her blouse and pulling it over her head.

Paco gasped, swallowed the lump in his throat and said, "Oh, Sarita."

She pressed a finger to his lips and whispered, "Shhhh, Paco. Shhhh … say nothing." Then she reached back, unhooked her brassiere and let it fall to the blanket.

The moonlight gleaming off Sarita's perfect breasts paralyzed Paco. He couldn't breathe, he couldn't swallow. He couldn't speak.

She took his hand and cupped it over her breast and whispered, "Do not worry, Paco – I love you – and see the yellow and purple luciérnagas? See how they kiss? The legend tell us when the fireflies kiss our love is for real and it is forever. You have not to worry, Paco," she whispered again. Then she smiled and took his hand. She took his hand, spread her legs and pressed it between the wet lips of her aching vagina.

Paco felt a hand squeeze his right elbow. "Mr. Sánchez," the voice said rocking his arm back and forth. "Mr. Sánchez. It's the nurse, Mr. Sánchez. I have to take your blood pressure and vital signs."

Paco opened his eyes and looked up at the nursing assistant. Her breath smelled of old coffee and stale cigarettes. "Fuck you, puta. Go away! I do not need you to take my blood pressure!" he shouted pulling his arm back.

"Okay. *Okay*, Mr. Sánchez. But I'll have to report this."

"I do not care. Report it, puta!"

The nurse swirled around and stormed through the door and out of room 413, shaking her head and reaching for her Spanish to English dictionary wondering if she could spell 'puta' to discover *and* report what Paco had called her.

Paco pulled the covers over his shoulders and tried to go back to his dream, although he discovered it was useless.

Conversation 135
Los Angeles County Hospital
Monday, August 5, 2002; 8:46 a.m.

Sutherland's research into Guillain-Barré both monopolized and muddled his thoughts; a gloomy cloud had dominated his mood from the moment he read the conclusions in Raphaël's manuscript. *"Plasmapheresis is the first and only treatment that has been proven to be superior to supportive treatment alone in Guillain-Barré syndrome. Consequently, plasma exchange should be regarded as the treatment against which all new treatments, such as intravenous immunoglobulin, should be judged .... Plasma exchange is more beneficial when started within seven days after disease onset rather than later."*

"Tick-tock. Tick-tock. As a medical student, what *can I* do?" he anguished.

When he entered Paco's room he found Sarita at Paco's bedside caressing his hand and quietly repeating, "It is okay, Paco, it is okay." She did not turn to his footsteps and Sutherland delayed his intrusion to absorb firsthand the uncommon bond between these two helpless people. It served to further kindle Sutherland's omnifarious sentiments, yet he did his best to suppress them with a feigned and ingenuous smile.

"Good morning, Mrs. Sánchez. Buenos días, Paco."

Sarita startled and then scrunched her shoulders, put a free index finger to her mouth and whispered, "Shhhh. Shhhh … he is finally sleeping."

Sutherland tiptoed over to Sarita and apologized, "I'm sorry."

"No problema. You did not wake him, but he need to rest."

Sarita looked up at Sutherland and said, "When we did not see you, I thought that maybe you were gone."

"No, no. I took the weekend off to research the treatment of Guillain-Barré and study for the United States Medical Licensing Exam – it's a test we need to pass before graduation. I should have told you. How is he doing?"

"He is not very well. He have a very bad night. The nurses say he was mean. He is better one minute and worse the next. So up and down. I do not understand. Dr. MacDougall say now that he have to have plasma – what you call it?"

"Plasmapheresis?"

"Yes, that and Dr. MacDougall say that the Guillain-Barré is creeping up to Paco's lungs and that his breathing is worse."

Sutherland had reviewed Paco's vital signs and the morning's lab results, but couldn't decipher MacDougall's illegibly scribbled chart note from the day before; even though the paralysis appeared to be worsening, Sarita's news provoked welcome relief – Paco would finally benefit from the evidence based standard of care for Guillain-Barré. Sutherland contained his delight, took Sarita's hand and said, "Let's sit down."

When they were comfortable, he continued, "Apparently the Guillain-Barré is advancing, although slowly. The plasmapheresis *will* help Sarita. Yesterday I did an in depth literature search to learn more about Guillain-Barré," he boasted. *"Evidence based* research establishes plasmapheresis as the mainstay therapy for the disorder."

The color drained from Sarita's face, "Then why did not Dr. MacDougall begin it sooner? Does he not know what he is doing?"

Sutherland's irresponsible faux pas hit him square in the solar plexus. He felt a wave of nausea and for the moment sat speechless realizing his braggadocio served no worthwhile purpose except to undermine MacDougall's credibility, erode Sarita's confidence in Paco's care and further unsettle her nerves. Moreover, he kicked himself for violating an ethical principle first articulated by Hippocrates – *To hold him who has taught me this art as equal to my parents and to live my life in partnership with him.* What was I thinking he wondered? Professor Dornwyler would kick my butt big time if he knew this.

"Well, like Dr. MacDougall explained, and the literature confirms," he backpedaled, "plasmapheresis has certain risks and complications. Until now Dr. MacDougall thought the risks outweighed the benefits. Medicine is not exact science Sarita. You have to consider all the issues. The challenges are considerable. Dr. MacDougall is an excellent physician; believe me he knows what he's doing."

Sarita's shoulders sank in frustration. "How can this nightmare be?" she asked shaking her head. Then she looked back to Paco and said, "Just tell me, Dr. Sutherland, that he will get better."

"He'll recover. We just need more time," he reassured her. "The plasmapheresis should do the trick."

Sutherland's words lingered in a moment of stony silence. After several uncomfortable seconds, the medical student broke it, "How long have you and Paco been together?"

Sarita looked away from Sutherland and over to Paco. At first she didn't answer, then she took a deep breath and began. "We meet when I am eighteen," she smiled. "He have already moved to the United States and he came to visiting Mamacita in Guadalajara from there. My mother and Mamacita they are friends and Mamacita she invite us to dinner when he came. Right away I think he is so handsome. I never see anyone so good-looking. He have the big muscles from working so hard with the bricks and he have such beautiful skin. Paco also have such a smile and he have a moustache, so he looks like a caballero. I like that and I like that he have a pretty smile. But most of all, I love that he have wonderful blue eyes. Paco he look at you like no one I have ever known. His eyes they are so gentle but they are – how do you say – at the same time so strong. He have eyes that never lie to you."

Sarita reached up, took Paco's hand and continued. "When he is there that very night he ask me to go for a walk after we have dinner and I get all nervous, but my mama and Mamacita they smile and look at each other like they were planning to have this anyway and say it is okay. So we walk around the city. Guadalajara is so beautiful, especially at night. It is in May but the weather this day it is so nice like the summer and there is a full moon.

"Many people are in the streets, but I do not see nobody but Paco. When we get to the Plaza de Armas, he take my hand to hold it. My heart it is beating so strong I think it is to jump out of my chest. He have rough hands, but the way he hold mine he is so gentle. Like he hold it now," she said wiping away her tears. "Tell me he will get better, Dr. Sutherland."

"He will. He just needs time. But please … go on. Tell me more about you and Paco."

"When he hold my hand, we walk around the Plaza and finally we climb the stairs up onto the portico. It is dark in there and we can see the luciérnagas – how do you say in English – the fireflies?"

"Yes, fireflies."

"Well the fireflies they are dancing yellow and purple in the air and they are kissing. In Mexico, Dr. Sutherland, we have a legend that when the luciérnagas find you, and they kiss, you have true and ever-lasting love. So Paco, he take both my hands and kiss them. And then he kisses me. I have never been kissed before. But Paco he kiss me, and right there he look at me with those eyes and he says to me I am so beautiful. He asks me to be his princess and he wants me to come to the United States."

"What did you say?"

"At first I do not know what to say to him. My face it is so red and I find it hard to breathe. Then I see the luciérnagas kiss again and tears come to my eyes and I know what to say. When he kisses me once more, then I say yes."

Sutherland looked away from Sarita catching his own breathe and forcing back his own tears. When finally he regained his composure, he took Sarita's hand and said, "That's a beautiful story."

"It is our story," she blushed. "Tell me again, Paco will get better."

"He will, Sarita. The luciérnagas say it is so," Sutherland smiled. "But I want to hear more. When did you come to the United States?"

Sarita leaned forward and gently petted Paco's arm, "I think it was 1995. We get married first and then the immigration police they give us a very bad time. We tell them we are married and Paco is to be a citizen, but they would not listen. Then when I show them I get pregnant with Miguel, they say it is okay. Paco he never give up. But I never see him so worry."

"You have three children?"

"Miguel, José, Angelina and this one," she beamed pointing at her stomach. "I am so anxious to know Paco will get better."

"I understand, Sarita. He will," Sutherland reassured again.

Sarita frowned, "But just yesterday, Dr. Overstreet say he have a strange germ causing the infection, E. coli or something I think he call it. And that he will have to start some very big antibiotics, and they will have to guess at which one would be the best, because Paco he have a germ from the garbage truck they have never seen before."

Sutherland released Sarita's hand and folded his arms over his chest, "Well, actually that's what I came to tell you."

"Yes. What?" Sarita asked.

"More polymerase chain reaction results came back from Nashville this morning. Just now in fact. There are no E. coli, and this isn't herpes."

Sarita jumped up, "Paco, did you hear that? You have no bad germs! You have no bad germs!"

Paco stirred, but her celebration didn't wake him.

"Well, at least we don't think so, Sarita," Sutherland cautioned. "He could possibly still have some strange bug, but the PCRs say otherwise and I'm hopeful."

Sarita's head drooped and her shoulders sagged again. "But I thought … you say Nashville …"

"Because Paco's case is so complicated, Dr. Overstreet got studies for fungi, mycoplasma and treponema after all. They're still cooking," Sutherland apologized. "I'm sorry. I realize this is hard. You have to be – can you be patient just a little longer?"

"Paco say that this is worse than when he have the spider bite. Yet he tells me to be patient too. I have no choice do I, Dr. Sutherland?"

Sutherland ignored her question and instead looked deep into her eyes. Worry, Paco's vacillating symptoms, and the inexplicable complications had sucked the beauty from Sarita's exquisite face. How dare he ask her to be patient? She was dying inside. Then suddenly it came to him. The spider bite! Of course!

Conversation 136
Los Angeles County Hospital
Monday, August 5, 2002; 10:14 a.m.

Dr. Overstreet sat at the nursing station with Paco's chart. After reading the lab and X-ray reports he wrote: *According to the nurses, he slept fitfully during the night. His wife claims he continues to see things and wakes up frightened. Apparently he called one of the nurses a bitch and told her to "go fuck herself" in Spanish. Still not out of bed, but ataxia seems better. He had chicken soup yesterday, some apple this morning, but not much of either. Mrs. Sánchez states she is bringing in some burritos. Exam is pretty much the same. Temp Max: 100.6 degrees. Blood pressure 151/97, heart rate 108. Respirations 24. Heart and lungs: clear, shortness of breath seems a little better. Neuro: un-changed. Polymerase chain reactions definitely negative for E. coli and herpes. Still waiting on the cytomegalovirus, mycoplasma and treponema results. Dr. MacDougall has ordered plasmapheresis and is treating presumptively for delirium tremens with Ativan, even though Mrs. Sánchez adamantly denies alcohol abuse. If all infectious disease studies return negative, I recommend transfer to a specialized neuro rehab facility at Humanitarian or University Hospital. Add Haldol to Ativan as necessary to treat spikes in agitation. Discuss with Dr. Mac-Dougall.*

Conversation 137
Los Angeles
Monday, August 5, 2002; 10:34 a.m.

"Jack? Hey, Charlie Overstreet here. Great. You? Good, great. Say listen, if Paco Sánchez remains stable from an infectious disease stand-point, I think we should transfer him to a specialized neuro rehab unit. Yeah. Like Humanitarian or University. Right. Sure. Agree. Watch him for a few days, start the plasmapheresis and then transfer. Okay, got it. We're on the same page and shooting at the same target."

"By the way, have you been invited to the GlaxoSmithKline din-ner tomorrow night? No? Well, listen you get a $250.00 honorarium, filet mignon and lobster, and all the Opus One you can drink for just attending and listening to a lecture on Retrovir in the treatment of HIV disease. I can't go. Want my invitation? No ... well think about it. You know my number. I can have my girl run the invitation over to you if you change your mind."

Conversation 138
University Hospital Medical Library, Los Angeles
Monday, August 5, 2002; 12:22 p.m.

The shilly-shallying manifestations of Paco's illness spawned Jus-tin Sutherland's insomnia. Most nights he could not fall asleep, when he did, it came with distorted, fitful dreams. His mentors seldom preached – but of course it made sense – that bedside medicine required

262

a substantial appetite for the arcane as well as capacity for science. Admittedly he was a novice. Who was he to challenge the likes of Drs. Rodríguez and Overstreet or the stature of Dr. MacDougall? Still, the questions outnumbered the answers and Paco's condition was *not* improving. Why? His fluctuating mental status and array of symptoms didn't fit any pattern. *Why?*

The notion that a defect in Paco's blood brain barrier might hold the answers came to Sutherland out of the blue during his conversation with Sarita that morning. He vaguely recollected the complexities of the barrier from his neuro-anatomy lectures two years ago – and he might have it flipped upside down – but curiosity had the cat, and Sutherland had to set it straight.

He skipped lunch and ran to the library.

There wasn't time to do a PubMed MeSH search on this one, so he dug into Victor's *Principles of Neurology* and Walton's *Diseases of the Nervous System*. Taken together he found the information he sought and drew some measure of satisfaction that he had remembered most of the features correctly. The blood brain barrier or BBB comprises a system of unique endothelial cells that restrict certain ions and microscopic elements like bacteria from entering the brain; viruses, due to their minute size, enter more easily. The BBB consists of capillary beds with tight junctions of high electrical resistance that promote the active transport of molecules like glucose and alcohol and caffeine into the brain, while simultaneously preventing penetration of neurotoxins.

The blood brain barrier serves an essential neuro protective role.

Inflammatory processes, especially certain infections, act to break down the barrier, disrupt homeostasis and permit the influx of noxious elements. Was this the reason for Paco's fluctuating symptoms? Sutherland thought it might be, but thus far he had not discovered the explanation he sought. So he scoured the texts for more.

He found what he was looking for in Walton's discourse on neuro-anatomy in the second chapter. Sutherland re-learned that the entire brain was encased by the blood brain barrier *except* the region of the pituitary gland, where a tiny bed of capillaries permitted the efflux of essential secretory substances like human growth and thyroid stimulating hormones into the blood stream. *There*, the brain was exposed. And

263

there, just in front of the pituitary fossa and anterior to the sphenoidal sinus, sat the nasal passages. Normally, these two structures formed an impenetrable wall, isolating the pituitary capillary bed from external influences. *Normally*. But maybe Paco Sánchez was not normal? As a child a spider had crawled up his nose and bit him. Had *Loxosceles reclusa* venom disrupted the wall? Was *reclusa* back to bite Paco again? Maybe.

And Sutherland knew that only one person might hold the clue.

Conversation 139
Los Angeles
Monday August 5, 2002; 12:36 p.m.

While Justin Sutherland combed medical textbooks for the answers to Paco's enigmatic illness, Geoff Boyer sat on the terrace at Nick & Stef's Steakhouse tapping his foot. He looked at his watch – 12:36 p.m. – "Where for Christ's sake is MacDougall?" he wondered.

He jumped when a skylark flew by his face darting for a chunk of soda cracker the women at the table in front of him threw down for it. "Stupid bitches. Can't they read the 'Please Do Not Feed the Birds' sign?" he whispered.

Looking over the menu he glanced at his watch again, took a sip of his martini and spotted Jack MacDougall coming through the doors. He stood up catching his napkin with his left hand and shaking MacDougall's with his right. "Hey, Jackson, how's it going? Thanks for coming on such short notice."

Dr. Jack smiled and said, "No problem, Geoff – sorry I'm late. Patients, you know. What's up?"

"First tell me what you are drinking – I'm having a Grey Goose martini – then sit down. We need to talk."

MacDougall sat, spread the napkin across his lap and said, "I'll have the Grey Goose too; patients can't smell vodka."

Boyer signaled to the waitress for two more and said, "Hey, I got a bottle of the Chivas 18 you recommended. You are right. That *is* good shit."

"I thought you'd like it. Smooth isn't it? I've been a Johnnie Walker Black guy all my life – the Chivas 18 has me switching."

"Very smooth – what do you like here – when do you have to be back?"

"I usually get the steakhouse burger – one-thirty. I told Stephanie I might be a little late," MacDougall answered.

"The waitress brought the martinis and set them down. Boyer polished off his first and handed her the empty glass. "Can you come back in a second? We're not ready to order lunch yet, Crystal."

"Sure, Mr. Boyer. I'll be back in a few minutes," she smiled.

Boyer's eyes followed her as she disappeared. "Sweet ass. Very sweet - I wouldn't mind a little of that," he chortled under his breath.

MacDougall munched on one of the two olives in his martini, nodded his head in agreement and asked, "So what's up? You sounded anxious on the phone."

Boyer surveyed the other patrons in the room, sat forward and asked, "Did you buy any HHC?"

MacDougall examined Boyer. Early fifties, looking no more than late forties, cutting the mark of executive success – diamond cuff links, Robert Talbott Sevenfold ties, Ermenegildo Zenga hand-stitched Italian suits. Zelli ostrich leather shoes. Full head of hair, perfect complexion, ideal body weight, and groomed to the hilt. Dressed top to bottom. The total package. Nothing's missing, he thought. I wonder where he gets his jollies. Then he said, "HHC stock? Not yet. Still considering …"

"Good. Listen, Jack, what I have to say I couldn't say or ask over the phone and as I said, I'll deny under oath I uttered it, if I ever had to testify. Remember Saturday on the golf course? I told you and Pinkerton about Humanitarian – claimed you were both dumb fucks if you didn't buy as much HHC as you could get your hands on before Wednesday?"

MacDougall drank from his martini looking over the rim of the glass at Boyer, "Uh-huh."

"Well Wednesday our year-end financials …"

"You gentlemen ready?" Crystal interrupted.

Boyer looked up at the waitress, flashed a perturbed smile and said, "We're both having the steakhouse burgers, medium rare with bleu cheese and the rest of the works. You want another martini, Jack?"

MacDougall shrugged his shoulders, smiled and looked at his wristwatch, "Might as well. It's five o'clock somewhere."

"And two more martinis, Crystal."

Boyer's eyes followed the waitress into the kitchen, and then turned back to MacDougall. "Not bad tits either. Wouldn't you say?"

"Nice," MacDougall smiled. "Very nice."

Boyer finished his second martini, leaned into MacDougall again and whispered, "Jack, when you call Wasserman – whatever you order – add in ten-thousand for me."

"Ten-thousand *shares*?"

"Ten thousand shares."

MacDougall massaged his nose from side to side with the edge of his index finger and cleared his throat, "This morning HHC listed at $23½. That's $235,000 and Wasserman gets nearly $8000 for his share of the transaction ..."

"Here we go!" Crystal said carefully setting the martinis on the table in front of MacDougall and Boyer. "Your burgers should be out in five minutes."

That she had freshened her lipstick and the second button on her blouse had mysteriously come undone did not escape MacDougall. That she leaned ever so slightly into Boyer to make eye contact and reveal some cleavage didn't miss him either. When she was out of earshot MacDougall said, "She's fucking hitting on you, Geoff."

"Bullshit. You think so? Jesus, I wish she'd hit on me. That's one delicious woman I tell you. One delicious woman. I wonder if she's married."

"What difference does that make?" MacDougall chided.

"Doesn't, does it?" Boyer chuckled.

"Anyway. Enough pussy talk for the moment. Back to business. Ten thousand shares," Boyer repeated, reaching into his brief case and coming up with a polished, hand-crafted 3" x 4" x 8" koa wood case.

He rubbed his fingers across the velvet finish and extended it to MacDougall. "I picked this up on Maui. Don't open it here. You will find it's all there, plus the commission and a little something for your trouble."

"It's beautiful, Geoff. The grains are terrific. Thank you. I'll treasure this always," he smiled turning it over to further inspect it. "It's amazing. Concealed hinge. The finish feels like satin."

"My pleasure, Jack."

"Ten-thousand *shares*?"

"You're a fast learner," he winked.

"How do you propose I give the stock back to you?"

"Easy. You donate it to the 501(c)(3) not-for-profit Foundation I set up for prostate cancer. That way it's a tax deduction too."

MacDougall swallowed hard and broke out in a sweat. Boyer's diabolical scheme was a federal crime. They could go to prison for ten, maybe twenty years for money laundering. Nevertheless, he said, "You've covered every angle, Geoff. I'm impressed."

"How else can you make it rich in this fucked up, heavy-handed, government regulated economy?"

"You can't, mi amigo," MacDougall flip-flopped. "I'm in. Consider it done."

"Excellent," Boyer grinned hoisting his Grey Goose toward MacDougall.

"Here's to beautiful women, fabulous food, great wine and – Jack-my-man – good fortune!"

Conversation 140
Los Angeles
Monday, August 5, 2002; 4:32 p.m.

Later that same day, Sarita entered the offices of Republic Waste. Adjusting her handbag, she walked up to the counter and said, "Good afternoon, I am Sarita Sánchez. I am here to pick up Paco's check. I call ahead."

A haggard, fifty-something office assistant smiled and said, "Oh, hi, Mrs. Sánchez. I'm Sandy Miller, the person you talked with on the phone. I've got it right here. How's Paco doing? Is he still in the hospital?"

"Not so good. I worry so much, you know. He have paralysis from the germs and cannot walk. They tell me he cannot go home until he is better."

Without looking up, Miller rifled through a drawer of sealed envelopes and pulled the one labeled Paco Sánchez. "Here it is ... paralysis? I've never heard of that. From germs?" she asked, handing the paycheck off to Sarita.

"The doctors change their minds all of the time about him. First they say he is better. He will be going home. Then the next day he is worse. He have fever and headache. Every day they change what he have. They give him all of the medicines – he have what you call the IVs in every arm. Then on Saturday and Sunday he say he see purple and yellow and brown spiders," she frowned. "Have anyone here been sick besides Paco?"

The clerk reached for a Salem Light, lit it and said, "No, not like Paco ... just a day or two. Most of the time I figure it's a hangover or making a three-day weekend out of two. Why, Mrs. Sánchez?"

Sarita looked about the drab interior, sparse furniture and faded off-white paint. Employee notices on top of employee notices covered the bulletin boards behind the assistant's desk. One of the notices read: *Heads up! Always wash your hands before eating or handling personal items.* "I just ask. They are checking Paco for something they call E. coli or some other germs that maybe he get off the garbage truck."

Sandy Miller took a long drag from her cigarette, blew smoke from the corner of her mouth, furrowed her brow and said, "No, nothing like that. Nobody else has been hospitalized, that's for sure."

Sarita shook her head, "Okay. Well, I guess this is Paco's last check."

"I'm afraid so. Hopefully, Paco will get well and come back soon. He is so nice and polite. Most of the guys here are real rough. Cussing and swearing. Using the f-word three times in every sentence if you know what I mean. Not Paco. Manny the Super likes him too. Says he is a very hard worker. Tell Paco he is in our prayers."

Sarita wiped her eyes. "Thank you," she said and turned to walk out the door, "goodbye."

"Let us know how he's doing," Sandy Miller called out as Sarita closed the door behind her.

Sarita crawled into Paco's pickup and opened the envelope. "$176.32?" she whispered. "How long can I make this little bit work? Even the house payment have been over $1000.00."

Conversation 141
City Centre, Los Angeles
Monday, August 5, 2002; 4:39 p.m.

"This is Kathleen Carrier, Executive Assistant to Mr. Geoff Boyer President and CEO of Humanitarian Hospital Corporation. How may I ..."

"Dr. Jack MacDougall, calling for Geoff Boyer."

"May I ask the nature of your call?"

"I'm returning his call."

"Your name again?"

MacDougall wondered why Boyer put up with this bitch. Carrier knew God-damn well Geoff and Jack were good friends *and* business associates. He called Boyer several times a month. Does she treat everyone like this or just me?" he asked himself.

"*Doctor* Jack MacDougall," he harrumphed.

"One moment, Dr. MacDougall."

MacDougall rocked back and forth, cradling the phone between his chin and shoulder while drumming his fingers on the arms of his chair. Finally Boyer came on.

"Geoff Boyer."

"Hey Geoff, Jack. Thanks again for lunch today."

"You're welcome. Anytime," Boyer responded.

Switching to cabalistic code, MacDougall squirmed in his chair like a proselyte espionage agent and continued, "Listen. On the way back to the office this afternoon I stopped by the Country Club pro shop. Wasserman – you know Wasserman – showed me the new Ping G10 driver. What a beauty; the feel is fabulous. I took a couple of practice swings in the virtual range. All I can say is 'WOW!' He only has two in stock and, as you know, the demand for them is high, so I got one for myself and picked up the other one for you ... figure if you don't want it, you can always take it back."

Boyer picked up on MacDougall's ruse immediately. Not to be out done he concocted his own confabulation, *"Ping G10 driver?* Are you crazy? That's the one they designed using a Cray Supercomputer. Titanium – the whole wazoo. You know I want one. Perfect. Thanks for thinking of me. What do I owe you?" Boyer asked.

"It came to $235 plus tax."

"Bring it Friday evening and I'll come with the cash."

MacDougall smiled, knowing unscrupulous minds think alike, "You already paid me and then some, Geoff."

"What?"

"Our friendship is priceless. Consider the debt paid – or a gift – if it makes you feel better," MacDougall countered.

"Wow! Thanks, Jack – see you Friday for dinner and on the links Saturday."

"Hey, wait a minute," MacDougall countered. "I forgot to ask at lunch. How are the designs for the HHC multi-specialty clinics progressing? I haven't heard from Jacoby."

"Fabulous. The Innovations Group will have drawings for you to review next week. Anyway, that's what they promised." Boyer hesitated, "They've incorporated all of your concepts. You'll like it."

"Super. Can't wait to go over them with you. Listen. I've got to get back to my patients. Just thought I'd buzz in to let you know about the Ping driver. I'll see you Friday."

"Great, and on the links Saturday."

MacDougall hung up and secured his office door. From the bottom drawer of his desk he removed the koa wood box, examined its velvety finish one more time and opened it.

He counted the money again and laid it out in separate stacks. Two-hundred and thirty-five crisp $1000 dollar bills, eighty one-hundred dollar bills and one-hundred $50 dollar bills. Two-hundred and forty-eight thousand dollars in all.

MacDougall squirmed in his chair gawking at the pile of money. Now what, he wondered? How do I get cash like this to Wasserman? Maybe I'll just walk into his office and plunk it on his desk. Swagger in and say, "Hey Stevie boy, came in to clean up my margin account." Shock the shit out of him. Wait! I know – better yet – walk it in

270

clutched under my arm in a wrinkled, well worn brown paper bag like a little old lady. Sit down and hand it to the stupid cocksucker without a word. Savor the look on his dumbfuck face when he opens it.

A knock on the door wrestled MacDougall from his fantasy.

"*What ...?* Stephanie, you know when the door is closed, I'm busy and not to be disturbed."

"But you've still got patients, Dr. MacDougall. They're waiting," Stephanie said from behind the door.

"Don't you think I realize that? I was born at night, but not last night. I've told you what to say. *But I'll tell you again.* '*He* had to go to the hospital for an emergency and he just got back. He'll be *right* with you.' Can you at least remember that, Stephanie?"

"Yes, sir," she said walking away.

Mumbling under his breath MacDougall replaced the Koa box and locked it away. Glancing at the schedule for his final patients he saw the name Velma Richardson. "What is she doing here?" he asked himself. "I just saw her last week. Jesus H. Christ."

Conversation 142
University Hospital Clinics, Los Angeles
Monday, August 5, 2002; 5:09 p.m.

When Justin Sutherland finished his Emergency Room shift at four p.m., he hurried to University Plastic Surgery & Reconstructive Consultants hoping to discuss his blood brain barrier theory with Dr. Alexandre. Despite the impropriety of arriving uninvited, Sutherland considered time of the essence. Somehow he knew Alexandre would understand.

The receptionist rebuffed Sutherland at first, but when he explained his intentions, what it involved and who it was for, she let down her guard. Yes, Dr. Alexandre could give Sutherland five minutes *after* he saw his last patient. Could he wait?

Sutherland fidgeted in the reception room chair for nearly an hour, biding his time, albeit impatiently. Eventually, Alexandre's nurse called for the medical student, led him back to Alexandre's office, and introduced him to the surgeon. Alexandre was everything Sutherland ex-

271

pected. Tall, athletic, good looking, and most importantly, affable and receptive. Yes, Alexandre knew Paco Sánchez and yes, he had performed plastic and reconstructive surgery on him many years before. Yes, he had heard Paco was sick. But no, he didn't know the details. Could Sutherland elaborate?

"It all started with an upper respiratory tract infection that rapidly progressed into a picture suggestive of meningitis with fevers, vomiting, and delirium. He bounced between Humanitarian and County Hospitals when he first got sick – Humanitarian wouldn't treat him without insurance – which delayed his diagnosis and care. Eventually he came into the County ER. That's where I met him – Dr. Mack and I performed his spinal tap, made the diagnosis of viral meningitis and admitted him. Even though it looked viral, Dr. Overstreet started antibiotics. Initially Paco improved. But for the last several days his condition has been up and down, better one day, worse the next – agitation, headaches, visual changes, hallucinations – he's seeing spiders. Now he has Guillain-Barré syndrome."

"You mean he has post-viral polyneuropathy?" Alexandre inquired.

"Exactly."

Alexandre looked puzzled, "I'm no neurologist, but I thought Guillain-Barré followed the infectious phase by two or more weeks?"

"That's my point. The way Paco's illness waxes and wanes; the bizarre progression; the disconnected array of symptoms – I figure there has to be a reason. So I'm scratching my head. Thinking of everything. Knowing we're missing something. Then on Monday I'm talking with Sarita and she brings up the spider bite. Mentions again how Paco suffered. Then this crazy idea about a defect in Paco's blood brain barrier pops into my head."

Alexandre's face suddenly grew ashen. It finally occurred to him where Sutherland was taking this. Sutherland wondered, what he now wondered. Had the spider's venom etched an undetected tunnel – no matter how miniscule – that penetrated the sphenoidal sinus, connected with the pituitary capillary bed and left Paco vulnerable to the intrusion of noxious neurotoxins, bacteria and viruses?

He wondered as well, "After two years of reconstruction and countless procedures *did I miss something?"*

Alexandre rose from his chair, rubbed his palms together and began to pace. Scratching his forehead he walked over to the window and stared out. When he didn't speak, Sutherland grew uneasy. Was Alexandre angry? Have I overstepped my bounds? The silence was deafening.

When Alexandre finally turned and walked back to his desk, the color had reappeared in his face, "Who are the attending physicians?"

"Drs. Rodríguez, Overstreet and MacDougall ... Dr. Rodríguez is on vacation."

Alexandre reached for the phone and speed dialed.

"Yes, sir."

"What's Charlie Overstreet's number?"

After a brief moment the receptionist said, "I've got it right here sir. Can I put you through?"

"Please."

"This is Dr. Charles Overstreet."

"Hey, Charlie. George Alexandre. How are you?"

"Well I'll be damned. To what do I owe this long lost call?"

Alexandre looked up at Sutherland, "I'm sitting here in my office with a fourth year medical. Justin Sutherland. Know him?"

"I do. He's been following along on a case that, quite frankly, has got us by the balls."

Alexandre cleared his throat, "So, he comes to me this afternoon with the cockamamie idea that maybe the spider bite Sánchez had as a kid may have created an anatomic defect in his blood brain barrier."

"Spider bite?"

"Spider bite – probably a brown recluse species. You didn't get the history? Took me two years to reconstruct the fistula that ran from his nasal floor to his palate. Had to repair the necrosis along the nasal passage and his upper lip as well."

"Oh, yeah, yeah, yeah," Overstreet lied. "I remember. Go ahead."

"I think he may have something."

"Who?"

"Sutherland. The medical student. I've not seen Sánchez, but Sutherland could be on to something and it sounds as if we don't address it, Sánchez could be in for it. Is he in any condition to tolerate nasopharyngoscopy? I'd like to take a quick peek."

"He's pretty sick. What were you thinking?"

"I can do it at the bedside. A little Versed for conscious sedation. Use a pediatric nasopharyngoscope. Monitor his vital signs. Get in. Get out."

"When?"

"As soon as possible. Unfortunately, I'm leaving on a flight in a couple of hours. Won't be back until late tomorrow night. I've got cases booked for Wednesday morning; so Wednesday afternoon would be the soonest."

"Can I think on it? Noodle over it with MacDougall? Get back with you?"

Alexandre shook his head, "Of course, you're the attending. Let me know. You've got my numbers."

When Alexandre hung up Sutherland blurted, "What did he say?"

"What internists always say – 'I need to think on it'. And of course as he is the attending physician, it's his prerogative."

Conversation 143
Los Angeles County Hospital
Monday, August 5, 2002; 6:32 p.m.

Uncle Raphael stuck the Wal-Mart bag dangling from his right hand out toward Paco. "I have something for you," he smiled. "I know how much you like music, so I buy this to help you get better."

Paco rubbed sleep from his eyes, looked toward his uncle, and then away.

"Wake up, Paco. Look, Uncle Raphael buys you something," Sarita pleaded.

Paco massaged his face, gave them both a vacant stare and looked back at the television.

Sarita reached for the bag and peered inside. There were three items. A Sony Walkman, a Carlos Santana's *Abraxas* CD and a four pack of AA batteries. She gave Raphael a hug and said, "These are perfect. Thank you. And where is Emilio, Raphael?"

Raphael shrugged his shoulders, "I go to his apartment to pick him up and he is not there like he promise. I try to call his cell phone, but he does not answer. So I came to the hospital without him."

"I do not see. I do not see ..." she choked picking at the plastic wrap on the CD, "I do not see how his own twin brother can be so sick and he does not care for nothing."

Raphael shrugged his shoulders again, "Emilio is who he is, Sarita. You cannot change him. He have always been like this."

Frustrated with the protective plastic wrap, she tossed the CD on the bed and wiped her eyes. "That does not make it better," she said staring at Paco. "Emilio he should be here for his brother," she declared walking toward the door, "I go to the nurses to get some scissors."

Conversation 144
Los Angeles County Hospital
Tuesday, August 6, 2002; 8:54 a.m.

On Tuesday morning traffic backed up for miles and came to a standstill. Sarita slid her sweaty fingers over the steering wheel worrying that no one had taken time to help Paco with his breakfast. In a brown paper bag next to her she carried two fresh green chili-bean burritos for his lunch. She turned the radio to the traffic channel and discovered that a semi-tractor trailer carrying chickens had overturned on the rain drenched freeway. The announcer warned the accident might take hours to clear.

"Mother Mary, Joseph, Jesus," she said to herself. "I have to talk with the doctors and I must help Paco. This is very bad."

She turned her indicator signaling right and inched the pick-up little by little onto the shoulder. Other drivers had done the same with marginal benefit, but Sarita had a different plan. She put the Toyota into 4-wheel drive, shifted into low, steered the truck over the curb and climbed the embankment back toward the last exit ramp. Rain made the unpaved terrain slippery, but the pick-up caught traction, jostled over incidental potholes and within minutes she found freedom.

When Sarita finally entered Paco's room she found him sitting up in bed listening to the Santana CD and eating. "Paco?"

A piece of scrambled egg dangled from Paco's lips. "Buenos días, Sarita."

Her eyes opened wide. She kissed him on the forehead and asked, "What happened? You look better!"

"This morning I feel better," he smiled. "I still cannot move my legs, but my arms they are better."

"What happened?"

"I do not know. I just woke up feeling better and I am hungry."

"I came as fast as I could. It is raining and there is a very bad accident with the chickens and a truck and I could not get the traffic to move so I went over the road off the freeway and onto the streets. I bring you some burritos," she apologized.

Sarita jumped when Dr. Jack MacDougall burst through the door, muttering under his breath, examining Paco's chart.

"Look, Dr. MacDougall! Paco is better. The plasma it must have worked."

"Couldn't be the plasmapheresis," he mumbled. "He didn't get it, the machine is down. Worse yet bio-engineering has no idea when it will be back up. They are waiting on a part," he fumed.

MacDougall pushed the bedside tray away and tested the reflexes and sensation in Paco's arms and legs . "Can you lift your arms above your head, Mr. Sánchez? Good, great. Can you lift your legs? No? Can you wiggle your toes? Okay better. Fine. Good," he declared.

MacDougall returned to Paco's chart, made a few notes and said, "Actually, you do look better, Paco. Your respirations seem better too. Did you sleep okay?"

"Yes, better. I am very hungry and I ate breakfast. It is – how do you say – a relief?"

"I'll say," MacDougall said glancing at his Rolex. "Look I've got a meeting over at University Hospital and have to get out of here. I think you've finally turned the corner on this thing. Maybe the plasmapheresis won't be necessary," he mumbled heading toward the door. "Just some neuro rehab."

"Neuro rehab? What is that, Dr. Mac ...?"

"I'll check back this afternoon," he said, pulling the door closed and ignoring her question.

Sarita stood next to Paco's bedside staring at the door shut in her face. "You say he is better right now. Yesterday it was something different. You say his breathing is worse. Now he is not to get the plasma treatment Dr. Sutherland say he have to have. If tomorrow or the next day he is not better or he cannot breathe, what will you have to say then?" she whispered.

Conversation 145
The Grove Mall, La Brea
Tuesday, August 6, 2002; 1:38 p.m.

Carolyn MacDougall ordered the Coquille St. Jacques. When it arrived, she asked for another glass of Pouilly-Fuissé figuring one more wouldn't hurt. Gray skies and a steady rain drove her funk. Besides, she worried about her daughter. Alyssa's telephone call earlier in the day centered on Jack's chiding her for not making grades good enough for entrance into medical school and Alyssa's indecisive outlook on medicine as a career in any event.

"What's the big deal mom? Dad's not happy. He hates what he does. Why should I want to follow in his footsteps? Besides, *John* didn't have to."

Carolyn lost her appetite despite the remarkable flavor and tenderness of the scallops. She pushed them to the side, concentrating instead on the wine. Looking from the dreary skies into the crowded restaurant, she wondered how many of La Fleur's clientele were happy. Not many she surmised. Too caught up in themselves and their station in life – how big to build the house, what model Mercedes to buy, what private university to send their children to.

She finished the wine, paid the tab and made her way to the mall. Bored with Saks Fifth Avenue and Nordstrom, she drifted into Victoria's Secret.

She examined several lacey undergarments hanging on two or three racks in the front of the store not at all certain what she might be looking for, or for that matter, why she found herself shopping at Victoria's Secret. She certainly didn't need lingerie.

277

A thirty something beauty of Brazilian-Italian mix approached her. The clerk possessed deep brown eyes and shiny dark hair that flowed to her shoulders. Her warm smile heightened the shop's alluring ambience.

"What's that smell? I really like it," Carolyn asked the woman.

"Nice isn't it – *Sexual Secret* – our new eau de parfum. We lightly mist it through a system of atomizers that continuously refreshes the air. Victoria advertises it as 'luscious to the core.' Very sexy – don't you think?"

Indeed, very sexy Carolyn thought and wondered: How is it I can *feel* the scent down *there*? Wow! "Yes, I like it. The essence is … is *aphrodisiac*," she blushed.

"Um-hmm," the clerk winked. "Ve-r-r-ry aphrodisiac – so, my name is Chloé. May I help you with something this afternoon?"

Working up her bravado, Carolyn feigned a cough and cleared her throat, "I'm looking for nightwear. Something seductive. Something devilish and sinful – something provocative, yet mysterious," she smirked.

"Are you looking for a nightgown or a babydoll … or did you have something more risqué in mind?"

Carolyn frowned, "Risqué – but not too risqué – I guess."

"Come this way. We'll start with the babydolls and go from there."

Soft jazz emanated from the ceiling speakers. Otherwise the store was quiet. Not another customer in the place. Nice, Carolyn thought. It makes this kind of shopping more private. Chloé led her to the sleepwear and showed her a lipstick red, pleated lace babydoll and a black satin one with a v-neckline finished off with a satin bow at the point of cleavage. Carolyn inspected each of them holding them up and rotating them front to back.

"These are nice. What else do you have?"

"Let me show you our absolutely irresistible lingerie. Victoria has just come out with a new line."

Carolyn followed her down the row of drawers and asked, "If you don't mind telling me – what's the music overhead? It's so comforting."

"Isn't it just? Romantic too. I adore Chris Botti. This piece is entitled "The Way Home" and if you like this, just wait for "Regroovable" to come up. I listen to this CD over and over all day and never tire of it. It's called *Midnight Without You.* We have it for sale at the counter if you want."

Chloé opened a drawer and pulled from it three garments. One, a lacey jet-black point d'espirit teddy, the other a white cutout teddy and the third a black and magenta lace slip with garters. She held up the black point d'espirit, "This one is open at the crotch," she winked. "Kind of convenient, if you get what I mean?"

Carolyn blushed, but picked up the lace slip anyway, turned it about and then shook her head, "Uh-uh. This looks like bordello wear. I like the others though. Let me look them over and think about it. Can I try them on?"

"Sure – you are a ... ?"

"Medium."

Chloé dug out mediums in each of the styles and showed Carolyn to the dressing rooms. "Here you go. I'll come back and check on you or you can look for me on the floor when you're through. Make certain you bolt the lock."

Carolyn secured the door and disrobed. She agreed with Judi Pinkerton about one thing – George Alexandre had given her perfect boobs. She looked down at the lingerie and back to the mirror smiling. "Let's see," she whispered.

She decided the point d'espirit and the cutout teddy sent too provocative a message – Judi seemed enthralled with their new found relationship – but Carolyn didn't want to push her luck. She put them aside and tried on the satin teddy and lace babydoll, turning from side to side, inspecting the look from front to rear, and then again from side to side. After considerable deliberation, trying each on twice, she chose the lipstick red, pleated lace babydoll thinking, Jack's speaking in San Francisco tomorrow – gone most of tomorrow *and* tomorrow night – perfect.

She found Chloé folding panties and bras and said, "I like this one."

"Beautiful. You are lucky lovers," Chloé sighed.

Carolyn managed a lame smile and said to herself, "Yeah. Lucky all right – one unrequited; the other repulsed."

Lingering, she ran her fingers through her hair and inquired, "Chloé? Do you have another medium? It's my friend's birthday tomorrow. I think I'll get one for her. She likes to – how shall I say – play concubine, too? Oh! I almost forgot. I want a bottle of *Sexual Secret* and the Chris Botti CD as well."

Conversation 146
Los Angeles County Hospital
Wednesday, August 7, 2002; 8:30 a.m.

Dr. Overstreet wrote: *Mr. Sánchez slept overnight. Nurses report no confusion or hallucinations. Still unable to get out of bed. Cannot stand or walk. Denies shortness of breath today. Able to feed self with wife's assistance. Ataxia is better. Low-grade fever at 100.6. Chest: clear. Heart: regular rhythm, question of a faint murmur. Abdomen: benign. Conversant and mostly making sense. No fixed gaze. Nystagmus improved. No apparent hallucinations on my exam. Foley cath still in, draining well. Antinuclear antibodies negative. Sed rate normal. All cultures including fungi, mycoplasma and treponema are no growth. Polymerase chain reactions on all fluids negative as well. Assessment: Infectious meningoencephalitis with Guillain-Barré. Question source. Question organism. Now stable with slight, but progressive improvement. DTs resolved as well. Consider stopping antivirals and antibiotics. Continue immunoglobulin therapy. As per Dr. MacDougall, hold the Ativan and Haldol for now. Transfer to neuro rehab when medically stable. Dr. MacDougall states the plasmapheresis unit is down, so hold that as well. Call Alexandre to approve the nasopharyngoscopy.*

Overstreet closed the chart and whispered, "I certainly hope we've turned the corner on this animal." Then he sighed, "I haven't a clue what else to do."

280

Conversation 147
Los Angeles
Wednesday, August 7, 2002; 12:13 p.m.

Dr. MacDougall ignored his hospitalized patients altogether on the morning of August 7th, 2002. He had a flight to catch. As he settled into a first class seat on United's flight 2564, he checked his watch and took a deep, cleansing breath. The morning patients had left him wrung out – 13 of them all together, with his albatross, Velma Richardson to boot. "This evening's little San Francisco sojourn ought to be just what the doctor ordered," he smirked.

A flight attendant with sapphire blue eyes approached him, "Good afternoon, Dr. MacDougall! Welcome aboard United Airlines. May I get you a pillow and something to drink?"

"Yeah, sure. Make it two pillows and a Johnnie Walker Black – no wait – do you have Chivas 18?"

"No, I'm afraid not sir," the flight attendant smiled. "But we do have Johnnie Walker Black."

"I'll take that," MacDougall answered.

MacDougall watched the attendant walk back to the galley appraising her up and down. As he dialed his cell phone he said to himself, "Mmmm ... beautiful. She's got a nice ass, too."

On the fourth ring MacDougall began tapping his foot. On the sixth ring he muttered, "Where the fuck is she?"

After the eighth ring she picked up. "This is *Jasmine*," she whispered.

MacDougall looked down at his lap, then up at the ceiling and, turning his head right, out the window of the aircraft, "Uh, hi. Hello – uh, this is Ed Pinkerton. Calling to confirm our appointment this evening," his voice trembled.

"Oh, hi, Mr. Pinkerton. I was getting worried you'd never call. I'm *so* looking forward to our evening together – champagne – dinner in bed, chocolate for dessert. Oooh ... you are coming, aren't you, Mr. Ed?"

The flight attendant unfolded MacDougall's tray and set the Johnnie Walker on it, interrupting his train of thought. "Just a second," he stammered into the phone and then set it on the vacant seat next to him. With the cocktail napkin he wiped his brow, took a drink from the scotch, swallowed, picked up his phone and continued the conversation.

"Jasmine? You still there?" he asked.

"Yes, I'm here."

"Good. Okay. Sorry about that. The flight attendant brought my drink and I had to put the phone down."

"Is she pretty?" Jasmine asked. "She must be pretty."

"Actually, she is," MacDougall answered.

"Is she blond or brunette, Mr. Pinkerton?"

"Blond," he said wondering where this was leading.

"And she has a nice figure?" Jasmine asked.

"Hard to tell in her uniform, but I'd say so, yes."

"Do you prefer blondes or brunettes, Mr. Pinkerton?"

MacDougall took another drink from the Johnnie Walker, swallowed without tasting and answered, "I love women – red heads, blondes, brunettes – they're all delicious Jasmine, but you know that, all delicious."

"Mr. Pinkerton, I've got a friend – Tiffany. Beautiful blonde. Drop-dead, knock-out body and a smile that melts your insides. She could join us tonight if you like."

"Dinner and everything?" MacDougall asked, wondering what it would be like to have sex with two women as gorgeous as Jasmine at the same time. Son-of-a-bitch he thought.

"I say if I bring Tiffany, we skip the dinner and just get dessert. How does that sound?"

"Uh. It sounds nice," he faltered. "How about I think about it and let you know when I get there."

"Mr. Pinkerton. You have to understand this business," Jasmine asserted. "Tiffany's in high demand. If you want the ménage à trois, speak now or forever hold your peace."

MacDougall polished off the scotch and signaled the flight attendant for another. Pulling up on his trousers to conceal his erection, he said to himself, "What the hell, MacDougall, you only live once."

Jasmine broke his silence, "You there, Mr. Pinkerton?"

"I'm here. I'm in. Let's go for it."

"Fabulous. You will *not* be disappointed, Mr. Ed. I promise. Call me when you arrive. I'll have it all set up," she said. "Cheers 'til then."

"Cheers," MacDougall said and closed his phone.

He leaned back on the headrest, and closed his eyes, suppressing that damned urge to defecate that came with every case of the nerves. MacDougall considered his irrepressible visceral reflex a personality defect, a weakness that perturbed him. But he couldn't go to the toilet with the plane still on the ground, so he took a deep breath, tightened his sphincters and exhaled slowly, slowly, ever so slowly. Carefully passing a short burst of gas, he felt relief.

When the flight attendant came down the aisle holding his second scotch in one hand, she gripped a piece of paper in the other. She set the drink down, and then startled him by asking, "Here you go. And just checking, sir. You are, Dr. Jack MacDougall, aren't you?"

"I am. Why?"

"We have to be certain of our passengers. 911 and all, you know. I'm sure you understand. I couldn't help overhearing your telephone conversation. You introduced yourself as Ed Pinkerton."

MacDougall blushed, looked away, took a drink and said, "I'm Jack MacDougall ... *doctor* Jack MacDougall. You must have heard me saying I was calling for Mr. Pinkerton. Would you like to see my ID?"

"I'm afraid so, yes. It's regulation."

MacDougall reached back, dug out his wallet and showed her his driver's license. She looked him up and down, checking his photo against the real thing. "Very good," she said. "I apologize for any inconvenience."

"No problem. You're just doing your job."

"Make sure you fasten your seat belt. We're about to taxi," she said as she turned to go.

MacDougall closed his eyes, pushing the attendant's interrogation from his mind and said to himself, "Son-of-a-bitch. What a way to start a perfectly great getaway. Nosey cunt."

CONVERSATIONS FOR PACO

Conversation 148
Los Angeles County Hospital
Wednesday, August 7, 2002; 2:15 p.m.

As Jack MacDougall cruised at 28,000 feet toward San Francisco, Dr. George Alexandre raised Paco's hospital bed, infused 2.5mg. of Versed intravenously and waited for Paco to descend into semi-consciousness. Not satisfied with its effect, he pushed an additional milligram IV and made final preparations for the procedure by engaging the teaching attachment to the nasopharyngoscope. Justin Sutherland gripped the instrument and stood at Alexandre's side, anxious to confirm his suspicions – certain what they would find.

Alexandre gently passed the scope first up Paco's left nostril, then the right. In both instances, he extended the exam well beyond the arch of the sphenoid sinus and pituitary fossa – even to the point that Paco's vocal cords came into view. Moving the scope's controls both left and right and up and down, he carefully and methodically examined every millimeter of Paco Sánchez's nasal anatomy. Much to his satisfaction, everything was clean. Not the hint of a fistulous tract, perforation or fibrous patch. In fact, the grafted nasal mucosa on the right looked strikingly similar to that on the left.

"Wow, this is way too cool!" Sutherland exclaimed. "You can see everything. The definition is amazing!"

"It is, isn't it? So what do you think?"

"Well …" Sutherland paused, "I'm certainly no expert, this is all new to me, but it looks normal."

"I think so. No disruptions. No cryptic portals. No occult fistulas. By the way, I reviewed his MRI with radiology after my surgical cases this morning. On high resolution three dimensional scanning there are no visible defects."

Sutherland's heart sank. His grandiose hypothesis was all wrong. The miraculous answer he sought eluded him yet again. He still couldn't explain Paco's puzzle.

That's the trouble with being a medical student, he decided.

JAMES LENHART

Conversation 149
University Quad, Los Angeles
Wednesday, August 7, 2002; 4:32 p.m.

Sutherland made his way across campus to Falkner Hall and climbed the stairs to the third floor. Trudging down the corridor he found room 314 marked Peter Dornwyler, PhD Professor of Philosophy and Medical Ethics.

Absorbed in re-reading a manuscript prepared for publication, Dornwyler did not look up when Sutherland entered. When at last he finished the final paragraph, he stood, extended his hand and a warm smile, "Ahh-ha! Mr. Sutherland. Right on time. Come in. Sit down. To what do I owe this pleasure?"

Sutherland's gloomy mood permeated the atmosphere, "I need to talk sir."

"Talk?" Dornwyler persisted. "Okay ... but I'm no psychiatrist."

Sutherland cleared his throat, "I don't know who to trust – so I came to you."

Dornwyler leaned back in his chair, wrapped his hands behind his head and waited for Sutherland to continue.

The reason for his visit, and Dornwyler's silence, derailed Sutherland. He fidgeted and wondered if maybe he should excuse himself or even discuss something less personal like the principles of autonomy or truth telling, but finally he got his gumption and said, "I'm having second thoughts about medicine."

"Second thoughts? *You?* Why? What do you mean?"

"I like it and all ... at least most of it. Then again it's not what I thought it would be. I thought ... I thought it would be more like our ethics classes," he deliberated. "Dr. Dornwyler, I mean no disrespect to my clinical teachers – many of them are brilliant – it's the way they treat some patients and the slurs."

"Slurs?"

Sutherland wrung his hands, looked down to the floor and back to Dornwyler. "Slurs, sir. I've got this patient – well he's not really *my* patient. I did his spinal tap with Dr. Mack in County Hospital emergency, and since he's been admitted, I've been following him with the

285

attendings. Yesterday, the neurologist called Mr. and Mrs. Sánchez 'whining fucking wetbacks' – not to their faces of course – but in front of me. The patient is out of it half the time, his wife is delirious with worry, and the diagnosis is obscure. When I didn't respond, the attending glared at me – medicine is not what I imagined."

"The attending is no Marcus Welby I gather?"

"Marcus Welby?"

"TV series in the early seventies. Before you were born I'm guessing. Television portrayed Welby as the penultimate physician. A warm and fuzzy family doc; made house calls, delivered babies, cared about his patients. The whole shebang."

Sutherland hung his head, "I expected it to be more like that, yes."

Dornwyler leaned forward in his chair and stood, "I'm fixing some coffee, join me?"

"Yes, sir. Thank you."

The professor produced a bag of coffee from his credenza, unsealed it and held the opened container to his nose, "Ummm. Wait until you try this – half Sumatran and half Kona – very rich, very bold. All of that, yet velvet on the palate," he smirked. "I should have come up with this long ago."

Dornwyler dipped a spoon into the fresh grinds, measured six dollops of his blend into the filter and returned the basket to the coffee maker. From a pitcher he poured water into the percolator and flipped the switch. Dusting off his hands, he returned to his chair and said, "Well, well, Mr. Sutherland, reality sets in. The romance fades. It happens to most medical students – for different reasons I might add."

"It's just that ..."

"Hold that thought," Dornwyler broke in. "What's after graduation?"

"You mean residency?"

"Yes. Specialization."

"Family or emergency medicine. I haven't decided yet."

Dornwyler turned to the beep of the coffee maker, rolled his chair to the credenza and poured two cups. "Hmmm. So the internist and surgeons haven't gotten to you? Uh, cream or sugar?"

"They've tried. I've always seen myself as a family doctor. Even before I applied to medical school ..."

"Cream or sugar?" Dornwyler asked again.

"I'm sorry. Black, sir."

"The way God intended," Dornwyler chuckled and handed off the coffee. "You started to say a moment ago, and I interrupted."

"I started to say – actually, I don't remember what I was going to say for certain."

Holding the cup with both hands, Sutherland stared into the coffee, speechless. Tears welled into his eyes. "Dr. Dornwyler, it's the disrespect. Like they're better than the patients ... and the arrogance," he choked.

Sutherland wiped the tears with the back of his hand, sniffled and drank from the coffee.

"Like it?"

"Very good, sir. Thank you."

"You're welcome. Please, go on."

"The patient and his wife I mentioned. Mexican immigrants. The nicest people. He's very sick. His condition waxes and wanes – sometimes from hour to hour. Everyday it's something different. The attendings hurry in and hurry out, never taking time to sit down with him or his wife. Mrs. Sánchez is so frustrated. I try to fill in the gaps ..."

"Hmmm. Why do you suppose they do that?"

Sutherland looked into the coffee and took another drink. "I don't know. It's almost as if they cover the uncertainties and their inadequacies by talking down ..."

"Disgusting isn't it?" Dornwyler interrupted again. "Many physicians unglue with the dubious and struggle when patients don't respond like textbooks. And you're right – many, but not all, cover their frustration with airs of superiority and arrogance. As a family doctor it's something you'll have to get used to."

"What?" Sutherland scowled.

Dornwyler set his coffee on the scattered papers covering his desk and leaned forward, "How's the coffee?"

"Like I said. It's good, thank you. What do you mean ...?"

"Next time we'll have Ethiopian."

"Ethiopian?"

"Ethiopia is coffee's birthplace."

"I see," Sutherland nodded, "But what do you mean, I'll have to get used to it? Get used to what?"

"If you're 'just' a family doctor," Dornwyler signed quotes with his fingers, "It's my guess they'll likely talk down to you too."

Conversation 150
City Centre, Los Angeles
Wednesday, August 7, 2002; 5:22 p.m.

Geoff Boyer picked the tattered copy of Real Estates International off his desk and skimmed the pages. When he found the earmarked page marketing Villa Mira Mar Cortez in Cabo San Lucas he leaned back, put his feet on his desk and reviewed the advertisement for the umpteenth time.

Waterfront refined, tropical luxury. Private two and three bed-room villas. Choose from 2,232 to 2,869 square feet of extraordinary comfort. Breath taking views of the Sea of Cortez and Land's End over your own infinity edged pool. Spa, golf, tennis. Luxury homes by the sea. "That's it. Decision over. I'll call tomorrow and give it to Cindy for her birthday," he said out loud.

He threw the glossy on his desk, leaned forward and speed dialed Appleton. "You coming, Ralph? I've got the Dom on ice. If you don't get your ass in here you'll miss the news."

"Shit, Geoff, the time got away from me. I'm on my way."

Ralph Appleton knocked and entered just as Brian Williams on NBC Nightly News announced, "On Wall Street today, Goldman Sachs reported year-end results for Humanitarian Hospital Corporation that surprised even the most optimistic analysts. Despite the economic downturn created by 9/11, the nation's largest for-profit hospital chain reported earnings of $2.93 per share. Skeptical Wall Street brokers had predicted *losses* as high as $2.59 per share. Geoff Boyer, CEO and President of Humanitarian, cited improved revenues across most sectors and tight operations oversight for HHC's stellar performance. On the New York Stock Exchange today jubilant investors bid HHC higher. The hospital giant closed at $27.67, a gain in excess of four-dollars per share."

Boyer popped the cork on the Dom Pérignon pouring one glass for Appleton and one for himself. He handed Appleton his flute and toasted, "Outstanding, Mr. Ralph Appleton. Just out-fucking-standing."

Conversation 151
Marina del Rey
Wednesday, August 7, 2002; 6:56 p.m.

The heavy heat of a humid summer day had begun to fade when Ed Pinkerton answered his door, "Hey, Geoff. Come on in, we're back here in the den," he said leading Boyer to the rear of the house. "I was just telling Charlie that MacDougall flew to San Francisco this afternoon and won't be here tonight so I asked Richard Steinberg, my lab Director, to stand in. I hope that's okay."

Boyer concealed his disappointment, but was dismayed that he wouldn't get to high-five MacDougall over their good fortune. Besides, he wanted Jack's face to face reassurance that he had indeed placed the order for 10,000 shares of HHC before pulling the trigger on the villa in Cabo. "Of course it's okay. This is your poker night, Ed. What's Jack doing in San Francisco?"

"The American Neurological Society invited him to give a talk," Pinkerton said over his shoulder, "so he jumped on it ... Geoff Boyer, shake hands with Richard Steinberg my lab Director. Richard, Geoff Boyer CEO of Humanitarian Hospital Corporation. Of course you know Charlie Overstreet, Geoff."

Boyer shook Steinberg's hand, smiled and said "Hi Richard, Geoff Boyer." Then he turned to Overstreet, took his hand, gave him a bear hug 'n pat on the back and asked, "Hey Charlie, how they hanging? Good to see you again."

Pinkerton hiked up his pants for good measure and looked around at his guests, "All right. Before we begin. Judi's not here tonight – *girl's night out* with Carolyn MacDougall," he smirked. "So she set up the booze, chips and a platter of cheese and crackers on the table. I've got Tanqueray Ten, Chivas 18, Greygoose, Crown Royal and Remy

Martin X.O. There's Corona in the frig and a bucket of ice on the table. Help yourselves and we'll get rolling."

Boyer poured Chivas 18 over rocks, while Pinkerton and Steinberg took Tanqueray Ten. Charlie Overstreet settled for a bottle of Corona. They set their drinks and munchies on the poker table, Pinkerton shuffled the cards and Overstreet cut them.

He looked around the table and from his pink, puffy paws dealt the cards face down, "Okay, gents. Five card draw, five dollar ante, jacks or better to open."

After an hour of play Boyer had amassed a sizable pile of chips. "You play poker like you run HHC Geoff," Overstreet chided tossing in two reds. "I heard on the Nightly News this afternoon that Humanitarian had its best year ever. How did you manage such a stellar performance? You must be a freaking genius."

"Genius?" Boyer deadpanned. "Thanks, but it's not quantum physics Charlie – I'll raise you ten – how did I do it? Simple. First, I created a sense of urgency among all my hospital CEO's – scared the shit out of them really – and communicated throughout our entire organization my vision for Humanitarian's future *and* the corporation's dire straits if we didn't butt heads with this screwed up economy. In response, *they* voted to increase the nurse-to-patient ratios from 8 to 1 to 10 to 1, reduce healthcare benefits for employees, eliminate overtime and close the door on your quote unquote, self-payers – the uninsured. I flat out told them up and down the line, it's ludicrous to think HHC can make margin taking care of patients who have no payer source. Finally, I attacked supply costs. Medical devices like internal cardiac defibrillators and titanium joints drop directly to our bottom line – and they cost a fortune. Since January our policy states that no patient may have implantable devices placed without prior insurance company authorization *and* the patient's signed declaration to pay any and all implantable device deductibles. Genius? I'm no genius. We reduced expenses, improved our receivables, managed supply costs and filled beds with paying patients. As I said – simple."

"How do all those reductions affect patient care? I should think it would …"

"Look," Boyer broke in. "Sophisticated patients demand – and we provide – state of the art, high resolution imaging, the finest surgical robots and cyber knives money can buy, genetic analysis beyond compare. You can't have everything in the competitive marketplace of healthcare. Something has to give, which often means reductions in nursing to patient ratios and closing our doors to patients without a payer source."

Steinberg folded. Charlie Overstreet and Pinkerton matched Boyer's ten. "So what's the bottom line, Geoff? How much profit?"

Boyer smiled, "It's not profit, Ed, its 'contribution to margin' – just north of 90 million on revenue of two point two billion."

Overstreet whistled, "Wow-e-e-e-e!"

Pinkerton dealt cards to Boyer, Overstreet and himself, "Pretty impressive results I'd say, Geoff."

Boyer looked over his cards and back at the table, "Some analyst predicted we'd lose up to $200 million. Given this stinkin' 9/11 crap, I'm pretty happy – raise you twenty – it puts Humanitarian at the top of the heap nationwide amongst all the for-profits."

Overstreet called Boyer, Pinkerton folded and asked, "So, Mr. President and CEO, what's it mean to you?"

"What do you mean? Compensation?"

"Yeah," Pinkerton asked again, clearing his throat. "How does Humanitarian reward you?"

Boyer couldn't believe Pinkerton's gall, but chose to ignore it. "The system plays pretty straightforward. All our CEOs work on a base plus incentives. Depending on the size of the unit and budgetary responsibility, incentives push down as a percentage of margin – of course HHC strictly forbids disclosing incentive policies. Let's just say where I reign between base salary, stock options and bonuses they take pretty good care of me. Way more than I thought I'd ever make."

Pinkerton dealt fifth cards to Overstreet and Boyer, "Just for grins, Geoff, let's say your bonus is 10% of margin," Pinkerton snorted. "That comes out to over $9 million."

"Ed Pinkerton, you're an obnoxious bastard, an obnoxious fucking bastard you are, Ed Pinkerton," Boyer blushed. "And Charlie – it'll cost you another $20 to my see my cards."

Conversation 152
Bellflower
Wednesday, August 7, 2002; 9:03 p.m.

Sarita Sánchez cut an apple into several slices, poured a chilled mandarin Jarritos into a tumbler and sat at the kitchen table before a stack of unopened mail. Miguel and José bathed and tucked in, Angelina fed and fast asleep, she sorted through the mail, mostly junk, and sipped on her beverage. The bills she stacked in one pile, throwing the junk mail in the trash.

She read a letter from her sister in Guadalajara, finished the Jarritos, poured another, and returned to the bills. Barking neighborhood dogs had Muchi whining at the backdoor, so Sarita let her out to join their chorus before digging through the invoices.

She sat back down, fingered a piece of apple into her mouth and chewed on it. Working her way through the pile, she came to a thick envelope, return addressed *Pinkerton Pathology Associates.* Page one read:

Pinkerton Pathology Associates, Edmund M. Pinkerton, MD, LLC
"Health through Laboratory Medicine since 1994"

Itemized Statement For: Paco R. Sánchez
Date of Birth: March 14, 1973
Employer: Republic Waste
Insurance: None (self-pay)
Account Number: PRS03141973BFD
Dates of Services: July 26, 2002 – July 31, 2002

Sarita scanned page after page of itemized charges for metabolic profiles, complete blood counts with differential, complete blood counts without differential, anti-nuclear antibodies, polymerase chain reactions, sedimentation rates, urinalysis, blood cultures, cold agglutinins, urine porphyrins, serum protein electrophoresis, spinal fluid analysis, specimen acquisition, handling fees, specimen preparation, and fecal occult blood. On page 14, she came to the five day total and the disclaimer:

Total charges for period: $8,176.32

Conversation 153
Marina del Rey
Wednesday, August 7, 2002; 10:33 p.m.

Pinkerton shuffled the cards and passed the deck to Geoff Boyer, "Cut."

Boyer cut the cards and begged, "Treat me right, honey."

"Okay," Pinkerton announced. "Final hand, seven card stud, Jacks or better to open, ante upped from $25.00 to $50.00."

Boyer drew from his cigar, picked up two green chips and tossed them to the center of the table. "I'm in."

"Me too," countered Steinberg.

Pinkerton added his. Charlie Overstreet tossed his in as well. With the ante set, Pinkerton dealt the cards, two each face down to all four players, "Jacks or better to open" he reminded them.

Richard Steinberg picked up his cards, surveyed them, emitted a groan and scratched his head, "So Geoff I've been muddling over this all night. I follow healthcare securities pretty close. Stock market analysts pegged HHC for substantial losses. Instead you turn in a huge profit. I'm impressed, but I still don't get how you did it."

Boyer sipped the Chivas 18, chewed some ice, and peeked at his hand. "Uh-huh. Two queens," he said to himself, then cleared his throat and threw in four greens, "I'll open for $100.00."

Overstreet folded. Steinberg countered with $100.00. Pinkerton followed, then dealt one card each to Steinberg, Boyer, and himself face up.

"Queen high, your bet, Geoff."

Boyer chuckled, "First off, Richard, tells you something about stock market analysts – mostly they got their heads up their ass and don't know shit – here's another $50.00 for the gipper," he stonewalled. "Second, I ground the corporation on a matrix model. As a radical departure from heavy handed, top-down thinking, the matrix creates cultural confusion at times, but senior leaders *and* middle manag-

293

ers love it. As an important side benefit, matrix models improve corporate dialogue. Really, as I think on it, internal communication keyed the success ..."

"Richard?" Pinkerton asked.

"I'm in," he said, checking his cards and tossing in two greens.

Pinkerton looked over his cards, a seven and a nine in the hole, king showing. "Here's my $50.00 and I'll raise you $50.00," he bluffed.

Steinberg paused, looked at his hand, and tossed in $50.00 more.

Boyer threw in his chips and continued, "Remember that 'sense of urgency' I talked about? Back in January I wrote a 'dire straits' memo to all our hospital CEOs. I impressed upon them the unfavorable outlook if we operated status quo. Even floated the rumor we might need to sell the corporate jet. I didn't threaten them with their jobs and I didn't have to. They imagined that. The matrix spread the word, magnified the sense of urgency. Leaders took charge; I re-fueled their anxiety from time to time – and bingo! – June 30, 2002."

"Here they come, around the horn." Pinkerton declared dealing a six of hearts to Boyer, a jack of spades to Steinberg and a king of hearts to himself.

"But where did market analysts get the idea HHC was headed for the crapper?" Steinberg persisted.

"Easy. I labeled the dire straits memos strictly confidential. Gets the word out every time!" Boyer chirped.

"And for that you make nine-million bucks?" Pinkerton chided.

Boyer's face reddened. He wanted to kick Pinkerton in his big fat belly, or better yet his balls, but bit his tongue and countered, "How many shares of HHC have you got Ed?"

"Fifteen-thousand. Why?"

"What did you buy it at?"

"Around twenty-three bucks a pop."

"So my math says you made $60,000 today. Not bad for doing nothing while sitting on your fat fucking ass," he smirked.

Pinkerton cleared his throat, threw in a black and said, peering over the rim of his eye glasses, "Well, Geoffrey Boyer, I guess you set me straight. But enough of this corporate blah, blah, blah. My kings are riding high gentlemen and that'll cost you another $100.00."

Steinberg shook his head, took a long sniff of Remy Martin and folded. Boyer hesitated, rubbed his brow, and said, "You lucky bastard Pinkerton, Who shuffled these cards? I'll stay and raise you $50.00."

"You bluffing?" Pinkerton asked, pulling a swig from a fresh Corona.

"Yours to find out, Dr. Pinkerton. Yours to find out!" Boyer warned him.

Pinkerton tossed in two greens. Boyer looked at the pot mentally adding – eleven hundred bucks – not bad.

Pinkerton cradled the deck in his palm, "Just you and me, Geoff. You ready?"

"Ready."

Pinkerton tossed a six of clubs toward Boyer dealing himself a two of diamonds.

"A pair of sixes never beat a pair of kings, Boyer; I'm in for another $100."

"Me too, Ed ... 'cuz I've got you beat in the hole," Boyer responded looking over the queens and the sixes.

Boyer took another drink from the Chivas 18 and said, "Hey, Ed. I think I found the perfect hunt."

"Oh yeah. And I suppose we'll have to ride on the back of a mountain cat to get there," he said, looking toward Steinberg and then back to Boyer. "You ready?"

"Ready."

Pinkerton dealt Boyer a four of clubs and himself another king, "Oooh! Look out. Got you now big guy, and that will cost you two hundred big ones."

"Steinberg, did *you* cut these cards?" Boyer scowled.

"*You* know damn well who cut the cards, Boyer. So where's the hunt?" Pinkerton asked.

"Missouri."

"Missouri? Are you fucking kidding me? Hunting in Missouri?"

"Missouri. It's 100 miles southwest of St. Louis. *Prime Adventure Big Game Hunting Ranch*. Right in the heart of the Ozarks."

"You in, Geoff, or folding?" Pinkerton queried.

"Raise you $100.00," Boyer answered.

"Get this gents, he's living on the edge. I'll match you, Geoff."

Boyer sniffed the Chivas, took a drink and continued, "As I said, they call it *Prime Adventure Big Game Hunting Ranch*. There's another one – *Renegade Hunting Ranch* – in northern Michigan. Personally, I like *Prime Adventure*."

Boyer looked over his cards and went on, "I found it on the inter- net. We fly to St. Louis, stay overnight, drive down the next day – looks like a beautiful lodge – and they take care of everything. You can hunt deer or elk – even Rocky Mountain big horn sheep and water buf- falo. And they guarantee you'll bag your game."

"Jesus! Judi would shit if I hung a water buffalo's head in here!" Pinkerton laughed.

"Down and dirty, Geoff?"

"Down and dirty, Ed me bucko."

Pinkerton dealt Boyer an ace of diamonds and himself a three of clubs. "Three kings bet, and it'll cost you another $200.00."

Overstreet and Steinberg stared at the mound of money. Over $2,000.00. Nice pot, Charlie thought.

Boyer picked up six blacks, rolled them between his fingers and scratched his head, "Hmmm. Tell you what Ed, I'll meet your $200.00 and raise you $400.00."

Pinkerton looked over his glasses and down his nose at Boyer, "My $400.00 says you're bluffin' big shot."

"Try me fat bastard."

"Let's see what you got," Pinkerton countered.

Boyer uncovered his hole. "Three queens, two sixes."

"Son-of-a-cocksucking bitch," Pinkerton snorted, throwing down his cards. "You motherfucker, Boyer, I thought you were bluffing! Oh hell with it, there's more where that came from. Anyway as they say – easy fucking come, easy fucking go. How about a nightcap, gents?"

Conversation 154
Los Angeles County Hospital
Thursday, August 8, 2002; 9:32 a.m.

The next morning Sarita stood at Paco's bedside trying to feed him when Dr. MacDougall came in beaming. "Well, well. How's our patient today?"

Sarita had slept in fits and she was in no mood for condescension. Pinkerton's bill had unraveled her. The baby's somersaulting in her uterus, compounded the sleeplessness as well. And something gnawing at her sixth sense that she couldn't put her finger on, made her toss and turn all night. When the sun finally came up, she showered and rushed back to the hospital, where her fears were realized.

"He seems worse again. He will not eat and he is more confused, and see his right arm. It is twitching. The nurses say that he have a very bad night. They say that they try to call you, but that you did not answer."

MacDougall's thoughts flashed on Jasmine and her friend Tiffany. He smiled inwardly and countered, "I presented at the American Neurological Society in San Francisco last evening, and just got back this morning. Let's have a look. The nurses told me his respirations and temperatures were up again – of course fever always causes increased respirations – they use it to fight the fever."

"They?"

"Yes. Patients – it's a physiologic mechanism to reduce fever," MacDougall said placing his stethoscope to Paco's chest.

"Paco is not a 'they' and he is getting worse again."

"Mrs. Sánchez, I've told you, Guillain-Barré behaves this way. The syndrome fluctuates up and down. All in all he's better. We saw this all the time at the Mass …"

"I do not care about the Massachusetts General," Sarita insisted. "I care about Paco. Better yesterday, worse today. Everyday something new. Up and down. Look at him sweat. Paco he never sweats like this. And he is more confused and sometimes when you talk he say nothing. It is like he is not here."

"The sweating? Reflex sympathetic dystrophy … its part of the picture. Excuse me. Could you move so I can finish my evaluation?"

Sarita moved away. Folding her arms across her chest, she felt her heart racing and her legs growing weak. A headache pounded like a hammer between her eyes and spread through to the center of her skull.

And she couldn't take a full breath. Standing at the back of Jack Mac-Dougall – just looking at him – made her blood boil. "He does not care for my Paco," she said to herself.

When MacDougall finished, he raised up, turned and faced Sarita, "Well, I must admit his lungs sound like he may have a little pneumonia. I'll call Overstreet and get his take. In any event, his breathing seems labored again."

"What about the plasma treatment?"

MacDougall pulled a handkerchief from his coat pocket and wiped the moisture gathered on his upper lip, "I checked when I came in. The unit is still down. Let me go call Overstreet. I'll be right back."

While Sarita waited, Paco lay in wet, sweat laden bed clothes staring at the ceiling. She held his hand, praying the rosary over and over, asking God what to do, when MacDougall returned.

"I spoke with Overstreet. He'll be here in thirty minutes or so. In the meantime, we'll get a chest x-ray."

"I want him in a more better hospital," Sarita declared. "He is not better. You do not understand what is wrong or how to treat him. When I go to the library and read from the family medical encyclopedia about this thing you call Guillain-Barré, it says Paco should have a heart monitor and be in the Intensive Care. It says *you* should not let Paco get pneumonia. You have done none of these things. And the machine it is broken. I want him moved to Humanitarian Hospital."

"Mrs. Sánchez, encyclopedias are very basic; they generalize. I myself value science. I practice in a world where every patient is unique and, as I am certain you can tell, I pride myself in personal attention and care tailored to each individual. Besides, transferring him is not so easy. He's unstable."

Sarita's wrath unleashed, "Unstable? You said he was better, that this is part of his sickness. Now you say he have pneumonia. That does not sound better to me. I want Paco moved to a hospital and to doctors that can get him well."

MacDougall yanked a paper towel from the dispenser and blotted the beads of sweat welled up on his forehead. He then made an unapologetic about face, glared at Sarita, harrumphed and growled, "I'll call social work and see what we can do. But don't forget who's the doctor here, Mrs. Sánchez. I'm ordering the chest x-ray."

Sarita's faced turned scarlet. Looking MacDougall straight on, eye ball to eye ball, she lashed out, "And what will that cost? $8,000.00 like Pinker Patho Associates?"

MacDougall shifted his weight from one foot to the other. He wished he were back in San Francisco with his consorts. Sarita's *non sequitur* muddled his thoughts and took his tongue. Finally he responded, "Mrs. Sanchez, nobody said the best health care in the world was inexpensive. You must understand …"

"I understand only this," she asserted. "My Paco is worse. You now say he have pneumonia. In this hospital he cannot get the treatment that Dr. Sutherland say is the most important …"

"Dr. Sutherland?"

"Yes, he tell me he did research and he say that the plasma treatment …"

"Mrs. Sánchez, Justin Sutherland is a medical student. He's no doctor *and* he's not even assigned to this case …"

"It does not matter. He comes to see Paco every day. He answers all of my questions. He read about the Guillain-Barré and he tell me everything."

MacDougall's smirk could not camouflage his anger. His face turned blood red. "You put your trust in a medical student over me? Well, we shall see about this, Mrs. Sánchez. Certainly, we shall see about this," he declared storming from the room.

Conversation 155
Los Angeles County Hospital
Thursday, August 8, 2002; 11:13 a.m.

A comfortably dressed woman with a soft face and warm smile entered Paco's room. She shuffled over to Sarita and extended her hand. "Hi. I'm Lucille Stufflebeam. I'm one of the social workers here at County Hospital. I reviewed your husband's chart and came to see you. From what I gather, you and Paco have had a pretty rough time – you are, Mrs. Sánchez, aren't you?"

Sarita stood up and said, "Thank you. Yes, I am Sarita Sánchez. This is my husband Paco. He is so sick," she said releasing Stufflebeam's hand and reaching for Paco's. "Look at him. He does not know who I am half the time. Today he does nothing but sleep and he is very hard to wake up. He have fever, and look how he breathes. Dr. MacDougall now say he have pneumonia."

"I know," the social worker sighed. "The nurses told me. How are *you* doing?"

"It is awful," Sarita's face reddened. "I hate this hospital. I hate doctors who do not do nothing, who talk down to you, who do not look you in the eye and do not tell you nothing. This hospital is for poor people, they have no machines or the machines they are broken. Paco and me we are not poor. But he have been without a steady job and he have just gone back to work when this happened."

"Dr. MacDougall said you want him transferred."

"I want him transferred to Humanitarian Hospital. That is our hospital. That is where our babies are born," Sarita insisted.

Stufflebeam motioned to the chair and extended her hand, "Let's sit down. Maybe you can tell me about your family. Do you have children?" she asked.

Sarita pulled the chair over to Paco's bedside, sat down and, leaning forward, took Paco's hand, "Yes. We have Miguel, who is almost 7. Then there is José, he is 4. Angelina is 6 months, and I have one on the way," she said curling her arm around her abdomen.

"I bet they are beautiful."

"Next to Paco, they are my life. Miguel he looks just like Paco, big, strong and brave ... the same with José. Angelina – well like her name – she have to be an angel. I will show you the photographia," she said reaching for her purse. "I have one in here," Sarita said digging through it until she found what she was looking for.

Stufflebeam took the photograph from Sarita and examined it. "They're darling," she smiled. "Who is the woman?"

"That is Mamacita. She is Paco's mother. She lives with us. Thank God for Mamacita at this time," Sarita declared signing a cross over forehead, abdomen and chest. "I cannot take care of the children with Paco like this. I have to be in the hospital as much as I can."

"They're beautiful, Mrs. Sánchez," Stufflebeam said handing back the picture. "What's your dog's name?"

"Her name is Muchi. Paco pick Muchi up before I came to the United States you know as a – how do you say – 'stray'?"

"Yes," Stufflebeam nodded, "stray."

"Thank you."

Sarita wrung her hands, folded them in her lap and continued. "Paco pick her up when he first came to the United States. He is working with his uncle Raphael when he find Muchi. Paco say she is all skinny and dirty and very afraid. But Paco feed her some food every time he have a chance, and little by little she comes to Paco and he have her ever since. When Paco is laying bricks, he take Muchi to work with him every day. Every day I come home, Muchi she wag her tail and look at me like she want to say, 'where is mi padre?' When I say, 'Paco he is very sick and still in the hospital, Muchi' her tail droops and she hang her head and goes to sit by the door waiting for Paco, like he is going to come through it any minute."

Stufflebeam wiped a tear from her own eye, looked at Paco, then back to Sarita, "I checked on the transfer. Humanitarian claims you have an unpaid, outstanding bill."

"Yes, for Angelina. Paco lost his job – and the insurance – just before she have been born."

"I realize it must be hard to understand this, Mrs. Sánchez, but Paco can't transfer to Humanitarian unless the bill is paid." She paused, "In full."

"I do not, I cannot, we do not. He have to stay here – at the County Hospital?"

"I am checking with University Hospital. That's an option. They have the best ..."

"I want Humanitarian," Sarita declared. "When we have insurance, they always treat our family so good."

"I understand, but would University be okay?" Stufflebeam asked.

Sarita looked over at Paco, around the room and out the window, "No experiments. No way do I want Paco to be an experiments. When Paco is eighteen or nineteen he have a very bad problem with the scar and Dr. Alexandre he spends two years at the University doing experiments they have never done before. Paco say he is very happy, but he never want to have that again. I do not want Paco to have the experiments. Paco he is not an experiment."

Sarita's declaration intrigued Stufflebeam. Although she wanted to hear more, time was short; she needed to get cracking on the transfer and decided she could fill in the rest of the story later. "No experiments, Sarita," Lucille Stufflebeam reassured her. "I will get them to promise."

Conversation 156
Los Angeles County Hospital
Thursday, August 8, 2002; 12:15 p.m.

Sarita massaged Paco's face, running her hands across his brow and brushing the hair off of his temples. "Paco? Please keep fighting. Somehow I get you transferred to Humanitarian and to the right doctors. Keep fighting for me. I love you so much. Say something Paco. Say something," she whimpered.

Paco blinked half-shut eyes and swallowed, but looked neither in Sarita's direction nor answered her plea. She watched him breathe. Deep, heavy breaths. He hiccupped. Then he sneezed. Showering mucus down his nose and mouth and onto the bedcovers. Indifferent to it, he made no attempt to wipe it away. So Sarita wet two washcloths, cleaned the mucus with the first, and washed his face and neck with the second.

She thought she detected a smile but couldn't be certain, so she rinsed the cloth and repeated the process including his chest and arms, "Does this feel good ... does this feel good, mi amor?"

When she finished she took his hand and prayed, "Dear Lord and Jesus, please answer my prayer. Help Paco to gain your strength and give him the power to heal this awful sickness and, dear God, give me the strength and wisdom to be ever present at Paco's side and to know what I must do to help him. Bless Mamacita for her help. Bless and protect my little ones, all – Miguel, José, Angelina, and Muchi – and bless the baby inside of me, dear God. Amen."

Sarita repeated the Lord's Prayer and the rosary over and over, the beads tumbling through her fingers one by one when the scheme came to her. She slid the Walkman headphones over Paco's ears, pushed play, picked up her purse and scurried from the room saying, "I can be right back, Paco, and I bring you some other music. I think that maybe God he have answered my prayers."

Conversation 157
Los Angeles
Thursday, August 8, 2002; 3:08 p.m.

Sarita Sánchez charged frantically through traffic to her destination, while Jack MacDougall carried Paco's chart to the physician's lounge shaking his head. He poured a cup of coffee, took a deep breath and sat down to write.

More pronounced cognitive changes coupled with increasing respiratory difficulties. This afternoon the nurses called to report sudden onset of bizarre unexplained movements. On my evaluation, he indeed demonstrates loss of speech, episodic agitation, and now, of all things, finger snapping. A Foley cath is in place. For the most part, has not been out of bed since admission. His exam reveals no purposeful response to stimuli, but he does startle. His respiratory rate has increased. He moves his upper extremities, but not purposefully, and withdraws legs to painful stimuli. In the intermittent episodes without agitation, he is quite lethargic.

Assessment & plan: Unstable, deteriorating. Guillain-Barré with pneumonitis superimposed, as the most likely explanations for worsening symptoms. Condition is guarded. County's plasmapheresis device still not in operation. Needs transfer to Humanitarian or University. Discuss moving him to IMC or the ICU with Dr. Overstreet, until transfer can be arranged. I looked for Mrs. Sánchez to review his condition, but nurses said she left just before he took this turn for the worse. Will try again later.

MacDougall closed the chart, threw the pen on the table, leaned back, rubbed his eyes and yawned. His brain ached from lack of sleep, too much champagne and cavorting until dawn with Jasmine and her delicious friend.

He shook his head to break the cobwebs and confessed, "For all sorts of reasons, I need to transfer this guy."

MacDougall yawned again and stared mindless out the window. The billboard across the freeway advertising *The Soprano's* reminded him of Tiffany and Jasmine and the hard-on he got watching the two of them kiss. Then he thought of Tiffany's delicious body and chuckled, "Jesus Christ, what a great night."

Conversation 158
Los Angeles
Thursday, August 8, 2002; 3:22 p.m.

The sign on the parapet of the building advertised:
PAYDAY LOANS
Signature – Paycheck – Car Title
LOANS
And bold red letters with bright orange background on the plate-glass window to the left of the entrance advertised "Need a Loan, We Can Help"; letters to the right of the door, on the opposite plate-glass window, translated the words into Spanish "Necesita Dinero, Le Podemos Ayudar" – these words Sarita Sánchez understood.

Sarita parked Paco's pickup, entered the building and greeted the woman behind the counter. "Buenas tardes," she said. "My name is Sarita Sánchez. I would like to make a loan?"

"Buenas tardes," the woman smiled, "I am Carmen Aguilera, what kind? Have you had a loan before?"

"No, not before. Not here. I want to borrow on Paco's pickup," she said, handing a piece of paper to the woman.

"This is the title?" Aguilera asked examining the document. "Good. Let's see, 1997 Toyota Tundra. Is that it out there?"

"Si ... I mean," Sarita's voice trembled.

Carmen smiled and walked from behind the counter, "Let's have a look."

Sarita followed the loan officer out to the parking lot. Carmen pushed back her hair and walked around the Toyota, checking the tires one by one and then the exterior. She opened the door and checked the interior and the odometer. "68,367 miles. Nice, real nice – clean. Your husband takes good care of it."

"Paco, he bought it new. We finish paying in last December. Paco, he love his truck."

Carmen climbed in behind the steering wheel and asked, "Do you have the keys, Mrs. Sánchez? I want to start it up."

Aguilera took the keys from Sarita, turned the ignition, revved the engine three or four times and said, "Very good. You should see some of the trucks we get in here. I call them trash-ups. Couldn't loan money on them for anything. Let me get the serial number … J-P-X-Q-0-0-0-1-4-9-7-4-X-Z. Okay, let's go back inside."

The loan officer studied the title, strumming her nails on the counter, comparing the serial number for a match. "So, held jointly in the names of Paco and Sarita Sánchez, 1997 Toyota Tundra, correct serial numbers," she said feigning a cough. "Everything's in order. The truck looks good as new. How much did you want to borrow?"

"How much can I borrow?"

"Maximum is 60% of value. Of course, we have to verify employment and check for bankruptcy. Ever declare bankruptcy, Mrs. Sánchez?"

Sarita floundered and then said, "No."

"Credit okay?"

"I think so. Paco he pay the bills. When they lay him off, we got a little behind."

Carmen smiled, "Uh-huh … okay. You make out the application, while I do the credit check and determine its value. You can have a seat over there. Here is a pen, clipboard, and application. Want some water or soda? Oh, I need your social security numbers and you said something about when Paco was laid off. Is he working now?"

"Yes, he is working," Sarita lied.

"Where?"

Sarita's face reddened. She looked down and then back at the loan officer, "Republic Waste. He works picking up the garbage."

"Oooh. Sounds like hard, miserable work."

"It is very hard. But the money it is pretty good and they have insurance. Paco, he is a mason but there have been no jobs and he never complain. I fill out the paperwork," she said avoiding any further discussion.

CONVERSATIONS FOR PACO

Conversation 159
Los Angeles County Hospital
Thursday August 8, 2002; 6:42 p.m.

When she returned to the hospital, Sarita wiped Paco's face and neck again with a warm, wet wash cloth. Each time he smacked his lips and snapped his fingers she trembled. "What is this?" she said to herself.

"Paco," she whispered stroking his forehead and hair, "It is okay. You rest. I give you some new music."

She removed the plastic wrapper from Luis Miguel's *Todos Los Romances* CD and put it the player. Adjusting the Walkman headphones over his ears she said, "See what I have for you, Paco?"

Sarita pushed play, turned the volume up just enough so she could hear the lyrics and observed his reaction; the music seemed to sooth his agitation. She released his hand, sat back, pulled a blanket over her shoulders and curled up in the chair listening. The lyrics from "Cuando Vuelva a Tú Lado" gave her some peace and half-way through "No sé tú," she fell asleep.

> *"No sé tú.*
> *(I don't know about you)*
> *Pero yo te busco en cada amanecer*
> *(But I look for you every morning when I wake up)*
> *Mis deseos no los puedo contener*
> *(I can't help my desires)*
> *En la noche, cuando duermo*
> *(In the night, when I'm sleeping)*
> *Si de insomnio, yo me enfermo*
> *(I'll get insomnia)*
> *Me haces falta, mucha falta*
> *(I miss you, very much)*
> *No sé tú.*
> *(I don't know about you)."*

When Sarita felt Raphael's hand on her shoulder, she woke with a start. Outside, night drew the curtain on day. She shook the sleep from her head, rubbed her eyes and welcomed him, "Buenas noches, Rapha-el!"

"Buenas noches, Sarita. I am sorry I am late. The traffic it is very bad. How is he doing?"

Sarita stood and took Paco's hand. "To me he seem worse. He is sleeping now but earlier he does not know where he is again and he smacks his lips and snaps his fingers. I do not understand Raphael," she exhaled. "I gave for him the Luis Miguel CD and when I play it he seem to be more better."

She pushed replay on the Walkman again and asked, "Can you sit down for a while, Raphael? I would like it."

Raphael pulled the straight back chair next to the bed. Dumb-founded, they both sat in silence staring at Paco. Finally, Raphael spoke. "This have to be some kind of mistake, Sarita. Paco, he is al-ways so healthy. When I bring him to the United States he is so strong. Even as a boy he work in circles around the men. They say you never have to worry about Paco when you have to have the mortar he is one step ahead, always keeping the palate full."

Raphael took her hand, leaned forward and looked into her eyes. "He love you so much Sarita. I remember when he came back from Guadalajara after he first meet you, he is so happy. His face turn all red and he say to me he has love for the most beautiful woman on the earth. He tells me all about you – your hair, your eyes, your smile – he say you look like the cameo and you are his princess. He is so excited he cannot keep his mouth from talking over and over. I almost get him to stop, it is so much, but I can never do that to him, so he keep talking and telling me. He thinks about nothing else. And he worry that you maybe forget him and he ask me what to do. I say write her the letters. I say the woman always have in their hearts the desire for the love let-ters. I say to him that is how I get Graciela to love me. I write her let-ters.

"I came into the kitchen that night and he is writing something. I look over his shoulder and he is copying the Spanish letters into Eng-lish. I say to him, 'You are estúpido, Paco. How can you tell her you love her if she does not speak or read English?' He look up at me with those eyes only he have and say to me, 'I send the letters in Spanish.

Then when Sarita comes to the United States with me, I teach her the English like you and the school teach me. I give her the English copies of my letters to learn from.' So I say nothing no more about the letters. Like Paco, he know what he wants and he know what he have to do to get it.

"But I do tell him if he love you very much he should write you the poems. I tell him, 'write her the poems and she loves you forever. I promise.' He only say to me with a red face and frown, 'Uncle Raphael, I am no Don Juan.' I tell him to try it. He just shake his head.

"The next night he is sitting at the table. He is writing the poems. Each one he grunts, crumples into a ball and throws away. I laugh at him and say nothing. He is so in love with you."

Paco stirred, smacked his lips and snapped his fingers. Sarita stood up and took his hand, "It is okay, Paco. Listen to the music. Everything it is okay," she reassured him and turned back to Raphael whispering, "You say a beautiful story, Raphael. Thank you for telling me."

"He never give you the letters?"

"The immigration get him so upset," she said wiping the tears that bobbed up in the well of each eye, "I think maybe he is just happy to have me here and know that I learn what I need because we both want it so much. It does not matter now. Look at him."

"Yes, I think so, Sarita," Raphael shrugged.

"The music calms him. He is resting."

"He has to sleep," Raphael said stretching his arms above his head and looking at his watch, "I tell Graciela I would not stay so long. She worry that I come home late and get up so early."

Sarita released Paco's hand and reached for Raphael, "Tomorrow I am to get him transferred. Call me before you come. I am hoping to have him at Humanitarian Hospital ... good night, Raphael. Thank you for coming and telling me the stories."

Conversation 160
Los Angeles County Hospital
Friday, August 9, 2002; 7:36 a.m.

On Friday morning charge nurse Priscilla Collins cornered Dr. MacDougall, "If you're going to put Mr. Sánchez in restraints, I need you to help me complete this form."

"What form?"

"A new policy on restraining patients – documents the thought process, conditions and alternatives – actually I think it's a good procedure. I'll fill it out, but need to review it with you as I complete it."

"When did he fall out of bed?"

"Cindy Dwyer gave report. At around 2:00 a.m. he pulled out his Foley and IV lines. When Cindy found him, he was on the floor screaming about spiders and snakes. They got him back in bed but he fought them all the way. We had to restrain him to get his IV and Foley back in. After they pushed 5 mg of IV Haldol, he settled down."

"Pardon the expression but what the fuck is going on with this guy? I keep thinking he is better, and then he's worse. His wife really gave it to me and this hospital yesterday – says she wants him transferred."

"The social worker tells me he can't go to Humanitarian – apparently an unpaid bill. She is working on University. I agree, Jack. He's been over the top. My nurses are going nuts too."

"Bizarre, nothing fits. I thought I would never say it but, I never saw anything like this at the Mass General."

"Forget the Mass General, Jack, and help me with this restraint protocol."

"I suppose you heard the Red Sox beat the Yankees again."

"Knock it off and get back to work – help me fill out this form – okay? Describe the behavior that places the patient at risk:

"Number 1: Unintentional, disorganized behavior/confusion that interferes with prescribed treatment modalities?"

"Check."

"Number 2: Patient requires medical immobilization to protect lines, tubes, drains?"

MacDougall scratched his neck and then frowned, "Check."

"Number 3: Danger to self/others/environment; combative, psychotic disorder."

"Check – wait, how did he get out of bed, I thought he's hardly out of bed since admission?" MacDougall asked.

"He hasn't been and I have no earthly idea how he managed it this time. You know how psycho patients get. Somehow he got out and Dwyer found him on the floor."

"Did he hit his head?"

"I asked Cindy. She didn't see anything. I checked too. Except for a little scratch on his arm, nothing, no bumps or bruises ..."

"Good."

"Okay. Let's finish this thing up."

"Number 4: Alternatives to immobilization: a) Verbal reminders?"

"Check."

"b) Alter environment/reduce stimuli?"

"Check."

"c) Family or significant other sits with patient?"

"Check."

"Last question Jack – Number 5: Notification schedule: per MDs directives?"

"Sounds good to me."

"Great. Sign it, and I'll chart it. Thanks, Dr. MacDougall."

MacDougall took the form, scribbled his name and said, "No problem. See you later. Oh! It's Pettitte on the mound against Pedro Martinez tonight – your Yankees don't have a chance in hell, Collins."

"We'll see. Pettitte's on a four game winning streak."

"So? Not a chance. No way Pettitte can outduel Martinez," MacDougall echoed heading down the hall.

Conversation 161
Los Angeles County Hospital
Friday, August 9, 2002: 10:13 a.m.

Justin Sutherland found Sarita sitting at Paco's side, holding his hand, staring at his restrained arms and legs. She didn't hear the medical student enter, and when he placed his hand on her shoulder, she startled, "Oh my God!" she exclaimed. "You scare me!"

"I am sorry, Mrs. Sánchez, I didn't ..."

310

"No, it is all right, I am in another world. I cannot think of nothing. Look at Paco. I was trying to comfort him, get him to settle down. Look at him."

Sutherland looked down. Paco lay in the disheveled bed, staring at the ceiling, repeatedly smacking his lips, rolling his fingers, and trying to lift his arms against the leather straps. Drool trickled from the corner of his mouth and, like a river, ran down his chin and along his neck, pooling in the pocket above his collar bone.

"He does not say nothing, Dr. Sutherland. Just noises and groans. I bring him the music we love for the Walkman and I put it on, but he still is restless. Every day he is worse."

Sutherland leaned on first his right, and then left foot, fidgeting. "I've been here most days; even sometimes late at night, Sarita. I keep missing you. I'm sorry."

"I tell the doctors he have to be in Humanitarian. They do not know what they are doing. Paco needs real doctors and nurses that keep him clean. Look at him. And how he smells – how do you say – sour? I do not think they have give him a bath since he have been here. They treat him like he is some kind of dirt. He have to be transfer."

Sutherland cleared his throat, "Mrs. Sánchez?"

"Yes."

"I hate to tell you, but I came to say goodbye. This is my last day at County. I rotate over to the University Hospital for my hematology rotation next. I wanted to catch you before I left."

"Now, I move Paco for sure. You have been the only one ..."

Sutherland cleared his throat again, "Thank you, I've done nothing to ..."

"Oh, yes, Dr. Sutherland, you do not know," Sarita insisted. "You never know how much what you do means. Every day you come here to see Paco, we feel better. You have explained to us, when the others did not.

"If now Paco could speak, he would say to you 'tell me I have said something' and that you have learned from caring for me. What I say to you, that you not someday become a big shot doctor who do not have time to sit for his patients."

"Thank you, Mrs. Sánchez, I'll ..."

"How do you call it 'hematolog'?" she interrupted.

"Hematology – it means the study of blood. I'll be working with Drs. Hardy and Saiki. They're the greatest. I am lucky to have the chance. Can I do anything for you before I go?"

"Get Paco some more medicine to quiet him down. I cannot stand it, Dr. Sutherland, when he struggles like this."

"I'll tell the nurses," Sutherland said extending his arms, inviting an embrace. Sarita leaned her head on Sutherland's shoulder, tears flowing down her cheeks.

"Thank you," she sniffled.

"You're welcome," he choked. "Paco is a brave, strong man, Sarita. They'll fix him up at Humanitarian, I feel it," he said, releasing her. "I'll ask the nurses to get him some more Haldol," he said and disappeared.

Conversation 162
Los Angeles
Friday, August 9, 2002: 12:56 p.m.

Sarita hurried through traffic, running a red light at the intersection of Jones and Marquesa. Lucille Stufflebeam had promised to complete the paperwork for transfer to Humanitarian as soon as Sarita paid the outstanding balance. She steered Paco's pickup into the Payday Loans parking lot, bumping the front tire against the curb.

When she entered, Carmen Aguilera was standing at the counter, "Hi, Mrs. Sánchez. All set?"

"I think so. Here is the title and the certificate."

"Great. Thanks. I got all the documents in order and the check is made out."

Sarita eyed the check, "How much?"

"Sixty percent of value, $6,736.52."

Sarita ran some rough calculations in her head. $5,000.00 for Humanitarian, $1,300.00 for the house payment, and a little left over for groceries.

"I called Republic Waste. Boy, do they like Mr. Sánchez."

Sarita's heart sank. "Who did you talk with?"

"Let's see her name is here somewhere. She verified employment; said Paco was the best, works hard every day. Here it is – Sandy Miller."

Sarita breathed a sigh of relief, "Paco he never complain. When constructions drop, he work anything to bring in the money. Then the job came up at Republic. He is no garbage man, Mrs. Carmen, Paco is a brick layer, but it is all there is for now. Paco never say no thing about how bad it is," Sarita said, pushing the title toward Aguilera.

"You're lucky. My ex is a lazy, son of a bastardo, if you know what I mean. He cannot keep a job for nothing. No way. So, I gave up on him," she said examining the title. "Okay, I need you to sign here as joint owner and I need his notarized signature or he needs to come to sign as well."

"Paco he is working. He does not get off until 4:30."

"Can he come in then? We don't close until 6:00. I'm here all day."

"You cannot give me the check, and I have him come in later?"

"I'm sorry. We need both signatures. It's the law."

Sarita eyed the check – $6,736.52! "I have got to have the money before 4:00. My little José is at County Hospital with very bad asthma," she fibbed. "He is not getting better and we want to transfer him to Humanitarian. They won't take him unless we pay our bill from Angelina. I need the money before 5:00. I can get Paco to come in right after he is off work."

Carmen Aguilar shook her head and frowned, "Like I said, Mrs. Sánchez, without his signature, I can't release the check. I'd lose *my* job."

Sarita fidgeted, avoiding eye contact with the loan officer. Then it came to her. She had another idea. She opened her purse and dug through it until she found Paco's wallet and driver's license. She examined his photograph, assuring herself that Carmen Aguilar would not be able to distinguish the photograph of Paco from his twin brother Emilio. Sarita took a deep breath, looked back at Aguilar and said, "I can go to find Paco at the job and bring him here to sign right away. We can be right back."

"Thank you, Mrs. Sánchez. I really appreciate your understanding."

Sarita hurried out the door and climbed into Paco's pickup, turned the ignition and dialed her cell phone. "Now if I can just find Emilio," she said.

Conversation 163
University Quad, Los Angeles
Friday, August 9, 2002; 1:00 p.m.

Dr. Samuel Zuckerman ran the School of Medicine consistent with the precepts of Wharton School of Business, his third alma mater after the University of Michigan for a Bachelor of Science in molecular biology and University of Pittsburgh for Medical School. Zuckerman dressed impeccably, which served to offset the effect of his balding pate, prominent proboscis and protuberant chin. Although he rarely let on, Zuckerman considered himself a medical mastermind and had relished the notion of a future as Dean of a top tier medical school. "When that happens, I'll show the Association of American Medical Colleges a thing or two," he had often grunted to himself.

So when Zuckerman's executive assistant called Justin Sutherland at 11:45 a.m. for an urgent meeting in the Dean's Office at 1:00 p.m. the student broke out in a sweat. What in the world could the Dean want, Sutherland wondered? "May I ask what this is regarding?" he got up the gumption to inquire. "I'm not entirely certain," she responded. "Just be here, and be on time."

Sutherland arrived at 1:00 p.m. sharp. After introducing himself, the receptionist led him back to the Dean's office where he found him thrumming his fingers on a brilliantly polished walnut burl desk, while discussing in muted tones an issue with Dr. Jack MacDougall. Neither stood for Sutherland. Their visages spoke a thousand words. Sutherland knew he was in for it and he broke into profuse perspiration for the second time that day.

"Sit down, young man," Zuckerman said motioning toward a chair alongside MacDougall.

The eerie silence held court like a funeral pall, but before Sutherland could get comfortable the Dean broke into his diatribe. "Dr. Mac-

Dougall tells me you are meddling where you have no business interfering. He tells me you have been visiting a patient for whom you have
been neither assigned nor authorized. He alleges you are undermining
his authority and creating chaos in the care of a seriously ill patient –
what's his name Jack – Sánchez? If his facts bear out, this is a serious
transgression, if not an unprecedented ethical violation, Mr. Sutherland.
I'll hear your side of the story momentarily, but it had better be con-
vincing. You're precariously close to being dismissed from this University and the School of Medicine. Do I make myself clear?"

"Yes, sir."

"So explain. We don't have all day."

Sutherland squirmed in his chair, staring at the Dean, but avoiding
MacDougall's gaze. "Well, sir, it is true. I have been following Mr.
Sánchez ..."

Zuckerman slammed his fist on the table, "God damn it! Who in
Jesus' name gave you permission?"

Sutherland shuddered, "Dr. Rodríguez, sir."

"What? Who is Rodríguez?"

"Mr. Sánchez's attending sir," the medical student responded wiping his sweaty palms against his trousers.

"Is that accurate, Jack?"

"Rodríguez is the Sánchez's family doctor, but I had no idea he
gave Sutherland permission to follow him. He said nothing to me."

MacDougall's fabrication floored Sutherland. They had discussed
Paco's case face to face on at least two occasions – just three days ago
MacDougall labeled them "whining fucking wetbacks" and at no time
did he suggest that Sutherland should be hands-off.

Zuckerman fiddled with the pen on his desk, staring aimlessly at
the walnut burl. Then he looked back at Sutherland. "How did this
come about?"

"I worked him up the night he made his third visit to the ER. Dr.
Mack let me do his lumbar puncture. Fascinated with his case, and his
unusual presentation, I asked Dr. Rodríguez if I could follow along during his admission. He said yes, so I thought everything was okay."

Dean Zuckerman cleared his throat, "I admire your recognition of the value in continuity of care and your interest in the patient's presentation ..."

"That's not the issue here, Sam!" MacDougall interjected. "What gets my goat is a fourth year medical student leading the patient and his wife into believing he is not getting world class care." Then he glared at Sutherland, "What business – pray tell – do you have suggesting that plasmapheresis is essential in the care of Guillain-Barré syndrome?"

"Perhaps you are unaware, Mr. Sutherland," the Dean interjected. "Dr. MacDougall is regarded an international authority on these matters. He is published in several scholarly journals on Guillain-Barré, aren't you, Jack?"

"Petersdorf and I practically wrote the book," MacDougall harrumphed.

Sutherland felt the perspiration trickling from his underarms; his mouth was as dry as the desert and he couldn't swallow for the life of it. Certain his days in medical school were numbered, he shrugged his shoulders in resignation, reached into his backpack and produced the Hughes and Raphaël Cochrane Database Systematic Reviews. "I admit my transgression in this matter, Dr. Zuckerman. My behavior may represent a serious breach of medical ethics. If it makes any difference, here is the basis for my opinion – the result of an extensive MeSH database search in PubMed," he explained handing the manuscripts to Zuckerman.

Samuel Zuckerman took pride in his reputation as an academic elitist. "Show me the evidence! Show me the evidence!" he often demanded. "I could care less about your *opinions* God damn it! Show me the evidence!" and when he took reign of the School of Medicine, he immediately imbedded a seminar on Medical Information Management into the curriculum. "*This* is a university and I intend to graduate scholars, not lunk-heads. There's no reason to have a bunch of dogmatic bullshit rattling around in your brain. But you better jolly well know how *and where* to find the evidence."

"Hmmm ... PubMed. MeSH database search. Cochrane Systematic Reviews. Interesting," he mumbled glancing at both articles, and then fast forwarding to the conclusions.

316

Sutherland sat back and took a deep breath attempting to quiet his racing heart. He realized he was lucky to not be standing, his legs were like rubber. True, he wasn't certain if he was cut out for medicine, but expulsion from medical school was not the answer to his conundrum.

"Hmmm ... have you seen this Jack? Raphaël's work? Just published in 2001? Systematic review of six randomized controlled trials. Says here and I quote, *'Plasmapheresis is the first and only treatment that has been proven to be superior to supportive treatment alone in Guillain-Barré syndrome. Consequently, plasma exchange should be regarded as the treatment against which all new treatments, such as intravenous immunoglobulin, should be judged ... . Plasma exchange is more beneficial when started within seven days after disease onset rather than later, but is still efficacious in patients treated up to 30 days after onset of the disorder.'*

"It looks like Sutherland has come across something. So what do you say to that, Jack?"

Conversation 164
Los Angeles
Friday, August 9, 2002; 1:32 p.m.

Sarita discovered Jorge and González vacuuming cars at Gabe's Swish and Shine Auto Wash. When she asked them Emilio's whereabouts, they shook their heads. González shrugged his shoulders and reminded her, "You know Emilio. He work only when he have to and many times he not come to work on Friday, Sarita. How is Paco?"

She shook her head, "He is very sick. That is why I must find Emilio. I am sorry I have no time to talk. Thank you. I have to call you later."

Sarita got back into the truck roasting in the hot summer sun. She rolled down the window, shaded the pad on her cell phone and dialed Mamacita who said she had not heard from Emilio.

She threw the phone on the seat, started the truck and drove off.

Making her way through the slow, afternoon traffic, Sarita finally exited off the Interstate, and gunned her vehicle toward Emilio's apartment. When she found it, she walked up the stairs to the second

317

level and knocked on his door. When he didn't answer she tried the knob.

It opened.

She found Emilio's living room dirty and unkempt. Although she expected no less, it surprised her. It reeked of wasted joints, stale beer, body sweat, cigarette butts and tequila. She squeezed her nose between a thumb and forefinger and stepped in.

"Emilio ... Emilio? It is Sarita."

No answer.

She tiptoed in and around the helter-skelter of dirty clothes, a pair of panties, empty beer bottles, a Penthouse magazine opened to the Pet of the Month and a used condom – dropped and left on the floor to dry. Unwashed dishes littered the sink, and a Domino's Pizza box with a leftover, aging mushroom and pepperoni slice sat on the kitchen table.

"Emilio? Emilio?" she called out again.

"He have to be here somewhere," she whispered.

Looking past the kitchen and down the hall Sarita spotted the bedroom door standing ajar. She walked toward it, pushed it open and there he was. Lying face down on the bed, naked except for his undershorts. His left arm cradled an empty bottle of tequila. His face lay immersed in a puddle of mucoid drool. A girl no more than sixteen or seventeen lay face up, completely naked, next to him.

Sarita shook her head, frowned and made her way toward the bed. "Emilio. Emilio. Wake up," she pleaded, "I need you."

Except for heavy, rhythmic breaths he made not a solitary sound.

She walked closer, placed a hand on his shoulder and shook him, "Emilio." She shook him again, this time harder, "Emilio!"

"EMILIO!" she yelled.

The girl startled, sat straight up in bed and shouted, "Get the fuck out, bitch!" and then fell back to the sheet-less mattress, covered her ears and rolled into a ball.

Sarita dug the fingernails of both hands into his skin, leaned within inches of his ear, shook him as hard as she could and screamed, "EMILIO, WAKE UP! WAKE UP!"

He groaned, swallowed hard, smacked his lips and caught his wind, but was otherwise lifeless.

"EMILIO!" she shouted and shook him again.

Nothing.

Sarita released his arm and stood upright.

With her arms folded across her chest she paced back and forth, glaring at Paco's twin brother, mumbling and cursing in Spanish. Finally, she turned and faced him, placed her hands on her hips, spit on his naked body and growled, "You estúpido Mexican bastard, Emilio. You are worse than gringo. You care no shit for your brother who gives you every chance. You cannot even come to the hospital when he is so sick he could die. I hope that you rot in hell. If Paco could see you he would say, 'Emilio, you go fuck you. Go fuck you, Emilio'. And I say that too Emilio, YOU GO FUCK YOU!"

Then she spit on him again for good measure and stormed out of his hell hole, too angry to cry.

Conversation 165
Santa Monica
Friday, August 9, 2002; 3:32 p.m.

As Sarita hurried back to County Hospital, Dr. Edmund M. Pinkerton parked his Dodge Ram alongside the Chevy dealership entrance and sauntered in. An anorexic blonde with spiked heels and a low cut blouse that exposed her gaunt ribs approached him with a toothy, factitious smile, "Welcome to Bunnin Chevrolet! Looking for a new ride?"

"No, I'm looking for that," he said pointing to the Corvette.

"Really?" she responded looking Pinkerton up and down. "It's a beauty, isn't it?"

"I've always wanted one … since I was a kid in high school," Pinkerton panted.

The saleslady extended her hand, "By-the-way. I'm Trisha."

"Pleased to meet you," Pinkerton winked.

"So this is Corvette's top of the line – the LS6 Z06," she said, leading Pinkerton across the show room floor. "Hydroformed frame, 5.7 liter engine, 405 horsepower, torque like you cannot believe. This baby will leave your eyeballs in the back seat if you floor it."

"Son-of-bitch – pardon my French – she's drop-dead gorgeous isn't she," Pinkerton grinned, opening the door. "Wow-ee!"

"Electron Blue is new for 2002. She's got high-performance suspension with aluminum front stabilizer bars too. Would you look at that leather interior? Something else, huh? And get this – Head-Up digital gauges that display on the windshield so you can keep your eyes on the road."

"What's the sticker price?"

"$74,956 including destination and dealer prep."

"That's not bad ... mind if I get in?" Pinkerton drooled.

"Of course not. Try her out."

Pinkerton crouched down, grasped the steering wheel with his right hand, slid his right leg over the seat, gripped the roof with his left hand and worked his enormous bulk in behind the wheel. Unlike the Maseratis, Ferraris and Porsches he'd tested, the Corvette was actually comfortable once he adjusted the seat for up and down. "Son-of-bitch," he whispered, again massaging the leather upholstery with one hand and the gear shift knob with the other. Then, licking his lips like a little kid, he blurted out, "What the hell. I'll take it!"

Conversation 166
Los Angeles County Hospital
Friday, August 9, 2002; 4:03 p.m.

Sarita looked up when Lucille Stufflebeam shuffled into room 413 and closed the door.

"Well, there's good news and there's bad news, Mrs. Sánchez. University can take him in transfer."

"So what is the bad news?" Sarita asked.

"They don't have any beds."

Conversation 167
Los Angeles County Hospital
Friday, August 9, 2002; 4:56 p.m.

Priscilla Collins dialed Jack MacDougall's cell phone. She tapped first her left, then her right foot on the tiled floor waiting for him to pick up.

"Come on. Come on. Answer ... answer damn it."

On the fifth ring she heard his voice, "This is Dr. Jack MacDougall."

"It's Collins. Where are you? Where's Overstreet?"

"I'm in the lounge having a cup of coffee, Charlie is with me. We're discussing Sánchez. You sound frantic."

"Well you'd better get up here. Paco Sánchez is in cardiac arrest!"

MacDougall sat straight up scowling, "What? I didn't hear, Code Blue."

"I didn't call it yet."

"Didn't call it? For Christ sakes, Collins, you call Code Blue and *then* you call me! We'll be right up!"

Overstreet and MacDougall arrived breathless to find Collins performing cardiac massage. At the head of the bed, a nurse anesthetist held an endotracheal tube and laryngoscope preparing to insert it into Paco's trachea. Sarita stood at the end of the bed, tears pouring down her face.

"Wait. Stop. Get out of the way and get *her* out of here!" MacDougall barked. "What are you thinking, Collins?!"

MacDougall pushed all comers aside, glared at Sarita and repeated, "I said, get *her* out of here."

Paco's eyes rolled back. His spine arched like a humpback whale, writhing in concert with facial distortions, tooth gnashing and vocal grunts. His arms and legs flailed purposeless against the restraints. When his body stiffened, it momentarily relaxed and the pattern began all over again.

"Jesus-motherfucking-Christ," Dr. Jack MacDougall blurted. "He's seizing. This isn't cardiac arrest. Get the crash cart in here and push 10 mg of valium STAT! Charlie, check his airway and insert a tongue depressor! Collins, order an EKG, and I want blood gases too!"

Conversation 168
Los Angeles County Hospital
Friday, August 9, 2002; 6:13 p.m.

An hour later MacDougall cradled his forehead in the palm of his left hand, took a deep breath and wrote in Paco's chart.

CONVERSATIONS FOR PACO

History: 29 year-old Hispanic male admitted late July 2002 for meningoencephalitis, thought to be viral, but organism never identified. He subsequently developed symptoms consistent with Guillain-Barré syndrome; as this progressed I ordered plasmapheresis for ascending polyneuropathy but unit not available (out of order, broken part).

On Thursday August 8th he developed increased shortness of breath, lip smacking and bizarre finger snapping. We made a diagnosis of pneumonitis, started him on oxygen, added Ancef to his antibiotic regimen and discussed transfer to either Humanitarian or University Hospital with his wife. At around 5:00 p.m. today, he developed a tonic-clonic generalized seizure convulsing for a prolonged period, Code Blue called. I finally resuscitated him with repeated IV doses of 10 mg Valium and a single dose of Dilantin 300 mg slow IV push. He vomited during resuscitation. Emesis tested positive for blood. He now rests comfortably on 2 liters of oxygen by nasal canula and the anti-convulsants. Post seizure labs revealed very low serum sodium at 122 (normal 135-145); blood sugar and complete blood count were, however, within normal limits. Attempted to get blood gases but seizure activity made specimen acquisition impossible. Oxygen saturation on room air 93%, corrected on nasal O2 to 95%.

Assessment: meningoencephalitis, Guillain-Barré syndrome, recent low grade pneumonitis with shortness of breath and hypoxia; severe depletion of body sodium, syndrome of inappropriate anti-diuretic hormone (SIADH) and evidence for gastrointestinal bleeding. Seizure probably secondary to underlying infectious process, SIADH or even acyclovir toxicity.

Plan: Move to our critical care unit for stabilization and intense monitoring. Carefully correct serum sodium. Continue Dilantin for seizure prophylaxis. Discuss with Dr. Overstreet. Get serum acyclovir levels. Transfer to University Hospital when stable. Critical care consultation with Dr. Pierpoint.

PS: Lucille Stufflebeam (medical social worker) reports he can't transfer to Humanitarian, outstanding past due bill; no bed at University, but requires intensive care unit, so will have her check on that as well.

Conversation 169
Los Angeles County Hospital
Friday, August 9, 2002; 6:26 p.m.

MacDougall stood next to Overstreet in the hospital hallway. "I'm getting Pierpoint to consult and checking on an ICU bed at University. I thought you were following his electrolytes, Charlie?"

"And I thought you were, Jack. Last time I ordered them was Tuesday."

"I ordered them Thursday," MacDougal admitted. "But I didn't follow up – too exhausted from the rush-rush presentation to the American Neurological Society in San Francisco. This case is going south, Charlie. Let's get him out of here and over to University. Let the medical house staff wallow over ..."

"Just a second, Jack, my cell phone," Overstreet gestured, flipping it open.

"Dr. Overstreet, here. Yes. Hi, Lucille. Wow. Great, good work. When? ICU right? Tonight. Perfect. We'll write the orders straight away. Dr. Pierpoint's coming in to see him as we speak."

Overstreet flipped the phone closed. "University has a bed," he smiled, "They've got an intensive care unit bed at University and can take him in transfer, Jack."

"Thank f-ing Christ," MacDougall frowned. "Charlie, can you talk with his wife? Go over everything. I can't take another round of her diatribe – yammering how we don't know what we're doing, this is a lousy hospital. Blah, blah, blah. Could you do that for me, Charlie?"

Conversation 170
Los Angeles County Hospital
Friday, August 9, 2002; 8:02 p.m.

Ellis Pierpoint rambled toward the ICU nursing station, shaking his head. Considered "the King" at County Hospital, Dr. Pierpoint ruled medical affairs with an iron fist and had little tolerance for breeches in care. Nobody, but nobody, gave Ellis Pierpoint backtalk. At 73, he still worked 12 hours per day, talked of nothing but medicine, rarely took vacations, and never played golf. "Golf is for idiots of social class, and a waste of productive time pandering over a stupid little white ball on a wooden peg," he often said.

Born and raised in North Dakota, he took internship in general practice at the University of Minnesota following medical school, moved southwest to relieve his wife of her rheumatoid arthritis and establish a general practice in 1958. Respected for his dedication to patient care, Pierpoint studied assiduously, maintaining certification and hospital privileges on the general medical wards, as well as the intensive care units. When the request came to consult on Paco Sánchez at 6:15 on Friday evening, he left home despite a torrential summer downpour and drove immediately to County Hospital.

Pierpoint sat with Sarita at Paco's bedside and took a detailed history. Then he examined Paco from top to bottom. At the nurses' station he carefully reviewed the voluminous accumulation of records. Finally he opened Paco's chart, mumbling, "What a mess," and began to write.

Paco Sánchez is 29 year-old Mexican American male cared for by Drs. Jack MacDougall and Charlie Overstreet since admission. Hospital course has been rocky with no definitive diagnosis and, therefore, no directed, specific plan of care. Patient's wife is delirious with the situation and wants her husband transferred immediately. Although I reinforced that everything humanly possible was being done – and done correctly – she is adamant about transfer.

Pierpoint set his pen on the counter, removed his bifocals and rubbed his eyes with the knuckles of both index fingers. He sighed, glanced back at his watch and started writing again. For the most part he repeated the somber details set forth in MacDougall's note, describing the chronology of Paco's current admission, his past medical history, today's seizure, and the resuscitation. However, at the conclusion of his chart note entry, he added the following:

Mr. Sánchez is responsive, but disoriented to person, place, time, and events. He responds to verbal cues with nonsensical words and utterances. He is agitated and restless; they've got him in 4-point restraints. His heart sounds normal, although I detect the presence of a low grade murmur at the apex. Breath sounds are coarse, and as noted above, he does have increased heart and respiratory rates. He presently does not move his legs to command.

Assessment: Critically ill, 29 year-old male with meningitis, encephalitis, Guillain-Barré syndrome, pneumonitis, seizure disorder, gastrointestinal bleeding, and hyponatremia. His prognosis at best is guarded.

Plan: Continue stabilization in our ICU unit. Transfer to University Hospital ASAP. Console wife. Conduct candid case analysis with Drs. MacDougall and Overstreet.

Conversation 171
Rancho Palos Verdes
Friday, August 9, 2002; 8:13 p.m.

Pierpoint dialed his cell phone, after several rings a voice answered, "Dr. MacDougall."

"Jack, Ellis Pierpoint. Say, your man Sánchez is pretty sick."

MacDougall cleared his throat. He knew what was coming. "I agree. When I left the hospital they were sending him over to University."

"Where are you?"

MacDougall paused, twirled the pen on his kitchen counter and took a sip of St. Emillion La Gaffelière letting it linger on his palate. He wanted to say "Home, as if it's any of your fucking business, Pierpoint," but thought better of it, bit his tongue and instead lied, "I'm over at University making arrangements for his transfer."

"Good. So how the hell did you let it get away from you like this, Jack? He could have died on your watch."

"You know how these viral meningitis cases go, usually watchful waiting and they are better. I treated hundreds of these at the Mass General. This is that one in a thousand you read about that falls beyond two standard deviations, Ellis."

"It's Dr. Pierpoint to you, Jack, and as far as I'm concerned you can shove the standard deviations up your ass. You and Overstreet let him go down the proverbial toilet. Why didn't you call me sooner?"

"That seemed unnecessary. He was getting better. Like I say, we saw this all the time ..."

Pierpoint's face turned scarlet. "Jack, I don't give a rat's ass what you saw or when you saw it. I care about the here and now, one patient, one disease, one presentation, one diagnosis, and one treatment at a time."

MacDougall gazed out the kitchen window at his swimming pool and paced back and forth swirling the Bordeaux. He had nothing to say.

"Jack, are you there?"

MacDougall closed his eyes, set the wine down and took a cleansing breath.

"*Jack*, are you there?"

MacDougall resisted with all his might telling Pierpoint to go "f" himself, instead he retorted, "Look, Ellis, I've busted my butt for this guy and most likely I'll not get a fricking dime for my time. The system is crazy ..."

"Jack, Jack, Jack, Jack, *Jack!* I harbor no umbrage you getting paid and paid well – making a *damn good* living – for what you do. For that matter, I'm not critical of the for-profit hospital giants making a buck or two, but *not at the expense* of best practices medicine or at the risk of human life. Giving topnotch care to everyone, irrespective of lot in life and financial means, is what you signed on for when you got accepted to medical school."

MacDougall knew this was an argument he could not win, but continued it despite the futility. "Ellis, he *got* topnotch care."

"If you call a serum sodium of 122 topnotch care, you and I have a serious difference of opinion. It's no wonder he seized and has been delirious out of his mind."

"Ellis, he *got* topnotch care!"

"That's your perspective. But it's not mine. And you can bet your sweet bippy I'm going to have a morbidity conference over this one, Jack. What's gone on is horseshit and it's unacceptable. Pure and simple. This young man could have died."

"I didn't think ..."

"You're right for once, Jack," Pierpoint asserted. "You *didn't* think."

Conversation 172
University Hospital, Los Angeles
Friday, August 9, 2002; 11:13 p.m.

A thoroughly intoxicated Jack MacDougall flopped into bed that night when Dr. Tobi Guillen stood at the side of an Emergency Room gurney looking down at Paco Sánchez. What she saw gave her goose bumps. Dull, bloodshot eyes. Dried spittle in his moustache and at the corners of his mouth. The shadow of handsome facial features twisted by illness. The dimmed portrait of young man with work-hardened muscles gone to atrophy. The smell of human illness. What had gone wrong? How did it get this way? The records from County Hospital didn't paint a clear picture. Why should someone this age be so sick? Fate, she decided, made it her charge to find out.

She took a deep breath, shook her head and began a thorough exam. Vital signs showed a heart rate of 126, respirations 24, blood pressure 152/94, temperature 99.7°, and oxygen saturation 93 to 94%. His pupils reacted to light and the retinas looked normal. Examination of his ears and eardrums revealed nothing out of the ordinary. On his lower lip and tongue she detected bite marks. "I guess he bit his lip when he seized," she murmured. She found the reflexes over his legs depressed, but brisk and symmetric in his arms.

Guillen rolled Sánchez to his side, noted the Foley catheter and checked his skin. It was red over his buttocks and imprinted by the folds of bed clothing, but there were no apparent ulcers. Dried feces clung to folds of his buttocks. She shook her head and let him roll back, pulled the stethoscope from her white coat and listened to Paco's lungs; and then his heart. Just below his left nipple, she thought she heard a faint swish, swish, swish sound. "Hmmm, Dr. MacDougall didn't say anything about a murmur in his report," she said to herself.

She moved the instrument back over his chest, listening first on the upper right, then on the upper left and down along the sternal borders. No abnormal sounds in those areas. She placed the scope back on the spot below the nipple and heard the faint swish, swish, swish noise again. "I wonder if they got an echo at County?" she said out loud, continuing her examination. Guillen placed her hand over his heart to feel its beat. She detected no lifts or heaves, but when she removed her hand, it stuck to his chest. Coupled with his sour odor, she asked herself, "Did County ever bathe this poor man?"

"Mr. Sánchez? Mr. Sánchez?" she said, rocking her closed fist over his sternum. "Mr. Sánchez?" she asked again using more pressure.

"Uh-huh."

"Mr. Sánchez? It's Dr. Guillen. Mr. Sánchez? Mr. Sánchez? Where are you?"

"Uh-huh."

Dr. Guillen looked up when Sarita's head peaked around the emergency bay curtains and asked, "May I come in? I am Sarita Sánchez. I am Paco's wife."

"Oh, hello, Mrs. Sánchez. I'm Dr. Tobi Guillen, 4th year neurology resident here at University Hospital," she smiled. "Sure, come on in. I have some questions anyway."

"Thank you. How is he?"

"I was going to ask you that, Mrs. Sánchez. How was Paco before he got sick?"

"He was very strong. Never sick. He work every day."

"What kind of work?"

"He is a mason – you know what I mean – he lays the bricks, but with the slowdown, he have been working with the garbage. I hate him to do that. I ask him not to, but he said we have to have the money, so I say okay."

"Did the doctors at County say anything about his heart? Get any kind of heart tests?"

"No, I do not think so, but I do not remember. It is hard to say, so many tests. They never say, but after a few days it seem like they never even examine him. Dr. MacDougall and Overstreet come in and tell me about the tests, tell me that he is getting better, tell me not to worry, and walk out. I know Paco is not right. Look at him."

"What about his breathing?"

"Dr. MacDougall say his breathing is getting worse – that the Guillain-Barré it is causing him troubles with his breathing, so they were going to start the – how do you say it – plasma?"

"Plasmapheresis," Guillen answered.

Sarita's shoulders sagged. She glanced around the room and back at Dr. Guillen. "Yes, plasmapheresis – but the machine at the County

Hospital it is broken and so they cannot give him the treatments. And yesterday or the day before he says he thinks he may have pneumonia."

Sarita sniffled, wiped away welled up tears and continued, "I am sorry. I am so confused. I cannot remember when anything happens. Do they have that machine at University?"

Guillen reached for Sarita's hand, "Don't worry, Mrs. Sánchez. It's my job to put the puzzle together. And yes, we do have a plasmapheresis unit, and yes, it is working."

Sarita blew her nose and asked, "Can you start it tonight?"

"Probably not tonight. First, I have to get more tests and a solid picture of exactly what is causing this; start a PICC line," she cleared her throat continuing, "Mrs. Sánchez is he like this all the time or is he sometimes awake?"

"Sometimes he will say, 'Sarita, Sarita?' Sometimes he looks at me and smiles, but the last few days it has been mostly like this. Kind of blank. He have been out of it like this."

"Has he eaten?"

"Some days Paco he eat and some days he push it away. The last two days – I think – he have nothing."

"Okay. I've got to look over his record again – see if they got an echo of his heart – review his labs. I'll be ordering more tests, calling in an infectious disease doctor, and I would like cardiology to see him too."

"Thank you, Dr. Guillen."

"Are you going to be here awhile?"

"Oh, yes. I will be here all night. Mamacita has the kids."

"Great. I'll be back. And, oh, we'll admit him to intensive care until we are confident he is stable."

"Thank you. You have to do whatever. Just get my Paco back to me."

"We'll do everything possible, Mrs. Sánchez. I'll see you in a few minutes."

Tobi Guillen shook Sarita's hand, turned and headed down the corridor pushing back her own emotions, "Just bring my Paco back to me," she said to herself. "Mrs. Sánchez, I'll try, but you're asking for a freaking miracle."

Conversation 173
University Hospital, Los Angeles
Saturday, August 10, 2002; 12:32 a.m.

Tobi Guillen sat in the residents' conference room drinking a cup of burnt Maxwell House and leafing through Paco's record from County Hospital. Words like – hallucinating, altered consciousness, 4-point restraints, no bowel movement since admission, meningoencephalitis, viral PCR, unable to get out of bed, low serum sodium, respiratory rate of 26 – popped out at her. Finally, she ran her fingers through her hair and wrote.

Admitting Orders: *Saturday, August 10, 12:32 a.m.*
Name: *Paco Sánchez.*
Admit: *ICU.*
Condition: *Serious, guarded prognosis.*
Diagnosis: *Meningoencephalitis, post-viral polyneuropathy, syndrome of inappropriate anti-diuretic hormone, hyponatremia and pneumonia.*
Diet: *Arrange for total parenteral intravenous nutrition; begin in a.m., nothing by mouth.*
Activity: *Position bed at 30 degrees. Patient to remain upright 30 degrees with bedrails in place, out of bed when able. No restraints.*
Vital signs: *Every hour. Call ICU Attending Physician for respiratory rate greater than 28, heart rate greater than 140, blood pressure greater than 160/90, temperature greater than 101°, oxygen saturation less than 92%.*
IVs: *D5, 3 normal saline at 175 cc per hour; infuse via IVAC.*
Consultants: *Cardiology - Dr. Young in a.m., Pulmonary - Dr. Fredericks in a.m., Gastroenterology - Dr. Sweeney in a.m., Neurology - Dr. MacDougall in a.m., Infectious Disease - Dr. Overstreet in a.m.*
Labs: *CBC with differential, comprehensive metabolic profile, 24 hour urine for creatinine clearance, electrolytes and Bence-Jones proteins, Dilantin level in a.m. (see also labs obtained in ER at 11:13 p.m.)*
Medications: *Hold all antibiotics until evaluated by Infectious Disease. Continue Dilantin 300 mg. slow IV push daily. Dilantin level daily.*
Other: *Seizure precautions.*
Call me for significant changes in status. Okay for wife at bedside.

Guillen rubbed at the headache between her eyes, looked over the orders and then declared, "Wait a minute. This is baloney. Mr. Sánchez needs a fresh opinion, a new set of eyes." She crossed out MacDougall and Overstreet, writing instead Dr. Carpenter for Neurology, and Dr. Irving for Infectious Disease.

Conversation 174
University Hospital, Los Angeles
Saturday, August 10, 2002; 8:07 a.m.

Sarita slept fitfully in the ICU Family Room. She checked on Paco every hour. Each time she found him sleeping. Each time the nurse reassured Sarita he was doing fine. She dozed heavily from six to eight a.m. but when she woke up felt an eerie sense of doom. So she went to the restroom, quickly splashed water on her face, rinsed her mouth and headed to his cubicle. When Sarita entered Paco's ICU enclosure she found him sitting up, limply wiping his hands and face with a damp cloth. Her worse fears were allayed. Sarita couldn't believe her eyes. "Paco?" she hesitated. "Paco?!"

Paco set the washcloth on his lap and looked up at Sarita, "Buenos días, Sarita."

"Paco, is that you? What happen?"

"Happen? What do you mean?"

"You are so much better. I cannot believe it. What have they did to you?"

"Corrected his serum sodium," came the voice from behind.

Sarita turned. "Dr. Guillen, good morning! What happen? It is Paco. Look at him sitting up!"

"When he came in here, his sodium was 122. They drew it on Tuesday when it was trending down at 126. It appears they didn't see it. Anyway, this morning it's back up to 133, and voila! He's better! Amazing isn't it?" she smiled.

"Thank God. Thank you, Dr. Guillen. Mi Paco es mucho mejor!" she exclaimed, throwing her arms around Dr. Guillen. "Soon you come home together with Mamacita and the children and the baby and me," Sarita said wiping away her tears. "I am so thankful you are at the University where they can make you better, Paco!"

"He *is* much better, Mrs. Sánchez. However, he still has a ways to go before discharge," Guillen cautioned, paused and continued. "His respirations are still elevated," she warned. "Although I must say, Mrs. Sánchez, *I* feel better and *he* looks better. Right Paco?"

Paco managed a weak smile, "Uh-huh. I feel better."

"I still want all the other consulting doctors to see him, just to make certain we are not missing anything. Oh, Paco? Anyone ever tell you, you had a heart murmur?"

"Heart murmur? No, in Jalisco we go to the Pharmacia for the medicines."

"When you immigrated, you saw a doctor then?"

"Yes, but he never examine me. Just fill out the papers. That is all."

Conversation 175
University Hospital, Los Angeles
Saturday, August 10, 2002; 8:14 a.m.

A gentle breeze swirled around Justin Sutherland walking on the cafeteria patio at University Hospital carrying a tall cup of fresh Starbucks in one hand and Harrison's *Principles of Internal Medicine*, 14th Edition in the other. He found a quiet corner drenched in morning sun, set his coffee on the table and sat down to read. A skylark flew in on the chair opposite, checking for food. Seeing none, it flew off for better pickings.

Sutherland rubbed his eyes, took a drink of coffee, and opened the book to his first hematology reading assignment: "Disorders of Coagulation." The chapter read like a repair manual for Sunbeam toasters and Sutherland found it difficult to stay on track. He thought he might call Jennifer later to see about dinner and a movie. The morning paper advertised two movies they wanted to see – "Road to Perdition" and "The Pianist." Maybe he would go for a bike ride in the afternoon. Then he remembered he needed to wash and iron his white lab coat for Monday. He waded through the text, turning the pages and slapping his cheeks to stay awake. Near the end of the chapter, the final paragraphs caught his attention.

"Emergent Consequences of Disordered Coagulation – Pulmonary Emboli"

"Rudolph Virchow postulated more than a century ago that a triad of factors predisposed to abnormal clotting of blood in the vessels of the lungs. These are: (1) trauma to the blood vessel wall, (2) abnormal clotting mechanisms and (3) stasis of blood in the vessels per se."

Sutherland drank his last bit of coffee, set the empty container on the table and read on.

"We now believe that many patients who suffer from pulmonary emboli may have an underlying inherited predisposition that remains clinically silent until a stressor occurs. Common stressors include surgery, trauma, obesity, pregnancy, cancer, chronic illness and immobility for significant periods of time."

Sutherland's pulse quickened. He drank from the empty cup, set it back down and continued.

"The most frequent inherited predisposition is resistance to activated protein C associated with a gene mutation designated Factor V Leiden. When venous clots become dislodged from their site of origin they migrate to the blood vessels of the lungs. In cases of certain congenital heart malformations, they may accumulate and pass into sites distant from the heart and lungs like the brain or other major organs such as the liver and the kidneys."

Sutherland massaged his brow with the fingers of both hands and said out loud, "What the ...?" and read further.

"On physical examination, young, previously healthy individuals may appear deceptively well. In cases of prolonged crescendo embolization, patients may progress from states of mild anxiety to fluctuating agitation, altered mental status, delirium and coma. Undiagnosed and untreated, pulmonary emboli are, of course, serious and carry with them a significant incidence of death."

"Holy shit," Sutherland declared, slamming the book closed, rising from his chair and running to the ICU.

Conversation 176
Rancho Palos Verdes
Saturday, August 10, 2002; 8:31 a.m.

While Justin Sutherland frantically raced to the ICU, Edmond M. Pinkerton looked out over the green on the 5th hole, leaned on his wood, and said, "So, have you gents thought anymore about hunting this fall?"

MacDougall cupped the ball and tee in his right hand, pushed it into the turf, took a couple of practice swings, and addressed it. "I like Boyer's idea," MacDougall grunted, hitting the ball 200 yards straight and well down the fairway. "Did you learn anything more, Geoff? Not bad. Pinkerton, your shot."

Boyer adjusted his cap, "I surfed the web some more. I really didn't come up with anything I liked any better than the Missouri gig."

"What's the name?" MacDougall asked.

"*Prime Adventure Big Game Hunting Ranch.* Its 100 miles southwest of St. Louis in the heart of the Ozarks. We fly non-stop from here on my corporate jet. Arrive in St. Louis Thursday, drive down to the ranch early Friday morning; hunt Friday afternoon and Saturday morning. Return to St. Louis and fly back on Sunday."

Pinkerton rearranged his trousers, teed up, and fired his shot, hooking it left and into the brush off the green. "Sh-h-h-it. Playing like this, I'll never win the pot today … unless of course you assholes handicap my big, fat butt. The hunt sounds good to me. I can't do wilderness any more. Plain and simple."

"What do you think, Charlie?" Boyer asked Overstreet.

"You guys know me; I'd rather go to the Bob Marshall Wilderness. What's *Prime Adventure* cost Geoff?"

"Who cares," Pinkerton interrupted.

"It's not bad, really. $200 bucks a night accommodations in the hunting lodge – which by the way looks beautiful – including meals. They've got gazelles, Hawaiian Black Rams, Wildebeests …"

"What the fuck? Wildebeests?" Pinkerton snorted.

"Wildebeests. They import them young, raise them up – and we hunt them from a pick-up truck. They guarantee you bag your game. No game, no pay. And they even process the meat."

"Arghh!" growled Pinkerton. "Who wants to eat Wildebeest?"

Overstreet teed up next and whacked the ball. "What's it cost to hunt?" he asked hooking it to the right and landing it just shy of the stream.

"Depends on your game. If I remember correctly a Hawaiian Black Ram costs you something like $950.00 – not bad, and what a trophy that'd make," Boyer declared.

The foursome put their clubs back in their bags, got in their carts, and drove toward Pinkerton's foul lie. "I'm in for *Prime Adventure Big Game*. No muss, no fuss," mumbled MacDougall.

"Me too," Pinkerton laughed elbowing MacDougall. "Besides, I'll bet St. Louis has some pretty good – uh, shall we say – *Gentlemen's Clubs*? Gentlemen!"

Conversation 177
University Hospital, Los Angeles
Saturday, August 10, 2002: 8:39 a.m.

Nurse Maureen Stoyakovich had deep blue eyes and the frame of a seasoned marathon runner. When she entered Paco's intensive care unit cubicle, she smiled at Sarita, looked at Paco, and said, "Feeling better, huh?"

Paco looked up, managing a shallow smile. "Yes, better."

Sarita grimaced, "But he just say his headache came back. Not as bad as he have it before, but back."

"Are you hungry? I could order you something to eat. That might help," Stoyakovich suggested.

"Maybe. What do you think, Sarita?" he frowned.

"You have not have anything for two days. We can see how it helps."

Stoyakovich placed her hands on her hips, "What would you like? I'll call Dr. Guillen and get it approved. After some breakfast, I'll get the aid to give you a nice bath."

Paco squeezed his eyes shut, rubbed his forehead and frowned, "Oooh, the headache it just get worse *again*."

Sensing the depth of his pain, Stoyakovich leaned toward Paco, "Are you okay, Mr. Sánchez? What's wrong? Mr. Sánchez?"

Paco shook his head "You have some … you have some huevos … you some huevos …" he asked and looking toward Sarita exclaimed, "Where are you, Sarita? I cannot see you! Sarita! I cannot *see!*"

335

"Mr. Sánchez, what's wrong?!" Stoyakovich repeated.

Wild eyed Paco clutched his chest, "Now it is my breathing and I *cannot* see! Sarita, I cannot breathe," he wheezed. "I cannot see! I cannot breathe! I cannot breathe!" he gasped turning shades of deep, dark purple. "I cannot breathe!" he choked. "I love you, Sarita! Hold me, Sarita! I love you!"

Stoyakovich ran for the telephone and dialed Code Blue. Sarita threw her arms around her husband and screamed, "Paco? No, Paco! Dear Jesus. No, Paco! I love you too!"

Conversation 178
University Hospital, Los Angeles
Saturday, August 10, 2002; 8:42 a.m.

Justin Sutherland ran into the ICU groping for breath, "Where's Mr. Sánchez?"

The receptionist shook her head and pointed, "Over there, the code."

"The code? What happened?"

"He was sitting up in bed talking with his wife and the nurse and bingo – just like that – he coded."

Sutherland peered behind the glass enclosure of the ICU cubicle. Nurses and doctors frantically crowded around Paco barking orders, pushing intravenous medications, and conducting cardiopulmonary resuscitation. The resident leaning over Paco performing chest compressions stopped momentarily, permitting the anesthesiologist to insert an endotracheal tube. Then he began the compressions all over again. "One thousand-one, one thousand-two, one thousand-three, one thousand-four, one thousand-five – bag him; one thousand-one, one thousand-two, one thousand-three, one thousand-four, one thousand-five – bag him!"

"I can't believe this is happening," Sutherland blurted. "Where's Sarita?"

"Sarita?"

"Mrs. Sánchez, his wife, where is she?"

The receptionist shrugged her shoulders, "I'm actually not certain. Out in the hallway, I guess."

CONVERSATIONS FOR PACO

PART IV

"Differences in health status among population groups that are unnecessary, unfair, unjust and actionable are referred to as health inequities. Health inequities affect life chances and are not inevitable or caused by behavior or genes; they are the result of deep social divisions associated with racism, class structure, and sexism."

~ *Richard Hofrichter, 2009*

Conversation 179
Los Angeles County Hospital
Monday, August 12, 2002; 11:07 a.m.

The smell of death pervaded the dank and dreary basement of County Hospital. MacDougall made his way down an endless hallway, until he reached a door marked with the lettering **Private – Anatomic Pathology.** He entered without knocking and found Pinkerton leaning over Paco Sánchez, peeling back the dead man's scalp.

"Hey, Ed. What have you found?"

"Jack! Come on in. Have a seat. I'm not finished yet. Just getting to the brain, then I'll be done with the gross. If you can hold on a minute, we'll have a look together."

MacDougall took a place on the stool and sat while Pinkerton cut through Paco's skull with a Stryker saw. With the circumferential cut complete, Pinkerton inserted a wide blade chisel between the sawed surfaces, gave it a single brisk twist and with a crack the skull popped off. Pinkerton set it to the side and said, "Hmmm. Interesting."

"What – what's interesting?"

"Hang on. Just a second."

The pathologist took his scalpel, made two lengthy crosswise cuts through the meningeal membranes overlying the brain and folded them back. He then lifted the edges of Paco's brain upward with the fingers of his left hand, inserted the fingers of his right hand along the margins of the skull, and gently blunt dissected the connecting tissue from the base of the brain.

"Hmmm … the meninges came away easy," he remarked. Then picking up a fresh scalpel and rolling the handle through his fingers Pinkerton said, "Let's get it out so we can look at it."

MacDougall stared at the autopsy table. A dead man's body. Open abdominal and chest cavities and a bunch of body parts – Paco's heart, his lungs, his liver and his spleen, even his kidneys and intestines – all carefully placed out next to his torso. MacDougall wondered how anyone could make a career of this work, but then again he reflected on Pinkerton's personality. No wonder it didn't turn his stomach. "It certainly churns mine," he whispered to himself.

Pinkerton inserted his fingers under the cerebrum, this time exploring Paco's brainstem. Lifting the brain forward, he cut it from its root.

"Here we go," he said, lifting the brain free, and holding it out on display for the two of them to examine.

"I thought you said he had the worst case of meningitis you had ever seen?" Pinkerton remarked rolling the organ over and examining the undersurface.

"He did."

Pinkerton deliberated. "Minimal evidence here. Of course, I have to section them and do the microscopics, but on gross the brain and the meninges look okay to me, Jack."

"What do you mean?"

"Just what I said. If this were bacterial, viral, or even fungal, you'd see adherent sticky substance all over the coverings. Separating the meninges from the brain surface would be difficult if not impossible. Again, and as you can plainly see, Jack, the surfaces are white and glistening. They look good to me. Your diagnosis of encephalitis may be correct – microscopic will confirm that – but I see no meningitis here."

MacDougall's face flushed, "I'm telling you, Ed, this guy had raging meningitis. That's how we signed it out at County."

"Not here. Oh, by-the-way, did you get a Factor V Leiden?"

"Factor V Leiden? No, why?"

"Just wondered. On gross it looks like he died from massive pulmonary emboli."

"You're shitting me."

"I wouldn't shit you, Jack," Pinkerton glowered. "You can see for yourself," he said picking up Paco's lungs. "Look. Various stages of organized clot throughout the vessels," he said spreading the lung tissues and pointing to the pulmonary arteries. "No pneumonia here either," he hesitated. "Want me to submit blood for Factor V."

MacDougall scratched the back of his neck, cleared his throat and sputtered, "No way. Do all the microscopics you want, but no Factor V. We can call it an oversight – or better yet, blame the lab techs for losing the specimen."

"Whatever you say, good buddy," Pinkerton winked. "Whatever you say."

Conversation 180
University Quad, Los Angeles
Tuesday, September 3, 2002; 11:13 a.m.

Wind lashed at the trees in the quadrangle as a hot summer squall pelted Dornwyler's windows. The professor ran his fingers through his beard, analyzing the rivulets serpentine dribble to the sill. He glanced back to Sutherland, then turned his attention to the coffee maker at the sound of the beep. He poured two cups, extended one to Sutherland and declared, "Ethiopian as promised."

Sutherland leaned forward taking the cup. He held the coffee to his nose with both hands, inhaled the aroma and blurted, "He died."

The furrows on Dornwyler's brow rolled up, "Who died?"

"Paco Sánchez."

"The Mexican patient we talked about?"

"Yes, sir. Massive pulmonary emboli and we never diagnosed it."

"Really?"

Sutherland looked down shaking his head in disgust. "Not a fricking clue. No one even entertained it. And the morning he died I was sitting in the plaza having coffee, reading a chapter in Harrison's on clotting disorders when it came to me. I ran to the ICU and, get this, when I arrived they were coding him. It was surreal," he sighed. "Now it's a ghoulish nightmare."

"What did you do?"

Sutherland wriggled in his chair and sipped at the coffee, "Found Mrs. Sánchez. Comforted her. What could I do? There must have been fifteen-hundred nurses and doctors trying to resuscitate him."

"It's plain to see you've been jolted."

Sutherland extended his neck and gazed at the ceiling. "Yes, sir," he said looking back to his mentor. "You never think anyone *you* care for will die – especially from misdiagnosis. It's a rude awakening. One you never thought about when applying to medical school. In that fantasy you're all the while saving lives and rescuing patients from the brink of death."

Dornwyler turned to a gust of wind that slapped rain against the window, "Quite a storm … so, how can I help?"

"I intended to come sooner. Time slipped away and it didn't seem right until now."

Dornwyler stared into his cup and then drank from his coffee, "Like the Ethiopian?"

"It's a little earthy for me. Personally, I liked the Kona and Sumatran better."

"I suppose. Anyway you said, 'It didn't seem right until now'?"

"Yes, sir. I've decided on Family Medicine. I wanted you to know and to thank you. Strange as it may seem my experience with Mr. and Mrs., Sánchez helped define my career aspirations."

"How so?"

"I like people. I like helping. But even more, I value the relationships that develop. It makes medicine at once both personal and rewarding."

Dornwyler nodded his head, "Family Medicine seems a good fit. You've hit on a core value that should serve you well and last a lifetime."

"There's something else. In Paco and Sarita Sánchez I discovered – at least from a family doctor's point of view – death is a lot like birth. It's the celebration that's different."

The professor looked puzzled, "Really? I'm not certain what you mean."

"Sounds kooky, huh?" Sutherland smiled. "Ponder it for a moment. Birthing frightens expectant mothers. The foreign environment of the hospital separates a mother from her reality *and* the people that anchor her life; the one constant in the experience is the relationship with her doctor that develops during prenatal care. It gets her through labor and voilá! New life is celebrated.

"In death, the bond between the family doctor and the family is the constant that carries everyone through the agonizing anguish. In the end, the decedent's life, as in birth, is celebrated. By establishing trust and developing strong relationships with patients, family physicians accrue permission to facilitate the two most predictable and important events in everyone's life."

"Hmmm," Dornwyler broke in, "conceptually and theoretically I like it. It's a bit idealistic ..."

"Like Marcus Welby?" Sutherland smiled.

Conversation 181
University Hospital, Los Angeles
Thursday, November 7, 2002; 7:29 a.m.

Dr. Ellis Pierpoint strode into the auditorium holding a Styrofoam cup of fresh coffee while he chewed the last remnants of a glazed chocolate Dunkin'Donut. He squeegeed the corners of his mouth with the back of his hand and in turn wiped the back of his hand on the side panel of his white coat. When he reached the podium, the drone of multiple conversations ceased and the room grew quiet. Pierpoint harrumphed, stared at his audience and began.

"Good morning ladies and gentlemen, welcome to November's Morbidity and Mortality Conference. Good to have you all here. I assume that everyone has coffee and is settled in, so without further adieu, let's begin.

"Today, we are honored to have Dr. Frank Templeton, Chair of Internal Medicine at University Hospital present our case, followed by Dr. Edmund Pinkerton, the attending pathologist, who will review the postmortem findings. Finally, we are especially honored to have with us this morning Dr. Maurice Bollinger, Chief of the Division of Neurology at Stanford University who shall critique the case of P.S. a 29 year-old Hispanic male. Dr. Templeton?"

As Templeton took the lectern Jack MacDougall shifted in his seat. He knew Maurice Bollinger from the American Neurological Society and viewed him as an opinionated blowhard. Justin Sutherland sat with Dr. George Alexandre in the back of the lecture hall leaning forward, anxious to hear what the presenters had to say.

"Thank you, Dr. Pierpoint. Good morning ladies and gentlemen. This morning I am indeed honored – none the less saddened – to present the case of P.S. a 29 year-old Mexican male who died at University Hospital on August 10, 2002.

"P.S. was first admitted to County Hospital from the Emergency Department by Dr. Michael Mack on 30 July 2002, with a diagnosis of viral meningitis, dehydration and altered mental status. He was assigned to Dr. Miguel Rodríguez his family physician.

"He initially presented to Humanitarian Hospital on or about 26 July 2002, with the symptoms of sore throat, fever and malaise. Although no cultures were taken, his doctors made a diagnosis of Streptococcal pharyngitis, started antibiotics and sent him home. When he didn't improve, he returned to both Humanitarian and County Hospitals on a number of occasions and, as I stated, was finally admitted on July 30th.

"At first he seemed to improve; however, late on the 31st he developed nystagmus as well as a broad based gait, complaining that he could not walk. Dr. Rodríguez and Dr. Charles Overstreet (consulting for Infectious Disease) entertained a presumptive diagnosis of postviral polyneuropathy or Guillain-Barré syndrome and called neurologist Dr. Jack MacDougall in for consultation. Dr. MacDougall concurred with their findings and ordered an MRI, polymerase chain reactions to numerous microbes (E. coli, herpes, cytomegalovirus, toxoplasmosis and Strep), and in consultation with Dr. Overstreet, started the patient on antibiotics and acyclovir.

"On Thursday, August 1st P.S. complained that the headaches were worse. He could not get out of bed, nor could he walk without falling. Furthermore, his bladder was found to be markedly distended. A urinary catheter was placed to bag drainage. The diagnosis was modified to viral *meningoencephalitis* with polyneuropathy and Dr. MacDougall began intravenous immunoglobulin G.

"On Friday, August 2nd Dr. Rodríguez signed out to Drs. Overstreet and MacDougall to cover while he vacationed during the first two weeks of August.

"Saturday, August 3rd the patient developed hiccups, agitation and increased confusion. He spiked a temperature *and* complained of seeing spiders. Nursing noted that he had not been out of bed since admission. Dr. MacDougall wrote that the patient slept poorly, couldn't urinate, but denied shortness of breath. His vital signs were heart rate 78, respirations 22, and temperature 99.8° with a T-max of 102.4° in the preceding twenty-four hours. He noted that P.S. was lying in bed, the nystagmus was some improved, his heart and lungs were clear, but he was unable to stand or walk. He felt a mass in the left lower quadrant of the abdomen which he thought to be stool. The patient's labs were unchanged. Dr. MacDougall reaffirmed the diagnosis of viral meningoencephalitis with Guillain-Barré. He continued the IV immunoglobulin G, and ordered a Fleet enema for constipation, Ativan to cover possible delirium tremens and physical therapy for range of motion exercises.

"The agitation waxed and waned on August 4; the patient continued to complain of seeing yellow and purple insects – predominately spiders. The hiccups got worse – he intermittently gulped for air – and his respiratory rate increased, presumptively due to the ascending paralysis. Dr. MacDougall continued the immunoglobulin G and ordered plasmapheresis. Provoked by a soapsuds enema, the patient had what the nurses described as a quote- unquote 'enormous' bowel movement.

"His condition seemed improved on Monday, August the 5th. He actually fed himself and sat up in bed. Bio-engineering reported that the plasmapheresis unit at County was out of order.

"On Wednesday, August the 7th the nurses noted that P.S. slept overnight, the confusion and hallucinations were improved, but he was still unable to get out of bed. Dr. Overstreet wrote that the patient denied shortness of breath and, for the most part, was conversant and making sense. He further reported that the antinuclear antibodies were negative, the sed rate normal and that the cultures and polymerase chain reactions on all fluids were negative. He reaffirmed the diagnosis, noting progressive improvement, and considered stopping the antivirals and antibiotics and transferring to a neuro rehab when medically stable. Dr. MacDougall did not leave a note in the patient's chart on Wednesday, August 7th.

"P.S. took a turn for the worse again Thursday, August 8th. He spiked a fever, increased his respiratory rate and began sweating profusely. Dr. MacDougall attributed these symptoms to reflex sympathetic dystrophy and possible pneumonia. He ordered a chest x-ray, called Dr. Overstreet and wrote in the chart and I quote: 'More pronounced cognitive changes coupled with increasing respiratory difficulties. This afternoon the nurses called to report sudden onset of bizarre unexplained movements. On my evaluation he indeed demonstrates agitation, loss of speech, and now, of all things, finger snapping. A Foley cath is in place. He has not been out of bed since admission. His exam reveals no purposeful response to stimuli, but he does startle. He is quite lethargic between episodes of agitation.'

"With this turn of events, the patient's wife 'demanded' transfer to either Humanitarian or University Hospital the afternoon of August the 8th.

"Early Friday morning August 9, the nurses found the patient on the floor. There were no apparent head injuries. Dr. MacDougall ordered four point restraints.

"Friday afternoon the patient suffered a tonic-clonic, generalized seizure and was found to have serum sodium of 122. Dr. MacDougall was in the hospital and successfully managed the Code Blue. He resuscitated the patient with repeated IV doses of 10 mg Valium and a single dose of Dilantin 300 mg slow IV push. The patient vomited during resuscitation; the emesis tested positive for blood. Dr. MacDougall's assessments included: meningoencephalitis, Guillain-Barré syndrome, low grade pneumonitis with shortness of breath; severe depletion of body sodium, syndrome of inappropriate anti-diuretic hormone and gastrointestinal bleeding. He concluded that the seizure was most likely secondary to the underlying infectious process, SIADH or even acyclovir toxicity.

"They transferred the patient to University late Friday evening. On the morning of Saturday, August 10th his serum sodium had corrected to 133 following judicious infusion of 3 normal saline. He was alert, and although lethargic, able to converse. At 8:39 a.m. he sat up in bed, screamed that he could not see or breathe, plummeted into respiratory arrest and coded. Valiant attempts to resuscitate him failed and he was pronounced dead at 9:11 a.m."

Templeton took a deep breath, scratched his nose and looked about the somber faces in the auditorium. "Any questions?"

A first year medical student sitting in the front row raised her hand and asked, "What is the syndrome of inappropriate anti-diuretic hormone?"

"Excellent question," Templeton nodded. "SIADH is a complex condition where paradoxical secretion of the hormone vasopressin enhances the reabsorption of water through the kidneys, thus concentrating the urine and diluting the serum. The excess free water causes low serum sodium or what we call hyponatremia. The causes for SIADH are many and include cirrhosis of the liver, lung cancer, kidney disorders, certain medications and – get this – Guillain-Barré syndrome. When the sodium drops below 125 or less, alterations in mental status are common.

"Make sense? Any other questions?" Templeton hesitated while scanning the audience. "Hearing none – Dr. Pierpoint."

Pierpoint walked to the podium, took the microphone and introduced Ed Pinkerton.

"Most of you in the audience know Dr. Edmund M. Pinkerton, Chief of Pathology at County Hospital. Dr. Pinkerton trained at Johns Hopkins and Harvard and has been on the medical staff of our sister institutions for more than twenty well-respected years. He will now review the pathological findings."

Pinkerton waddled to the lectern and grasped both edges of the podium to support his bulk. "Good morning to all of you," he puffed. "It is my pleasure as well to provide insight into the unfortunate case of a 29 year-old Hispanic male who died of complications secondary to his underlying illness. I will not bore you with details that do not have a direct bearing on this case. In other words, I will not elaborate on normal findings unless of course they somehow are interrelated to his cause of death or have educational merit. Having said that, permit me to focus on the heart, the lungs and the brain.

"I performed a post-mortem examination on patient P.S. on August 12, 2002. In summary, here is what I found.

"Major organs – exclusive of the heart, lungs, circulatory and nervous systems – were all normal on both gross and microscopic evaluation. The kidneys, liver, spleen – all normal," he paused to catch his breath.

"Evidence for meningitis was surprisingly, if not dramatically, absent on gross. Certainly the classical findings of the meninges adherent to the brain per se or evidence of sticky substance were nowhere found. The brain did, however, demonstrate changes consistent with a low grade, sub-acute encephalitis on microscopic sections.

"Due to the clinical presentation of Guillain-Barré, I followed and dissected out isolated peripheral nerves in the arms and legs. Microscopic changes consistent with post-viral polyneuropathy were noted in both lower extremities, confirming that diagnosis.

"Of considerable surprise, post-mortem examination of the heart demonstrated small foci of fibrinous alterations on the mitral valve with attendant, organized clot surrounding the valve and its cordae," he continued, "which of course is consistent with infectious endocarditis and accounts for the fever and finding of a heart murmur first documented at University Hospital when he was transferred."

Pinkerton took a deep breath, a drink of water and went on. "Examination of this patient's lungs provides significant information pertinent to his cause of death," Pinkerton stated while simultaneously projecting graphic Power Point slides on the large screen behind him. "As these photomicrographs demonstrate, throughout the pulmonary vasculature multiple clots in *various stages* of organization were identified. You can see them here, on this slide and this one as well," he asserted, laser pointing the pulmonary arteries on several projected images. "Most importantly," as demonstrated here, "large, fresh blood clots were discovered in the branches of the main pulmonary arteries establishing death due to massive pulmonary emboli on Saturday, August the 10th. Moreover, I discovered the source of these emboli in various branches of his femoral, iliac and deep pelvic veins.

"One final note. Given his sudden, acute loss of vision I traced the ophthalmic arteries from their origins discovering embolization along the tracks of vessels to both eyes. There were, as well, emboli in many of the small arteries supplying the cerebrum and the cerebellum, which may account for the cognitive changes witnessed throughout hospitalization, as well as some of the disturbances in balance and gait. The source of these emboli was, of course, the alterations previously described on the heart's mitral valve. Dr. Pierpoint."

Pierpoint stood, made his way toward Pinkerton, took the microphone and said, "In the interest of time I ask you to hold questions for

Dr. Pinkerton until our discussant, Dr. Maurice Bollinger, completes his comments.

"As many of you know Dr. Bollinger sits as the Chief of the Division of Neurology at Stanford University and enjoys an international reputation in his chosen field. Dr. Bollinger is first author of more than 70 peer reviewed publications and thirteen book chapters on infectious meningitis and encephalitis. In addition to the degree Doctor of Medicine, Dr. Bollinger holds a Master of Public Health degree from the University of Washington. Please welcome Dr. Bollinger."

Conversation 182
Bellflower
Thursday, November 7, 2002; 7:51 a.m.

As Bollinger adjusted his necktie and prepared to deliver his analysis, the metro bus carrying Sarita Sánchez to her destination at the Westin Hotel rumbled north on 59th street. On a good day the 12 mile journey took more than thirty-five minutes, but Sarita had no alternatives. She simply could not afford driving the Caravan or the $18 per day to park it in the downtown district. Housekeeping paid $9.25 per hour and she counted herself lucky when she got $40 a day in tips.

Sarita reached into her handbag, pulled out a tattered 5" x 7" notebook, and turned past her grocery list to another page where she rehashed the billed charges for Paco's sickness for the umpteenth time.

Global Emergency Physicians, Inc.	$643
County Hospital Emergency Services	$2,167
Humanitarian Hospital Emergency Services	$912
Emergicare Physicians, LLC	$1,374
Dr. MacDougall	$2,456
Dr. Overstreet	$2,193
University Hospital	$13,634
County Hospital	$209,768
Radiologic and Imaging Consultants, Inc.	$27,832
Pinkerton Pathology Associates, LLC	$23,967
Edmund M. Pinkerton, M.D. (autopsy)	<u>$3,200</u>
Total	$288,146

"More than $19,000 a day," a day she whimpered peering out the window. Actually, Sarita wondered why she had not received statements from Drs. Rodríguez and Alexandre, but then again she was too embarrassed to inquire, and what difference did it make in anyway? The total already amounted to more than she could earn as a hotel maid working 60 hours per week, 52 weeks per year for 10 years. Inside her uterus, she felt the baby kick; at 32 weeks it was getting difficult to make beds and clean toilets. Then again, what choice did she have? She'd already sold Paco's pick-up truck to keep up the mortgage, but that would soon run out. *What choices did she have?* Move in with Raphael and Graciela? Sell the house and move to Project Housing? Work two jobs? She *could* do that.

Nearer the downtown area the bus meandered past the Déjà Vu Gentleman's Club. She'd heard she could make more than $500 per night stripping. Two good nights per month could make the house payment. The thought made her blush and brought tears to her eyes. She knew she had the body and the looks. But Paco would never forgive her. Then again, she was desperate. Did she have a choice? Sarita stared back at the notebook.

The bus stopped abruptly at a traffic light three blocks from the Westin, jostling Sarita in her seat and interrupting her train of thought. She looked out the window and glimpsed up at a billboard advertisement that she'd seen, but paid little attention to, a hundred times. Perhaps it was her mood. Perhaps the jostling had rattled her numb senses to life. Maybe she'd reached her capacity to tolerate the stress of Paco's death, the devastation to her family and the pressure of financial ruin. No matter what, the billboard *pointed* to a plan. Her shoulders stiffened, she sat up straight and a sardonic smile spread over her lips. For the first time since Paco's death, she felt a wave of relief and then, although bittersweet, a sense of calm.

Conversation 183
University Hospital, Los Angeles
Thursday, November 7, 2002; 7:56 a.m.

When Maurice Bollinger took the lectern to dissect Paco's case, Jack MacDougall rose from his chair and refilled his coffee wishing his cell phone would ring. When it didn't, he returned to his seat feeling the weight of silence in the entire auditorium.

Bollinger took a sip of water and began, "Thank you, Dr. Pierpoint. Ladies and gentlemen; esteemed colleagues. Thank you for inviting me to discuss this very unusual and complex case of a previously healthy male construction worker who died from complications of his illness on August 10, 2002. Before I delve into my remarks, please permit me to divulge the preparation for my discourse. I, of course, spent several hours reviewing the patient's medical records, including Dr. Pinkerton's very thorough post-mortem examination. In addition, Dr. Pinkerton and I discussed the case of P.S. face to face for more than one hour.

"This case stands out for the remarkable fluctuations in the patient's condition throughout hospitalization. For example, he seemed to be progressing quite predictably on August 1 and August 2 when, on August 3rd, he began hiccupping and became confused. Both nurse and physician chart entries document hallucinations (claiming he saw brown spiders) and agitation. These symptoms gradually improved and by Tuesday, August the 6th he ate breakfast on his own.

"On August 8th and 9th, he went south again, this time developing increased respiratory rate, profuse sweating and a seizure on the afternoon of 9 August. Following correction of his serum sodium on Saturday August 10th, he conversed with his wife, the nurse and the 4th year neurology resident at University Hospital. He complained of hunger, then suddenly collapsed into respiratory arrest and died.

Bollinger took another sip of water, looked out into the audience and continued, "Reviewing the differential diagnosis of altered and fluctuating mental status seems appropriate at this juncture as it is substantial and multi-faceted.

"First – trauma. Open and closed head injuries. Of course there was no history of trauma in our patient nor was any identified on multiple MRIs or at post-mortem.

"Second – substance abuse, both street and prescribed. Alcohol, opiates, cocaine, amphetamines, benzodiazepines, barbiturates, even beta-blockers. As in the case of trauma, there *was no history* of drug or alcohol abuse in this individual. He did, however, receive central nervous system depressants for hiccups, agitation and the presumptive delirium tremens – despite lacking the evidence or history for it – during hospitalization.

"Third – autoimmune and inflammatory etiologies like systemic lupus erythematosis, primary and metastatic carcinoid syndromes. Dr. MacDougall ruled these causes out through MRI imaging and laboratory diagnostics. The patient's anti-nuclear antibodies and complement levels, for example, were normal.

"Fourth – psychiatric. Acute psychosis, extreme bipolar disorder, and acute exacerbations of major depressive disorder may all cause fluctuating mental status. Mr. P.S. had no history of depression nor to my knowledge did he suffer from mental health disorders. He may well have been victim of acute hospital psychosis, however, which, we all understand, frequently occurs in patients with prolonged confinement in intense hospital environments. Given his cultural background and the enigma that swirled around his multiple diagnoses – including the bizarre manifestations of Guillain-Barré – it is almost certain that our patient's delirium took some of its roots from this well established phenomenon.

"Fifth – disturbances in glucose metabolism. As you all learned, hypo- and hyperglycemia as well as altered osmotic states can cause dramatic shifts in orientation to person, place, time and events. Repeated serum glucoses during hospitalization were all within normal limits.

"Sixth – electrolyte derangements. Alterations in sodium and calcium levels impair cognitive functioning. Certainly, Mr. P.S. had a substantial reduction in serum sodium on day 9 of his hospitalization, which exacerbated the underlying conditions and provoked his seizure; however, during the initial presentation of his altered mental status, his sodium was normal.

"Seventh – liver and kidney failure. Chronic hepatitis with elevated ammonia levels and chronic renal failure with elevated blood urea nitrogen levels may cause altered mental states. This appears not to have been a factor for P.S. as repeated laboratory evaluations of his liver and kidney functions were normal.

"Eighth – infectious diseases. Encephalitis, meningitis, brain abscesses. As Dr. Pinkerton detailed, our patient demonstrated microscopic evidence of sub-acute viral encephalitis, but neither significant meningitis nor brain abscess on post-mortem examination.

"And finally, cardiopulmonary etiologies – cerebral vascular accidents, acute myocardial infarction, embolic phenomenon or any other condition leading to reduced oxygen – hypoxia – to the brain, including infection of the heart valves as was the case in our patient today." Bollinger took another sip of water and continued.

"It seems apparent after the fact, that our patient began 'throwing' progressively more and substantially larger blood clots from his femoral and pelvic veins to his lungs, which ultimately lead to his demise. From my discussions with Dr. Pinkerton, we may surmise that this first occurred around August 3rd when he began hiccupping and hallucinating yellow and purple insects and brown spiders. Then again on August 4th and August 8th, when he developed detectable shortness of breath. As he was previously very healthy, a non-smoker and physically fit, he tolerated hypoxia that might have killed others in short order. Although cerebral hypoxia caused him to hallucinate, become disoriented and agitated, he endured it remarkably well – from a life and death standpoint – until August 10th, when massive pulmonary emboli killed him.

"In conclusion," Bollinger summarized, "the cause of yo-yoing mental status in this patient was encephalitis early on, followed by high fevers, acute hospital psychosis, vacillating episodes of undetected hypoxia secondary to blood clots thrown to his lungs and brain, and of course, low serum sodium or hyponatremia. With respect to his mental status, meningitis and alcohol abuse were never factors.

"Dr. Pierpoint?"

Pierpoint rose from his seat, took the podium alongside Dr. Bollinger and asked, "Questions for either Dr. Pinkerton or Dr. Bollinger?"

After a brief pause, a hand rose in the audience. "Dr. Bollinger? What do you propose as a cause for deep vein thrombosis and pulmonary embolization in this young, previously healthy male?"

"Well, as you are all well aware, Rudolph Virchow postulated more than a century ago that a triad of factors predispose to abnormal clotting of blood. And, as most of you know, they are trauma to the blood vessel wall, abnormal clotting mechanisms and stasis of blood in the vessels per se.

"Stasis of blood in the vessels per se stands out as the likely etiologic factor in this case. Mr. P.S. had a significant underlying illness that caused him to be immobilized and confined to bed for several days. Indeed, the attending physician restrained him on hospital day 8 or 9. Blood pooling provided the opportunity for clot development in his lower extremities and pelvis, which eventually broke off and traveled to his lungs. We also know from autopsy, infectious vegetations or endocarditis on his heart's mitral valve produced an opportunity for platelet aggregation, clotting and subsequent embolization to the arteries of his brain and his eyes. This explains the dramatic and sudden loss of vision on August 10th and may also have contributed to the neurologic symptoms seen several days prior to his death ..."

"What is the difference between a thrombus and an embolus?" the first year medical student broke in.

"A thrombus is the formation of a blood clot in a blood vessel. It becomes an embolus when it breaks off and travels to a distant site. So in this instance, our patient had a deep vein thrombus that broke off, and traveled to his lung as a lung blood clot aka a pulmonary embolus."

"I have a question for Dr. Pinkerton," a participant interjected. "Dr. Bollinger dismissed the issue of alcohol abuse in the decedent. Dr. Pinkerton, did you find any microscopic evidence for Wernicke's encephalopathy or what I call alcoholic psychosis in the patient's brain?"

Pinkerton stood and answered briefly, "None whatsoever."

Another voice rose from the audience, "What was his Factor V Leiden?"

"Good question," Bollinger responded. "Factor V Leiden as you all learned is resistance to activated protein C associated with a gene mutation designated as Factor V Leiden. This mutation is the most frequent inherited predisposition to abnormal clotting.

"Factor V Leiden was not obtained during his hospitalization. Dr. Pinkerton asserts he ordered it post-mortem. The lab apparently processed the specimen incorrectly, the test was never performed and, unfortunately, those results are not available."

"I have another question for Dr. Pinkerton," a voice came from the corner of the auditorium. "Did the lungs demonstrate changes consistent with pneumonia?"

Pinkerton stayed glued to his chair and answered, "No."

"So what was the source of the persistent fever?"

Pinkerton remained seated, "Like I said, probably infection on the heart's mitral valve – the endocarditis."

"But like the pulmonary emboli, endocarditis was never considered in the differential diagnosis, was it?"

Bollinger cleared his throat, looked down at the podium and said, "Apparently not."

"Drs. Pinkerton and Bollinger? Do these findings suggest the patient's death was preventable?"

Bollinger paused and pursed his lips. MacDougall squirmed in his seat. Dr. George Alexandre watched, while tears welled up in Justin Sutherland's eyes. Pinkerton didn't budge and offered no opinion. Finally, Bollinger came out with it, "It's hard to say, but we all understand this. With attention to detail and careful consideration of every issue, pulmonary emboli are preventable. No one suspected them in this vigorous young man. Why would they? Nevertheless, I would have to say so ... yes. This patient's death *was* preventable."

Bollinger's declaration dropped on the participants like a pall.

Eventually, he broke the dead silence, "However, before anyone in the audience accuses me of Monday morning quarterbacking or attacking my physician colleagues, permit me to don my Public Health hat for a moment and speak the unspeakable. Early in the course of our patient's illness, P.S. sought care at Humanitarian Hospital's Emergency Department. But he had neither insurance nor money; so he received a cursory exam, was diagnosed without the benefit of supporting laboratory studies and given antibiotics for an infection that he did not have. To confound matters, he was told he would have to seek care from the County Hospital if his symptoms did not improve. As the saying goes in healthcare inner circles, Humanitarian Hospital *treated and streeted* Mr. P.S.

"Do we place profits before patients in the United States?" Bollinger paused, surveyed the audience and continued. "I ask you again. *Do we place profits before patients in the United States?* This case certainly suggests that we do for remember when Dr. MacDougall ordered plasmapheresis to treat the patient's Guillain-Barré at County Hospital, the unit was in disrepair, further delaying best practices care for the complications of his illness.

"How is it the richest country on the planet can put a man on the moon, deploy space shuttles, fund the human genome project and million-dollar military missiles to annihilate rogue states, but can't find the heart and wherewithal to adequately finance healthcare and public hospitals to make topnotch medicine accessible to all her citizens? Sentinel research by Andrulis, Hadley and Weissman unequivocally establish that delay in care results in longer hospital stays, dramatic increases in cost of care and – get this – mortality rates *as much as 124% higher* compared to those who get right timed care. The case of P.S. presented here today puts a punctuation mark on that reality ... personally, I find it astonishing, if not disgusting."

The lull that followed rattled even the usually unflappable Dr. Pierpoint, who promptly rose from his seat to intercept Bollinger's rant when a voice from the assembly broke the verbal impasse.

"Dr. Bollinger? Any significance in the hallucinations?"

Bollinger scratched his head, "Hypoxia of course – uh, maybe I don't understand what you're asking?"

"Hallucinating yellow and purple insects – the brown spiders?"

"Well, let's see," Bollinger paused, "yellow and purple insects – brown spiders? No ... none that I am aware of."

Sutherland glanced at Dr. Alexandre who by now sat shaking his head in anguished contempt, wondering like Bollinger how all of this could be? Then on the plastic surgeon's cue, they both stood and exited through the rear entrance of the auditorium.

Conversation 184
Burbank, California
Monday, December 23, 2002; 9:16 a.m.

Geoff and Cindy Boyer followed their children up the steps of Humanitarian's Gulfstream GIV-SP corporate jetliner. Stubblefield secured the cargo bay, checked the hydraulics a final time and boarded the airplane. With everyone settled, the flight attendant locked the cabin down and brought magazines, pillows and crystal flutes filled with mimosa all around. Within minutes they taxied down Million Air's executive jet runway and cruised at 37,000 feet – one hour and 46 minutes from their Christmas vacation destination in Cabo San Lucas.

Geoff took a drink of his mimosa, nudged Cindy and whispered, "Did you tell them?"

"Tell them what? About the villa?" she persisted. "Of course not, it's your gift. I thought *you* should tell them. I got a card. You can write something nice and give it to both of them."

"What do you think they will say?"

"What can they say?" she asked, then plugged her nose between the thumb and index finger of her left hand and continued in a nasal falsetto, 'We don't want the crummy deed to a villa at Mira Mar Cortez in Cabo San Lucas'? Honestly, Geoff, sometimes you *are* silly."

Boyer leaned his head back, closed his eyes and smiled. He certainly would never reveal that deeding the property to his children slid the financial windfall from insider trading on HHC under the radar. None of their business – no never mind and that's for sure.

He polished off the mimosa, smiled one last time and said to himself, "Merry Christmas everyone. Mer-r-r-ry Christmas!"

Then Geoff Boyer, President and CEO of Humanitarian Hospital Corporation, took a snooze.

Conversation 185
Bellflower
Wednesday, December 25, 2002; 3:36 a.m.

The Boyer clan nestled snugly in their Cabo San Lucas beds two nights later, when nine hundred miles north the unmistakable pressure of uterine contractions woke Sarita Sánchez from profound sleep. For a moment Sarita thought she must be dreaming, but as the wave began its spiraling crescendo, she knew it was real. Rubbing her eyes, she crawled to the edge of the bed moaning while wrestling the sleep from her head and waiting for the pain to subside. When the contraction passed, she rolled out of bed, splashed water on her face and pulled on a maternity dress. After brushing her teeth, she alerted Mamacita and then called the hospital. When the next contraction came, Sarita glanced at her watch. Four minutes apart. She threw on a long coat, grabbed her purse and keys and raced out the door.

The dashboard clock timed the next two contractions exactly four minutes apart, but they didn't take her breath away. Relieved, she got on the expressway and headed toward County Hospital.

The next contraction came three minutes later and with such force Sarita pulled the Caravan off the Interstate to the side of the road. She closed her eyes, holding her breath as long as she could, and then screamed, "Holy Mary, Mother of God! Holy Mary, Mo-mo-mother of god! Holy Mary Mother of God! I-i-i Holy Mary-Mary. Mother-mother of God-d-d-d!" Finally it let up.

Sarita leaned her head on the seat back, attempting simultaneously to take a breath and swallow what little saliva moistened her mouth. When she caught her breath, she quickly massaged her face and then shifted into gear. Releasing the brake, she sped back onto the Interstate.

At this time of day, and on Christmas morning, the traffic was light. Most everyone else was dreaming of sugar plums. But not Sarita; she was alone and the hospital was nowhere in sight. Gripping the wheel, she accelerated to 90 and alternating lanes, passed everything in her path. "If I can just make it another five miles," she whispered.

Two miles from the hospital exit, a contraction built again, this time faster and stronger. She drove to the shoulder of the Interstate and just as she shifted into park, her water broke. What seemed like a gallon of the slippery fluid gushed between her legs, over the seat, and onto the Caravan's floor.

The salubrious odor of budding life that enveloped the vehicle renewed her resolve and provided clear counterpoint to the extraordinary force that started high in her uterus, spread downward, speared her pelvis and exploded into her vagina. And with it came the disarming memory of the extraordinary need to push despite the piercing pain. She wanted to run from it, but instead she screamed, "I-I-I have to push!"

She remembered too that last time the nurse's soothing voice told her what to do, "Mrs. Sánchez! Look at me! Mrs. Sánchez! Listen to me! Don't push! Say hee-hee-hee-hee! Hee-hee-hee-hee!"

So she said, "Hee-hee-hee-hee! Hee-hee-hee-hee!" but the need – *the irresistible urge* – to push overwhelmed her. "Uugghh," she groaned as she pushed. "UUGGHH!"

For a moment it let up. She caught her breath. She gathered her wits. She panted, "Hee-hee-hee-hee! Hee-hee-hee-hee!" It was back, "Uugghh," she grunted. "Hee-hee-hee-hee! I-I-I-I-heeeee-I-I-I-hee-hee-hee!" she cried.

When the contraction at last subsided, she combed back her hair with both hands, wiped her brow and looked down. Her feet swam in the pool of amniotic fluid. Her dress, her coat and the seat were soaked with it. Sweat ran into her eyes. She could barely see. She wiped her eyes, slammed the gear shift into drive and rushed toward the hospital – soaking wet from top to bottom.

Sarita Maria Sánchez took the exit and made the off ramp traffic light when the contraction came back. Her face scrunched up like a gargoyle. Wide-eyed, she grimaced, "Hee-hee-hee-hee." She panted, trying at once to not push and still steer the vehicle straight, "Hee-hee-hee-hee! I-I-I-I-heeee-I-I-I-heee!"

Taking the last turn toward the hospital, Sarita cut it too sharp, hit the curb and jumped it, losing control of her vehicle. It swerved left, then right heading toward a lamp post. She grasped the wheel, accelerated slightly, steered against the wayward direction and regained control, just missing the pole. But two blocks from the emergency entrance, the pain exploded; she could take it no more. "Hee-hee-hee-hee! I-I-HEE-HEE-HEE-HEE!"

Sarita pulled the car to the curb, rammed the seat back, and pushed, "Uugghh! Uugghh! UUGGHH! Holy Mary Mother of God! UUGGHH!"

When the contraction hit an unexpected lull, she took a breath and reached between her legs to sooth the fire that filled her vagina. She found instead the crown of her baby's head. "Holy Mary Mother of God! M-M-MOTHER OF GOD! SHI-I-I-T!" she screamed. And the contraction came back.

Sarita raised her pelvis, but lost her footing on the amniotic fluid-drenched floor. So she hunkered down, braced her foot against the brake pad, and lifted her pelvis again. This time her feet held. She raised her buttocks, hooked her thumbs under her panties and slid them down. "Hee-hee-hee-hee! Hee-hee-hee-hee!"

Flipping up her dress, Sarita got her panties around her ankles just as the pressure roared back. "Hee-hee-hee-hee! Uugghh-uugghh! Uugghh-uugghh!"

She caught her breath and felt between her legs again. Holy Mother Mary! The head was out. She could feel the whole thing! "HOLY MOTHER MARY!" she cried, "Holy Mother Mary! Hee-hee-hee-hee!" she whimpered.

And then from interstices of her memory she heard the consoling voice of Dr. Rodríguez. It was as if he was there. "Sarita the head is out now. You're doing great. The baby is fine. We're almost done. But I need you to listen to me. As hard as it is, I need you to resist pushing until I tell you to push. Then we'll work together to gently deliver the shoulders and your baby. Okay? You're doing great. Lift your buttocks while I put this towel underneath to help with the delivery. We're almost done."

Calmed by the resonant recollection of Dr. Rodríguez's voice, Sarita Sánchez took a deep breath, reclined the seatback and raised her feet. Panting "Hee-hee-hee-hee!" she took off her panties, threw them to the side and like Dr. Rodríguez, fashioned with her coat a hammock between her buttocks and the steering wheel to catch her baby just in case she couldn't hold on. Then she locked her heels and the coat into and between the steering wheel prongs and waited. When the contraction came back, she took a deep breath and pushed. She pushed evenly and progressively just like Dr. Rodríguez instructed with Miguel, José and Angelina. "Push just a little, Sarita. That's right gently push. Good. The baby is almost out."

Sarita placed her hands between her legs grasping the baby around its head and neck and pushed. "Uugghh! Uugghh! Holy Mary Mother of God. Uugghh-uugghh! Hee-hee-hee-hee!" she panted. "Uugghh!" The baby's top shoulder popped out and with it came more fluid. She smelled blood too. "What if I tear?!" she cried.

The other shoulder slid out next. Her baby felt like a big, slippery fish. "What if I drop you!" she screamed, but somehow held on and pulled – vernix, amniotic fluid, blood, baby and all – up and out to rest on her abdomen. She looked down. Her baby had a full head of hair. Its nose and mouth were perfectly formed – there was no cleft. Choked up, she began to weep. But between her emotions, she lifted the umbilical cord and looked between its legs, *"You are a boy!"* she whispered. *"You are a boy!"* she whispered a second time. Then baby Paco grimaced, took his first breath and cried. Sarita's tears flowed non-stop too. She was all alone. By herself. In the middle of the night. Holy Mary Mother of God.

Conversation 186
Los Angeles
Friday, January 10, 2003; 4:46 p.m.

Two weeks after the Christmas and New Year holidays, Jack MacDougall leaned forward in his office chair going through a stack of mail. Correspondence needing attention he sliced open with the sterling silver letter opener Carolyn had given him for Christmas and set it aside. Junk mail, he sailed like a Frisbee into a trashcan three feet distant.

Making his way down the pile, MacDougall came to an envelope marked CONFIDENTIAL: TO BE OPENED BY ADDRESSEE ONLY. The return address read *Saitherwaite, Levisan and Thorne, Attorneys at Law*. He inserted the blade of the letter opener, cut open the envelope and removed the missive.

MacDougall leaned back reading and re-reading the letter. "Jesus-H-Christ," he muttered. Picking up the phone, he dialed Pinkerton.

"Ed Pinkerton."

"That cocksucking Mexican cunt is suing me."

"What? What are you talking about?"

"Sarita Sánchez – she's suing me for medical malpractice."

"No shit? Who are the attorneys?"

"Saitherwaite, Levisan and Thorne ..."

"Ouch – the ambulance chasing bulldogs. Really, no shit – huh?" Pinkerton interrupted. "Have you seen the billboards they've got spread all over town?"

"Fluorescent *'Wrongful Birth? Wrongful Death? Call the Experts!'* bullshit? Yeah, yeah, yeah," MacDougall retorted shaking his head.

"I've been telling you all along, Jack. It's why we need tort reform. Frivolous law suits like this should be legislated DOA – dead on arrival."

"Exactly. Fucking cunt."

"Just hope she scattered the ashes far and wide, Jack."

MacDougall paused, "Why? What do you mean?"

"I know she cremated him. We dispatched his body to Hammersmith's," Pinkerton explained. "So he can't be exhumed. If she scatters his ashes, there's no DNA. If there's no DNA they can't prove Factor V Leiden deficiency or show causation. Could be a bitch of a trial, Jack. They'll put your balls through the motherfucking wringer. But without conclusive DNA, they've got no case. My way of thinking, you're home free."

Conversation 187
La Brea
Friday, January 10, 2003; 4:47 p.m.

Persistent rain fell from a gloomy winter sky, but Judi Pinkerton and Carolyn MacDougall shook it off, folded their umbrellas and walked into the offices of Platinum Travel. They introduced themselves and asked the receptionist for Vicki Falkner.

The agent appeared from behind a filing cabinet and greeted the couple with a warm smile, "Hi, Judi. Hi, Carolyn. Come on in and have a seat," she said leading them back to her desk. "I thought you weren't coming."

"I'm sorry. We got hung up at Neiman-Marcus," Judi Pinkerton sighed.

"Oh, well, no problem. I got caught up on some filing. Need a water? Something to drink?"

"Thanks, I'd like some," Carolyn answered.

Judi agreed, "Sure. That would be great."

The travel agent handed off two bottled waters, sat down and said, "Okay. So, Judi, I've researched several resorts that meet your criteria – sun, luxury, golf, tennis, a spa, adults only, a spacious suite or villa – does that about name the amenities?"

"Carolyn?" Judi asked, "Anything else?"

361

"In suite Jacuzzi and sunbathing privacy," Carolyn smiled.

"Right. Absolutely. I got that too."

"Let me show you *Las Brisas Acapulco*," she continued turning the computer screen in their direction and reading: "Master suites. Private pool and Jacuzzi. Panoramic view of Acapulco Bay and the Pacific Ocean. King bed. Plasma screen TVs with CD and DVD. Bathrobes. Gilchrist & Soames bathing amenities. Living room. Dining room. Covered outdoor lounge. Terrace with teak lounge chairs and umbrellas. No children allowed ...

"Look at those photographs," the travel agent paused. "Nice, huh?"

"And it's private?" Carolyn asked again.

"I've stayed there. Totally private," she winked.

"Golf?" Judi Pinkerton asked. "Ed and Jack *have* to golf."

"Not on property, but there are several championship courses within a short drive."

"Sounds perfect," Judi said. "What's the rate?"

"February is high season so it's pricey - $699 per night for two adults – but you get what you pay for and believe me *Las Brisas Acapulco* is worth every penny."

"Let's book it, Carolyn!" Judi exclaimed.

"What the hell, Judi. Let's book it!" she laughed. "And daily tee times for Jack and Ed, while we're at it," she giggled.

Conversation 188
Guadalajara
Friday, January 10, 2003; 5:12 p.m.

When Sarita Sánchez stepped off the airplane and onto the tarmac in Guadalajara, she pulled a wheeled overnight night bag behind her. In a front pack she swaddled her newborn. Under her left arm she carried a plain cardboard box measuring 8 inches x 8 inches x 17 inches. The weight of the contents got heavy, so she stopped, switched arms and continued on to Enterprise Rent-a-Car. For 260 pesos she rented a Volkswagen Jetta equipped with a car seat and began the winding drive along the banks of the Santiago River. The winter sun ducked just below the horizon when she neared her destination.

She made a sharp right turn along a steep curve and pulled into the staging area of the brick works. Relieved all the workers had disappeared for the day, Sarita steered the Jetta alongside a neatly stacked pile of pallets near the river's edge. Wind whipping through the trees along the river bank and the rushing water of the Santiago rattled the empty silence.

Sarita rearranged the baby's front pack, pulled the box from the front seat and got out. Cradling the carton between both arms she made her way to the river's edge. There she found an elevated, dry patch of grassy soil where she sat, watching the relentless water pass toward its journey to the Pacific Ocean.

Like the river, tears streamed down her cheeks and dripped onto the box. Finally, she sucked back the salty brine, blew her nose and wiped away her tears. She opened the box and twisted in reverse the tie securing the plastic bag and its contents.

"Paco," she choked. "Paco, I know how much you have love for Guadalajara. I understand how much you have love for the sun and the ocean and the smell of Night Jasmine, the luciérnagas and of the nature's things," she sobbed. "I know-know-know too, how much you have love and how much you have missed your p-p-papá. For just now I want you to-to go to be with him. And some day I have Miguel and José and Angelina and little Paco send me into the Santiago from this very place to be with you and Papá too."

Then she stood, dipped her hand into the box, cupped a handful of Paco's ashes and threw them into the river. Sarita Sánchez threw handful after handful of Paco's remains into the Santiago River repeating over and over until the box was emptied, "In the name of the Father, and of the Son, and of the Holy Spirit. Hail Mary, full of grace, the Lord is with thee."

Conversation 189
Bellflower
Saturday, January 18, 2003; 1:57 p.m.

At Wal-Mart, Sarita had the photo of Paco, José and Miguel building sand castles in the sun enlarged to 8" by 11". She choked and trembled when she first looked at it. "Paco playing with the boys he love so much," she whispered. "I cannot believe none of this – it is a like a nightmare."

"What?" the clerk asked, "I'm sorry, I couldn't hear you?"

"Nothing, nothing," Sarita apologized, "How much is it?"

"Comes to $5.67 with the tax."

Handing over the money, she managed a bitter-sweet smile, thanked the clerk and made her way to picture frames. There she found the perfect one – three-quarters of an inch faux driftwood with a narrow edge of gilded rope on the inside border. Finished with her shopping, she made her way through check-out and drove home.

The hammer she found in the kitchen junk drawer, but for the life of her, she could not find a picture hanger. Certain she had one, she dug through the drawer pushing thumbtacks, rubber bands, note pads, pens and pencils from one side to the other, not once, but three times. Finally she gave up in frustration, wishing she had the sense to get one at the store. "You are stupid, Sarita," she shook her head and muttered.

She put on her coat and went out to the garage, hoping she might get lucky and find one amongst Paco's nuts and bolts and things. Sarita opened drawer after drawer on the work bench scanning the glass jars filled with nails, screws and fasteners. No picture hangers. Not a one. She stared about the garage walls. Shovels, rakes, Paco's mattock pick – but no containers for small objects like nails or picture hangers.

Sarita opened the cabinet where Paco kept his hand tools, looking over, among and around them. There were trowels for every possible purpose. Three or four hammers. Masonry saw blades. Plumb bobs. No picture hangers. On the upper shelf she discovered paint thinner, window cleaner, and several containers of insecticides, car wax and Armor All, but no picture hangers. She got down on her hands and knees and surveyed the bottom two shelves. Hedge trimmers, the Hudson sprayer, blowers, and fertilizers on the bottom shelf. On the one above, a De Walt drill, a Milwaukee Super Sawzall, a hot glue gun and a worm drive Skilsaw. In the back corner of the same shelf, she spotted a small wooden box. Her eyes lighted up. "But why keep this in here?" she grunted reaching between the tools to retrieve it.

She pulled the box out, got off her hands and knees and opened it. What she found left her speechless – so when her cell phone rang, she just couldn't answer it.

Conversation 190
Los Angeles
Saturday, January 18, 2003; 3:31 p.m.

Justin Sutherland listened to the phone ringing, hoping Sarita would answer. After six rings an intercept picked up, "¡Hola! This is Sarita Sánchez. I am sorry I cannot answer the phone right now. Please leave me a message and I have to call you back when I can. Adios y muchas gracias."

Sutherland waited for the beep and left the following message, "Hi, Sarita. This is Justin Sutherland. I'm sorry I missed you and hope you are well. This is a quick call to let you know I am leaving on a red-eye tonight flying to Memphis, Tennessee for a month long, rural Family Medicine rotation in northwest Mississippi. I'll call you when I get back. Give Miguel, José, Angelina and little Paco a hug. And hi to Mamacita and Muchi too. I will see you soon. Goodbye for now."

Conversation 191
Bellflower
Saturday, January 18, 2003; 3:32 p.m.

Sarita's trembling fingers set the opened box on Paco's work bench and leafed through the letters. There were many of them. All written in English and dated in 1994. She picked one out and folded it open. Holding it close to steady her quivering fingers, she stared at Paco's words, slid down a cabinet door to the floor and read.

April 27, 1994
My dear Sarita,
When the plane flew away from Guadalajara I have never felt so empty like that. I ask myself. Where is Sarita? The seat next to me is someone sitting there, but it can never be you. Where are you Sarita? I ask again.

365

It seem like the days before we have to be together for a lifetime, but now you are not with me.

I work very hard today and it is not yet summer, but it is very hot. All day long I lay the bricks, wipe the sweat from my face and I am thinking of nothing but you. I think about you so much I cannot keep the bricks straight!

Uncle Raphael he kids at me. When I tell him about you right away he knows by my eyes that you are the perfect one. He tells by the sound of my voice that I have found my princess and everlasting love.

At night when I close my eyes I think of us together. You are so beautiful it is nothing for me to remember your soft skin, the sight of your hair and how the moon sparkles against your face and into your eyes. I can see the fireflies dance. Even now I can smell the Night Jasmines by the road. But they are nothing compare to the perfume of you.

Will you marry me Sarita? Will you be my princess for all my days. Can we make life and love together in the United States? You become a citizen and we have children. They become citizens too and I build a nice white house with tile floors and bedrooms for all of the children. We can have a good life together Sarita.

Sarita? Oh, Sarita. Are you happy because I call you my princess? Sarita my princess! I say to myself over and over.

I go crazy with my thoughts of you. When you take my hand and hold it to your breast my heart leaps for the joy inside of me. When you say the fireflies kiss and it is okay, I know it is, but I need to know you feel it too. When we make love there are four lights that shine – the lights of Guadalajara we can see far away, the lights of the moon above, the lights of fireflies dancing overhead and the lights that shine from my heart for you.

I love you Sarita and I hope you love me too, Paco

Sarita held the first two pages to her chest, scanning up and down the third. Tears streamed down her cheeks dripping onto her coat and Paco's letter. She tried to swallow back the tears, but couldn't. So she closed her eyes, put her head back and let her emotions spill. After several minutes, she took a deep breath, wiped her eyes and read his poem.

To my dear Sarita,
Deep in my heart,
There, lives my soul.
And when we met
I brought you in.
So you live there too,
Giving it the reason
to beat.
Every second,
Of every minute,
Of every hour,
Of every day.
All my love to you, Paco

Conversation 192
Los Angeles
Saturday, January 18, 2003; 5:14 p.m.

Dear Dr. Dornwyler,

This quick email thanks you again for taking time to mentor me and keeps you informed of my whereabouts. Tonight I fly to Memphis for a month long rotation in rural Family Medicine. The University connected me with a family doctor near Cleveland, Mississippi and I am really looking forward to the experience. I stopped by your office to say goodbye on Wednesday, but you had already left for the day.

I submitted my match list for Family Medicine and am hoping for either the University of New Mexico or the program in Santa Rosa, California.

When I return in February, I will call or come by your office. In the mean time, please take care. Thanks again for sharing your wisdom. You have been my alter ego (whatever that means) when I needed it most.

Sincerely,
Justin Sutherland

A warm winter sun piercing leafless trees cast long shadows over the dormant grass. Unlike summer, few people enjoyed the space and peace of Mancusso Public Park. Miguel and José ran ahead with Muchi, Emilio pushed Angelina in her stroller. Sarita's arms crossed over the front pack that snuggled little Paco next to her warm body. The fresh air and sunlight lifted Sarita's mood. Besides, Dr. Alexandre's office had called on Friday. His research grant received funding. They wanted to schedule Angelina's cleft lip surgery.

She looked down at her swaddled infant and smiled, "He look just like the pictures of you and Paco when you were niños pequeño, Emilio. He have so much hair, just like you and Paco. And the blue eyes too."

Emilio picked up a slender tree branch lying on the walk and tossed it for Muchi.

"Mamacita say so," he smiled. "Bebé Paco have to be handsome niño, like his padre and his uncle Emilio, she say!"

A burst of chilly wind blew Sarita's hair across her face. She pushed it back, cleared her throat and asked, "When do you go back to Guadalajara, Emilio?"

Emilio watched Muchi retrieve the stick and answered, "I do not know, Sarita, what do I have to go back for? I work in the agave fields for 40 pesos? Jorge and González they are back to work laying the bricks with Francisco and I have been working there too. Jorge say if I stay with him and it is okay with Francisco, he teach me to lay the bricks. Raphael say he know a man who teach me to lay tile. I like that to make a beautiful floor with my hands, Sarita. So I do not know. And if I go back to Guadalajara, who watches after you?"

Sarita looked up, smiled at Emilio and placed her hand over his, "We get by, Emilio. I have my money from the housekeeping at the hotel and waitress at the restaurant. Mamacita she help with the children, so they have someone at home for them. We are not your problem, Emilio."

Emilio frowned, "But, Sarita, Paco he want me to watch over you, I know. Maybe someday I can get the green card and then become a citizen."

Sarita looked straight ahead, walking in silence. Miguel and José darted in and out behind the trees.

"Bang, bang! Pow, pow! I got you. You are dead, Pancho Villa!" exclaimed José. "You are dead, Pancho Villa! And now I cut off your head!"

Miguel grabbed his chest, swirled about, and fell to the ground, "Yes, I die. But I die for my country – just tell them I have said something," he groaned as his eyes fell shut.

EPILOGUE

Following the abuses of World War II, the Geneva Convention adopted and promulgated the first universal code of medical ethics written since Hippocrates in ~ 400 B.C. Like me in 1976, many U.S. medical students today recite the Declaration of Geneva upon graduation from medical school as affirmation of ethical conduct. Last revised in 2005, the Declaration now reads:

Declaration of Geneva
At the time of being admitted as a member of the medical profession:

I solemnly pledge to consecrate my life to the service of humanity;

I will give to my teachers the respect and gratitude that is their due;

I will practise my profession with conscience and dignity;

The health of my patient will be my first consideration;

I will respect the secrets that are confided in me, even after the patient has died;

I will maintain by all the means in my power, the honour and the noble traditions of the medical profession;

My colleagues will be my sisters and brothers;

I will not permit considerations of age, disease or disability, creed, ethnic origin, gender, nationality, political affiliation, race, sexual orientation, social standing or any other factor to intervene between my duty and my patient;

I will maintain the utmost respect for human life;

I will not use my medical knowledge to violate human rights and civil liberties, even under threat;

I make these promises solemnly, freely and upon my honour.

According to Jones (2006), "The declaration of Geneva is an affirmation of ethical medicine agreed upon at the second general assembly of the World Medical Association in 1948. It was a revision of the ancient Hippocratic Oath that sought to restate the moral truths of the ancient oath in a form that could be understood and accepted in the twentieth century."

Conversations for Paco chronicles a love story that intersects with the avarice, injustice and malfeasance of U.S. healthcare. Inspired by a true account, *Conversations* dramatizes the travail and tribulations of Sarita and Paco Sánchez, two simple Mexican immigrants, caught up in the sordid underbelly of healthcare in America and the hubris of the physicians and professionals who perpetuate it.

Consider this:

- In November 1999, the Institute of Medicine (IOM) released a report estimating that as many as 98,000 patients die as the result of medical errors in U.S. hospitals each year (AHRQ, 2008).
- In July 2006, the Institutes of Medicine reported that medication errors harm at least 1.5 million people every year. The report concluded that the extra medical costs of treating drug-related injuries occurring in hospitals alone conservatively amount to $3.5 billion a year.
- In the United States, the National Practitioner Data Bank (NPDB) functions as the clearinghouse for malpractice awards and adverse actions toward physicians. In 2006 the NPDB reported the following data:

Malpractice Claims Payments	15,843
Adverse Actions	
State License	4,452
Clinical Privileges	836
Professional Society Membership	35
DEA	22
Medicare/Medicaid Exclusion	1,699
Total Adverse Actions	7,044
Total All Reports (Malpractice & Adverse Actions)	**22,887**

- The prevalence of physician impairment is not known as it often goes unrecognized and is underreported to "protect" health professionals. None-the-less, the above data speaks to the incidence of disciplinary events in the United States. Various researchers have estimated impairment due to substance abuse (alcohol and others) in the range of 8 to 10 % of practicing physicians. 15% of the general population suffers from personality disorders. Certainly physicians are not immune to these psychiatric conditions to include histrionic, borderline, narcissistic and obsessive-compulsive personality types. Dr. Jack MacDougall, a central character in *Conversations for Paco,* exhibits narcissistic traits as well as various forms of impairment.
- According to CNN Money, Universal Health Services, Inc., a Fortune 500 corporation and one of the United States' largest hospital management companies made $170.4 million on revenues of $4.751 billion in 2008.
- Forbes reported that Universal Health Services compensated Chairman of the Board and CEO Alan B. Miller $12,006,675 for 2009.
- "Forty-seven million Americans went without health insurance in 2006, an increase of 2.2 million people from the year before, according to a report issued by the U.S. Census Bureau. It marks the sixth consecutive year the ranks of the uninsured have grown. For the second year in a row, the percentage of children without medical coverage also increased. The Census Bureau estimates 8.7 million children – or 11.7 percent – had no insurance, an increase of 700,000 over the year before." (U.S. Census Bureau as quoted on Stateline.org)
- According to the Commonwealth Fund (2007) "Despite having the most costly health system in the world, the United States consistently underperforms on most dimensions of performance relative to other countries. This report—an update to two earlier editions—includes data from surveys of patients, as well as information from primary care physicians about their medical practices and views of their countries' health systems. Compared with five other nations—Australia, Canada, Germany, New Zealand, and the United Kingdom—*the U.S. health care system ranks last or next-to-last on five dimensions of a high performance health system: quality, access, efficiency, equity, and healthy lives. The U.S. is the only country in the study without universal health insurance coverage, partly accounting for its poor performance on access, equity, and health outcomes (italics added).* The inclusion of physician survey data also shows the U.S. lagging in adoption of infor-

mation technology and the use of nurses to improve care coordination for the chronically ill" (Commonwealth Fund, 2007).

- When President William Jefferson Clinton rolled out the *Patient Bill of Rights* in 1998, he intended that it stand as an enduring document comparable to the venerable Bill of Rights that anchors the U.S. Constitution. Initially embraced by the American Hospital Association, in five short years the Association distilled it down and rebranded it *The Patient Care Partnership*. The Association's actions effectively eliminated the human rights protection afforded by the original declaration and shifted healthcare responsibility from the provider to the consumer (Health and Human Services, 1999 and the American Hospital Association, 2003).

Given these facts, is it any surprise that the drama played out through the lives of Sarita and Paco Sánchez resonates to some degree, and on some level, with each and every one of us? Is it any wonder we shake our heads and ask: "What went wrong with healthcare in America and how can this be?" Or do we question: "Has healthcare in the U.S. lost its ethical compass?"

Most patients I encounter desire the same thing. A physician who sits down to listen, treats them with respect, acknowledges their grief and shows empathy for their suffering; they want a physician who stays abreast of new knowledge, honors the unrelenting drive to understand and treat their maladies and finally, a physician who admits, "I'm not certain," but has the resolve and resources to pick apart the unknown. In the end, they want physicians, and a health system, that cares.

References:

1. American Hospital Association, 2003. The Patient Care Partnership. [Internet] Available at: http://www.aha.org/aha/content/2003/pdf/pcp_english_030730.pdf [Accessed 25 August 2008].

2. American Neurological Association, 2008. Current News. [Internet] http://www.aneuroa.org/ [Accessed 31 December 2008].

3. Andrulis, D., 1998. Access to care is the centerpiece in the elimination of socioeconomic disparities in health. *Ann Intern Med*, 129: pp.412-416.

4. CNN Money, 2008. Fortune 500 Snapshots: 485 Universal Health Services. [Internet] Available at: http://money.cnn.com/magazines/fortune/fortune500/2008/snapshots/2874.html [Accessed 17 August 2010].

5. Davis, K. 2007. Mirror, Mirror on the Wall: An International Update on the Comparative Performance of American Health Care. *The Commonwealth Fund*. [Internet] Available at: http://www.commonwealthfund.org/publications/publications_show.htm?doc_id=482678 [Accessed 25 August 2008].

6. Forbes, 2009. Alan B. Miller Profile. [Internet]. Available at: http://people.forbes.com/profile/alan-b-miller/82993 [Accessed 17 August 2010].

7. Gillon, R., 1994. Medical ethics: four principles plus attention to scope. *British Medical Journal*, 309: 184.

8. Hadley, J., 1991. Comparison of uninsured and privately insured hospital patients: condition of admission, resource use, and outcome. *JAMA*, 265, 3, pp. 374-379.

9. Hughes, R. Intravenous immunoglobulin for Guillain-Barré syndrome. *The Cochrane Database of Systematic Reviews*. [Internet] Available at: http://www2.cochrane.org/reviews/en/ab002063.html [Accessed 17 August 2010].

10. Jones, D. 2006. The Hippocratic Oath II: The declaration of Geneva and other modern adaptations of the classical doctors' oath. *The Catholic Medical Quarterly*. [Internet] Available at:

http://www.catholicdoctors.org.uk/CMQ/2006/Feb/hippocratic_oath_i
i.htm [Accessed 25 August 2008].

11. MayoClinic.com, 2006. Mental Health: Personality Disorders. [Internet] Available at: http://www.mayoclinic.com/health/personality-disorders/DS00562 [Accessed 26 August 2008].

12. Medical Errors & Patient Safety, 2008. *Agency for Healthcare Quality and Research.* [Online] Available at:
http://www.ahrq.gov/qual/errorsix.htm [Accessed 25 August 2008].

13. National Practitioner Data Bank, 2006. Annual Report. Health Resources and Services Administration. U.S. Department of Health & Human Services. [Internet] Available at:http://www.npdb-hipdb.hrsa.gov/pubs/stats/2006_NPDB_Annual_Report.pdf [Accessed 26 August 2008].

14. News from the National Academies: The Institute of Medicine, 2006. Medication Errors. [Internet] Available at:
http://www8.nationalacademies.org/onpinews/newsitem.aspx?recordi
d=11623 [Accessed 12 March 2011].

15. Office of Communications and Public Liaison, n.a., 2008. Guillain-Barré Syndrome Fact Sheet. *National Institute of Neurological Disorders and Stroke. National Institutes of Health.* [Internet] Available at:
http://www.ninds.nih.gov/disorders/gbs/detail_gbs.htm [Accessed 4 April 2009].

16. Pancho Villa, 2008. Wikipedia: The Free Encyclopedia. [Internet] Available at: http://en.wikipedia.org/wiki/Pancho_Villa [Accessed 23 March 2008].

17. Raphaël, J., 2001. Plasma exchange for Guillain-Barré syndrome. *The Cochrane Database of Systematic Reviews.* [Internet] Available at:
http://www2.cochrane.org/reviews/en/ab001798.html [Accessed 17 August 2010].

18. The United States Department of Health & Human Services, 1999. The Patients' Bill of Rights in Medicare and Medicaid. [Internet] Available at: http://www.hhs.gov/news/press/1999pres/990412.html [Accessed 25 August 2008].

19. Vock, D., 2007. U.S. Uninsured Rate Climbs Again. Stateline.org. [Internet] Available at:

http://www.stateline.org/live/details/story?contentId=235948 [Accessed 25 August 2008].

20. Weissman, J., 1991. Delayed access to health care: risk factors, reasons, and consequences. *Annals of Internal Medicine*, 114(4) pp. 325-331.

JAMES LENHART

acknowledgements

I must first acknowledge and humbly thank my medical school alma mater, the University of New Mexico, which gave me the opportunity to study the science and art of medicine when at times it seemed no other institution ever would. Wow! What an honor.

Of course without the friendship and support of many individuals, *Conversations for Paco* would not have been possible and I gratefully acknowledge everyone who nurtured it and helped make it come alive. My hat is forever off to the following very extraordinary people:

My medical school mentor: *Dr. Diane Klepper*

Manuscript preparation & word processing: *Ms. Kathy Finn*

My special friends from Guadalajara: *Ixtabay and José Márquez*

English to Spanish Translations: *Ms. Rosamari McNulty, Ms. Ixtabay Márquez and Dr. Norma Cadena*

Critique, instruction, editing and advice: *Douglas Unger, Professor and Chair of Creative Writing, the University of Nevada Las Vegas; Jessica Roberts, from the Charlotte Gusay Literary Agency; my good friend and extraordinary patient Bruce Andresen; Barbara Agonia and my extraordinary daughter Melissa*

Inspiration: *My comrade in letters Beverly Rogers, who from the very beginning said, "I couldn't put it down!"*

Advocate: *James Earl Rogers*

Creative insights and technical labor: *Jonathan Sturak*

Sleeping Giant Publishing: *Who, like the University of New Mexico, believes in my passion*

Legal: *COOPER/COONS J. Charles Coons & Jeremy K. Cooper*

Magic: *Bill Gates (How did the likes of Melville, Faulkner and Hemmingway do it?)*

Words of wisdom and undying love: *My extraordinary best friend, soul mate and wife Nancy, who gave up days, nights and weekends to bring Conversations for Paco to life. Thank you, thank you, thank you! (She is also a terrific editor).*

CONVERSATIONS FOR PACO

about the author

James G. Lenhart, MD, FAAFP, MPH

One of America's most accomplished family physicians, James Lenhart claims Montana as his birthplace. He was raised in Helena and received his early education from the University of Montana. He graduated from the University of New Mexico School of Medicine, took residency in Family Medicine at Brown University, and completed an academic medicine fellowship at University of North Carolina-Chapel Hill. In 2010, James earned a Master's of Public Health from the University of Liverpool, England where he researched the social determinants of health and health policy. He Board Certified in Family Medicine in 1979 and Sports Medicine in 1999.

Dr. Lenhart holds the distinction of Fellow in the American Academy of Family Physicians and in 2007 was named Nevada's outstanding family doctor. In addition to many years in the private practice of medicine, Dr. Lenhart has held academic positions as full professor of Family Medicine at the University of Nevada, the University of North Carolina-Chapel Hill and the University of Arizona. From 2007-2009, he served as Vice Chancellor for Health Sciences Academic Affairs in the Nevada System of Higher Education. "Dr. Jim" hosted *Dr. Jim's Healthline Today*, KSNV Las Vegas' NBC affiliate health headline segment, which reached intermountain markets of over 3 million viewers and gained national exposure to the 37 million tourists who visited Las Vegas annually between 2010 and 2013. For his contributions to the advancement of Hispanic cultures, Dr. Lenhart was selected to The Latino American Who's Who in 2011. He now cares for the underserved in Tacoma and writes from his home overlooking Puget Sound and the Olympic Mountains in Gig Harbor, Washington.

Writing with unrelenting candor, Lenhart's fictional works are inspired by true stories and real life characters gathered from over 30 years of patient care, healthcare experiences and academic medical center rituals. *Conversations for Paco* is his debut novel.

James is married to his beloved wife Nancy and is the father of two grown children.

For further information visit James at his website http://jameslenhart.net

jameslenhart.net